Dr Ribero's Agency of the Supernatural:

The Case of the Secret Spirit-Half

TITLES IN
DR RIBERO'S AGENCY OF THE SUPERNATURAL
SERIES

Dr Ribero's Agency of the Supernatural:

The Case of the Secret Spirit-Half

Lucy Banks

AMBERJACK
PUBLISHING

Chicago

AMBERJACK
PUBLISHING

Copyright © 2023 by Lucy Banks
All rights reserved
Published by Amberjack Publishing
An imprint of Chicago Review Press Incorporated
814 North Franklin Street
Chicago, Illinois 60610
ISBN 978-1-64160-825-1

Library of Congress Control Number: 2022942094

Cover design: Jonathan Hahn
Interior design: Jonathan Hahn and Elizabeth Sheffield

Printed in the United States of America
5 4 3 2 1

Kester stood still and strained to listen.

He couldn't hear a thing, no early morning birdsong, no breeze rustling the surrounding leaves—nothing. The surrounding wood was perfectly quiet, much like the daemon who was currently floating in the air before him.

In any other circumstance, he would have laughed at the sheer absurdity of it all. He knew how it must look—a pasty, bespectacled young man, standing next to one of the most powerful creatures in existence. The mere idea was ridiculous, in many ways. But the situation was too hopeless for laughter. There was nothing funny about the mess he was in, and as far as he could tell, there was no easy way out of it.

The silence was unnerving. He'd fled Dr. Ribero's house only a few minutes ago, but already, the trees had blotted out the reassuring sight of the wood-clad ranch. He'd never felt more alone than right now, in this place.

Alone, apart from Hrschni, who was waiting patiently for him to make his decision, hovering in the air, exuding lava-hot energy, expressionless but patient. A creature that once filled him with fear but over time he'd come to trust.

Only a few hours ago, Kester had the opportunity to capture the daemon—to hand Hrschni over to Infinite Enterprises and help his father's agency win back some respect. It was the biggest case they'd been given and the most important of their careers.

Instead, he'd helped Hrschni to flee. His colleagues now loathed him, a fact that hurt so badly it almost felt physical. Although he'd only been working at his father's agency for a few months, he'd come to regard them almost as family. A bickering, inept, and often irritating family, admittedly, but people he cared deeply about, nonetheless.

To make matters worse, he suspected, despite his father's optimism, that he was now a wanted criminal too. He'd assisted the escape of an identified spirit terrorist, and Infinite Enterprises were hunting him down. Their van was currently parked on Ribero's driveway, and even now, they were probably knocking on the front door, demanding to be let in.

They're coming for me, and I mustn't forget that, he reminded himself. Although the towering pines offered good coverage, Infinite Enterprises were experts at this sort of thing. They caught secretive spirits for a living, so he'd pose them no problems at all if he didn't manage to stay one step ahead at all times.

He closed his eyes, fighting to block out the futility of it all. He hated the thought of being seized by the Infinite Enterprises crew. He'd worked with many of them in the past; they were people he'd previously considered to be friends. He didn't want to see the accusation and anger in their expressions, nor how let down they felt by his actions.

"Are you ready?" Hrschni asked, bringing him back to the present.

Kester nodded, though it felt like a lie. He'd chosen to trust the daemon and asked to see the truth. There was no going back now—not that he wanted to, anyway. He *needed* to know about his mother, and all the secrets she'd held back from him. It was either that or surrender completely.

He wasn't afraid, or not of Hrschni at least, though things might have been easier if the daemon had still been inhabiting his human form. *Mind you,* he thought ruefully, *even as Billy Dagger, the mighty rock star, he was fairly intimidating. It probably wouldn't have made much difference.*

The daemon's blazing silhouette quivered as he extended his hand towards Kester's forehead. Kester was aware of the pressure of the daemon's finger between his eyebrows. He felt the heat of it, penetrating deep into his skull. The sensation penetrated his nervous system—a sharp, metallic throb, though strangely, it was rather comforting.

Then, as though a switch had been flicked within his brain, the outside world drained away. The trees that surrounded him, the bitter cold of the winter morning, all of it faded entirely, leaving him in calm, motionless darkness.

"I am the key," Hrschni's voice reminded him, from somewhere far, far away. Kester nodded, or at least, thought he did. His body felt detached—a rigid, cold thing that no longer belonged to him. He let himself drift and felt the pressure of the last few weeks slide from him like oil. The disappointment of his team, after he'd let the daemon go free. The anger in Serena's voice, when she'd told him he'd ruined everything. The knowledge that he was a wanted man and potentially faced imprisonment.

None of that matters right now, he thought, listening to the slow hiss of his own breath, easing in and out. *Now, it's time to finally learn the truth.*

"I'm going to take you deeper," Hrschni whispered. "Don't be afraid, Kester. This will be easy for you, and in time, you'll understand why."

"I'm not frightened," Kester heard himself say.

"Good. You've spent too long living in your own shadow. It's time to free yourself and be who you're meant to be. But first, I'm going to show you who your mother was and the choices she made. I owe you that much, at least."

Kester thought of his mother, the rosy-cheeked, curly-headed *cosiness* of her, before the cancer had left her haggard and hopeless. He thought of Dr. Ribero too, the father he hadn't even known about until a few months ago. The strange and terrifying cases he'd worked on with the team. Miss Wellbeloved's gentle chastising, Mike's crude banter, Pamela's kindly attention, Serena's ceaseless sarcasm. Then of course, there was Anya. They'd been happy together, until she'd got caught up in all the mess with the daemons and the Thelemites. He should have listened to her, but instead, he'd pushed her away.

He'd been cruel to her. And he'd let his team down, but he hadn't had a choice in the matter. He just wished he could make them understand that.

Infinite Enterprises have been killing spirits in secret, he reminded himself. *That's why you let Hrschni escape; always remember that.*

"Are you ready to see your mother, Gretchen, as she was back then?" Hrschni asked.

Kester didn't reply. He didn't need to; the daemon already knew the answer. Instead, he focused on relaxing and slipping silently into visions of the past.

CHAPTER 1 – GRETCHEN AND THE SSFE

Gretchen had repeatedly pored over the brochure for the School of Supernatural Further Education over the last few months. She'd studied the expansive building in the photos and examined the students posing in various classrooms, mastering a variety of skills that sounded so alien to her. She'd also spent many quiet evenings imagining what it might be like, studying in a place that, technically speaking, was one of the country's best-kept secrets.

I'm sure I'll get used to it, she reminded herself, though the words always rang false. How could anyone get used to spirits unless they'd known about them from a very early age?

Until recently, she hadn't even believed in the supernatural, much less imagined that she'd be learning about it. But then, she'd always known that she was different. It wasn't just the lack of friends or the peculiarity of her parents or even the strange things she regularly experienced, late at night. It was an innate understanding, deep within herself, that she would never fit in with society's idea of normal. She was *odd*, and now she was going to study alongside people that were every bit as unusual as she was. People only studied at the SSFE if they were supernaturally gifted in some way.

On the morning of her first day, she woke early, feeling composed and well-prepared. A few hours later, as her parents' car rumbled along the motorways and roads, she focused on gathering her thoughts, readying herself for the experience that lay ahead. True, she hadn't grown up with the supernatural, as many of her classmates would have done. But she'd taken the time to mentally adjust. She would cope; she always did.

However, the moment the car rumbled through the towering iron gates, her confidence drained away. She stared open-mouthed out of the window, taking in the sight of the sweeping gravel driveway, the expanse of lawn to either side, and the huge trees, towering over the walls that surrounded the school itself. Then, she wondered if it was too late to beg her parents to take her back home again.

It wasn't just the size of the building that was intimidating, nor the austere gothic pillars flanking the façade. It wasn't even the steep granite steps leading to the enormous front door, or the multitude of narrow, stained-glass windows that lined the walls. It was more the sheer *darkness* of it, sucking colour out of the surroundings, like a black hole. It looked like the sort of place people wandered into, then never escaped from.

"Hurry along, dear," her mother said, flapping a hand in her direction. "We've not got long; there's already a queue of cars behind us."

"Yes, Mutti." Gretchen bit her lip, then pushed the car door open. She felt small and observed, like a mouse in a laboratory. Her suitcase was tatty compared to the students around her, and her clothes too prissy and bland. Already, she stood out and for all the wrong reasons.

Her mother rolled down the window and blew her a kiss, just as the car started to roll away. Gretchen gave a timid wave, noting how her father nodded briskly from the driving seat but kept his eyes on the steering wheel.

He's incapable of showing emotion, even as he sends his own daughter off to college for the first time, she thought, as she watched them leave. Still, that's what he'd always been like. Mutti told her it was because of the war and the horrible things they'd seen. Mutti always assured her that her father loved her very much. It just didn't feel like it at times.

She lowered her hand, then turned deliberately back to the building. This was it. She was here, for better or for worse. Now she needed to summon the bravery to climb the steps and register her arrival at reception.

They all know each other, she thought, watching the other students mingling outside. Their chatter and laughter filled the air, a stark contrast to the hostile college building that acted as their backdrop. She wondered if she'd be the only one who didn't know anyone else.

It was time to get moving, whether she wanted to or not. Besides, she'd always been the outsider. It wasn't as though this was a novel experience for her.

"I'm a survivor," she muttered, as she marched towards the front door. "My parents were survivors. I can do this."

It's just a matter of telling myself I'm not an imposter, she added silently. *While wondering when everyone will realise that I don't really belong here.*

Registration was an efficient, speedy process. After only a few minutes of filling out paperwork, she was approached by an older student, who promptly ushered her through a warren of narrow corridors and communal areas and up several flights of spiral staircases.

Finally, he deposited her outside a narrow wooden door. A small plaque was mounted beside it, with the number *134* etched across its tarnished brass surface.

"Here's your room," he said, handing her an oversized key, then a folder containing an intimidatingly large bundle of papers. "The welcome event is six o'clock, down in the main hall. Smart attire only."

The student turned and scurried away before she had a chance to thank him; his footsteps echoed down the dingy hallway before dwindling into silence. *Here goes nothing*, she thought, sliding the key into the lock and shoving the door open.

The first thing she noticed was that the room was tiny, with barely any space to move around in. The window was small too, its narrow pane of glass allowing only a limited trickle of light to slip through. Then, her gaze rested on the single beds flanking each side of the room, each with a single flat pillow and plain quilt. An angular, pointy-nosed girl was already sitting on one of them.

"Hello?" Gretchen said uncertainly.

The girl smoothed down her hair, which had escaped from her plait like a set of dark, unruly springs, then stood, adjusting her skirt. She was narrow, her posture self-contained, but her expression was open; welcoming even.

"You must be my roommate," she said, holding out an awkward hand. "I'm Jennifer; I hope you don't mind that I've already bagged a bed."

Gretchen slung her suitcase on the empty mattress. "It's not a problem. They both look as uncomfortable as each other, don't they?" She quickly accepted the girl's hand and shook it. "I'm Gretchen, by the way."

Jennifer smiled. "Pleasure to meet you. As for the beds, I know what you mean. I already miss mine, back home. My father did warn me that this place was a bit *severe*."

"Did your dad come here too then?"

"He did, and my grandfather too."

Wow, Gretchen thought, releasing the latches on her case. *Yet another person who's going to settle in far quicker than I will.* "Did they like it?" she asked, as casually as she could.

"They both said it was hard work. Some of the teachers are scary too, but I'm sure it'll be fine. I'm lucky I suppose; a good friend of mine started today too, though he's over in the boys' quarters." She sat back down again, picking at an invisible bit of lint on her cardigan. "So, what course are you studying?" she asked, eventually.

Gretchen pushed her suitcase to one side, then sat down too. "Spirit Sensing and Communications, though I don't really know what to expect."

"Spirit Sensing and Communications? That's the same course my friend is on."

"What's his name? I'll look out for him."

"Julio. Julio Ribero." She smiled. "He's a live wire, but very sweet really. I'm studying Conversant Skills, like my father did. He runs a supernatural agency down in Exeter."

"You've really grown up with it all, then?" Gretchen shifted uncomfortably. "My dad only told me about my skills recently. Until then, he just let me believe I was strange."

"I suppose parents sometimes find it difficult to accept that their child isn't like everyone else."

Gretchen shrugged, then started pulling out some clothes from her suitcase. The truth was, she didn't really want to talk about her father. All her life, she'd been told by Mutti to *make allowances for him, to try to understand the way he was.* The only problem was, he'd never tried to understand her in return.

"What do you think we should wear for tonight's social, then?" she asked, neatly changing the subject.

Jennifer pulled a face. "I was just going to wear this. Do you think we have to dress up?"

Yes, unless you want people to think you're wearing clothes your mother picked out for you, Gretchen thought, appraising her housemate's outfit. She grinned, then gestured to her case. "I've got a few things you can borrow, if you like."

"Really? That's ever so kind of you."

"It's nothing, really."

Their eyes met, and they examined each other properly, for the first time. In Jennifer's gaze, Gretchen could sense kindness and an open, honest nature. She seemed like someone who'd led a sheltered life and who, in her own way, was every bit as terrified about being here as she was.

I like her, she thought, with something like surprise. It was unusual for her to warm to someone so quickly. She spied the luggage tag on the girl's case. *Jennifer Wellbeloved.* The name matched her new roommate perfectly, as far as she could tell.

By contrast, her own name had always sounded grating to her own ears. *Gretchen Lanner.* The foreigner. The outsider. The one who would never truly be accepted.

As they made their way to the social event, Gretchen began to speculate what the main hall would look like. A cathedral-like space came to mind, complete with soaring ceilings, candelabras, and banquet tables. Or perhaps it would be a gothic affair, with polished wooden panels on every wall and intricate carved gargoyles peering from the rafters above. Either way, she felt certain the room would be grand and reflect the sombre nature of the building itself.

Jennifer paused in the middle of the central atrium, squinted around herself, then pointed.

"It's that way," she said, patent shoes clacking against the floor. "There's a sign on the wall; that's the tunnel that leads down to it."

Gretchen blinked. "Down? As in underground?"

"Yes, beneath the building."

It wasn't what Gretchen had expected, but then again, she was already getting used to the SSFE being full of surprises. She followed her roommate, surveying the other students around them; some dressed smartly, others wearing robes that wouldn't have looked out of place in a fancy-dress store.

They both made their way through the large entrance, which as Jennifer had claimed, led to a tunnel, a low-roofed space lit only by a series of sconces on the walls. The path was steep and uneven, and Gretchen couldn't help but stare with increasing wonder, aware of the sheer weight of the ground above her.

"How big is this college?" she said, moving aside to let a group of other students hurry past.

Jennifer smiled. "Daddy said it's huge. People have got lost down here, you know." She pointed to a smaller tunnel leading off into semi-darkness beside them. "The private study rooms are down there. The training rooms too, from what I've heard."

Eventually, they reached the bottom of the sloping path. Two oak doors were held open with oversized iron hooks, revealing the main hall within and the crowds of students thronging inside. Gretchen paused, stunned into silence by the sight in front of her. The space was more a cavern than a cathedral, vast and craggy, with a stone floor polished to alabaster smoothness and a raised stone stage at the furthest side. Instead of electricity, the hall was illuminated with hundreds of burning torches, which flickered with an eerie blue light.

"Daddy told me all about this place," Jennifer whispered. "Isn't it amazing?"

Gretchen looked down at her feet. She could see a blurry outline of her own reflection in the floor. "It's certainly something," she agreed.

Suddenly, a male student grasped Jennifer by the arm, then planted a kiss on each of her cheeks. Gretchen watched with astonishment, momentarily spellbound by the shine of his black hair, which was swept carelessly back across his forehead. His eyes glittered with excitement—and with impish amusement.

This must be the friend Jennifer mentioned, she thought, with a vague pang of envy. He wasn't like she'd imagined him to be.

Jennifer prised him away. "Julio," she began calmly, unfazed by his exuberance. "This is Gretchen, my roommate. You're on the same course as her."

Julio appraised her solemnly, then beamed. "That is good! Now we both know someone, and we won't feel like the idiot, sitting in class all on our own."

"That's true," Gretchen said, smiling in return. It was impossible not to; the young man's energy was infectious.

"We have a strict teacher, I have heard," he continued. "But at least it is not the djinn, Dr. Barqa-Abu, right? Jennifer's father, he said everyone was frightened of her, back when he studied here. They all ran away like little children when she floated down the corridors. I won't be scared, of course, because I am scared of *nothing*." He winked at Jennifer, who, in turn, winked at Gretchen.

"Did you grow up together?" Gretchen asked. She was finding it difficult to imagine how two such different people ended up as close friends.

Julio shook his head. "No, I came to this country two years ago. My English, it was very bad. I had nothing, just the clothes on my body, and I was in trouble. Jennifer's father took me in. The kindness of that man is magnificent; he truly is a saint."

"That was very generous of him."

"It wasn't entirely generous," Jennifer corrected. "Daddy realised Julio could pick up spirit intention. So basically, he saw him as the perfect addition to our agency." She patted her friend's arm. "Once he's got his qualification, of course."

Julio's eyes narrowed. "So," he began, edging closer, until Gretchen could smell the warm spice of his aftershave. "What skill do you have, Gretchen?"

She shrugged and hoped the dimness of the lights would conceal her blushing. "My Dad recently decided I've got some talent with sensing spirits. I'm new to all of this; I didn't even know about the supernatural until a few months ago."

Jennifer and Julio glanced at each other.

"It's a lot to take in," Julio said after a moment, just as music started to play from the loudspeaker above them. "But I am sure you will be fine. I will help you in class, yes?"

She grinned, then accepted his offered arm, letting him gallantly steer both her and Jennifer closer to the stage. She couldn't help but notice how the crowds seemed to part, with students edging aside to make room for him, seemingly without being aware that they were doing so. Though Julio wasn't particularly tall or well built, he had a presence that commanded respect, or at least attention. She could see why Jennifer liked him so much.

The music ceased as a heavy-set, shock-haired man walked onto the stage and held his hand up for silence. At once, the crowds stopped talking.

"Welcome, first years!" he boomed, in a rich timbre that echoed around the space. He let the words settle before taking a deep breath and continuing. "For those of you who don't already know, I am Professor Thaddeus Boe; headmaster of the SSFE. This evening is your chance to talk to your fellow students and to hopefully make dear friends that will last you a lifetime. Tomorrow, you will knuckle down to your studies and help us to maintain the formidable reputation that we've built over the last hundred and ten years. But for now, enjoy yourself. And remember, *Visio Omnia Vincit*. Vision conquers all. Those words are as true now as they ever have been. Seek the truth, students, and there, you'll find true understanding of the world."

"Truth," Julio declared, nudging Jennifer on the hip. "That is the most important thing, yes? That, and love."

Gretchen caught the look between them. It was the unmistakable gaze of two people very wrapped up in one another, who had been together for a while, who were so familiar with each other that they could almost intuit the other's thoughts. She looked away, uncomfortable in the realisation that she was the unwanted third person, the single to their pair.

Freeing her arm gently from Julio's own, she forced a smile. "I'm going to get a drink," she said, pointing at the line of tables against the opposite wall.

"Good idea," Julio announced, oblivious to her awkwardness. "Though it will be horrible English drinks. My parents drank only Argentinian wine, the proper stuff that tastes of the pines, the clouds of the Andes, the pampas grasses."

"It doesn't," Jennifer whispered to Gretchen as he strode off. "It tastes like red wine, surprise, surprise. But don't say anything; he's exceptionally proud of his heritage."

As I should be too, Gretchen thought, as they wandered after him.

But unlike him, I choose to hide it. I don't want to reveal myself because then, people have cause to judge.

By eleven o'clock, both Gretchen and Jennifer were tucked up in their narrow beds, the loud music from the social event still ringing in their ears. Gretchen yawned. It had been a long day, but it had gone far better than she'd anticipated.

Jennifer reached over to turn off the light, then paused. "What did you think about tonight?" she asked quietly, leaning closer.

"What do you mean?"

"You know. The people. The college. Everything."

Gretchen thought about it carefully, then answered truthfully. "I'm not sure. It's a lot to take in."

"You're handling it very well, considering you're new to all of this."

"Thanks."

"Why didn't your father tell you earlier? I mean, about your abilities?"

"I don't know." Gretchen lay on her back, staring at the ceiling. "Dad never tells me much, to be honest. He and Mutti—Mum, I mean—they were German Jews. They managed to escape, but it was hard on them both, especially as they were so young at the time. I think that's why he's so secretive; he had to be back then, in order to survive."

"That's terrible. I can't imagine what it's like, living through something like that."

"Let's hope we never see any more wars, eh?"

Jennifer nodded, then turned off the lamp. "Good night, Gretchen."

"Good night," Gretchen replied. A few minutes later, she heard the soft, even sound of her roommate breathing and wondered how anyone could fall asleep so quickly. She'd always struggled with sleep, even as a child. Her nightmares had been vivid and terrifying: doorways splitting open in the air before her and *things* slipping in and out.

On occasion, she'd even imagined that she'd had control of it, that she'd been able to command the air to come apart at the seams, and that it was somehow all her fault. Those were just childish fantasies, of course. Even though the supernatural had turned out to be real enough, there was a limit to the world's possibilities, after all.

The alarm startled Gretchen out of a deep sleep. It took a while to emerge from dreaming, a muddled and dark succession of doors opening and closing around her and the sense that creatures were emerging before disappearing again. She opened her eyes, winced, then reached for the clock to silence it. Instead of the usual posters of her favourite bands above her, she found herself staring at featureless white wall. Then she remembered where she was.

Quickly, she flipped over to see Jennifer already climbing into a charcoal-grey dungaree dress.

"We should hurry up," her roommate said softly, grabbing her cardigan from the wardrobe. "We've only got twenty minutes until class."

Gretchen groaned. "It'd be just my luck to be late on the first day."

Lurching out of bed, she raced to the communal bathrooms to wash, then tore back to her bedroom, tugging on various items of clothing and hoping they didn't clash too badly. On reflection, a novelty jumper featuring a cat playing with a ball of yarn probably wasn't the best way to make a good first impression, but there was no time to choose another one now.

"Which way do I go?" she asked, closing the door behind her.

Jennifer, who was already halfway down the corridor, paused mid-march. "Did you bring your map?"

"No, it's back in the room."

"Have mine. I already know where to go." She squeezed Gretchen's shoulder. "Don't worry, it'll be fine. I'll catch up with you later."

Gretchen watched her scurry away, then stared blankly at the map. The place was enormous, a multi-levelled labyrinthine behemoth, and by the looks of it, her classroom was right over the other side of the main building.

I'd better start running, she thought, and started to jog.

It was easy to underestimate the size of the place and the effort involved with racing down corridor after corridor. Two wrong turns and one chaotic collision with a crowd of third-year students later, Gretchen finally reached the right hallway. She was sweaty, out of breath, and suspected that her face was roughly the same colour as an overripe strawberry. Hurrying along, she scanned each door in turn—then without warning, crashed into something large, solid, and, judging by the muttering, angry too.

"Careful!" the something snapped, prising her off his chest. "Other people exist, you know."

"I'm sorry," Gretchen said, taking a deep breath. "I'm late for class."

The student, who was surveying her as a cleaner might observe a particularly disgusting toilet, sniffed. "You're precisely on time," he said, rapping at his watch. "See? Eight fifty-nine exactly."

Without waiting for an answer, he opened the door beside them. She glanced at the sign beside it, then followed him in.

The teacher, who sported an enormous chignon hair-bun and a harassed expression, peered at them both over her spectacles.

"I've just completed registration," she said, waving her pen at two empty seats. "Sit down quickly, please."

To Gretchen's annoyance, the large male sat down at the desk nearest the back, which happened to be next to Julio Ribero. Supressing a sigh, she swiftly placed herself at the front, cursing her luck. It was her own fault for getting up late, not that it was any consolation.

The teacher coughed, then studied her registration book. "Let me guess," she said, tapping the desk. "You're Gretchen Lanner?"

"That's me."

"Hmm. That must make *you*," she pointed expansively at the other latecomer, "Larry Higgins."

"Absolutely correct, ma'am."

"Mrs. Trow-Hunter is perfectly adequate, thank you. I'm not landed gentry."

The class sniggered, and Larry turned puce around the cheeks. Gretchen wasn't sure whether to feel sorry for him or relieved to see him taken down a few pegs. Certainly, he'd established himself as a bit of an idiot, which, considering he'd only been in the classroom for a minute or so, was quite an achievement.

Her gaze travelled to Julio, who met it evenly. He gave her a mischievous wink, and she grinned. It was obvious that he thought exactly the same about Larry too. She wished she'd managed to get the seat next to him. He'd be fun to work with, she could tell—albeit overexcitable. But there was nothing she could do about it now. Instead, she was stuck under the watchful eye of Mrs. Trow-Hunter for the next term, if not longer.

Once the first few days had passed, Gretchen found herself falling into a routine. Her timetable was packed with lessons, but there was still plenty of time to spend with her friends in the SSFE's social area, a jarringly modern room with a bar and dozens of comfortable sofas. After a few weeks, it began to feel as though she'd been studying there for far longer.

She called Mutti every day from the hallway telephone, as promised. Her mother's tone was always anxious, but that was to be expected. Mutti worried about everything, from spiders in the bathtub to the price of bread in their local bakery. As usual, they both avoided talking about Dad, though occasionally, Gretchen heard her father grunting and coughing in the background. It sounded like he was getting worse, but that was hardly surprising, given the fact that his pipe was seldom out of his mouth. It was a miracle his lungs even functioned at all.

During the second week, Gretchen, Jennifer, and Julio finally ventured into London, revelling in the fact that the centre of the city was only a short train journey from the school. The busy streets and crowds seemed impossibly removed from the insular confines of the SSFE, but they soon adjusted, visiting as many of the ancient pubs as they could and exploring London's alleyways, passages, and hidden squares.

She loved it all, in spite of herself. All her life, she'd lived in Cambridge and had spent an entire childhood soaked in its scholarly, tranquil ambiance. Here, in the capital, there was life. Electric energy galvanised every building, every street, every person. There was chatter, commotion, occasional boisterous disturbances. She felt that she'd never really lived *properly* until now, and she'd never been happier.

Then, after three weeks of being at the SSFE, her nightmares returned. At first, she wasn't too alarmed. She supposed, on reflection, it made some sort of sense. This was all so *different*, and bad dreams were perhaps her brain's way of processing it all.

However, after a full week of disturbed sleep, Gretchen felt exhausted. The dreams were almost identical, aside from the fact that they were becoming progressively more vivid. They always followed the same pattern: Firstly, she would find herself sitting up in bed, quite without knowing when she'd done so. Then, her eyes would fix at the shimmering rip in the air in front of her. Sometimes, she'd even stand, without wanting to, and her hand would stretch out to touch it.

They're just dreams, she kept reassuring herself. In time, they'd go away, just as they had before. She threw herself into her studies, which certainly helped to take her mind off things. Julio seemed to find the assignments much easier than she did, and she often had to ask him, during quiet study sessions, the meanings of specific terms. Having friends helped. When the days were enjoyable, it was easier to forget about what she had to endure when she was asleep.

"You look tired," Jennifer informed her one day, over lunch.

Gretchen took another bite of her tuna sandwich, then swallowed hard. "It's because we're working so hard," she said, fighting to make herself heard over the thrum of conversation in the canteen. "And we've been going out a lot. I'm probably due an early night."

Jennifer sighed. "I know what you mean. Julio loves being around people, and I find myself going along with what he wants, a lot of the time."

"You're your own person, Jen."

"I don't mind, really." She picked at her pot of salad, delicately spearing lettuce on her fork. "The truth is, I just like being with him. Does that sound silly?"

"No, not at all. You're in a relationship with him; that's how you're meant to feel."

"I know. But it worries me sometimes, how much I rely on him. I still remember the first time Daddy brought him home. He was such a brooding, nervy teenager; I couldn't take my eyes off him. We'd always lived so quietly, and then he came along. He was like a firework being let off in a church."

"Or a bull in a china shop," Gretchen added. "But I get it. He's a handsome guy, I suppose."

"He asked me to marry him, you know," Jennifer whispered, looking around her.

Gretchen sat up sharply. "When?"

"A while ago."

"Why didn't you tell me sooner?"

"I didn't know what you'd think. I was worried you'd see me as a silly, lovesick teenager."

"Does it matter what I think?" Gretchen asked, more sharply than intended. "If you love him, that's all that's important."

Jennifer nodded. "You're right, of course. Daddy approves. I sometimes wonder if that's what he had in mind all along. He only ever had a daughter; then Julio came along, like the son he never had, and now he can pass the business on to a male heir."

"That's an outdated view. Why can't he pass it on to you? Females are perfectly able to run companies, you know."

"It doesn't work like that. People working in the supernatural industry, they're quite *traditional*, you know. That doesn't mean they don't respect women, of course."

"If you say so." Gretchen picked up her sandwich, studied it, then lowered it again. "Don't take this the wrong way, but aren't you a bit young to marry Julio?"

"I'd marry him tomorrow if I could. But Daddy and Julio have an agreement. Julio needs to prove himself first, then the wedding can go ahead."

"Isn't it better to wait anyway? I mean, you might meet someone else, and—"

"I don't think I would. You just know when it's the right person, don't you? You might think Julio's a bit crazy, but he's one of the best men I know."

"He's only just a man. He's young, like you."

Jennifer smiled. "You disapprove. Don't worry, I understand. By modern standards, I suppose it is a bit soon to get engaged."

A deafening bellow distracted them both, followed by the distinctive crash of a tray landing on the floor, complete with a food-laden plate and a glass. They both swivelled round, eyes widening. A large figure was sprawled behind them, attempting to haul himself up, before slipping over again.

"Who left half a bloody mushy banana on the floor?" he shouted, glaring at everyone in the vicinity.

"Larry," Gretchen whispered, rolling her eyes. She stood up, then offered a hand to him. "Here, grab on tight."

"I don't require assistance, thank you very much! I'm perfectly capable of—" His next words were cut short, as he scrabbled over yet again and landed on the nearest plastic bench. "It's the banana," he said furiously, lifting his shoe to show her. "Look, it's smeared all over me. What halfwit left that there?"

"Dunno," one student called out from a nearby table. "But you've just deposited a plate of spaghetti hoops and toast all over the place. Not to mention that apple juice."

"That was my sodding lunch!" Larry snapped back. "I've got nothing to eat now."

"Try eating that banana," someone else chorused. Gretchen sighed, then led him over to where she and Jennifer were sitting.

"Here," she said, rummaging in her jeans pocket for her purse. "I can loan you money to buy more food, if it helps."

"No! How humiliating, accepting charity on top of everything else. I'll have you know that my father has supplied me with plentiful funds, which is unsurprising, given how high-up he is, and—"

"Suit yourself," Gretchen interrupted. She glanced at Jennifer, who looked half-shocked, half-fascinated. "Jen, this is Larry Higgins. He's in my class. And he's got banana-mush on his shoe."

"I hardly see why you felt the need to share that information," Larry glowered. He nodded at Jennifer, then rearranged himself in his seat. "I am indeed in Gretchen's class. She's all right, I suppose. Better than that idiot I have to sit next to, anyway."

"Larry," Gretchen said warningly.

"Honestly, if you see *that* moron, I'd steer well clear. Full of himself, he is. Interrupts every five seconds with a ridiculous story about his childhood in Argentina, keeps waving his hands around like they're going to take off at any second. And he keeps interrupting me when I'm saying something important."

Gretchen raised an eyebrow. She'd yet to ever hear Larry say anything important, but she didn't like to correct him.

Jennifer leaned forward. "You mean Julio Ribero."

"That's the one. Ugh, what an intolerable little weasel of a man."

"He's my boyfriend."

Larry paused mid-rant, then paled visibly. "Your boyfriend?"

"Yes, that's right. I've known him for years."

"Ah. Right. I see. Well, when I called him a *little weasel,* I was merely referring to his stature, you see, not—"

"What about when you called him a moron and an idiot?" Gretchen asked.

Larry chewed at his nail. "Yes. Well, he does behave like an idiot and a moron, to be fair." He leaned backward, then studied them both. "I'm surprised," he said finally. "I always thought he had the hots for *you,* Gretchen."

Gretchen stiffened, then quickly glanced at Jennifer. Her expression was impassive.

"That's crazy," Gretchen said. "I only know Julio through my friend here."

Larry raised an eyebrow. "If you say so. It's just you're always thick as thieves, you two. Anyway, I shall leave you to continue your lunch. I need to purchase more food, before the rest of the greedy students strip the canteen bare. It's like competing with a swarm of locusts, sometimes."

They watched him leave, then Gretchen hastily turned to Jennifer. "He's a stirrer," she said quickly. "He loves rustling up trouble. Just ignore him."

"Honestly, don't worry. I trust Julio completely, and you too. It's nice that you get along."

"I'm glad that you trust me," she said, breathing a sigh of relief. "It's important; it means a lot."

Jennifer nodded. "That's good," she said finally, then frowned slightly, before returning to her lunch.

At first, all Gretchen was aware of was the dark. It felt thicker, almost sticky somehow, pressing against her bare arms, weighing down upon her body. She sat up, straining to see, then caught sight of the *rip*, shining wetly in the air, only a few feet from her bed.

This is a dream, she told herself, closing her eyes, forcing herself to be calm. *If I lie down, it will go away. It always does.*

She could sense something peering through the rip, waiting in a place that was somewhere else, not here. Unsure whether to slip through or not.

I hate this, I hate this, she thought to herself, over and over. She would give anything to be free of it. Although all she wanted was to go back to sleep and try to forget it had ever happened, her legs swung slowly over the side of the bed, against her will.

She opened her eyes, feeling her arm rise slowly towards it. Just a few more inches, and it'd be within her reach; she could push her fingers *through* and finally get a sense of what lay beyond.

It doesn't pay to be curious, her father had always told her. *Sometimes, it's better not to know.*

He's right, she thought, in a dreamy, detached way, while at the same time thinking, *he's wrong. This is the truth; this is what needs to be seen.*

"Gretchen?" The whisper was muffled, coming from somewhere a great distance away. "Gretchen, what *is* that?"

"It's a door," Gretchen whispered back. "It's calling to me."

She felt a cold hand on her leg and gasped. Immediately, the air resealed itself with a gargled *whoosh*, shivering slightly before stilling. She turned to see the vague outline of Jennifer's face, dimly lit by the moonlight outside the window.

Gretchen wondered if she was still dreaming, about to wake up at any moment. This didn't feel like sleep, though. Instead, she felt alert, tense, aware of everything around her. A moment later, the room was flooded with a reassuring amber glow. She blinked at Jennifer, whose hand still rested against the base of the lamp.

"What's going on?" Jennifer muttered blearily. She moved over to Gretchen's bed and sat beside her.

"What was that thing?" she asked, waving at the empty space before them.

"You saw it too?"

"Of course I saw it! I know what it looked like too, but . . . *that's impossible.*"

"What did it look like? Please tell me, Jennifer; I need to know."

"Don't worry; there's a logical explanation, I'm sure."

"What explanation can there be?" Gretchen said, grabbing her hand. "I've been seeing them for years, and until now, I thought they were just in my dreams."

Jennifer studied her face carefully, opened her mouth, then frowned. Her jaw was tight, her eyebrows knitted in alarm. It didn't make Gretchen feel any better about the situation.

"It *looked* like a spirit door," she said finally, then shook her head. "But that's just me adding two and two together and coming up with five. There are hardly any spirit door openers these days, and it's hereditary too, so one of your parents would have been able to do it."

"There's no chance of that," Gretchen said, thinking of Mutti and Dad. Until recently, she hadn't even known that they'd been aware of the supernatural at all, let alone had any powers to open *spirit doors,* whatever those were.

Jennifer visibly relaxed. "It's just me being silly. But that *thing* in the air looked so much like an illustration in a book I've got at home, it startled me. It looked like the air had been torn open, and the spirit world lay just on the other side."

Gretchen thought of the *things* she'd sensed, the feeling that she was being watched by unseen eyes, that they'd been waiting for her to somehow tear the rip more and create a gaping hole. *There's an explanation to all of this,* she told herself, shivering. *There has to be.*

"Hey, you're the supernatural expert," she said, trying to inject some lightness into her voice. "You must have an idea of what it could have been."

Jennifer rubbed her forehead, blinking hard. "I don't know. We should get back to sleep, for now. Whatever it is, it can wait until morning."

It might not wait until morning for me, Gretchen thought, as she lay back down, tucking herself neatly under her sheets. A part of her was horrified that her friend had seen it too, because that meant it was real. But another, hidden part of her thrilled at the thought. She could do something *major,* create a tear in the air. Even if it wasn't a spirit door, it was impressive.

Maybe this is my talent, she thought, as Jennifer switched the lamp off again, leaving them both in darkness. *Maybe this is the real reason Dad was so keen for me to come here. Not that he'd tell me. He'd never tell me anything that I'd find useful.*

Chapter 2 – The Chase Begins

Kester's eyes snapped open, and he took a deep, shuddering breath.

He was disorientated, still partly lost in the cosy confines of his mother's student bedroom. He thought of the rip in the air, which had undoubtedly been a spirit door. *How could she not have known?* he wondered, blinking with confusion. *Why didn't my grandfather tell her?*

He turned to see Hrschni floating beside him, his form burning as brightly as ever, eyes blazing directly into Kester's own.

"Why did you stop?" Kester asked.

"You need to get away," the daemon replied, simply. "They're coming."

Infinite Enterprises, Kester realised. He spun around, peering through the bushy pine trees, straining hard to hear the sound of approaching footsteps. It wasn't a surprise; he knew his father would only be able to delay them for so long.

This was no time to dwell on the visions that the daemon had just shown him—or how time had shifted and stretched in the past yet seemed to have hardly passed at all in the present. Quickly, he turned back to Hrschni. "How far away are they?"

"You have a few minutes. If you walk in a northwesterly direction, you will find a path by a stream. Follow that, and it will take you to a village called Cowley. From there, you can catch a bus."

"To where?"

"Anywhere that's not here."

"What will I do? I've got hardly any money in my wallet, my phone's battery is low, I can't sleep outside because I'll die of cold, I—"

The daemon flared brightly, silencing him. "Don't worry," he said. "I will help you, as you helped me. Assistance will come; I will find you, and we will continue where we left off. But for now, you need to go."

The situation felt desperate, but Kester knew he had no choice. If he was caught by Infinite Enterprises now, they'd haul him in for questioning, and however hard he tried to explain why he'd let Hrschni escape, he knew they wouldn't understand. He'd be expelled from the supernatural world for good, most likely even locked in prison, and his father's agency would be ruined.

This is the only chance I've got to make things right, he thought, just as he heard what sounded suspiciously like a twig snapping not that far away.

"Go," Hrschni hissed. "If you don't make haste, they will find you."

Kester didn't need telling twice. Steeling himself, he began pushing through the trees, fighting his way past prickly branches that slapped hard against his body. The coldness had seeped through his clothes while he'd been lost in his mother's memories, and now his limbs felt leaden and unresponsive.

Yet again, I'm in a dire situation, he thought, as another branch whacked him on the nose, nearly knocking his glasses off. Under normal circumstances, he'd be able to muster a wry smile, but now wasn't the time. He had to get away—and fast.

As he shoved a path through the trees, his thoughts turned to his mother. Hrschni hadn't just shared a memory; he'd *taken him there*—transported him into the same places as Gretchen and allowed him to study her in depth. It hadn't just been her youth that had shocked him, but her natural exuberance too, and her energy. When he'd known her, she'd been far calmer and more introverted, happy to smile benignly as he sat on the floor reading his books or to listen quietly to his chatter while strolling around the park.

Seeing his father as a student had been less of a surprise. In fact, the young Ribero had been exactly as Kester would have imagined him to be. Impassioned. Charismatic. An unstoppable, sometimes infuriating force of nature. *It's no wonder Jennifer loved him so much,* he thought, as he finally emerged from the trees and into the open. *And my mother, I suppose.*

He spied a pebbly path ahead, with a fast-flowing stream beside it. He'd made it this far, which was an achievement in itself. Now, according to Hrschni, all he needed to do was follow the path until he emerged at a village. It was a clever strategy; he suspected that Infinite Enterprises would predict he'd make a beeline for the main road, which was in the other direction.

Don't think about it, just keep going, he ordered himself. It was hard; he'd spent the previous night walking from Exmouth to Exeter, and his legs were burning with exertion. However, he had no choice. All he could do was trust Hrschni and hope that everything would turn out right in the end.

Oh, Mum, he thought bitterly, as he continued onwards, wrapping his arms around himself to keep warm. *I wish I'd been you, instead of me. That I'd had good friends like yours and been able to focus on studying and enjoying life, rather than dealing with this. It isn't fair.*

He walked for another half an hour. To his relief, no one was following him—or at least no one he noticed. Finally, he emerged onto a main road and crossed over towards the row of cottages on the other side. A useful sign told him all he needed to know, even though it was partly obscured by ivy: COWLEY. True to Hrschni's word, there was a bus stop close by, and Kester sat on the wall beside it, resting his head in his hands.

A bus arrived only a few minutes later, chuffing to a halt beside him. He looked up at the driver as the door slid open, then stepped on.

"Where's this bus going to?" he asked, too exhausted to raise his voice beyond a hoarse whisper.

The driver gave him an incredulous look, then scratched his beard. "Well now, it goes all the way to Princetown, then stops off at—"

"Where's Princetown?"

"You're not from round here, are you? Princetown is in the middle of Dartmoor."

Dartmoor. Endless moors immediately came to mind, craggy tors rising from the hills like prehistoric beasts. Kester had heard plenty about the place but hadn't yet had the chance to visit. It seemed like as good a spot as any.

"How much does it cost to go to Princetown?" he asked.

"Fourteen pounds sixty."

Kester rummaged in his wallet. He had just under twenty-five pounds; this would use up most of his spare cash. He didn't dare pay by card either; Infinite Enterprises' surveillance team would undoubtedly be able to track him, then. He pulled out the money, handed it over, then headed to the back of the bus. To his relief, only one other person was on board: a hunched old lady who seemed more interested in her magazine than him.

As the bus rolled off along the road, he stared out of the window, watching as the houses gave way to open countryside. Everything relied on Hrschni keeping his word. If the daemon decided to leave him in the lurch, he'd be lost.

It's lucky that daemons are one of the more trustworthy higher order of spirits, he thought, resting his head against the seat and closing his eyes. *Even if they do love riddles and puzzles, they're usually good at keeping promises.*

He remembered how Hrschni had broken the rules of his spirit permit and chosen to slip under the radar—an illegal move that guaranteed deportation back to the spirit world. He also remembered that he was putting his trust in a daemon who had kidnapped him in the past, and who'd tried to convince him to release chaos in the world. A daemon who was the Grand Master of the Thelemites too—the organisation the government currently feared the most.

He decided not to think too hard about it, for now. He had far too much to worry about as it was. Besides, despite all that, he did trust Hrschni. He wasn't entirely sure why. It just felt right to do so.

Somehow, Kester managed to nod off, even though the bus kept stopping and starting on the narrow roads to let other cars pass. He awoke at last to the sound of the driver bellowing the name of the town and turned his attention to the view outside the window.

Princetown didn't look like much, from what he could tell. He'd been expecting quaint cottages and picturesque old pubs, like many of the other rural villages in Devon. Instead, the landscape was filled with row upon row of modern stone houses, most of them squat and practical, rather than characterful.

He rose from his seat, reluctant to leave the warmth of the bus. The slate-grey sky outside threatened rain at any moment, and his clothing was ill-suited for a soaking. Even worse, he had no spare clothes to change into and no money to buy any others. The situation seemed desperate, but he knew he had to keep the faith. It was either that or give up now and head back to Exeter and hand himself over to Infinite Enterprises.

Everything will be alright, he told himself, as he hurried towards the door.

The driver watched him in the windscreen mirror. "If you're interested in sightseeing, there's a good museum in town," he said eventually.

"What about a place to stay?"

"There's a hotel further along. Nice place, does a good fry-up. Don't know what the prices are like, but as it's out of season, you might be lucky."

Stepping off, Kester opened his mouth to reply, then closed it again as the doors slid shut behind him. A moment later, the bus grunted into action, then chugged slowly off into the distance.

Well, he thought, watching as it turned the corner and disappeared from view. *I'm in a new place, with about ten pounds to my name, and I've got nowhere to stay. This should be interesting.*

He wandered along the road, then saw what must be the high street up ahead, if the small row of shops and large car park were anything to go by. Beyond that lay a smartly whitewashed building, complete with a sign swinging in the breeze.

To his relief, he realised it was the hotel the driver had mentioned. Even better, it looked presentable, cosy even, with lamps in the windows and smoke rising gently from the chimney. At the very least, he could buy himself a drink and some food, then wait for help to arrive.

What if it doesn't, though? The thought nagged at him, like a nervous tic. He pushed it back down again and shoved the front door open.

The warmth of the air within was such a welcome surprise that Kester found himself pausing for a while, basking in it like a cat on a sunny window ledge. Then he remembered himself and peered around the dark, wood-panelled room.

A young man stood behind the bar, a tea towel in hand, staring at him questioningly. "You're a bit keen," he said, placing the towel on the nearest beer mat. "I've only just opened."

Kester forced a smile. "Do you have a payphone?"

"We do, out by the toilets." The barman's eyes wrinkled with concern. "Everything all right?"

I must look dreadful, Kester realised, shuffling forward. He hadn't slept, eaten properly, or washed for a long time.

"I've had a rough few days," he said. "Can I order some food? I'm starving."

"Kitchen's only doing breakfasts, and those are usually reserved for guests. But I can ask our chef to rustle something up for you, if that helps."

"It really does. I just need to use your phone, but if I could have a sausage sandwich or something, that'd be wonderful."

The young man saluted. "Right you are, sir. I'll throw in a free cup of tea; how does that sound?"

Kester nodded gratefully as the man slipped back through a passageway, presumably to alert the kitchen. He made his way in the direction of the toilets, where, as promised, he saw a battered old payphone mounted on the wall. He knew it was risky to call his father, but at least it wouldn't be from his mobile phone. The truth was, he wasn't really sure how extensively Infinite Enterprises was trying to track him, nor how much access they'd have to things like phone lines and CCTV images.

To his relief, Ribero answered swiftly. Kester felt guilt wash over him again. His father sounded fragile and exhausted; this was the last thing he needed, given his current state of health.

"It's me," Kester announced in a low voice, glancing over his shoulder to check he was alone.

Silence echoed down the line. He waited, winding the telephone cord around his finger.

"Ah, you are the plumber, yes?" his father said eventually, in a too-loud tone. "It's about time you phoned about my kitchen sink." Obviously, he had the same concerns as Kester and wanted to be sure that if the conversation was being listened to, they wouldn't give too much away.

"Have you spoken to the daem—to the you-know-who?"

"I spoke to your colleague, yes. They filled me in, and I will pay the extra money. Though I do not like how you operate; it is sneaky, yes? A sneaky contractor is not a good thing."

Kester grinned. He could always rely on his father to over-egg the performance. Still, it was pretty convincing, he had to admit. It was *exactly* the sort of hard time Ribero usually gave people who came to do work for him, regardless of whether they did a good job or not.

"Princetown," Kester said, saying the word as softly as he could.

"Yes, I understand. I already know this. You will get your money; it will be sorted soon. Now, come and fix my sink, please. Do you understand?"

"Thanks."

"We will speak soon." Ribero hung up without saying another word, and Kester breathed a sigh of relief.

A few minutes later, he was presented with a sausage sandwich, a round of buttery toast, and a steaming mug of tea. The meal, combined with the log-fire beside him, almost reduced him to tears. It was simple, unadulterated comfort, something he hadn't experienced in a long time. Instinctively, his mind travelled to other comforts that he now missed badly. Holding Anya in his arms—that was the first one that sprung to mind. Curling up beside one another on the sofa or nuzzling his face against the warmth of her neck.

The memories flooded through him, bright, sharp, and full of bitter nostalgia. Bitter, because all those times he'd been snuggled beside her, another creature had been there too. Fylgia had been inhabiting Anya's body at the time, so there'd been three in the relationship, not two. The mere thought of it made him flinch, especially as he knew that such unions occasionally produced children that were half-spirit, half-human. *What would they be like?* he wondered. *Would they drift and float around like spirits? Could they disappear at will?* The thought was discomforting, so he put it from his mind. Some things were just too bizarre to contemplate.

After he'd savoured the last bite of sausage sandwich, his gaze rested on the flames in the fireplace. Their ceaseless shifting and coiling reminded him of Hrschni. He remembered the first time he'd met the daemon, deep in the labyrinthine maze of Chislehurst Caves. Back then, Kester had regarded him as a deadly adversary—a sensible opinion, given that Hrschni had used Anya to lure him there, then threatened to keep him imprisoned within the caves until he agreed to create a permanent spirit door.

But now, he realised that the situation wasn't as clear-cut as he'd once thought. The truth existed in the grey areas between right and wrong—and was often open to interpretation. It was a tangled knot, and even thinking about it was exhausting.

After a few minutes, his eyelids started to droop. The warmth and the scent of the smoke were cocooning him in a fuzzy state of sleepiness, and he let himself give into it, resting his head against the back of the seat. It seemed like only a few moments later that a hand crashed down on his shoulder, shaking him hard.

"What?" He blinked in the light, momentarily confused by his surroundings.

"Lazy boy! Always with the nodding off, yes?"

He turned to follow the sound of the voice, then slowly grinned. Looming over him was the familiar face of his father, and instinctively, he reached upwards and pulled the old man into a tight bear hug.

"I'm so glad to see you," he muttered, mouth muffled against Ribero's collar.

His father half tumbled, half settled into the seat beside him. "I am not a teddy bear that you can cuddle," he said brusquely, smoothing down his jacket. "Also, we only saw each other a few hours ago. So, no need for the fond greeting, I don't think."

Kester chuckled. "How did you manage to get here without Infinite Enterprises following you?"

"Hrschni distracted them while I drove away. They followed him instead, then he disappeared, *poof!* They probably feel very stupid."

"I'm so glad you understood my message earlier on." Kester glanced around to check no one was listening. An elderly couple were propped up at the bar, but to his relief, they seemed more interested in their conversation than anything else.

"I knew where you were already. The daemon saw you getting on the bus, then he told me."

"Why didn't Hrschni just walk with me, rather than watching without me knowing?"

"Why don't you ask him yourself?"

Kester looked around, firstly over Ribero's shoulder, then to the door. There was no one there. Then, he met his father's eyes and saw the distinctive glitter of burning energy, hidden deep within.

"You let him enter your body?" he whispered incredulously.

"It was the only way. You don't have to make it sound like the kinky love thing."

"Sorry. I mean, Hrschni's here too? *Right here?*"

Ribero sat up straighter. "I am," he said, in a more solemn, measured voice.

Ingenious, Kester thought, *but unexpected.*

"I thought you two didn't see eye to eye," he said, studying his father's face intently.

"Desperate times call for desperate measures," the daemon replied, through Ribero's lips. "Although your father and I have not always agreed on things in the past, we're united in our concern for your welfare."

Kester longed to ask what it felt like, to have a daemon inhabiting your body, to sense it existing alongside your own thoughts and emotions. But now wasn't the time. Although no one appeared to be listening into their conversation, it was still a public place.

"You should stay here for a while," Hrschni continued smoothly, then pulled out an envelope from Ribero's jacket pocket. He slid it across to Kester. "There's a hundred and thirty pounds here; it's all the money your father had in the house. It should be enough for a few nights' accommodation, plus food. You must stay inside as much as possible; do you understand? Infinite Enterprises will try to find you."

"Can I use my mobile phone?" Kester asked.

"It's best if you don't. We don't know yet if they're monitoring it. However, we have some clothes and toiletries here for you. They are your father's clothes, of course, so they might not be to your taste."

Ribero's expression twisted and writhed, reminding Kester of a mime artist with a sudden bout of painful indigestion. "My clothes are not to be criticised!" he said, far too loudly.

Dad's back, Kester thought with a grin.

"I order my clothes from the finest tailors in Saville Row and my shirts from Argentina, because the quality is far better than your thin, falling-apart little English shirts, and—"

"Dad, can we move on from shirts? We need to think of a plan. Everything is hanging by a thread here."

"Good threads too, silk threads from the Argentinian silkworms that—"

"Dad?"

Ribero sunk in his seat. "Very well. We will leave now, myself and this daemon, and we will have private words about his nasty judgement of my clothes. But we will be back soon. I will not abandon you in your hour of need, my boy."

Kester smiled. He knew his father meant it, regardless of his bluster and indignant rage. "Thank you," he said.

"Do not worry. We will think of something, and everything will turn out well. Even though Serena sent me her resignation earlier, and Mike said he is thinking of doing the same. And his horrible brother Crispian stole my diary with my passwords and business contacts. Oh, and Jennifer and Pamela cannot stop weeping and wailing at me down the phone. But it will all be fine, you will see."

"Serena resigned?" Kester's stomach clenched. He knew she'd been furious, but he had never imagined she'd actually quit the agency.

Ribero's lips stretched to a rictus grin. "It's no problem, we will figure this out." He stood, patted Kester's head, then pointed to the door. "We will leave you to enjoy the pub food and nice hotel room, yes?"

And the knowledge that I've ruined at least five other people's lives, Kester thought, as he watched his father leave. As for everything being resolved in the future, he was starting to lose faith. Things had become too awful, too quickly, and he couldn't see a way to dig a path out of it.

The room was basic: a single bed, shower-room, and a battered wardrobe that looked as though it had seen better days. Still, it was cheap, which was the main thing.

Kester laid out his father's clothes on the bed and stared at them bleakly. He'd never really envisaged himself as the sort of person who'd wear a burgundy silk shirt, nor a pair of immaculately creased pinstripe slacks. As for the paisley cravat, he could only imagine how much Mike would roar with laughter at the sight of it. But it would all have to do. At least he could finally slip out of his dirty clothes and into something fresh, even if he did feel like he was attempting to emulate a silent movie star in his new attire. The brief nap on the bed was also welcome and left him feeling less muddy headed, though not any more positive about the situation.

Around mid-afternoon, he crept back down to the main bar and made his way to the payphone. He thought it unlikely that Infinite Enterprises would have tapped Miss Wellbeloved's home phone, but he reminded himself to keep it swift anyway, just in case.

She answered after a couple of rings. Her greeting, which was usually so strident and brisk, was shocking to hear. She sounded frail, weary, and most depressingly of all, completely devoid of hope.

"Miss Wellbeloved," he muttered, pressing the phone to his ear. "It's me."

"Kester?" There was a lengthy pause. "Where are you? What's going on, have you—"

"I can't tell you everything," he interrupted, "but I want to tell you as much as I can. You deserve to know the truth. You already know that Hrschni told me about Infinite Enterprises killing spirits in secret. Well, it's true. He sent me CCTV footage that proves it."

Silence rang down the line.

"Are you still there?" he asked, finally.

"Please tell me that's a lie," she said, her voice cracking midsentence. "Oh Kester, I couldn't bear that to be true, on top of everything else."

"I'm so sorry. That's why I couldn't let Serena capture Hrschni. For what it's worth, I don't agree with what he's trying to do. I don't believe spirits should be allowed to flood into our world in an uncontrolled manner. But I do think his intentions are noble. He wants to return to a time when spirits and humans helped one another."

"But Kester, what about all those things that he did to you? How can you be sure he's not being manipulative, twisting your thoughts so you agree to create a permanent spirit door with him?"

"I haven't agreed to anything, I promise." He paused, then took a deep breath. "Has Serena really resigned?"

"Yes. She won't answer my calls, or your father's. She accused us of siding with you. I spoke to Mike earlier. He's devastated too, Kester. I've never heard him like that. Of course, he's having to deal with his brother's betrayal too, on top of everything else."

"Dad mentioned Crispian had stolen sensitive information."

"God knows what he intends to do with it." Miss Wellbeloved sniffed loudly. "He might sell it to the highest bidder, I suppose. Imagine if it got into the wrong hands? Pamela is blaming herself; she was the last one to use Julio's book, and she thinks she might have left it on his desk, for anyone to see."

Kester thought of the ever-affable Pamela. He'd never met anyone like her before: kindly and completely unflappable, even in the face of catastrophe. He'd never met people like *any* of them, for that matter. They were all good people, and none of them deserved this.

"It's not her fault," he said. "It's mine, all of it. But I'm trying to put things right, I really am."

"That's a noble ambition, but I don't see how you can."

Neither do I, Kester thought, chewing his lip. He remembered Miss Wellbeloved as she'd appeared in his mother's memories, back when she'd been studying at the SSFE. She'd been fresh-faced, trusting, optimistic about the life that lay ahead of her. It was just as well that she'd had no idea about the trauma she'd have to endure in her later years.

"What has Larry said about it all?" he asked reluctantly. Since Larry Higgins' agency had joined forces with Ribero's, the atmosphere between them had been nothing short of combustible.

"I'm sure you can imagine. He's already phoned me three times today, and on the last occasion, he threatened to dissolve the contract between our two agencies."

Kester frowned. "Of course he did." It was exactly how he'd expected the man to react, throwing out accusations at the drop of a hat, without attempting to understand the truth of the matter.

"It's a disaster," Miss Wellbeloved went on. "Oh, Kester, I hate to be so negative, but I really don't see how we can bounce back from this. Infinite Enterprises want to talk to us all too, about our involvement in your treachery."

"Why? They must know you had nothing to do with it."

"They know I'm fond of your father. They probably think I'm protecting you for his benefit."

He rubbed his temples, unsure what to say. It was comforting to hear her voice, but her words were a torment.

"I'd better go," he said finally, hearing distant laughter from the bar area. "I wish I could tell you that everything will be alright, but I can't. What I can promise is that I'll fight my hardest to resolve everything, even if it kills me."

"Don't say that."

"It's true. You have my word. And Miss Wellbeloved?"

"Yes?"

He paused. For a moment, he'd been tempted to share what Hrschni had shown him and to mention that he'd seen her as a young woman. But instinct forced the words into silence instead. He would tell Miss Wellbeloved in time; just not quite yet. He couldn't articulate why; he just knew it didn't feel right to blurt it out now, in this place.

"Nothing," he said eventually. "Nothing that can't wait, anyway."

It was a relief to clamber into bed at the end of the day. Kester peeled back the duvet and settled on the mattress, then finally realised just how weary he was. His body ached all over. He wished for nothing more than to sink into a blissfully dreamless sleep, but to his frustration, his mind refused to comply. Instead, a riot of thoughts raced around his head and refused to be silenced.

He tossed from one side to the other and back again, flipped the pillow this way and that, then attempted to pummel it into a more comfortable shape. Finally, he sat up, glaring angrily around himself. A thin strip of moonlight cast a watery glow across the floor. Normally, he found the sight of the moon relaxing. Tonight wasn't one of those occasions.

Any further attempts at sleep were futile. With a sigh, he switched the main light on. He gazed at the wall in front of him, then gasped.

The wall *had a face*. Such a thing shouldn't be possible, but nonetheless, there it was: a sharp, narrow face made of smoke and sand, swirling restlessly and watching him with burning intent. Kester screamed, reared back instinctively, and cracked the back of his head on the metal bedframe.

"Please," the face said, not unkindly, "calm yourself."

It drifted from the wall before moving into clearer focus. Kester grabbed his glasses from the bedside table, then exhaled heavily. It was only Dr. Barqa-Abu, not that there was really any *only* about it. Barqa-Abu was his teacher at the SSFE and, more unsettlingly, an ancient djinn. She was also one of the most prickly, uncompromising creatures he'd ever met, which made her presence in his room even more unnerving. Still, according to most people, that was how she was with everyone, so he supposed he shouldn't take it personally.

"Why are you here?" he asked, wrapping the duvet around himself in an attempt to hide his pyjamas. Actually, they weren't his at all, but his father's, and they happened to be a bright purple satin with black piping at the hems. They also had an embroidered monogram on the breast pocket, which made them infinitely more embarrassing.

Dr. Barqa-Abu floated closer, then rested at the foot of the bed. He fought against the urge to retreat; the last thing he wanted was to be accused of prejudice against spirits. The djinn was notoriously stern towards anyone who displayed signs of being a spiritist, even if offence hadn't been intended.

"It was the earliest I could come," she said, curling restlessly beside the duvet. "I was busy teaching; then Infinite Enterprises requested my presence for an informal interview about what had happened."

"But you weren't even there that night," Kester said. "Come to think of it, why weren't you? Everyone thought you'd help capture Hrschni. Fylgia struggled to subdue his energy on her own."

"I've already spoken to Fylgia. She understands how deeply complex this situation is. It is beyond the understanding of humans."

Kester sighed. He had no real fondness for Fylgia. The daemon was mischievous and always frustratingly slippery with her answers. Admittedly, she'd been working undercover, trying to prevent Hrschni from achieving his goals. However, she'd also inhabited his girlfriend's body for several weeks without him knowing. He'd lost his virginity to Anya while the daemon was hidden inside her. Even thinking about it made him feel somewhat queasy.

The djinn drifted in and out of focus, like a smoke-cloud in the breeze. "I have always taken pride in my fearlessness," she said slowly. "But this time, I was too frightened to act. I am ashamed of this fact."

Kester took a deep breath. He hadn't expected such honesty or vulnerability from the usually ferocious spirit. "If you'd have been there, Hrschni would have been captured, and none of this would have happened."

"I believe he sent you a USB stick, which had some CCTV footage on it?"

"He did. Do you know what was on it?"

"He sent a copy of it to me too. Or rather, he ordered one of the human Thelemites to do so. Hrschni loathes technology with a passion."

"Is that why you didn't come?"

"Yes. I couldn't, not after seeing what was on that recording. I'd heard rumours in the past, that Infinite Enterprises were exterminating my kind, but everyone denied it. I'm a fool, because I trusted that they were telling the truth."

Kester winced. He'd trusted them too, but the evidence had been undeniable. He'd watched the footage that showed a spirit being torn apart and witnessed the machine capable of such a thing.

"How long do you think it's been going on for?" he asked softly.

"I don't like to imagine."

"Do you think they're all in on it? The whole organisation?"

She shook her head. "Most of Infinite Enterprises' employees are decent people. I don't believe they know anything about it."

Kester agreed. After working on a case with Ian Kingdom-Green and Cardigan Cummings, not to mention Lili Asadi and Tinker, he couldn't imagine any of them approving of murdering spirits.

"What should we do?" he asked, simply.

"I do not know. On the one hand, we have a daemon who is intent on causing chaos by unleashing spirits into the world. But on the other, we have a human organisation who have the audacity to slaughter spirts."

"Presumably they were repeat offenders who refused to stay in their own realm?"

The djinn whirled towards him, too quickly for him to react. "That is no excuse for this cruelty!" she hissed, her breath hot and dry against his face. "I have always had faith in humans, always believed that, in spite of everything, they would make the right choices. Now, I am not so sure."

Kester waited, fighting to calm himself, as she retreated slowly to the other side of the room.

"You're right," he said, choosing his words carefully. "But we *have* to decide what to do, and quickly. Otherwise, the situation could get a lot worse."

She sighed and drew nearer again. "All I know is that I have a job to do, and now is the time to do it."

"What's the job?"

"I'm your teacher, Kester; am I not? So that is what I shall do. Teach you."

He blinked. "You mean, continue my spirit intervention lessons?"

"No, those can wait. I mean something much more important. Your spirit door opening skills."

"Oh, those." He slumped back down. "Dr. Barqa-Abu, you know how useless I am at it. It takes me ages to achieve anything, if I manage it at all."

"That is because you've had no formal training." She hovered on the bed beside him, a hazy bundle of angular lines and whirling air. Her eyes rested on him, and he rather wished they hadn't because they were like two burning coals, burrowing deep into the heart of him.

"Okay," he said slowly, edging instinctively backwards. "When did you want to start?"

"Now, Kester."

"Now?"

A hint of a smile played at her lipless mouth. "As you humans say," she told him, "there's no time like the present."

It was past three in the morning when Dr. Barqa-Abu finally let Kester return to bed. This time, he felt his eyes close almost immediately, despite the fact that the djinn remained in the room with him, studying him intently. *Don't spirits ever sleep?* he thought irritably, as he finally slid into unconsciousness.

He awoke to see the wintery light of the sun pouring through the window. At first, he thought he was alone, but then his skin prickled with tension. There was a spirit nearby, though how he could tell, he didn't know. It was something of a gift, or a curse, more likely. Sure enough, the air shivered before him only a few moments later before congregating into the restless dark mist that he'd become so familiar with.

"Your father indicated you liked to sleep until late in the day," Dr. Barqa-Abu said humourlessly.

Kester rubbed his eyes. "It's only just gone nine; it's not that late."

"It's late enough for you to have missed breakfast, I'm afraid." A glimmer of a smile appeared on her face. "I suspect this will come as something of a disappointment."

He swore under his breath. A full English breakfast would have been welcome and, if nothing else, would have improved his mood. Nine o'clock may have been late in the djinn's opinion, but the fact remained, he'd still only had six hours sleep.

"Can I nip out to the shops, at least? A sausage roll would do the job nicely."

"We have more important things to attend to than food."

Oh, that. He sighed. "I thought I was doing well last night. I created those last few spirit doors quickly, didn't I? And I closed them again before you could get sucked through."

"Kester, for the hundredth time, *please* do not refer to it as being *sucked through.* I am not a particle of dust being removed by a vacuum cleaner." She shook herself in a gust of warm air, then stared at him. "I refer to something else, as a matter of fact."

"Not the spirit doors, then?"

"No. Hrschni will be with us soon. Very soon, in fact. I sense him drawing near."

Kester's mouth fell open. "Aren't you worried about meeting him again? After all, you and Fylgia were working against him, and—"

"Spirits don't hold grudges. He was angry, of course. Full of rage, in fact. Much as he was when he discovered I'd worked against him thousands of years ago. But he and I understand one another. We know we desire different things, and we accept one another's differences."

Kester shook his head. The lives of the spirits had never made much sense to him, though that wasn't surprising. They were strange entities, with attitudes, opinions, and emotions that were entirely alien at times.

"Could I at least buy a packet of crisps or something?" he asked instead.

"No. You only have about five minutes. That's just enough time for you to wash and do whatever unpleasant human things you need to do."

He winced. Five minutes wasn't nearly enough time to prepare himself for another encounter with Hrschni. Still, it looked as though he had no choice in the matter.

"Off you go," she said, waving a bony hand in the direction of the shower-room.

"Off I go," he repeated glumly and locked the door behind him.

Exactly four minutes and forty-five seconds later, Hrschni materialised in the hotel room. Kester was unaware of this at first, due to the fact that he was still on the toilet. However, the spirits soon made their presence felt, largely by tutting outside the door and passing comments about the *base nature of the human body*.

After another few minutes, he emerged, red-faced and irritable. "I was doing my best to hurry up," he snapped, reaching for one of his father's shirts.

The twist of the daemon's mouth suggested amusement. "I am glad Dr. Barqa-Abu is helping you to hone your skills," he said, edging closer. He burned almost too brightly for the room to contain, an intense coil of energy that seemed liable to detonate at any moment.

"That doesn't mean I'll be using my skills to help you open a permanent door to the spirit world," Kester reminded him.

Hrschni shrugged, then glanced at the djinn. "There are forces at work that are bigger than all of us," he said. "Now, would you like to show me how you're progressing?"

"No, because it needs more work. I'm still very slow, but at least I know how to go about it. It's my mother, you see. For some reason, when I remember her, it makes opening a spirit door much easier."

Hrschni's light dimmed for a second, like a candle sputtering in a breeze. "That doesn't surprise me," he said gently. "She was a formidable woman. Speaking of which, it's time we picked up where we left off the other day."

"You want to show me more of her life?" Kester guessed.

"Correct. The truth must be seen." He reached across and pressed his finger to Kester's forehead. "We may as well make a start now."

"I'm still hungry," Kester muttered, though his thoughts already felt scattered, his mind rapidly descending into nothingness.

"We'll feed you later," the daemon promised, seemingly from far away.

Darkness washed over Kester, as it had done before. This time, he was more relaxed and let it carry him deeper, down into the same place of emptiness that he'd been before.

Let go, Hrschni spoke, a distant whisper, deep within his head. *Then you'll find your mother again.*

With a sigh, Kester sunk down into the black and lost himself entirely.

CHAPTER 3 – A DAGGER IN THE BACK

Gretchen checked over her shoulder one last time before slipping through the door. She was definitely alone, but that wasn't surprising. Hardly anyone used the subterranean study rooms, mainly because they were all claustrophobic, dark, and more than a little bit sinister.

This particular room felt more like a cell than a study room, with a narrow wooden desk in one corner, a flickering light overhead, and not much else. It was also the perfect place to practice. There would be no interruptions down here—no distractions and no questions from inquisitive students. She could focus entirely on exploring this strange, confusing ability of hers.

Squaring her shoulders, she took a deep breath, then stared at the empty space ahead. *Come on,* she thought, glaring hard, until her eyelids ached. *If I can somehow open these air-rips when I'm asleep, I should be able to manage it when I'm awake.*

At one point, the air grew hazy, though she wasn't sure if this was supernatural or due to the soreness of her eyes. Either way, the effort was too much. With a frustrated grunt, she slumped against the wall. Perhaps there was no point trying; maybe it only happened when she was asleep.

That'd be typical, she thought, grabbing her bag from the floor. *It'd be just like me to have a talent that's no real use whatsoever.*

If she listened hard, she could hear the dim clatter of footsteps high above. It only served to make her feel more isolated, more *different* from everyone else. All the other students seemed to know their place in the world; they had purpose, ambition, plans for the future. She felt clueless by comparison.

I'm wasting my time here, she thought, as she marched back towards the door. *I might as well give up.* The ramp leading up to the main building was long and steep, but she scarcely noticed. Instead, her thoughts were clouded with disappointment and a growing sense of panic. She felt like a fraud. Someone was bound to notice soon enough, and what then? Would they throw her out of the school? Would she have to return to her parents' house and get a job as a secretary or a shop-worker? Now she'd grown used to the SSFE; she couldn't imagine leaving it all behind.

As she emerged into the central atrium, it took a moment to acclimatise. The chaos of multiple students in motion was a shocking contrast to the quiet twilight atmosphere of the rooms below. A moment later, a firm hand slapped down on her shoulder, followed by a distinctive rumbling laugh. She turned with a smile, already knowing who it was. *Julio.* If there was one person who could cheer her up, it was him.

He beamed back at her, then let his hand slide down to his side.

"You were meant to meet me for study period," he said, eyes glittering with mock-anger. "I had to sit in the library on my own like the sad clown with no friends."

Gretchen winced. She'd completely forgotten. "I'm sorry," she said. "I'm all over the place at the moment."

"It's no matter. Are you going back to your room?"

"Yes, I need to grab my things for the next lecture."

"I will come with you. I want to see if Jennifer got the tickets for that music thing tonight."

"The Billy Dagger gig?" She laughed. "Dream on. It's a tiny venue; I bet the tickets sold out within minutes."

"I don't even know who this Dagger is."

"You must have spent your life living under a rock."

"No, I just know what I like, and what I do not." He wrinkled his nose. "Like you. You are a person that I like. I know we will be lifelong friends."

She grinned. "You can tell that already?"

"I can. We will still be laughing together, even when we are old. I guarantee it."

They climbed the spiral staircase to the girls' rooms, then paced along the corridor together. Jennifer emerged from the door as soon as they reached it, flushed and wild eyed. She held some papers aloft, then waved them triumphantly in their faces.

"Three tickets, look!"

Julio winked. "See, Gretchen? You were wrong. Jennifer has ways of getting what she wants, you see."

Jennifer tittered, then gave him a peck on the cheek. "It was all very strange. I was right at the back of the queue and felt sure I didn't stand a chance, then a man in a suit came over to me, said I'd been selected as a *VIP* fan, and asked me how many tickets I wanted. Can you believe it?"

"Are they genuine?" Gretchen asked sceptically.

"I think so."

"I will endure this Dagger if it makes you happy," Julio declared grandly. He wrapped Jennifer in a hug, and Gretchen stood back, focusing her gaze deliberately on the wall behind them. She was happy for them both, but their displays of affection made her feel lonelier somehow. She'd never had a boyfriend, mainly because her father had insisted that she attend a girl's school. Opportunities to even talk to boys had been few and far between, let alone date any of them.

It's not jealousy, she reminded herself, just as someone tapped her on the shoulder, making her jump. She turned to see another student, pointing down the corridor.

"You're Gretchen, aren't you?" she said. "There's a call for you, on the payphone."

Gretchen sighed. It was her mother; it always was. She only had a few minutes before her next lecture, so at least the conversation wouldn't be too long.

"Catch you later," she said to Jennifer and Julio, then paced quickly to the phone. The receiver was dangling by the wall, and she scooped it to her ear.

"Hi Mutti," she said, unable to keep the weariness from her voice.

"Ah, Gretchen. Dein Vater, er ist—"

"Mutti, can we speak in English?"

"Your father is unwell. It's his lungs; you know how much he coughs all the time, and finally he saw the doctors because it was so bad, and they've found something, and—"

"Wait, hang on." Gretchen rubbed her forehead. "What are you trying to tell me?"

Her mother let out a sob. "He's very ill, darling. Very ill indeed. I am sorry, there was no easy way to tell you."

"Tell me what? You still haven't told me—"

"It's serious, Gretchen."

Both women fell silent. Gretchen rolled her mother's news through her head, trying to understand it all. Was her father just sick or something even worse?

"Is it . . . ?" she asked, unable to finish the sentence.

Mutti paused. "Yes," she said eventually. "Please, come home as soon as you can. I will pay for your train ticket; it's not so far to travel."

"How long have I got? I mean, do I need to come now, or—"

"No, but sooner is better. Do you understand?"

She understood very well. A leaden feeling washed through her body before settling in the pit of her stomach. *My father is dying,* she realised, fixing her gaze on the hallway beyond, at all the other students emerging from their rooms. They all seemed unfamiliar, suddenly—creatures laughing and talking on another planet, unaware of the drama playing out just a few feet from where they stood.

Her father, close to death. It didn't seem possible. His face immediately came to mind: hard, distant, judgemental. The man she'd tried to please as a child, only to see her own failures in the coldness of his expression, the stiffness of his demeanour. It was difficult to view him in a positive light. He'd never smiled when she told him her childish secrets. Never laughed at her attempts at jokes or praised her for her achievements. She'd always felt like a disappointment to him.

"Gretchen?" Her mother's voice chimed down the line, startling her back into the present. "Will you come back soon?"

"I can't this week," she heard herself reply, in a flat, wooden voice. "We need to submit the theme of our thesis; it's important. But I will come soon, I promise. Is that okay?"

"I suppose so. We have weeks, I think. But not months. Do you hear me? *Not months.*"

Tears prickled in Gretchen's eyes. *Not months.* Her father was dying quickly, then. She thought back to all those years that he'd coughed and spluttered, bringing up thick globs of phlegm that he quickly concealed in his handkerchief. He'd probably been unwell for years and had chosen to ignore it, rather than see a doctor. Now it was too late.

"Mutti," she said, wiping a solitary tear as it slipped down her cheek. "Take care, okay?"

"I love you, darling."

Gretchen paused. "I know."

The phone line went dead. She cradled the receiver in her palm for a few moments, then placed it gently back in its place. Then, she turned to see Jennifer and Julio, both staring at her with concern.

"We weren't eavesdropping, honestly," Jennifer said. "But we could tell something was wrong. What's happened?"

Gretchen shrugged. "My dad's dying."

At once, she was wrapped in a tangle of arms, both Jennifer's and Julio's. She felt another tear slide down her face and was mortified that her friends should see her like this: weak and uncertain, defenceless as a baby bird. But despite that, she appreciated that they cared. It warmed her, even though she felt cold to the core.

"We don't have to go to the Billy Dagger gig tonight," Jennifer said, as they walked along. "I'll stay here with you."

"Absolutely not," Gretchen replied, pulling out a hankie and blowing her nose. "I know how much you like him; you have to go. I'll be all right here."

"No, I'm not leaving you."

"Honestly, I'll be fine."

"Ladies," Julio said, easing between them like melting butter. "The plans should carry on as before. Gretchen, you will want something to distract you, yes? That is the thing to do when you are in pain. That is, if you are not going home to your papa?"

"Not just yet," Gretchen confirmed.

"Well, then. This will help. Some loud music that hurts your ears and pushes out any sad thoughts, I think this is what any doctor would prescribe."

"I'm not sure that's what she needs," Jennifer added, as they reached the main atrium. "I'd be devastated if I'd just received news that my father was—"

Julio held up a finger. "Why doesn't Gretchen tell us what she needs, eh?"

Gretchen paused, taking in the vast space around her: the crowds, the footsteps clattering on the polished floor. Finally, she nodded. "I know it sounds callous, but I want to go. At the very least, I can have a few drinks to numb the shock of it."

Jennifer's tight expression suggested she thought the gig would be anything but helpful, but then, she wouldn't understand. She enjoyed a warm, loving relationship with her father, something entirely removed from Gretchen's own experiences.

"I'll see you two later, then," Jennifer said eventually.

Julio kissed her on the cheek, then put an arm around Gretchen's shoulder. "I will look after her, don't worry," he said loudly. "You have my word."

Jennifer's smile was watery and uncertain. "That's good," she said, before she was lost in the swarms of people pacing around them. When the crowd had cleared, Gretchen saw that her friend was already some distance away, scurrying towards a hallway on the other side of the atrium. She felt a pang of guilt but wasn't sure why.

My emotions are a mess, she reminded herself, as she and Julio headed in the opposite direction. *One thing's for sure; life is about to get a whole lot more complicated.*

The lecture was long, the minutes stretching impossibly, the hands of the clock above the teacher's desk seemingly frozen in place. Gretchen absentmindedly took down notes, without knowing what she'd written. She wished she'd stayed in her room instead, burrowed her head into her pillow, and shut out the world around her. Anything would have been better than attempting to feign normality while her thoughts were in turmoil.

Afterwards, Julio scurried to her side. "Are you sure that you're okay?" he asked, as they left the lecture room and pushed through the doors to the main square.

She waved his comment away. "Please, let's talk about something else. Tell me something exciting. Something happy. Anything to take my mind off things."

"As you wish. The big news of the day is that I have decided what I will do my thesis on," he announced grandly. "It is a very progressive idea. I think I will get excellent marks for it."

She smiled, in spite of herself. She wished she had even a fraction of her friend's natural confidence. "What's your idea, then?" she asked, taking a moment to breathe in the fresh air. The main building was across the square, and the lawns were crammed with students enjoying the afternoon sun. She envied their carefree afternoon, the simple pleasure of just lying on the grass, nibbling sandwiches, and sipping fizzy drinks. By contrast, her own life felt like it was getting messier by the day.

"My thesis," Julio continued, snapping his fingers in front of her face, "will be an examination of shamanist ritual and how it is used, even to this day, in the world of the supernatural."

"Don't you think other people will have done that in the past?" she said doubtfully.

"Ah, but I will link it to the modern day. This will not be a dull paper all about the history. This will be new and exciting."

"If anyone can pull it off, it's you."

A loud snort from close by startled them both. They looked over their shoulders to see Larry following them, leather briefcase swinging in one hand, immaculate ring-binder file in the other. Gretchen caught Julio's eye, then groaned quietly.

"I just overheard what you said," Larry declared, panting as he fought to keep up with them. "Shamanist ritual? That subject's as old as the hills. Why would you choose something so unutterably tedious for your thesis?"

"This will not be tedious," Julio said stiffly. "And it is none of your business."

"Keep your hair on, I was only trying to assist."

"I would worry about your own thesis rather than mine. Because you have reason to worry."

Larry reddened. "What's that supposed to mean?"

"Mrs. Trow-Hunter thinks you are the pillock."

"She thinks no such thing. Why would you say that?"

"Because she muttered the word *pillock* when you asked that silly question in the lecture today. Yes, I am sure of it. *Pillock.* That is what she said. It may have been *big pillock,* in fact—"

"I'll have you know that woman thinks I show enormous promise."

"As an even bigger pillock in the future," Julio whispered to Gretchen, who giggled.

Larry poked Julio squarely in the chest, stopping him in his tracks. "You do know I can hear you, don't you? You've got a voice like a bullfrog."

"Thankfully not the face though, eh? Still, you may grow out of it one day."

The strangled noise issuing from Larry's throat would have been enough to concern most people, but Julio's glee seemed to increase alongside his classmate's rage. Gretchen tugged on his arm, hurrying him away. She knew, if left to his own devices, he'd continue to goad Larry for hours.

"Let's go and find Jennifer," she suggested. "Then we can get prepared for going out tonight."

"Ah yes, the Dagger thing." He gestured at his body. "Do you think what I am wearing is okay? Is this what the people wear to the music thing?"

She studied him, taking in the polished shoes, the smart suit trousers, and the flowing silk shirt. On anyone else, it would have looked ostentatious. Ridiculous even. But somehow, as with everything else, he managed to pull it off.

"You'll do," she said, giving his arm a squeeze.

The music venue was hidden down a narrow alley, its entrance already overflowing with people, all fighting to wedge themselves through the doors. Gretchen shivered and pulled her denim jacket more tightly around herself. Although it had been a warm enough day, the temperature had now dropped, and the distinct bite of an autumn wind gusted around them all.

Am I coldhearted for doing this? she wondered, as she jostled her way to the front of the queue with Jennifer and Julio. Her father was at home now, perhaps already rigged up to a breathing apparatus, and here she was, out having fun. Mutti had asked her to come home straight away, and she'd refused. The truth was, she couldn't face him. She understood the severity of the situation; the word *death* had been chiming around her head all day, but the reality hadn't sunk in yet. Her lack of emotion disturbed her, more than she wanted to admit.

"Are you okay?" Jennifer asked gently, startling her from her brooding.

Gretchen shook herself and forced a smile. "I'm fine."

"Let me know if you want to go back. I wouldn't mind, honestly."

"You're sweet. But this will be good for me."

"See?" Julio said, interrupting. "It will be good. Stop reminding her of it, Jennifer." He wrinkled his nose, peering at the people around him. "This is a stinking place, is it not? Bad smells. People not washing."

Gretchen winced as the surrounding crowd glared at him in unison. "I'm sure everyone's washed," she whispered. "It's just that kind of place, that's all."

"The ground is sticky too. Sticky with what? With nasty vomit? With the body fluids, all spilling out?"

"It's a music venue, not an operating theatre," Jennifer hissed. "Keep your voice down. You're getting attention, and not in a good way."

Julio shrugged, his expression mutinous. Thankfully, the queue started to move before he could say anything more, and soon, they found themselves being shoved forward into the foyer. They handed over their tickets, then joined the surging crowds inside.

"Someone spilled their beer on my shirt," Julio groaned, as they fought to find room in the packed venue. "This is finest silk and is not easy to clean."

"Please stop fussing," Jennifer said. "The support act will be on in a minute, and I don't want you moaning all the way through it."

Gretchen nodded to the bar, which was just about visible over the sea of heads. "Shall I get us some drinks?" she shouted over the noise.

"That is my job, as the man," Julio said.

"I'm perfectly capable, as the woman."

"But the man does the—"

"Julio, don't push it," Jennifer said. "We live in the twentieth century, not the Victorian era."

Gretchen snaked a path through the multitudes of pressing bodies. To her dismay, the bar was enveloped in a crowd of people, all waving their money at the barman and shouting orders. She spied a gap at the far end and forced her way towards it.

A group of girls barged in front of her, and she sighed. It was at times like this that she wished she was a foot taller, and a stone heavier too. Still, she was out to have fun, and it was taking her mind off things, which was the main thing.

Except I'm not having fun yet, she thought glumly, as she was jostled aside by yet more people. *And I can't stop my thoughts going to dark places.*

Suddenly, a flash of movement caught her eye, something *different,* unexpected, in a way she couldn't immediately identify. Turning towards it, she glimpsed a vague outline of a figure, concealed in the shadows of a doorway by the stage. She squinted to see better, but all she could make out was a hint of cheekbone gleaming in the light, and a hand, slung casually into a pocket. The person stepped forward, as though sensing her attention, and revealed himself fully.

It was a face she recognised immediately—hardly surprising, given that it graced a poster in her bedroom back home. *Billy Dagger!* Her heart quickened with excitement. She was surprised that no one else had noticed him, but then, his movements were slow and surreptitious. Perhaps he liked to survey his fans before performing. It must boost his ego, knowing they were all here to see him.

He turned his head and met her gaze squarely, with casual interest. She blushed and quickly looked away. The last thing she wanted was to be thought of as just another lovesick groupie. After a few seconds, she dared to glance back, expecting him to be gone, but he was still there, albeit concealed in the shadows again. He raised a hand, finger curled in her direction. It took her a while to realise that he was beckoning her to come closer.

How is no one else seeing this? she thought, looking around. Every other person's gaze seemed to be fixed in a different direction, as though they were wilfully, deliberately ignoring the rock star's presence. It made no sense.

Slowly, she walked towards him. The crowds parted with surprising ease, and the thrum of conversation seemed suddenly muted, as though the volume had been turned down. She herself felt like she was under some sort of spell.

Maybe this is a hallucination, she told herself. After all, things like this didn't happen to people like her. But the explanation didn't ring true. Although she was emotionally overwrought, she felt calm, level-headed. All the details were in sharp focus: from the smell of beer and too many human bodies to the stuffiness of the room and the faces of the people around her. This was real, she was certain of it.

"Hello?" she said, creeping through the doorway and into the passage beyond. Billy Dagger had edged back into the darkness, and she could only just detect the silhouette of his body. That and his eyes, which were gleaming almost unnaturally in the limited light filtering from the bar area.

Slowly, he extended a hand. "Pleased to meet you."

She paused, then shook it. His skin felt warm, hot even, but not clammy, and strangely smooth too. If she hadn't known better, she would have thought his skin had been carved from stone.

I'm touching Billy Dagger! she thought, adrenaline surging through her limbs. Quickly, she pulled her hand away, aware that her grip had already lingered for too long.

"Aren't you worried people will see you?" she said. "You'll be mobbed."

He smiled. "I'm not worried. Just pleased to meet you, as I said."

She studied him carefully. Even though he was motionless, he exuded energy: an imperceptible wave of heat that radiated from his person. *I suppose this is why people call him a rock god,* she thought, stifling a smile. There was something almost inhuman about him, though she couldn't say what, exactly. Perhaps this was what geniuses were like in person: different, in a multitude of confusing ways.

"I'm pleased to meet you too," she replied quietly. "Surprised but pleased."

"I was watching you, earlier."

"Watching me?" Gretchen grimaced. "Why? I'm nothing special."

"I don't know about that. You attend the SSFE, don't you?"

"Excuse me?"

He stepped into the light, then leaned casually on the wall beside her. She swallowed hard, feeling trapped by his presence, like a butterfly pinned to a specimen board. It wasn't just that he was handsome; it was the way his eyes fixed her in place and insisted on holding her gaze in return.

"I apologise, Gretchen," he said. "You're probably wondering how I know about the SSFE."

Her eyes widened. "And my name."

"That too, but don't be alarmed. I'm not a predatory celebrity, looking for a good time with a starry-eyed fan. You interest me, so I wanted to meet you."

"I interest you?" She took a step back. "I don't understand. I'm not interesting at all."

"That's not true." He grinned, a mischievous twist of the lips that made her cheeks burn. "I find you interesting, and I know you're capable of great things."

She edged back. The situation was out of her control; she felt as though she were sinking slowly, unable to pull herself to safety. But she wasn't a foolish school girl, goggle eyed and naive. She was an adult, albeit a young one, and needed to start acting like one. *He may be famous,* she reminded herself sternly, *but he's just a human, like me.*

"It was incredible to meet you," she said stiffly, folding her arms. "I should probably return to my friends now; it sounds like the support act are on."

He nodded. "I understand. It's been an honour to finally talk to you. I sense that our paths will cross again, someday soon."

"I can't imagine they would. You'll be touring around the country. I'll just be getting on with my studies and muddling through life."

He leaned closer, so close she could feel the heat of his breath on her cheek. "Something has happened," he said, frowning. "You're worried. Unhappy."

"I've got to go," she said firmly, stepping away. She was unsettled by his manner towards her and by the response he provoked in her. She felt *driven* towards him, in a way that baffled and excited her in equal measures.

He's right, we will see each other again, she thought incomprehensibly. She closed her eyes and tried to gather her thoughts. When she opened them again, Billy Dagger had gone.

It was impossible for someone to move so fast. Frowning, she peered down the corridor. It was dark down there, which would have made disappearing easier. But still, she hadn't heard his footsteps, nor sensed his departure.

Strange. Very strange. Now that he'd gone, it was beginning to feel less and less like reality and more like something she'd only imagined. After waiting a while longer, she turned reluctantly back to the bar. Her friends were still waiting for a drink, and judging by the deafening music, the support act was already in full swing. Her instinct was to tell Jennifer and Julio what had happened, but she knew they wouldn't believe her. They'd laugh, presume she'd made a mistake, or somehow been taken in by an imposter. It *had* been Billy Dagger, though. She was willing to stake her life on it.

Still, it would be pointless to tell them, and there wasn't much to tell anyway about that brief, peculiar conversation. *Besides,* she thought, as she squeezed back through the crowd, *I've got enough to be concerned about at the moment without adding to my worries.*

It had just been one of those odd occasions, that was all. Something to tell the children in the future: the *bizarre* time she'd had a conversation with the legendary Billy Dagger, just before he'd rocked the room to a crowd of delighted, baying fans. It would never be repeated, despite what he'd said. She was nobody, after all, and nobodies scarcely got to talk to their heroes once in their lives, let alone twice.

The week passed in a monotone of tedious lectures and library research. Gretchen's thoughts often drifted back to what had happened at the gig, though she felt guilty about it. She knew she should be thinking about her father, not a man she'd only talked to for a few minutes in a darkened passageway. She craved solitude, even more than usual. It wasn't that she didn't enjoy spending time with Jennifer and Julio; in fact, in the short time she'd known them, she'd grown to see them as integral parts of her life. But she needed silence, a place to just exist and to understand herself a little better. At the SSFE, where the corridors constantly rang with the noise of thousands of students, finding some tranquillity was almost impossible.

The following weekend, she packed her rucksack with a few clothes, said goodbye to her friends, then walked to the local station. She couldn't delay going home any further, even though the thought of sitting with her father in their dingy living room, listening to the mantlepiece clock ticking while he coughed, glared, and shifted about in his armchair wasn't pleasant. But she had to see him, despite her reservations. She *needed* to see it for herself, for it to finally sink in.

She caught the tube to London Liverpool Street, then boarded the train to Cambridge. *Here's the alone time I wanted,* she thought, as the train started to pick up speed, racing away from the capital. *Funny, now I've got some peace and quiet, I don't like it at all.*

As she watched the fields fly past, she thought again about Billy Dagger. She was embarrassed by how regularly he'd invaded her thoughts in the last few days. Anyone else would call it a silly crush, a girlish fantasy about someone unattainable. It was more complex than that, though. She remembered the intensity of their exchange, the eerie inevitability of it, as though he'd been waiting there, just for her. The warmth of his hand still seemed to linger on her skin—though of course, she knew that was impossible.

I need to focus on my father, not him, she reminded herself. *That's what matters right now.*

"I am so glad you are here," Mutti said, reaching for Gretchen as soon as the front door opened and pulling her into a stiff hug. "I knew you would come soon."

Gretchen reluctantly stepped inside. She was overcome by how *small* the house felt, even though she hadn't been away from it for long. There was a smell to it too: a dank, stale odour that permeated from the wallpaper, the patterned carpets, perhaps from her mother too. She heard a wracking cough coming from the lounge and winced.

"How is he?" she asked, prising herself from her mother's arms.

"I want you to prepare yourself. Things have gotten worse, very quickly, and—"

"Let me see him." Gretchen entered the lounge, then stopped abruptly. As expected, her father was in his armchair, only now, he was bundled in a blanket, oxygen mask strapped to his face, hands curled around the armrests like claws. He looked diminished, a shrunken husk of what he'd been before, and the sight stole her breath away. She didn't just see a man who was dying; she saw a creature who had become death itself—a skeletal, cold thing, inhabiting the body of the father she'd once known.

He raised his head at her arrival, then closed his eyes.

"Good afternoon, Gretchen. You are back."

"Mutti asked me to come back," she clarified, awkwardly.

"Yes. I told her not to."

I told her not to. The words echoed in her head, along with her own added subtext; *he didn't want me here.* He'd never wanted her, really. She perched on the sofa beside him, unsure what to say. His pain was evident in the tightness of his jaw and the tense hunch of his posture, yet she still found it difficult to summon any feeling towards him, apart from vague, disconnected pity.

"It is bad," he said finally, in a conversational tone. "They have not given me long."

She kept her gaze focused on the floor. It was easier that way.

"How long have you got?" she asked.

"A few months if I am lucky. But we will not talk about it, because there is no point. Death is a part of life, and I must accept it. To be honest, I believed that your Mutti and I would die in the war. I never thought we would survive beyond that."

"What do you want to talk about?"

He coughed again, then pulled the mask away. "I did not think it was a good idea at first for you to come. But now I know I must tell you some important things, Gretchen. I should have told you years ago, but I did not have the right words. Sometimes, the longer you leave something, the harder it is to do."

She waited. This was a side to her father she hadn't seen before. Expressive. Keen to share information. Usually, any questions she asked were met with a monosyllabic response or a request to stop bothering him with meaningless matters.

Just as he opened his mouth, her mother poked her head around the doorway.

"Would you like some tea and cake?" she asked, eyes flitting anxiously between the two of them.

"No, I'm fine," Gretchen replied, glancing back at her father, sensing his rising irritation.

Mutti was not deterred. "Gerhard, we need to give you the medication in ten minutes."

"I know!" her father snapped, before breaking into a fresh round of coughing. "Mein Gott, woman, please let me have this moment with my daughter. You know this has to be done."

Mutti's lips pressed together in disapproval, but with a curt nod, she retreated to the kitchen. Gretchen waited again, studying her father with curiosity and confusion. She'd expected some sort of intense conversation during her visit, but this wasn't what she'd anticipated.

Her father took a deep breath, then continued. "Do you know how your mother and I escaped Germany?" he asked eventually, scratching at the worn fabric on the armrest.

She nodded. "Mutti told me you had help from a war hero."

"Yes, Captain Monty Fletcher. He was my dearest friend. Do you understand, Gretchen? I loved him, very much."

"What are you trying to tell me?"

"That I owe my life to him, but the price of his help was too high."

"What do you mean?"

"He asked me to do a terrible thing." Her father leaned forward, finger pointed in her direction. "He wasn't who he seemed, and—"

"Dad, are you telling me he was homosexual? Or that you both were? That's not a 'terrible thing,' but you have to tell Mutti, because it's not right to—"

"No, not that. You have drawn the wrong conclusion, but I cannot blame you for it. What I am trying to say is that Monty was *not human.*"

Not human? Gretchen frowned, sitting up straighter. "What was he, then?" she asked, cautiously.

Her father massaged his forehead, as though the memory of it pained him. "He was a daemon who wanted to use me to change the world," he said eventually.

"Wait a minute," she said, interrupting. Her father had obviously planned a speech and was ready to rattle through it, but she couldn't grasp what he was trying to tell her. A *daemon?* Did he mean a monstrous person? It was impossible to tell.

He glowered at her. "It cannot wait."

"But I don't understand what you're saying."

"Captain Monty was a daemon, a highly advanced type of spirit. He was so clever, so full of zest and passion; I was almost convinced. He wanted my help because of what I can do. I am a spirit door opener, Gretchen. A very rare thing. And I—"

"Spirit door?" Gretchen immediately thought of her own experiences: the endless nightmares she'd had throughout her life, her instinctive fear of doorways leading to places unknown. She tensed, hands pressed hard against her knees.

"Please, stop interrupting me. This is hard for me to say."

She forced herself to take a breath, then sat patiently, rearranging her features into a neutral expression. Of all the things he'd ever taught her in life, the most useful skill was to conceal her thoughts and emotions, even when they raged inside her like a turbulent ocean.

"I said no to Monty," he continued. "Or *Hrschni*, I should say, because that is his real name. He was angry with me. He felt betrayed, and when I think of it now, I do not blame him. I made promises to him that I did not keep. But I could not open that spirit door, Gretchen! I could not do it! So, I broke the daemon's heart, and he left me in peace. Until you were born, that is."

"Me?"

"He returned, briefly. He told me that you had the same talent, that you were *full* of ability. More than me, perhaps. Oh Gretchen, why did you have to inherit it? It is a dangerous gift; that is why I didn't tell you for so long. I thought if you didn't know you could open spirit doors, you would never use your talent, and it would fade and die."

"All those years, I was scared about the rips in the air," she said heavily. "I thought they were terrible nightmares, and I was afraid, all the time. If you'd have told me, I could have understood things better. Why didn't you?"

"I waited until you were old enough, then sent you to SSFE," he said, flinching at her anger. "I gave you the chance to learn about the supernatural world and understand its perils a little better."

"I still don't understand anything, and the air keeps ripping up, Dad. There are *things* hidden in those rips; they could have hurt me, and you were happy to let me take that risk?"

Her father sank back in his chair. "I thought if we pretended it did not happen, it might go away. Then you could be safe. *We* could be safe."

"You should have told me sooner. All these years, I thought there was something wrong with me; you could have made my childhood a lot easier." As the words tumbled out, Gretchen could see the pain they caused him, but she couldn't hold them in. He'd *known*. All this time, he'd kept it a secret when he could have been helping her. As always, he'd focused solely on his own perspective, rather than hers.

"You blame me, and I cannot do anything about that. But listen to me, because this is important. You must—"

"No." She rose from the seat. "I *mustn't* do anything you say anymore. I'm your *daughter*, and you've let me down in the worst possible way."

"Gretchen, stop this childishness. There are bigger things to be concerned with. If you are truly opening spirit doors, then you are in danger, and—"

"Oh, spare me. You're a spirit door opener, and you've been fine all these years. The daemon left you alone after a while, you said so yourself. Don't worry about it, I'll be fine. Now that I know what I am, I can find someone else to help me understand myself better."

"Ach no, this is not what I want you to—" His words were interrupted by a series of barking coughs, followed by a guttural choking sound. Quickly, he reached for his oxygen mask and sucked on it greedily.

Mutti rushed into the room, casting a suspicious look at Gretchen as she passed.

"What did you say to him?" she hissed.

"Nothing that he didn't need to hear."

Sighing, her mother knelt beside him. "Gerhard, take deep breaths. It is not good to get so excited. You said this would be a calm conversation!"

"Don't worry," Gretchen said, resting a hand on her mother's shoulder. "It's better if I leave now, anyway. I'm only upsetting him."

"Nonsense, you only just got here. You cannot leave; your father needs you."

"I'll come back another time, when things are calmer."

"There may not be another time; look at him, my sweetheart! Please, it took a lot for him to say these things; there is more he needs to tell you and—"

Gretchen shook her head. "Not now. Please, I can't bear it."

"But you were going to stay the night. Please, we need you here."

Her father tugged of his mask, grabbed a tissue, and spat into it. "Let her go," he said heavily. "If she will not listen, I cannot tell her these things."

"Gerhard, you said yourself that it was important to—"

"There is no point. Not now, anyway."

"See?" Gretchen waved a hand at her father. "For once we agree."

Mutti clutched her face with her hands, defeated. "This is not how it was meant to be," she said, gazing at her daughter imploringly.

Gretchen shrugged. "But that's the way it is." She grabbed her rucksack on the way out and strode to the front door. Her mother scuttled after her, still entreating her to stay.

Her father could open spirit doors, and so could she. It was *real*; she now had irrefutable proof. The knowledge was terrifying, but she couldn't deny it thrilled her too, in a strange, indefinable way. Perhaps it was the sheer power of the ability that was exciting. It was a skill that could achieve so much more than just conversing with spirits or sensing their intentions.

But it's a power I have no control over, she thought, as she tugged at the front door handle. *And if I'm creating spirit doorways, that means spirits can slip through them, and they can get to me.*

She turned, then dutifully kissed her mother on the cheek. "Let me know if he gets worse."

Her mother shook her head in disbelief. "Please be less hasty. Give him some time to calm himself, then you can talk again."

"There's no point. You know what he's like."

"I do, but *you* don't know why. He is frightened for you. His hard words, they come from a place of love."

Gretchen snorted. "I'll take your word for it. See you soon, Mutti."

A place of love. As she walked back down the road, the words ran around her head, over and over again. Her childhood home had never felt like a *place of love,* but she understood that her father loved her deep down, in an awkward, uncompromising way. However, she couldn't forgive him for hiding the truth for so long. He must have known what she was going through, but he'd done nothing to ease her fear. Instead, he'd left her to suffer on her own.

Her thoughts turned to the daemon he'd mentioned: Captain Monty, or whatever his spirit name had been. Her father had indicated the creature had been interested in her as a baby; was he trying to warn her that she might be in danger?

I think I'd notice if a daemon was lurking around, she thought, quickening her pace. Also, she spent most of her time in SSFE, with several students who were adept at picking up the presence of a spirit. She felt sure someone would warn her if she was being stalked by a supernatural entity.

With a sigh, she glanced back over her shoulder. The house looked almost ludicrously small from this distance, squeezed in between two other near-identical buildings. It seemed inconsequential, as though one hard shove would bring it tumbling down. She'd return soon, she vowed, once she'd come to terms with the news. Her father was dying, she understood that. But she couldn't face him right now. The implications of what he'd just revealed were too overwhelming, and she needed some time alone, to think about it all.

CHAPTER 4 – ON THE RUN

Darkness again.

Kester opened his eyes slowly. He found himself staring up at the ceiling, struggling to catch his breath. His heart was thudding against his ribs too, but worse than that, he felt utterly wrung out by what he'd witnessed. His mother had *met* Billy Dagger. Through her eyes, he'd seen the rock star up close—not the ageing man he'd been when Kester had seen him in concert a few months ago, but young, vital, and attractive.

More importantly, that had been the moment she'd first met Hrschni. From Kester's viewpoint, it hadn't looked like a chance encounter either. As Gretchen had intuited, the daemon had been waiting for her.

He rubbed his eyes, then looked around him. Hrschni had departed, though at what point, he wasn't sure, and Dr. Barqa-Abu had gone too. Presumably, she'd recognised his need to recover.

They understand how I need to be alone, he thought, remembering how his mother had felt, back in the swathes of those borrowed memories. He hadn't just witnessed her emotions; he'd lived them too. He'd experienced firsthand the rage at her father and the bitter sting of his coldness towards her. He was ashamed. In all the years he'd spent with her, he'd had no idea that her relationship with Gerhard had been so painful. Now, more than ever, he realised that he hadn't really known her at all.

After a while, he sat up. His stomach churned in response—hardly surprising, given it was well past lunchtime, and he still hadn't eaten anything. He wondered if Hrschni or Dr. Barqa-Abu would be returning any time soon. For all he knew, they could be here already, hiding from view, though he didn't think so. Usually, he had an inkling when they were around.

"Anyone there?" he called out tentatively. "If so, is it alright if I nip downstairs for some food?"

He waited. There was no response, which as far as he was concerned, was as good as an affirmative. Smoothing his hair in the mirror, he slipped out of the room and headed downstairs. The bar area was full of people, mostly elderly tourists, who were chattering loudly. Squeezing past them, he finally reached the barman, who nodded in recognition.

"If you want food, it'll be a while," he said, waving around the room. "These people have all just ordered, and there are a lot of roast dinners on the list, I can tell you."

"I'd die for a roast dinner," Kester said yearningly. "Can I order one too?"

"With the trimmings?"

"And more. Extra trimmings laid on top of the existing trimmings, if possible."

The barman laughed. "Right you are. Want a drink while you're waiting?"

"Yes, a tea please. And two bags of cheese and onion crisps."

"Are you expecting company?"

"No, they're just for me."

"Wow, you really are hungry." The barman slammed the packets of crisps in front of Kester, then pointed to the table by the door. "That's the only one that's free; I'd get in quick before it's gone. Go on, I'll bring your drink over in a moment."

Kester scuttled quickly to the table, then sank down. Judging by the excited thrum of conversation around him, the tourist group had just returned from a tour of the prison. He'd heard of the famous Dartmoor Prison, of course, but so far, had yet to see it.

Perhaps that's somewhere I could visit while I'm stuck here, he thought, then imagined his colleagues' reactions. Serena would probably remind him that he wasn't here on holiday, and Miss Well-beloved would undoubtedly mutter something about needing to be more frugal with money. He smiled ruefully. He missed them all badly and wished they were all here now, regardless of how angry they might be with him.

He missed his mother too, more than ever. Seeing her alive again was agonising, even if it was only an echo of who she'd once been, trapped in visions of the past. She might have had her secrets, but she'd been his world, back when he'd been a child. The ache of her death hit him afresh, and he swallowed the lump in his throat, reluctant to show emotion in a room full of strangers.

The barman placed a mug of tea in front of him, then hovered for a moment, studying him with interest.

"Have I got something on my face?" Kester said eventually, wiping at his cheeks.

"No mate, I'm just curious about you." Without warning, he sat down beside him and leaned in closer. "Hope you don't mind me asking, but are you in trouble with the police?"

"Of course not! Why do you ask?"

The barman frowned. "We had a funny phone call earlier. A woman claimed she was from a government organisation and said they were looking for a young male with glasses and brown hair. I thought of you, and it made me wonder."

Kester stiffened. *Infinite Enterprises*, he thought, fighting to keep his expression neutral. *It has to be.* "What did you tell them?" he asked, keeping his voice light.

"I didn't say anything, don't worry. I mean, it's a pretty loose description, isn't it? It could be anyone. They wanted my email address so they could send a photo through, but I said I didn't have time for all of that."

They're coming for me, Kester realised, swallowing hard. He should have known they would, eventually. This was *Infinite Enterprises,* the biggest and best-funded supernatural agency in the country. If they wanted to track him down, they would, sooner or later.

The barman stood, making Kester startle. "I'd better get back to it," he said, pointing at the bar. "I hate busy days like these."

"Yes, thank you," Kester replied distractedly. His instinct was to run out of the pub straight away, to catch the next bus, regardless of where it might take him. But he knew he needed to *think* first. If Infinite Enterprises had managed to track him here, the big question was *how.* What had given him away, and how long would it be until they arrived in person?

Waiting until the barman's back was turned, he slid carefully from the table and dashed back up to his room. To his relief, Dr. Barqa-Abu was already there, weaving restlessly in the air like a storm cloud. Hrschni appeared too, only moments later, a bright flash that lit up the room before dimming to a smouldering glow.

"Why were you down in the bar?" the djinn snapped. "We have a situation here."

"How did you know I was down there?"

"We saw you, of course."

"Why didn't you say something?"

Hrschni's eyes narrowed. "I suspect our presence may have raised some eyebrows. We have no time to lose; we must—"

"I know, Infinite Enterprises are coming," Kester interrupted. He seized his father's clothes from the floor and started bundling them back in the bag.

"I have been to Exeter," Hrschni said, watching him race around. "Your father is unable to fetch you. His illness is bad today; he's in no state to drive."

"I'll get the bus."

"No, that won't do. Infinite Enterprises know you caught the bus here, and they will be checking all buses leading out of the area. Miss Wellbeloved will be assisting us instead."

Kester stood up abruptly. "Miss Wellbeloved?"

"Yes. She is on her way already and will be here shortly."

"Won't they be following her?"

The daemon nodded solemnly. "Quite possibly. But we will try a new strategy today. Dr. Barqa-Abu will be talking to them."

"That's right," the djinn added. "I won't be able to convince them to drop the case, I'm sure. As far as they're concerned, you've broken the law of supernatural conduct and let a dangerous spirit loose. However, I may be able to help them see things from your perspective."

"It will also distract them while you escape," Hrschni said. His left eye momentarily ceased glowing before reigniting again. Kester wondered if it had been a daemonic version of a wink.

With a sigh, he continued packing, then suddenly straightened. "What about my roast dinner?" he said, looking first at one, then the other. "I'm very hungry."

Dr. Barqa-Abu sharpened to angular focus. "You can't sit down and enjoy a big meal!" she hissed. "Now is not the time!"

"At least I could ask for it to be put in a doggy bag?"

"No doggy bags, Kester! This is serious."

He pouted. "Fine," he said eventually, wondering if he'd get to eat anything at all today. The way things were going, he didn't fancy his chances.

Miss Wellbeloved's car rolled into the main car park ten minutes later, and Kester scrambled into the passenger seat, throwing his bag onto the seat behind. Immediately, the car screeched off in a squeal of tires as it careered down the road.

He scarcely dared to look at Miss Wellbeloved, even though they'd spoken only yesterday on the phone. When he finally summoned the courage to glance over, he was instantly struck by how gaunt she looked. *These last few days have taken their toll on her,* he thought, feeling guilty all over again. Even though he wouldn't have done anything differently, he still bitterly regretted that things had turned out the way they had.

"How have you been?" she asked eventually, offering him a tight smile.

He grimaced. "Things have been better."

"Tell me about it."

"I'm sorry," he blurted. "I did what I thought was right, and perhaps I was wrong, because now we're—"

"Don't be silly. If Infinite Enterprises are putting spirits to death, that's an unspeakable crime. I've already told the others about it."

"What did they say?"

"Pamela and Mike understood at once. In fact, Pamela kept going on about longing to give you a big hug, so I'd watch out for that when you next see her. She'll probably never release you."

The knowledge that they were no longer angry made him feel immediately better. "I could do with a big hug, to be honest," he said with a smile. "What about Serena?"

Miss Wellbeloved shrugged. "Serena is *being Serena*. She thought you were lying. Then she argued that some spirits might deserve to be exterminated. You know what she gets like."

"I do."

"There have been other developments too," she continued, as they wheeled around a tight corner, throwing Kester painfully against the door. "Which unfortunately, spell even worse news for the agency."

"What now?"

"Crispian. Infinite Enterprises informed us that he's registered himself as a sole trader, operating as a professional spirit-sighter. He's apparently already used your father's stolen diary to email all our contacts, offering his services. He also used the confidential pass-words to log on to SpiritNet and has registered to bid for work."

Kester whistled. "Mike was right about his brother then. He really is a colossal git."

"We wondered if it was an act of revenge, to show Mike up. You know how they feel about each other."

Kester did. It was sad really, that the two brothers loathed each other so deeply. In fairness, Crispian had extended the olive branch since he'd come down to Exeter, but the resentment between them had been too intense to overcome. Plus, he could see why Mike disliked Crispian so much. The man was oily, self-satisfied, and enormously irritating.

"We were already the scourge of the supernatural community, thanks to letting Hrschni escape," Miss Wellbeloved continued, as the car zipped around another corner. "Now, thanks to Crispian's actions, we're a laughingstock too. It's a shame; his talent would have actually helped our agency considerably."

"It wouldn't have helped Mike's sanity much."

"No, that's true." She glanced at him over her glasses. "So, I'm hoping you've already come up with a master plan on how to fix all of this?"

He gulped. "Not quite yet. Dr. Barqa-Abu spent most of last night teaching me to hone my spirit door opening abilities, though."

"So I heard. I fail to understand why that's a focus at the moment, though. I thought she was working against Hrschni. Now it rather looks as though she's helping him achieve his goals."

"Things are never that clear-cut though, are they?" Kester said. "You taught me that."

She smiled slightly. "Yes, I suppose I did."

He wondered whether to tell her about the visions that Hrschni had shown him, of her and his mother as students, but decided against, for now. It felt uncomfortably like spying, even though Miss Wellbeloved wasn't the focus of his attention.

"Where are you going to hide me, then?" he asked, as the car swerved to miss a fallen branch in the road.

"Nowhere very exciting, I'm afraid. There's a bed and breakfast in Exeter that'll do fine for tonight. But first, we're going to Pamela's house."

"Why? Won't it be risky?"

"Less risky than mine; Infinite Enterprises are already aware that I'm helping you. Whereas, as far as they're concerned, the others are still furious with you. Besides," she added, eyes twinkling, "Pamela wants to see you. Mike too, and Luke and Dimitri. They're all worried, and they want to find out what your plans are."

"I don't have a plan!" Kester squeaked.

"Well," she said, putting her foot on the accelerator, "you'd better think of one, and fast."

They arrived outside Pamela's house just as the sky was starting to darken. Kester surveyed the homely façade of the terraced Victorian house and chewed his lip with apprehension.

The last time he'd been here, he'd been using Pamela's computer to take part in an online lecture for the SSFE. He'd felt cosy and comfortable, even though Pamela's dog had deposited his usual carpet of hairs over Kester's trousers. Now, things felt very different indeed. It was reassuring to know that most of them understood why he'd helped the daemon to escape, but that didn't change the fact that he'd brought chaos down upon them and ruined their livelihoods in the process.

"Come on," Miss Wellbeloved said, switching the engine off and opening the door. "There's nothing to be worried about."

He followed her dutifully to the front door, waiting behind her as she rang the bell. A moment later, Pamela's familiar face appeared before them, along with Mike's, who was peering over her shoulder with great interest.

Both of them look tired, Kester thought, stepping tentatively inside. But then, he knew he looked a wreck too. The last few days— the last few weeks in fact—they'd taken their toll on all of them.

"Mate," Mike said in a perfunctory matter.

"Er, hello," Kester replied, shuffling awkwardly from one foot to another.

"What's with the fancy get-up? You look like a 1920s lounge singer."

Kester cringed. "They're my dad's clothes, not mine. Hello to you too, Pamela."

With a strangled gasp, Pamela tugged him into an exuberant bear hug. "Oh, Kester," she squeaked. "You mad, brave boy! Why didn't you *tell* us what was going on? We're your friends; that's what friends are for!"

"I'm sorry," Kester said, hugging her back. The relief was enough to make his eyes prickle with tears, which he hastily blinked away. "I wasn't sure what to do for the best. After Hrschni showed me the footage of the spirit being slaughtered, I knew I couldn't let him be captured."

"Yeah, we know, and he promised to show you the truth about everything, whatever that is," Mike added, padding back down the hallway. His tone was gruff, but not hostile. Kester suspected he hadn't quite been forgiven yet, but that it wouldn't take too long. Generally speaking, Mike wasn't the sort of person capable of holding grudges, especially when distracted with either food or alcohol.

They all went through to Pamela's snug living room. To his great delight, he noticed a selection of cakes laid out on the coffee table, plus a few bowls of crisps. *If this had been Miss Wellbeloved's house, those would have all been healthy snacks,* he thought, sitting down on the sofa. Thank goodness he'd come here instead.

"So," Mike continued, slumping down in the sagging armchair, "what truth did he show you, then? It had better be worth it, because as it stands, we're all out of a job because of you."

"Mike, don't start," Pamela chastised—just as the doorbell rang again. Kester stiffened, straining to listen as she paced back down the hallway to answer it, then relaxed. It was Luke and Dimitri, by the sounds of the voices drifting through. Then he heard Larry's booming tones and flinched. He really wasn't in any frame of mind to endure a round of sarcasm and derision from the co-owner of the agency.

He waited until the newcomers had entered, preparing himself for their reactions. Luke gave him a cheery thumbs-up, which under the circumstances, seemed odd. But then, Luke was always upbeat and never seemed to be much fazed by anything. Dimitri's greeting was taciturn and reluctant, but that was to be expected. Larry's eyes narrowed dangerously at the sight of him, and Kester braced himself accordingly.

"This had better be *bloody good*," Larry snapped, wagging a finger in Kester's direction. "We're up certain foul-smelling creeks without certain vital steering devices, and if you don't come up with a radical solution in the next few minutes, there'll be hell to pay."

"Perhaps not the most productive way to get results," Miss Wellbeloved remarked dryly.

"Not productive? I'll tell you what's not productive. This young *wally* here deliberately siding with the biggest threat mankind has ever seen! That's what's not productive, Jennifer!"

Kester recollected his encounters with the younger Larry via his mother's memories. He'd been equally as awful at the SSFE as he was now, as far as he could tell. Perhaps he'd just been born that way, no doubt grumbling about the quality of his nappy fabric or the lack of fine ingredients in his baby food.

"Look, you know what happened that night," he said heavily, meeting all of their gazes in turn. "You know why I let Hrschni go. I had my reasons, and they were valid. But I know it's had horrendous impact."

"I'll say!" Larry exploded. "Everyone's calling for us to be closed down with immediate effect! Infinite Enterprises even had the audacity to interrogate me about what I knew about it all. *Me!* I'm an upstanding member of the community, not some low-life ne'er-do-well. I've never been so humiliated in all my life."

Privately, Kester doubted the truth of the statement. After all, he'd witnessed the younger Larry slipping on a mushed piece of banana and throwing spaghetti hoops all over the canteen. That incident had been pretty mortifying, as far as he was concerned.

"Larry, we'll achieve nothing by throwing accusations around," Miss Wellbeloved said calmly.

"I'll achieve pleasure. That's good enough reason for me."

"God, I don't want to think of that man achieving pleasure," Mike whispered, far too loudly. "It'd be like watching a roaring walrus, I reckon. All that quivering flesh."

Miss Wellbeloved's mouth twitched slightly. "We're not gathered here to make Kester feel worse than he already does," she said firmly, giving Mike a warning look. "We need to come up with a plan."

"Hand the little blighter over to Infinite Enterprises!" Larry said.

"That won't resolve anything."

"They'll get him anyway, in the end."

Kester cleared his throat, drawing all eyes to him. "If you want to take me to Infinite Enterprises, Larry," he began, "I wouldn't blame you. But we'll be more effective if we work as a team. I mean, that's when we've always gotten our best results, isn't it? When we stick together?"

"Yeah, but that was before you picked a daemon over us," Mike grumbled.

"It wasn't like that. When I saw the impact of what I did, it broke me. I hated myself for making you so upset. But if Hrschni had been captured that night, nothing would have changed. Infinite Enterprises would still keep on destroying spirits on the sly, and a great daemon would have been exterminated too. Because make no mistake, that's what they would have done to him, wouldn't they? He's *ancient*, Mike. Thousands of years old. His views are far too radical, but his motives aren't evil. He doesn't deserve to be pulled apart by a piece of machinery and sentenced to drift around in agony forever."

Dimitri sniffed loudly. "He is a terrorist, Kester. His methods are destructive, is that not true?"

"There's an argument for that, yes, but—"

"So you're siding with a dangerous terrorist, and you're trying to convince us to do the same!" Larry shouted. "Well, *no thank you.* Some of us have morals, you know."

"Which one of us is that, then?" Mike said.

"*Me,* you imbecile! I'll have you know that I—"

"Hired my brother without asking any of us, which gave him the perfect opportunity to steal all our sensitive information?"

"It was Pamela who left Ribero's diary lying around for anyone to steal, not me!"

Everyone jumped as Miss Wellbeloved's fist slammed down on the coffee table, making the cakes bounce on their plates. "Stop this *at once!*" she cried. "This doesn't help!"

Larry rubbed thoughtfully at his chin, then sat down beside her. "What do you propose we do, then? The agency is ruined, and none of us will ever get a career in the supernatural industry ever again. We may as well accept defeat and turn Kester in, mightn't we?"

"No, we may not." Miss Wellbeloved glanced up. "Kester, you've never let us down before. How much time do you need?"

Kester frowned. "Time?"

"To come up with a plan?"

"I don't know. This isn't like solving a supernatural case. There are no clues for me to follow or puzzles to solve. This is a big, tangled mess."

Mike reached for a cake, then stuffed half into his mouth. "But a tangled mess is just another way of describing a puzzle, isn't it?" he said, spraying crumbs over the carpet.

Kester pondered his words, then nodded slowly. Perhaps Mike was right. Maybe if he approached this as a mystery to be unravelled, rather than an insurmountable problem, he'd make some progress.

"Give me a few days," he said, with more confidence than he felt.

"A few days?" Larry scoffed incredulously. "Who do you think you are, the messiah himself, capable of great miracles that the rest of us mere mortals can only dream of? Come on, admit it. You're going to fail."

"That might be true," Kester acknowledged. "But I'll never know until I try."

"What about us?" Luke chimed from the corner. "You know we're here too. What can we do to help?"

"Absolutely," Pamela agreed, giving Kester a thumbs-up. "This isn't just your fight, it's ours as well."

"You can help, actually," he replied. "Keep track on where Infinite Enterprises are. Try to find out more about this spirit-extermination device and how long it's been in operation for. We might be the poorest, least-equipped agency in the country, but we've already proved we're resourceful when it comes to discovering things. In the meantime," he said, turning to Miss Wellbeloved, "I'd better get going. I need to stay hidden if I'm going to get anywhere with this."

"What, are you off to meet your daemon buddy?" Larry asked, as Kester rose from his seat. "Are you going to report back to him on what we said? Let me guess, will the Thelemites be posting flyers through our doors soon, offering special discounts for new members?"

Kester ignored him. "Goodbye," he said, swallowing hard. "It's been good to see you all, even though it was only a brief meetup. And sorry again. You know I'd give anything for things to have worked out differently."

"Shouldn't have freed a daemon, then," Larry muttered. "Go on, off you trot. Have fun turning to the dark side."

Miss Wellbeloved rolled her eyes, then gestured in the direction of the front door. "Let's go," she said. "After all, we haven't got much time. But take some cake with you, you look far too pale for my liking."

A few days, Kester thought bleakly, as he hurried down the hall-way after her. *That's all I've got to sort this out. Why didn't I say a week? Two weeks, even? I really wish I'd learn to make life less difficult for myself.* But it was too late now. He had to keep his word, even if that meant not sleeping or eating for the next forty-eight hours. They were relying on him to put things right.

"Can we stop off at my place?" Kester asked, as Miss Wellbeloved's car sped through the narrow streets of the city.

"Isn't that a bit risky?" she replied, swerving to miss a badly parked car. "You might be seen."

He nodded. "I know, but I need to gather some things."

"Very well." Biting her lip, she hastily turned a corner, then glanced at him. "You've got an inkling of a plan, haven't you? I can always tell. You get a particular look in your eye. It's distant, yet focused. Just like a bird of prey."

"That's what Mum always said. Hence my name. 'Little Kester,' she called me. 'He sees things that others don't.' It's only recently I've realised what she meant by that."

"Gretchen would be so proud—"

"Please, stop telling me that." He patted her arm to soften the curtness of the words. "She hid things from me, just like her father hid things from her. But it's okay. I understand she was trying to protect me."

"Yes, I think she was. But for the record, I do wish her father hadn't kept secrets from her. It made her believe that secrets were normal, that she should only share a small part of herself with the people around her. Look where that got us all, eh?"

"She really loved you dearly, you know," Kester said. "It was obvious."

She shot him a look. "I don't see how it would have been. She never even mentioned me to you. I'd been erased from her past, as easily as chalk in the rain."

"It wasn't like that."

"Kester, I loved your mother, but she broke my heart. Your father did too, as you know already. I'm begging you to not do the same, because I don't think I could take it. Don't let us down."

"I won't," he said, as they turned onto his road.

She nodded, then parked the car by the pavement. "What do you need to fetch from home, anyway?" she asked.

He grinned. "Just some books."

"You never change, do you?"

"Nope. In this instance, I'm hoping books might hold some of the answers."

She sighed as he clambered out of the car. "I only hope you're right."

To his relief, his housemate Daisy was out. While most people might have been at work, he knew this was unlikely to be the case with her. Daisy had an uncanny talent for avoiding any form of labour, by either failing to apply for jobs or simply getting sacked after a day or two. How she managed to find the cash to pay the rent, he had no idea.

Sadly, Pineapple was very much present, sitting on the kitchen unit, eating a block of cheese and an unpeeled carrot. Kester studied the familiar oversized topknot, lurid neon vest top, baggy trousers, and serenely vacant expression, mumbled a greeting, then escaped quickly up the stairs. He couldn't face getting into a conversation with Pineapple at present; at best, their chats were vaguely baffling, and at worst, completely incomprehensible.

He seized *A Historie of Spirits*, which Dr. Barqa-Abu had given to him only a short time ago. It contained the ancient story of the djinn and the daemon in Persia, telling how the daemon had ruled the Parni people but had craved too much power. It also told of how the djinn had betrayed him, in order to keep the peace. Only later did Dr. Barqa-Abu share the information that she'd been that djinn, and Hrschni the daemon.

He grabbed a few other academic texts from his course, plus some fresh clothes. He didn't think he could bear striding around in his father's impeccable shirts anymore; he felt like a total imposter in them, not to mention an idiot.

Then, he took a final look around his room. It was small. Smelly too, if he was being honest, though that was more to do with the mould around the window frame than his own personal hygiene. The carpet had a hole in it, and the wardrobe looked as though it had been built at least fifty years ago. But it was his little home. It was only now, as he realised how close he was to losing it all, that he truly appreciated it.

Pressing the books against his chest, he raced back downstairs. Pineapple held a hand up in greeting, and he waved back, resisting the unusual urge to hug his housemate hard. *We keep spirits at bay for people like him,* he thought, tugging the door open, grimacing as the winter wind hit him in the face. *We keep spirits at bay so they can enjoy an untroubled life.*

Or we tear spirits apart for an agonising eternity, he thought, thinking of the machine at Infinite Enterprises. *We slaughter sentient beings for the sake of maintaining the status quo.*

Things could be different, he was sure. He just needed to figure out how.

Miss Wellbeloved dropped him outside the bed and breakfast, then sped off into the distance. The irony of the location hadn't escaped him. It was the same establishment he'd stayed in when he'd first arrived in Exeter, searching for the then-mysterious Dr. Ribero. It had only been a few months ago, back in the summer. He'd travelled down from Cambridge, still grieving, and what he'd discovered here had flipped his world upside down.

I wouldn't have had it any other way, he thought, as he pushed the door open and made his way to the reception desk.

A woman emerged from a doorway at the back and gave him a friendly wave. "Hello there, you've got a room for a few nights, yes?"

"How did you know?" he asked.

"You're our only guest. A friend of yours booked you in this morning." She disappeared into another room, then returned with a key. "There you are, it's the first room on the left as you go up the stairs."

"I think that's the same one I stayed in a while back," he said, as he began to climb the narrow staircase.

"I thought I recognised you. Well, I'm glad you liked it so much that you came back."

"I've come full circle," he mumbled over his shoulder. Back then, it had been the start of it all. But this wouldn't be the end. It couldn't be.

He turned the key in the lock, then pushed the door open. It was the same room and just as he remembered it: the single bed by the window, the neat quilt and plump cushions, and the same little pink rug on the floor. Carefully, he sat on the bed and laid his books out beside him. Now was as good a time as any to make a start.

Just as he opened *A Historie of Spirits,* the air shivered beside him. Before Kester had a chance to groan, the familiar murky form of Dr. Barqa-Abu took shape, growing sharper and more distinct with every passing second.

"I've literally only just got here," he grumbled, looking up at her black, burning eyes.

"Yet you already have your books out, ready to read." She nodded approvingly. "That's what I call dedication."

"I wondered if they might give me some ideas."

"That is good logic, Kester. Especially that book. History often holds the answers."

He cleared his throat. "I don't mean to be rude, but—"

"Why am I here, so soon after you arrived?"

"Er, yes."

He gasped as the writhing smoke of the djinn flew suddenly towards him, bony hands visible only inches from his face. "It's time to continue," she told him, holding him fast with her unfathomable, ancient gaze.

"Continue what?" he squeaked.

"Your education, of course. The other night, we had great success with your spirit door training. It seems you have great talent after all, perhaps even more pronounced than your own mother. I am not surprised. I sensed it in you, right from the start, something very special."

"I'm tired. And I still haven't eaten anything."

"Very well. Go and buy a sandwich, eat it quickly, then return."

"I'll need more than that; I'm famished. To be honest, I was more thinking of a burger and chips or something like that; there's a restaurant just down the road, and—"

"A sandwich will be perfectly adequate."

He pressed his lips together. "Fine. Sandwich it is, then." *They'd better have a good selection,* he thought, resisting the urge to tut as he departed the room. *If there's only egg mayonnaise left or something horrible like that, there'll be hell to pay.*

"You are doing exceptionally well," Dr. Barqa-Abu commented, a few hours later.

Kester wiped his forehead. The djinn was right; he *was*. Everything seemed to be falling into place, and he suspected his teacher was largely responsible. Now, he could open up a spirit door with scarcely any effort at all, then seal it again immediately after. He'd never imagined that he'd be able to get the hang of it so quickly.

"Why is it so easy now?" he asked, perching on the end of the bed. "I found it impossible to begin with."

"That's because you didn't know what you were doing. Now, you understand it. You feel the ability deep within you, and you know how to use it. Every spirit door opener is the same. That will be enough for today, I think. Hrschni will be here soon, to continue your *spiritual* education." A glimmer of a smile played at her lips before she faded into mistiness again.

"Why are you training me?" he asked. "I mean, why now?"

"Because I feel you will need your skills soon. It will help you find the equilibrium within yourself. That is what is needed, you see. The scales have tipped; the world is out of control, and balance must be regained."

"This all sounds very esoteric," he said with a laugh.

"That's because it is."

Suddenly, a burst of intense red light filled the room, followed by the unmistakable scent of sulphur. *Hrschni,* Kester realised, amazed at how little the daemon's appearance disturbed him now. Only six months ago, he'd been frightened of virtually everything that lay beyond the cosy confines of his childhood home. Now here he was, casually conversing with two ancient spirits.

"Another day, another hotel room," he said, holding his hands up. "We must stop meeting like this."

To his surprise, the daemon laughed: a rough, crackling sound that brought to mind roaring fires and dancing flame. "One day, we will hopefully meet under more settled circumstances," he said. "I'm glad that you are starting to accept me, Kester. Trust me even, perhaps."

"Let's not get ahead of ourselves," Kester replied. "I suppose you want to show me more of my mother's life."

"I do."

"And show me what part you had to play in it? I'm presuming you two met a second time, back when you were in Billy Dagger's body."

"We did. Your mother and I were close. The next time she and I met was after your grandfather's funeral. She never had the chance to say goodbye to her father, and it tormented her terribly. She left the funeral, caught the train back to the SSFE, then stopped at the gates. That's when she next encountered me."

"Show me, then," Kester said.

"Very well." The daemon pressed a finger against his forehead. "But I must warn you; this time we'll be venturing more into your mother's secrets. It may change how you feel about her."

Kester didn't reply. It was something he'd been dreading himself, but he knew he couldn't stop now. He needed to see it through to the end, for better or for worse.

"Let's get on with it," he said gruffly, closing his eyes. The darkness descended, and he felt himself falling with it, right back into the past again.

CHAPTER 5 – SECRET MEETINGS AND HIDDEN TALENTS

Gretchen stood at the gates and rested her hand against the metal bars. She stared at the school beyond, its hulking form silhouetted against the night sky, and at the expanse of the main square in front of it. No one else was around, but that didn't surprise her. The time was close to midnight, the official curfew hour, and the other students would have all gone back to their rooms by now.

She suspected Jennifer might still be awake, sitting up in bed, anxiously waiting for her to return. She'd offered to come to the funeral, even though she'd never met Gretchen's father and hardly knew anything about him. Even though Gretchen appreciated her friend's concern, she couldn't face the inevitable questions at the moment nor the pressure of someone else's arm wrapped around her shoulders. She just wanted to be alone.

I should go in, she told herself, tapping at the gate. *I really should. I need some sleep, especially after the day I've had.* It would be the sensible thing to do, but instead, she turned away and started walking back down the road. An owl hooted from above, a mournful note that echoed the emptiness inside her.

She hadn't been able to shed a single tear at the funeral. She'd covered her face with her hands and hoped that no one would notice. As her father's coffin had been lowered into the ground, she hadn't felt much at all, apart from a sense of how things *should* have been between them and the loss of the relationship they might have had, instead of this one.

He was gone, and she couldn't mourn him. Maybe one day she'd feel differently, but right now, all she felt was disappointment and anger.

He despised me, she thought, stuffing her hands into her pockets. *Otherwise, why wouldn't he have wanted to help me, as a father usually does?* Perhaps Gerhard would have had an answer for it all, but whatever it was, it was too late now. All those unspoken words had been buried with him, and that was the end of it.

She turned the corner and headed towards the woodlands at the side of the SSFE's grounds. It wasn't sensible to be somewhere isolated so late at night, but she didn't care. Solitude was more important than safety now.

Silently, she paced along the pebbly path, which wound a route through the densely-packed trees. She could hear the rustling of nocturnal animals moving about in the darkness all around her. Eyes were watching her, and she could sense them staring warily before concealing themselves deeper in the shadows.

Out here, in the darkness, it was easy to imagine herself as an animal too: a creature of instinct, free from emotion and thought. She'd give anything to be free of her brooding, if only for a while.

A sharp, crackling noise made her freeze, suddenly as alert as the creatures in the woods around her. It had definitely been made by something larger than a fox or rabbit. Then, before she could react, it came again. She strained to hear better. Then, she heard the distinctive sound of pebbles crunching underfoot.

Someone was close by, hidden away by the dark. Following her, perhaps.

There was no point in running; she could hardly see her surroundings, and it would only be a matter of time before she tripped or veered off the path. Whoever it was, they made no attempt to conceal their approach, though she wasn't sure if that was a comfort or cause for panic. The footsteps were getting louder; the person was either in a hurry to pass her or wanted to catch her up. She swung around, just as a dark figure reached out to touch her shoulder.

"Who are you?" she hissed. "What do you want?"

The light from the moon was weak, but it was enough to make out the silhouette of a hood covering most of a face. That, and a hand, hovering in the air towards her.

"Don't be frightened," a low voice replied.

She raised her hand instinctively to protect herself, but instead, her fingers drifted forwards until they reached the stranger's own. *What am I doing?* she wondered, confused by her own actions. The hand she touched was warm, and smooth as alabaster. *I know that voice,* she thought, squinting at the figure. But where from? It wasn't anyone she studied with; she was sure of it.

"Who are you?" she whispered, lowering her arm. "Why are you following me?"

The figure lowered his hood. She recognised the angular jaw and cheekbones straight away—not to mention the eyes, which seemed to gleam, despite the dimness of the light.

"Billy Dagger?" His presence made no sense, but nonetheless, here he was. Alone, in this small woodland at night. Just like herself.

"Please, just call me Billy," he replied. "I wanted to see you again. I'm so sorry for your recent loss."

"How did you know about that?"

"It's a long story. Would you walk with me for a while?"

She took a deep breath, fighting to calm her racing heartbeat. "We're in the middle of a dark wood, which makes me vulnerable. Give me one good reason why I shouldn't start screaming, right now."

"I would never harm you, Gretchen."

"That's another thing. How do you know my name, and that my father's dead? Why are you here, stalking me at night? You might be famous, but that doesn't give you the right to behave like this."

"That's a fair point." He gestured ahead, along the path. "In spite of that fact, I'm asking you to trust me and walk with me. Just for a short time; you have my word."

She met his gaze in the darkness. His eyes seemed to swell as she stared, and she found her own eyes fixed to them, while the rest of the world faded to darkness around her. *I don't understand this,* she thought, forcing herself to blink, to try to break the spell. *Why does he make me feel like this? And why can't I stop thinking about him?*

"I need to go back," she muttered eventually, looking away. "I don't know what's going on here; it's too strange, it's—"

"Gretchen, listen to me. I *know* you're talented. I can feel your potential, seeping from you."

"But how? Were you once a student at the SSFE? Do you work undercover for a supernatural agency or something? What *is* this?"

"Let's say that I'm familiar with the spirit world. I can sense when someone is remarkable, and *you* are remarkable, Gretchen. It radiates from you, like a burning light. But your ability is wild and untamed. You have no mastery over it. If you were able to hone your skills, you could achieve astonishing things."

Gretchen shook her head. She couldn't get hold of her thoughts; he stirred up emotions in her that she couldn't control. Besides, this was all too unreal to be taken seriously. Famous singers didn't just *turn up* in the middle of the night, declaring themselves to be supernatural experts. It didn't happen—certainly not to people like her.

"I don't know how you know so much about me," she whispered, as she started to walk back down the path, "but it's unnerving. Please, don't think I'm not flattered by your attention. I know who you are, and—"

"Who I am is meaningless. Billy Dagger, what is he, anyway? A human who writes songs, that is all."

She frowned. The way he referred to himself was odd; perhaps he viewed his onstage persona as separate from himself. "I'm going now," she said firmly. "Please let me leave."

"Will you agree to see me again?"

"I'm not sure that's a wise idea."

"Next Sunday at nine in the evening, at this spot."

She laughed. "I'm not going to be ordered around."

"It's not an order, only a request. Please. We need to talk properly; it's important. And on a more personal note, I want to see you again."

A thrill of pleasure ran through her, and she blushed at her weakness. He was undeniably attractive, but she needed to remember that his behaviour was unsettling, predatory, even. Now was not the time to lose her head, regardless of who he was or the effect he had on her.

She didn't reply, only pulled up the collar of her jacket and quickened her pace. Billy Dagger made no attempt to follow her, and by the time she turned, the night had already swallowed him up. She was surprised, and a little disappointed. His presence had lifted her, and now, his absence weighed her down.

"I need to go to bed," she muttered to herself, as she finally emerged onto the road. That would help, for a while at least. She prayed that her roommate would be asleep. The last thing she wanted was a grilling from Jennifer, regardless of how kindly intended it might be.

She fell asleep more quickly than she imagined she would—a dark, dreamless state that freed her from her turbulent thoughts. When Jennifer's alarm clock eventually pierced through her unconscious, it took her a while to resurface. She groaned, then turned to see her housemate tucked up in the bed opposite, looking every bit as bleary-eyed and dazed as she felt.

"Morning, Jennifer," she said, reluctantly throwing the duvet off. "Well done for setting your alarm. I'd completely forgotten mine."

Jennifer peeled off her bed socks and placed them neatly under her pillow. "How was the funeral?" she asked. "I was worried about you."

"It was as horrible as expected."

"You poor thing. What time did you get in?"

"I'm not sure. You were asleep."

"I waited up for you. But when I saw it was gone midnight, I presumed you must have stayed with your mother instead." She leaned over and patted Gretchen's leg. "I suppose it's a relief that it's done, though? You were anxious about it, I could tell."

"No, I wasn't really. It's a part of life, isn't it?"

"What, death? I suppose so, but that doesn't make it easier to accept."

Gretchen grabbed her towel and headed to the door. She wasn't in the right frame of mind to talk. A hot shower would help, if there was a cubicle available in the communal block.

"Let's meet after morning lectures," Jennifer called after her. "I've got something to ask you."

Please don't ask me to be your bridesmaid at your wedding or something terrible like that, Gretchen thought. She kept her face neutral and smiled at her roommate. "Okay," she said in as upbeat a voice as she could manage. "Catch you later."

"Tell Julio to meet me too, will you?" Jennifer smiled. "He'll want to hear it as well."

Gretchen groaned as soon as she reached the classroom. Today was the deadline for submitting her thesis title, and she'd completely forgotten. She'd had a few ideas, but none of the subjects had particularly excited her. Now she'd have to pick something at random and hope she could carry it off.

Mrs. Trow-Hunter waited impassively at the front of the class as the students trickled in, then rapped on her desk for silence.

"Registration will be different this morning," she stated, taking a seat at her desk. "When I call your name, please confirm the proposed title of your thesis. Woe betide those who have come up with anything vague or tedious. You've had plenty of time to think about it and to ask me any questions, which incidentally, none of you saw fit to do."

She called out the first name on the register, and Gretchen leant her head against her palm. At least her surname was in the middle of the alphabet, which bought her some time. But every idea that rushed through her head seemed too predictable, too much like topics that countless others would have covered in the past.

"Larry Higgins?" the teacher called, peering to the back of the class.

"I'm most certainly here, ma'am."

Gretchen peered over her shoulder to see Larry looking even more pleased with himself than usual—quite an achievement, given that his default expression was typically exceedingly smug and self-satisfied.

"Yes, I can see you're here," Mrs. Trow-Hunter sighed. "What is the title of your thesis?"

"It is 'An Examination of Shamanist Ritual and Its Relation to Our Modern-Day World,' ma'am."

"Enough with the *ma'am*, thank you. Now—"

A loud, spluttering cough cut through the rest of her comment. "What is this? This is an *outrage!*"

Gretchen looked around again, just in time to see Julio leap out of his seat and shake a fist directly in Larry's face.

"Julio, do sit back down," the teacher sighed. "We've got a lot to get through today."

"But this sneaky *hog* of a boy, he has stolen my thesis idea!"

Larry smirked. "I'm perfectly able to come up with my own concepts, thank you very much."

"No, you overheard me the other day when I was telling Gretchen about my idea, and then you—"

"You're making a total fool of yourself, which I suppose isn't unusual."

"I am not the fool here; *you* are the fool, because you are —"

Mrs. Trow-Hunter smashed her board wipe on the desk, making everyone jump. "You're both behaving exceptionally foolishly," she snapped. "Silence, the pair of you. I've never witnessed such a scene in my class before."

"He started it," Julio muttered ominously. "I will get my revenge, just wait. One day, Larry, when you do not expect it, I will steal something from you, and—"

"Julio, that's quite enough!" The teacher's eyes glittered dangerously. "Do I need to send you from the classroom like a naughty schoolchild?"

Julio's expression contorted to impressive dimensions before he finally shook his head. "I will not be a naughty boy," he said, making the rest of the class titter.

"Good. Let's continue then. Moira Humphreys?"

Gretchen gave Julio a sympathetic smile, which he returned, albeit unenthusiastically. She felt sorry for him, especially as it was obvious Larry had chosen the thesis topic to antagonise his desk partner.

Finally, the teacher rested her gaze at the front of the class. "Gretchen Lanner?" she said, leaning forward. "What topic will you be covering?"

Gretchen folded her hands in her lap to keep them from twitching nervously. "Well, I thought about it, and—" she began.

"Yes, and your decision was?"

"I'm going to write about spirit doors," she blurted, then blushed. The rest of the class surveyed her with curiosity.

"An interesting topic," the teacher said approvingly. "What's the official title, please?"

"'Spirit Doors and Their Role in Fostering Spirit-Human Relations.'" Each word stumbled from her mouth without thought or preparation. She knew nothing about the subject, apart from her own limited experiences, but at least she'd managed to come up with something.

"Very well, I look forward to reading it." The teacher nodded, then glanced down at her register again. "Fatima Mwangi?"

Gretchen sighed with relief as Mrs. Trow-Hunter's attention

moved on to other members of the class. Now, all she had to do was write the thesis. All ten thousand words of it.

Still, she thought, *it'll be a good opportunity to learn more about this strange skill and how I can use it in the future. That's something, at least.*

Gretchen and Julio met Jennifer in the main square, just as she emerged from her own lesson.

"That was the most boring lecture on conversing with lesser spirits *ever,*" Jennifer said, as they picked a spot on the lawn to sit down on. "Honestly, it was all stuff I covered with Dad, years ago."

"But you're lucky, aren't you?" Gretchen reminded her, settling on the grass. "This is all new to some people, whereas you've had years of experience."

"I know. *Talking to a poltergeist,* though? That's basic, by most people's standards." Jennifer chuckled, then leaned against Julio's shoulder. "But listen to me, wittering on about my lesson. How did yours go? Did the teacher like your thesis ideas?"

"That revolting maggot of a man stole my idea," Julio said darkly.

"Is the revolting maggot Larry?" Jennifer guessed.

"Who else?"

"Can't you both work on the same subject?"

"No, I will look like the big idiot if I do that."

"And, if Larry's is better than yours," Gretchen added, "it'll show you up even more, won't it?"

"That nasty slug could not write a better one than me!"

"Wasn't he a maggot a minute ago?"

Jennifer giggled. "Stop teasing him, Gretchen. You know how he gets."

"Yes, this is no joke," Julio added, resting his head against Jennifer's. "That stinking blister of a man has stolen my future."

Jennifer and Gretchen glanced at each other and smothered a smile. Julio's reactions were often overblown, but on this occasion, he had justifiable reason to be upset.

"Anyway," Jennifer said, tapping both of them on the knee. "I've got an invitation for you, Gretchen. I spoke to Dad yesterday, and he asked if you'd like to come to stay for a few days, over half-term."

"Me? Really?" Gretchen was surprised. She'd never been invited to stay at anyone's house before, not that her parents would have let her go, even if she had been.

"Yes. I've told him lots about you, and he said it'd be wonderful to finally meet." She smiled. "You'll love him. Everyone does, even though he does have old-fashioned ideas about things sometimes. You can meet our resident spirit too. She lives in the old tree in our garden; she's the sweetest thing."

"You live with a spirit?"

"Jennifer has spent her life with spirits," Julio said. "That is why she loves them so very much. You should come, Gretchen. It will cheer you and make the world seem like a better place."

"It's a very kind offer." Gretchen considered it, then nodded. "I've never been to the southwest before. In fact, I've never travelled anywhere further than London, really."

"You should experience Argentina," Julio said. "Ah, the clouds as they hug the foothills, the scent of an asado, the clatter of hooves as a horseman rides past, it is—"

Gretchen laughed. "One step at a time, Julio. Exeter's far enough for now."

"So why were you back so late last night?" Jennifer asked, idly picking at a blade of grass. "I'm amazed you managed to sneak past reception; you must have returned well past the curfew."

Gretchen shrugged. "It took a while to get back here, that's all."

"The last train is well before midnight, though."

"I came by bus."

Jennifer frowned. "They don't run late unless it's a weekend."

"Well, that's how I got here." She shifted uneasily under her friend's scrutiny. "Not that it matters anyway; the main thing is I'm back."

Jennifer nodded, but the look that passed between her and Julio was clear. *They know I'm lying,* Gretchen realised, feeling her cheeks grow warm. *The worst thing is, this is obviously something they've discussed before.* She didn't like the idea of them talking about her when she wasn't there, even though she knew it was inevitable she'd come up in conversation from time to time.

"I'm going to head back to the room," she said after a while. "We've got a practical next lesson, and I still haven't read the relevant section of the text."

"Ah, you don't need to worry with that," Julio said. "I bet no one has read it, apart from that nasty stench of a human, Larry Higgins. I know that he will have read it and learnt every word so he can chant it back to the teacher, but—"

"Well, I'd like to be prepared," Gretchen interrupted, more sharply than she'd intended. "I'll catch you both later."

"Okay, if you're sure you don't want to enjoy the sun?" Jennifer said. "Autumn's on its way; don't you want to make the most of it while it lasts?"

Gretchen shook her head. That was the thing; she *wasn't* enjoying it. She wasn't enjoying much of anything at the moment; and her thoughts kept being derailed by the memory of meeting Billy Dagger, feeling the warmth of his hand, blushing under his stare.

"I can live without the sun," she said, forcing a laugh. "I'll leave you two to it."

The darkness was almost absolute as Gretchen made her way along the woodland path. This time, she'd come prepared with a torch, which helped somewhat but also made sharp shadows leap from the trees around her.

What am I doing? she wondered, peering ahead. This was madness, pure and simple. Perhaps Billy Dagger had been playing with her, luring her out at night, then making her look a fool by not turning up. Or worse, perhaps. Was he about to attack her? He hadn't seemed the type, but she'd only just met him.

"This is ridiculous," she muttered, just as a figure stepped out from the undergrowth beside her.

"You came," Billy said, standing in the beam of her torch.

She trained the light upwards to his face, then smiled reluctantly. "You piqued my curiosity," she said, drawing closer. "But I've risked a lot to come here. My roommate was suspicious. She knows something's going on; she's perceptive."

"Good for her," he replied, falling into step with her. "I have respect for those who take the time to see things as they really are."

This time, she was able to survey him more clearly. In the pale white light of the torch, he seemed made of marble, a man created of impossibly smooth planes and sharp angles.

"Go on, then," she said eventually. "Tell me everything."

He smiled. "What do you want to know?"

"Why is a musical legend so interested in a girl from nowhere, born to two boring parents? That'd be a good place to start. And how do you know so much about the world of the supernatural? Do celebrities get access to classified information or something like that?"

He smiled. "You're not even close. Also, don't call your parents boring; they're anything but that. Your father was a good man."

Gretchen froze. "What do you mean, a *good man*? Are you saying you knew him?"

"I'm surprised you haven't guessed who I am yet. I was certain your father would have mentioned me, though he may have waited until the very end, when he felt he had no choice."

She turned to him, focusing on his eyes and sensing that she'd find the truth hidden *there,* in the endless black of his pupils. Slowly, the world turned around them. The black *changed,* and instead, she saw flames, dancing.

Finally, she understood.

"You're the daemon," she whispered, pulling away quickly. "The one my father warned me about."

He reached for her, and she flinched. Slowly, he held his hands up, like a trainer calming a skittish horse.

"I understand why he warned you," he replied. "But he misunderstood my intentions. He twisted my words, then refused to listen to my explanation. I was devasted when he said he never wanted to see me again. He was my dearest human friend."

"You're . . . an *ancient* daemon," she repeated, struggling to wrap her head around the fact. Somewhere, hidden within the body of this young man, there was a spirit, hundreds, possibly thousands of years old. "But this doesn't make sense. Dad said you were a fighter pilot called Captain Monty, not a musician, and—"

"Did you give him a chance to tell you everything?" he said gently.

She paused, then shook her head. "I was angry. But I was right to be. All my life, he's let me believe that my abilities were all in my head—that they were bad dreams and that I should ignore them. Do you understand how awful it was, as a child, to constantly suffer from vivid nightmares?"

"I don't understand why he didn't tell you. His mother told him everything, before she died. The poor woman, to die so young. Still, she missed the horrors of the war, which is a blessing."

"How many people in my family do you know?"

He smiled. "To put it simply, we go a long way back. And now here I am, talking to you, Gretchen Lanner, and hoping that you will listen to me. That's all I ask for: a chance to explain. It's the one thing your father denied me."

"My father never was good at giving people chances," she said bitterly.

"He was a better man than you realise, but he was blind to the truth. Don't blame him for that. I don't hold a grudge against him, despite everything that happened."

He took her hand and squeezed it. The heat passed through her like liquid running through sand, warming her immediately. She shivered in spite of it. She was standing in a wood with a *daemon,* a creature presumably powerful enough to kill her in an instant, if he chose to do so. Her instincts told her to run, to escape while she had the chance, but something held her in place. Curiosity, perhaps. Or something deeper—an emotional response to him that she didn't yet understand.

"Let's walk for a while longer," he suggested, as though guessing her thoughts. "The truth is, I enjoy being in your company, Gretchen. You burn so brightly, for a human."

"I don't think I burn very brightly at all. Most people find me pretty easy to ignore."

"That's not true. When you're among your friends, you shine out, like a star surrounded by darkness. I think you'll find it easy to control your abilities once you know how to."

"That's the thing," she said, walking alongside him, hand still tingling from the echo of his touch. "I *don't* know how to."

"Self-confidence is an important aspect. Negative capability is another."

"What's that?"

He chuckled. "Have you never heard of John Keats, the poet?"

"I thought his poems were pretty dull, when we did them at school."

"That's where you're wrong. Anyway, he often referred to negative capability. It's the ability to experience great and mysterious things by remaining passive and letting the universe work through you."

She thought about it. It made sense, especially as she so often saw the spirit doors at night, when she was lying calmly in bed, somewhere between sleep and consciousness.

I'm talking to a daemon, she reminded herself again. *I can't let myself be sucked in by his charm.*

"Gretchen," he said, "please, trust me. I give you my word I shall never harm you, nor anyone that you love. I abhor hurting humans. It's because of my love for humans that I fight to restore harmony between us."

"I don't understand," she said weakly.

"Your father didn't either, at first. The truth is that humans and spirits are stronger together. We are the dark to your light, the necessary shadow that walks behind you and that guides your way. We are your strength in times of worry; you are our good cheer in times of despair. That is how it always was, in the past. But over the years, humans have pulled away, and the balance has been lost. That's all I fight for: to bring us together again."

She remembered what her father had told her. "So that's why you're interested in me," she said flatly. "You want to use my spirit door opening abilities to achieve your goal."

He turned to her and placed both hands on her shoulders. She gasped at the sensation and was tempted to simply give into it—to let him hold her and tell her that everything would be all right, that nothing else would matter ever again.

Resist, she told herself, without much force. *Your father didn't trust him, so neither should you.* But then, when had she ever believed what her father had told her?

"I don't want to use you," the daemon said seriously. "I care for you. But I do think *we* could achieve great things, Gretchen. I feel that we, like so many spirits and humans, are meant to be together. You feel it too; I can tell."

"Billy, I'm not sure; I need to think about it, and—"

"Please, call me by my real name. Hrschni. Of all people, you should be the one to know me as I really am."

Without warning, he pulled her close. This time, she let him and rested her head willingly against his chest.

Over the next few weeks, Gretchen met with Hrschni on several more occasions, each time under the cover of night.

She knew that her friends were growing suspicious, though as yet, they hadn't expressed it openly. They'd been discussing it amongst themselves, though; it was evident from the concerned glances that passed between them and the way they kept inviting her to *talk about things,* if she needed to.

On occasion, the truth hung at her lips, like a leaf ready to blow from its tree and into the wind. But each time, the words wouldn't come. How could she even begin to confide about something this significant? She had befriended a daemon, something she knew Jennifer would be anxious about. She might even tell her father, who in turn, might decide to bring his agency to the SSFE and banish Hrschni on the spot.

They wouldn't understand. To be honest, *she* didn't understand, or at least not yet. She continually wondered why she kept up their secret meetings, especially when she still had concerns about his motives. It was partly due to his tales of the past, which he shared with her whenever she requested it. She loved to hear about his time spent with the nomadic Parni people or the ancient Druids. It thrilled her to learn about his life with the alchemists in the Middle Ages or magicians in the Renaissance. His profound love of humans shone through every sentence, and it was obvious how much their union meant to him.

It was more than just stories, though. He had a hold over her, something she scarcely liked to admit to herself. He captivated her imagination and occupied her thoughts almost constantly. The intensity of her feelings was frightening but also exhilarating.

"I wonder if you've got a secret boyfriend you're not telling us about," Jennifer said one day, as they were queueing for dinner in the canteen.

"Don't be silly." Gretchen reached for a tray, hoping that her friend wouldn't notice the redness of her cheeks.

"Why else would you always be rushing off late at night?"

"That'd be telling."

"But you can tell me. That's what friends are for; we confide in each other. I told you my secret about being engaged to Julio." The hurt in Jennifer's voice was unmistakable.

"There's no secret boyfriend," Gretchen said finally, as the dinner lady slopped a spoonful of food onto her plate. "Honestly."

That much was true, at least. Hrschni might be inhabiting the body of a young man, but there was nothing of a *boy* about him at all. He was pure spirit, right to his core. And, on reflection, that was perhaps what she liked the most about him.

They boarded the train in the afternoon, armed with luggage, snacks, and plenty of reading material. Jennifer had warned her that the journey to Exeter took several hours, and Gretchen was well prepared to settle with a book until the train finally reached its destination.

She started reading, without much interest. Then, as the landscape outside the window changed from expansive fields to rolling hills, she stared outside instead. For Jennifer and Julio, the surroundings were nothing special; Jennifer had spent her entire life within the rural Devon countryside and hardly noticed the difference. But Gretchen was used to the city: the swarming streets of Cambridge, the soaring historic buildings that dominated the skyline. She was used to crowds and noise, not emptiness and quiet. The change was pleasant, but it made her aware of her *otherness* once again. Here was yet another place where she was different to everyone else.

She wondered what Hrschni was doing at that moment. It was easy to imagine him strumming his guitar or perhaps sitting at a desk, inspiring Billy Dagger to write new songs. She liked him best when he was concentrating, when the line of his brow became firm and his eyes full of intensity.

Stop it, she told herself firmly. The situation was precarious; it wouldn't be wise to start obsessing over him like a lovesick teenager. Besides, he was a daemon. He wasn't human. The face that pervaded her thoughts was a mask, nothing more.

The train pulled into the station, just as the sky was fading from blue to evening-grey. The platform was silent as they disembarked, and mostly deserted, apart from an old man asleep on a bench by the wall. The overhead lights made tiny amber puddles on the ground, but otherwise, the place was unnervingly dark.

Jennifer saw her friend's expression and giggled. "You seem surprised," she said, as they headed towards the exit.

"It's so quiet." Gretchen raised her chin and sniffed. "It smells different too."

"That's clean air," Jennifer explained. "You don't get so much of it in London. Come on, let's get moving. Dad'll be waiting for us."

They emerged from the main exit to find an elegant black car waiting by the pavement. Its silver hubcaps gleamed under the lamplight, and its paintwork shone like oil. Gretchen stared with fascination, then turned her attention to the driver: a long-faced man with a drooping moustache, who apart from his wiry grey hair and severe spectacles, was the exact image of Jennifer. When he spotted them, he climbed gracefully from the car, then enveloped his daughter in a tight hug.

"Goodness me, you look different already," he said, stroking her hair. "Already so grown up, after so little time away."

"And I have grown at least an inch, yes?" Julio said, waiting to be noticed.

The older man turned, then pumped Julio's hand energetically. "There's my favourite lad. You've grown in mind as well as stature, I can tell."

Julio simpered, then noticing the others' amusement, disguised it with a cough.

Slowly, Jennifer's father's gaze travelled to Gretchen. After studying her intently for a moment or two, he smiled. "This must be the famous Gretchen Lanner. My daughter has been singing your praises for the last couple of months, so I suspect we shall get on wonderfully. My name is Artemis Wellbeloved. Call me Artie; everyone does."

Gretchen accepted his outstretched hand, which was shaken every bit as enthusiastically as Julio's had been. Then, without warning, he pulled her in the direction of the car, ushering her inside.

"You must be famished," Artie declared, nestling back in the driver's seat while they stuffed their rucksacks into the spaces around their feet. "Your mother has put on a magnificent spread, Jennifer, and I'm sure you're all very hungry."

"A beautiful steak with some of your excellent farmhouse bread?" Julio guessed, as he settled into the passenger seat.

"A ham hock, obtained from the butcher's only this morning. Not to mention many other things to celebrate your arrival."

Their responses were lost as the engine suddenly roared into life. A moment later, they were speeding down the road, then around a particularly small roundabout.

This will be interesting, Gretchen thought, as she observed the streets of Exeter flying past outside the window. *This is a family that's been immersed in the spirit world for decades. Which, given that I've now got a secret friend that's a daemon, might be useful. Or dangerous—I'm not sure which.*

Her mind turned again to Billy Dagger, or Hrschni, as she now thought of him. She didn't understand the emotions he aroused in her, but on occasion, when she was lying in bed, staring into the darkness, a single word came to mind. It was one that both thrilled and frightened her. *Love.*

The meal on Artemis Wellbeloved's kitchen table was every bit as impressive as promised. Gretchen stared at the profusion of food on offer, momentarily lost for words. It was a banquet fit for several guests: a tureen of steaming soup at one end, various loaves of bread beside it, ham, cheeses, winter lettuces, jams, cakes, and cordial, not to mention many other types of food to nibble on. She'd never experienced anything like it.

Jennifer's mother, Carole, was the direct opposite of her husband: short and softly rounded, with an abundance of curly hair and a kindly expression. After chatting exuberantly for a few minutes, she ushered them into their seats.

"Is the guest bedroom okay for you, Gretchen?" she said, as she passed round a jug of lemonade. "It's a little draughty in there; we've been meaning to sort it out for years, haven't we, Artie?"

"It's lovely, thank you," Gretchen replied. She meant it too; Jennifer's entire home was beautiful. It had a rambling, labyrinthine quality to it, with dark, wood-panelled corridors leading off to unexpected places, and crooked doors opening to staircases, windowless passages or cupboards stuffed with fascinating items. Her own room was small, but she'd been awed by the details: the velvety patchwork quilt on her bed, the polished wardrobe by the wall, with impossibly ornate animals carved into the wood, and the rug under her feet, which had dragons and tigers woven into the silken material. It was all old and worn, but also rich, textural, and endlessly interesting to look at. She'd loved it on sight.

The kitchen had a similar feel: warm, eccentric, full to the brim with knickknacks and old furniture. She accepted the food as it was passed to her and started eating with great enthusiasm, as did everyone else. After a while, Artemis reclined back in his chair and surveyed her earnestly.

"Jennifer tells me that you have quite the gift, Gretchen," he said eventually. "I'd love to hear more about it."

"Daddy," Jennifer chastised. "I told you not to grill her on it."

Gretchen flinched. She hadn't realised that her spirit door opening abilities had been shared with others. She glanced at Jennifer, who had the grace to look abashed.

"I'm not sure I'd call it much of a gift," she said slowly. "It's a bit useless, unlike Jennifer's spirit conversing skills. They're coming on very well; she always gets top marks in her class."

"Jennifer has been lucky enough to grow up among conversants," Artemis said, winking at his daughter. "Whereas you, from what I hear, were denied that privilege. Do you understand how rare the gift is, Gretchen?"

"Sort of," she said, thinking of the many times Hrschni had reminded her. *Special,* that's what he called her. *Talented.* She smiled at the thought of it.

"I am doing very well in classes too," Julio said, pressing a finger on the table for emphasis. "Our teacher said she liked the way I so often contributed to the lesson, did she not, Gretchen?"

Gretchen was fairly certain the comment had been meant sarcastically, after yet another of Julio's interruptions, but she nodded anyway.

"I'm delighted you're doing well, my boy," Artemis said. "Keep working hard, then you can work with me." He turned to Gretchen. "Julio is intent on proving himself worthy of being Jennifer's husband. I commend it; it's the sort of thing I would have done myself as a young man. But going back to your ability, Gretchen, have you let the SSFE know what you can do?"

"She doesn't want to," Jennifer said.

"Not yet," Gretchen corrected. "I need to practice." Hrschni was helping her to hone her skills, and already, she sensed that she was improving.

"I'm sure you're doing a wonderful job of it," Carole said indulgently, passing her the breadbasket.

Artemis gave his wife a look, then smiled. "When you're ready to apply for jobs, Gretchen," he said, "you must talk to me first. I've got a good feeling about you. You're one of those people, I can tell."

"One of those people?"

"Capable of greatness." He sighed, leaning back in his chair. "Goodness knows our agency could do with a bit of greatness right now. That's the problem, you see. People believe less and less, these days. Spirit-human relations are becoming more strained, which makes our job much harder. In times like these, a spirit door opener could come in very useful indeed."

Gretchen blushed and quickly continued eating. While she appreciated his compliments about her talent, she hadn't realised she'd been brought down here to be offered a job. She had no idea *what* she wanted to do for a living. Up until a few months ago, she hadn't even realised the supernatural existed.

"I hope you don't think my husband is putting any pressure on you," Carole said quickly. "You must choose your own path in this world."

Gretchen caught sight of her two friends, both watching her carefully. "I know," she said in a low voice, then forced a smile. "This food is delicious, by the way."

Carole nodded. Gretchen couldn't help but notice that the gesture was more directed towards Artemis than her.

That evening, the Wellbeloveds hosted a dinner party in honour of their visit. By eight o'clock, the living room was filled with people, some whom were more peculiar in appearance than others. Gretchen, Jennifer, and Julio lurked in the corner by the armchair, watching the crowd with interest. Despite the oddness of it all, Gretchen found herself enjoying the event. It was refreshing to be around so many lively, interesting people, each with their own eccentricities. *Her* people perhaps, she wondered. The outliers in society. The ones who were different—but in an intriguing way.

"So, these are all members of the supernatural society your father's a member of, then?" she asked, studying one man in particular, who was wearing a voluminous velveteen dress, not to mention a vaguely self-satisfied expression.

Jennifer nodded. "They're an ancient organisation; these are the members of the Exeter Lodge. It's just an unofficial get-together, nothing important."

Sensing their attention, the man in the dress strode over and kissed Jennifer energetically on the cheek.

"My dear girl, how well you look," he said, holding her at arm's length. "You've quite shot up; you're nearly as tall as your father now." Releasing her, he turned and gestured to Gretchen. "Is this the friend I've heard so much about, with the remarkable talent?"

How many other people know about my abilities thanks to Jennifer blabbing about it? Gretchen wondered, blushing furiously.

"I'm certainly Jennifer's friend. I don't know about the talent, though," she answered politely.

The man beamed in response. "Well, I never—a spirit door opener. We haven't seen one of those for a while. You're a dying breed, my dear, a dying breed. I'm Bartholomew Melville, by the way. Please call me Barty."

"You know all about me," Gretchen said boldly, "but I know very little about you. What is this society that you're all a part of, anyway?"

"It's very old and very important. My role in the society is equally as important, I assure you. I'm sure Jennifer has already told you not to mention it to anyone else."

"She has, and I won't. But what do you actually do? Talk about supernatural things?"

"Sometimes. We believe in reintegrating spirits into the human realm, just as it was many years ago. It's an honourable cause, I assure you. Something that would benefit both humans and spirits alike."

Another man called from across the room, and Barty smiled apologetically. "I've deserted my friend over there," he said, pointing. "I should get back to our conversation. It was a delight to meet you, Gretchen. I feel certain we shall meet again one day soon."

They watched as Barty waddled back to his friend, then turned to each other.

"You thought he was a bit of an idiot, didn't you?" Jennifer said in a low voice.

"How could you tell?" Gretchen replied.

"You narrow your eyes, like you'd enjoy nothing more than to shout 'you're an idiot!' in their face. That's how I can tell."

Julio burst out laughing, drawing all eyes towards him. "Yes! She does pull that face, doesn't she!" Suddenly he paused, expression straightening. "Hang on. You make that face at me too, sometimes. Are you calling me the idiot?"

Gretchen hastily shook her head. "Of course not," she lied, patting him on the arm. "Don't you worry."

Gretchen enjoyed her stay at the Wellbeloved house more than she'd expected. It wasn't just the warm hospitality that Jennifer's parents had shown her, nor the wonderful home itself. She felt, as they boarded the train to return to college, that it had been more to do with the sense of *belonging* she'd had while she'd been there. For the first time, she'd felt she'd been among like-minded people: those who didn't conform to normality any better than she did.

"So," Jennifer asked, once they'd settled in their seats. "Daddy was keen for you to join the agency, wasn't he?"

"I didn't know you'd told him about my ability to open spirit doors."

"Don't worry, he'll only tell people that can keep your secret."
She smiled. "It's true what he said, you know. Having a spirit door
opener would make us the best agency in the country. And it'd be
amazing to work with you. Can you imagine, us three working
together?"

In spite of her reservations, Gretchen couldn't help but smile.
"That would be nice," she said. *But only if I can bring a daemon along
with me,* she thought silently. *Those are my terms. It's just a matter
of finding the right time to tell them about Hrschni and how much he
means to me.*

They returned late in the evening, when most of the other students
had retreated to their rooms. After unpacking, Gretchen made her
excuses, then slipped out of the SSFE gates, making her way towards
the woods just beyond. As always, she was struck by the silence once
she was a distance from the college. The bustling world of her college
seemed to slide away like butter from a knife, melting into insignif-
icance with every step she took.

Hrschni was waiting for her, as she knew he would be. Instinctively, she ran towards him and into his outstretched arms. The heat
of his body radiated through to her, and she rested her head against
his shoulder, closing her eyes.

"I don't like being away from you," she whispered after a time.
"Is that silly?"

"You're never truly away from me," he murmured, touching her
hair. "I'm with you more often than you know." He lifted her chin
with his finger, guiding her gently nearer.

What is this? she wondered, as his lips met hers, and fire raced
through her. All she knew was that, whatever it was, she was powerless against it. Like a twig caught in a fast-flowing stream, she was
being carried forward helplessly, without a clue about where she'd
find herself in the future.

Chapter 6 – Revelations

One minute, Gretchen and Hrschni stood before Kester, wrapped in an embrace. The next, they were gone.

His eyes snapped open. He was back in the present; it was light, not dark, and he was in a hotel room with two spirits, not in the woods with his mother. His chest ached with the weight of what he'd witnessed, and the walls appeared to warp and twist around him, forcing bile to rise in his throat.

The daemon withdrew to a more respectful distance, sensing his turmoil.

"You . . . you *kissed* my mother," Kester stuttered, scarcely able to comprehend it. "You two were—"

Hrschni's glow flickered, for just a moment. "I loved her," he said quietly.

Kester sat down on the bed. Nothing had prepared him for this revelation. His mother and the daemon hadn't just known one another; they'd been in an intense relationship, and no one had known about it. Why had she gone to such lengths to hide it from

Miss Wellbeloved and Ribero, two people who had so obviously meant the world to her?

It's yet another secret she kept, he thought, sinking his head into his hands. *Another thing that she lied about. Who was she, really? And whose side was she on, all those years ago?*

"Why didn't you just tell me?" he asked. "You've had plenty of opportunities to; you didn't need to let me find out *like that.*"

Dr. Barqa-Abu drifted forwards and rested beside him on the bed. "Would you have believed him?" she asked gruffly. "Sometimes, we need to see things with our own eyes to accept their truth."

Kester thought immediately of the CCTV footage that Hrschni had shown him. She made a fair point; if he hadn't seen that, he would have always doubted what the daemon had told him. He'd needed to witness a spirit being destroyed, to sense its agony, to understand how truly horrific it was.

"Did she really love you?" he asked, after a while.

Hrschni nodded. "She did."

"But I didn't know that was possible. You're a spirit; she's human."

"Love doesn't recognise differences, Kester."

He thought about it. A sea of words jostled for supremacy inside his head, numerous questions and accusations too. But recrimination and morbid curiosity wouldn't resolve anything; he knew that.

"Can I be left alone for a while?" he asked the two spirits. "I need time to think about this." *A lot of time,* he added silently, mind racing. There was a *message* here, something he was missing, which was also important. But he couldn't muse upon it with others here. He needed peace and time to get his thoughts in order.

"Kester, I need to show you more," Hrschni protested. "Your mother's story is not complete yet. To leave it here would be to leave the truth untold, to—"

"Tomorrow," Kester said, holding up his hand. "Not now. I've seen more than I can cope with right now."

He slept uneasily, drifting in and out of consciousness, thoughts filled with images of Hrschni hidden inside Billy Dagger's body and how his mother had held him close. He wished that she was still alive, though now, the yearning was for all the wrong reasons. She'd died without telling him anything, and he longed to hold her to account for her actions.

Memories swamped him completely. He remembered all the times he'd sat with his mother in their tiny kitchen, eating in companionable silence. All the evenings spent relaxing on the sofa, with Mildew the cat between them. Endless hours of being with one another, endless chances for her to tell him everything. Instead, she'd chosen to keep him almost entirely in the dark.

Just like her father did to her, he thought bitterly. He supposed it was a blessing that he'd believed the best in her until she'd died, that he'd remained devoted until she drew her final, shuddering breath. Sometimes, ignorance truly was bliss.

He awoke the next day feeling irritable and unsettled. It was difficult to rid his mind of what he'd seen, and he suspected he'd drive himself mad with it all if he didn't find something else to focus on instead.

Rather than heading down for breakfast, he picked up *The Historie of Spirits* and started to read, remembering that Dr. Barqa-Abu had said it was a good idea to delve into the past. When he'd first received the book, he'd dismissed it as just another out-of-date educational text. Now, he viewed it in a different light. With a bit of luck, this might be the place to find some answers.

He flicked idly through the first few chapters. They covered the ancient history of spirits in the human realm—information that sounded largely like hearsay, combined with a fair bit of creative licence. However, the chapter *Early Shamanism* caught his attention. The book declared that the first shamans were undoubtedly spirit door openers who used their powers to welcome spirits to the human world. They were also responsible for constructing sun doors: permanent entry points to the spirit realm that enabled spirits to come and go with ease.

"The shaman's role was to encourage spirits to help humans," he read aloud, following the words with his finger. "In these early days, spirits assisted with controlling the weather, helping crops to grow, and even defending humans against attackers. When the occasional malevolent spirits entered the human world, the other spirits would assist with forcing the troublemakers back to the realm from which they came and preventing them from associating with humans ever again."

He tapped the page thoughtfully. Spirits were capable of policing themselves, or so this book seemed to suggest. Why had they stopped? When did increasing numbers of troublesome spirits start sneaking into the world? There were so many unanswered questions; it was difficult to know where to start.

The Historie of Spirits also suggested that the shaman presided over "spirit meetings," a sort of primitive parliament session, from what he could tell. During these meetings, problems were raised and resolved, and jobs were assigned to the spirits. If the book could be trusted, it seemed to suggest that the harmonious arrangement lasted for many centuries.

It certainly explained why Hrschni was so desperate to flood the world with spirits again. But the daemon failed to appreciate that times had changed. Spirits had proven that they couldn't be trusted—and besides, humans no longer wanted them here.

Kester couldn't help but wonder, though, if Hrschni was partially right. Had humans lost something when relations between themselves and the spirits had broken down? According to the book, spirits were once helpful and protective—an asset to humanity, in fact.

It's all so confusing, he thought, chewing his nail. *There doesn't seem to be any right or wrong answers, only strong opinions on either side.*

His phone started to ring, tugging him away from his thoughts. Quickly, he pulled it out of his bag. He was surprised that it had any battery left, though he supposed it made sense; he hadn't used it for a while. It wasn't a number he recognised, not that he could have answered it anyway; it was too risky. Finally, the ringing stopped. A message pinged on his screen, just a few minutes after.

Strange, he thought, frowning. His finger hovered above it, wondering if it could be from Infinite Enterprises and if opening the text would alert them somehow to his whereabouts. He didn't think that was possible, but then, his knowledge of technology was woefully poor at the best of times.

In the end, curiosity overcame him. He pressed the screen, then started to read.

Kester. Heard you're in a spot of bother. Am aware of your talents. Would like to talk about business opportunity, now you've been thrown out of the agency. Crispian.

He laughed out loud, then frowned. He had to hand it to Crispian: the man had nerve, if nothing else. It was tempting to type a sarcastic response, but he'd been told not to get in touch with anyone. Although he'd set his phone to ensure it couldn't be tracked, he didn't know what other sophisticated methods Infinite Enterprises might be using to try to find him.

He looked at his watch. It was only just gone ten. Even though it wasn't a sensible idea to go outside, he needed the fresh air. At least in the city, there would be crowds. He could conceal himself amongst others.

One little trip outside won't cause any harm, he reassured himself. *It'll be fine.*

He wandered the streets aimlessly for a while, marvelling at how strange Exeter felt now, even though he'd lived in the city for several months. Watching all the people hurrying around him, he felt removed from it all, an invisible alien surveying the world for the first time. Still, he was out of a hotel room, and it was a welcome change of scenery. He supposed that was the best he could ask for, really.

Instinctively, he headed in the direction of the library. It wasn't a surprise that his feet automatically followed the route to the building; it was his favourite place in the city, after all. Also, if he was being honest with himself, he was hoping that Anya might be there. He strongly suspected he'd blown his chances with her, but he couldn't help but hope that somehow their relationship could be saved.

Soon, the library came into sight: a large, modern building of brick and glass windows set a little way from the main high street. He passed through the automatic doors and entered the airy atrium within.

To his amazement, he spotted Anya immediately, standing by the welcome desk. She was talking to an elderly man, and he took a moment to bathe in the sight of her. Her face was so achingly familiar that it stole his breath away, and he absorbed every detail, from the patient crinkle of her eyes to the indulgent smile she gave the man as she pointed him in the right direction.

Desolation flooded through him again as he realised once more that he'd lost her. *How ironic,* he thought miserably, *that the most tender moments we spent together were when she was being inhabited by Fylgia. All those romantic times, I thought we were alone.*

She looked up, then locked eyes with him. Her shock was obvious and immediate.

It would be wise to leave the library, as quickly as possible. Even being here placed her in danger, not to mention himself. However, he couldn't help but remain rooted to the spot. Raising a hand, he attempted a smile, then stopped, feeling like an idiot. Her expression gave no clues on how to proceed; he wasn't sure whether she wanted him to approach or simply disappear from sight. This was a bad idea; it was wrong to put her in this position, especially at work. He turned, then realised that she was hurrying towards him.

"Kester, what are you doing here?" she whispered, glancing around herself, as though expecting someone to jump out at her at any moment.

"You know me," he said weakly. "I can't stay away from books."

Without warning, she grabbed him by the arm, then dragged him towards the corner of the room, behind the stairs.

"They're looking for you," she hissed, eyes wide with concern. "The other day, a woman started firing questions at me. She said it was important to find you, for everyone's safety. What's going on? What's happening?"

He realised how exposed they both were in the main atrium; there were windows to both sides, and it'd be easy for someone to watch them without detection.

"It's too long a story to explain now," he whispered, edging closer to the wall. "What did you tell them?"

"Nothing, of course. I know you still think I'm working against you, Kester, but I'm—"

"No, I don't think that. I know you've been pulled into this mess against your will, and it was wrong of me to blame you for it. I thought you'd deliberately betrayed me, that you were working with the Thelemites to—"

"It was never like that. I wasn't given a choice; they told me what to do and said you'd be in danger if I didn't comply and—"

He reached for her hand, quite without meaning to. "I *know*, Anya. I'm sorry. You tried to tell me, but I was so hurt, I refused to listen."

A small smile played on her lips. "I'm sorry too. What a way to start a relationship, eh?"

"You're telling me."

"We should talk properly, sometime. But not here; it's too risky."

"Where, though? Everywhere is risky at the moment."

"I know. It's a nightmare." With a sudden grin, she pulled him into a hug. "But I'm so glad to see you again. I don't want you to hate me; it feels horrible."

Breathing a shaky sigh of relief, he kissed the top of her head. "I never hated you," he whispered in her ear. "The only reason I was upset was because I cared about you so much."

"I care about you too." She pulled away reluctantly. "Which is why I'm telling you to go. The woman who questioned me yesterday made me nervous. She said they wouldn't harm you in any way, but I could tell she meant business."

"If I hid upstairs in the silent reading section, do you think they'd spot me?"

"Kester, that is *exactly* the sort of place they'd start searching for you."

He sighed. "I suppose you're right. I don't want to go yet, though." The truth was, this was the happiest he'd felt in a long time. *Screw everything else,* he thought, unable to take his eyes off her. *I'll risk the danger, because she's worth it.*

Then he remembered: this was how his mother had felt about Hrschni. He shivered, in spite of himself.

"I'm working on sorting things out," he promised her. "When everything is back to normal, can we start over again?"

"I'd like that, more than you could possibly know," she replied, squeezing his arm. "Now go. If you're dragged off by that scary woman, you won't be any use to anyone."

Kester obeyed. Anya was right, of course—not that it made it any easier to leave. He knew he should lay low, at least for now. He needed to focus his attention on becoming a better spirit door opener, because he suspected Dr. Barqa-Abu was training him for a reason. And he had to finish hearing all the secrets his mother kept from him. Hopefully, Gretchen's past might be the key to unlock the tangled mess he was in.

Either that, or Hrschni is using my mother's past to make me do what he wants, he thought. There was no way of knowing for sure. All he could do was try to muddle through it all, without having a mental breakdown at any point. At the present moment, he felt it was easier said than done.

Kester hastened back through the high street, bracing himself against the winter wind. The news Anya had given him was concerning, but he couldn't let it rattle him. It was important to keep his thoughts straight, to identify the heart of the problem, then find a solution.

Let's start at the beginning, he told himself as he hurried along. *Hrschni wants spirits to come and go as they please. The government don't really want spirits at all; that's why they hire agencies like ours, to send them back to their own world again. The traditionalist Thelemites, which Dr. Barqa-Abu supported, wanted to achieve balance between the two.*

Balance. He weighed the concept in his mind. It wasn't possible, though, or at least, not in any way he could imagine. Spirits were too diverse in nature. Some were unthreatening, sweet even, at times. Others, as he could personally testify, were terrifying. On rare occasions, they were capable of hurting humans and even killing them.

If a permanent spirit door were created again, especially in a prominent location like a city, spirits of all kinds would be able to flood through and mingle directly with humans. That could never be allowed; it would result in pandemonium. Humans would be fearful at first, then start to attack. *A war between spirits and humans,* he thought, shuddering. *Now that would be truly apocalyptic.*

What other options were there? People like him could create occasional, controlled spirit doors, which were far smaller and only open for a short period of time. But he knew only a few spirits would be able to slip through at a time, and that wouldn't suit Hrschni's desires. The daemon would continue to push for what he believed in and wouldn't rest until he'd achieved it.

It all felt rather hopeless. With a sigh, Kester continued on his way, lost in his thoughts. Suddenly, his gaze rested on a tall figure on the other side of the road wearing a cape.

A cape. He took a moment to digest the fact because he knew what it signified. *Ian Kingdom-Green.*

Kester was sure it was him, propped up elegantly against a shop window, studying his fingernails. It couldn't be anyone else; he was one of Infinite Enterprises' most recognisable members of staff, thanks to his flowing mane of hair and flamboyant dress sense. He was here to find Kester; there was no other explanation. Infinite Enterprises knew that they'd worked together in the past and that Ian would be able to recognise him in a crowd.

Kester observed the man carefully. As always, he was struck by his outlandish elegance: hair swept into a loose ponytail, a long black cape draped over his towering body. He longed to simply go over and talk to him, but that would be foolish. They may have got on well in the past, but as things stood at present, they were now working against one another.

He started to move away, at the exact moment that Ian lifted his head.

"Damn it," Kester muttered. His heart started to race, and he forced his body into action, pushing past the throngs of people walking in the opposite direction.

"Kester!" Ian shouted immediately, leaping forward. "Wait, please!"

To Kester's horror, the man started to jog across the road with alarming speed while still calling out to him. There was nothing else for it; he had to get moving, and fast. There was an alleyway between two shops ahead; he'd walked down it a few times in the past. If he could reach it in time, he might stand a chance of escape. It led out to a narrow road behind the shops, then to a large green space with plenty of trees and hedges to hide behind.

There wasn't a moment to lose. Taking a deep breath, he started to sprint up the alleyway, praying he wouldn't encounter anyone coming the other way, nor any overflowing bin bags to block his path.

"Kester, stop running! I need to talk to you!"

Ian's voice sounded a good distance away, but not as far as Kester would have liked. He powered ahead as the pounding footsteps behind him increased in volume. Ian was faster than him—he'd be willing to put money on it. The man's legs were practically double the length of Kester's own, and he was far more well built. But Kester had one advantage. He knew Exeter's streets well, and Ian didn't.

At the end of the alleyway, he took a sharp left down a narrow path, behind a boarded-up pub. There were some steep steps at the end, which eventually led out to the park by the remains of the old castle. If he could get there, he could hide for a while, at least until he'd managed to get his breath back again.

"Kester, please!" Ian's voice drifted after him. "Don't run; I have no intention of hurting you!"

Kester didn't believe for one moment that Ian would harm him. However, he was almost certain the man would capture him, then drag him to Infinite Enterprises' headquarters. If that happened, any chance he had of hearing the rest of his mother's tale would be ruined.

Speed was the most important thing. He raced up the steps, taking two at a time, even though his heart was pounding painfully against his rib cage. The clattering on the stairs below suggested that Ian wasn't far behind. He wanted to look back but knew it would cost him precious time.

Finally, he emerged at the top and sprinted through the old metal gates leading to the castle gardens. There were bushes here, plenty of them, and large trees too, with wide trunks that were ideal for concealing a full-grown person. He dived into the undergrowth directly beside him and edged silently towards the old stone wall at the back.

Ian thundered past, far too close for comfort. Kester held his breath and began to shuffle slowly along the wall.

"Kester, I'm sure you can still hear me," Ian shouted breathlessly, from somewhere close by. "I must speak to you. This whole situation is crazy. Infinite Enterprises aren't going to do anything terrible to you, I promise. We just want to talk, to try to understand what's going on. Kester?"

Kester kept on moving. To his relief, the bushes were denser and thicker the further he progressed, though their spiky branches ripped painfully at his face as he passed. The wind rustled noisily through the leaves—a fact he was thankful for, as it disguised the sound of his movement.

After a time, he paused, straining to hear any evidence to suggest Ian was nearby. To his relief, all he could hear was the mournful caw of a crow in the tree overhead. Other than that, the gardens were silent.

He emerged tentatively, then peered around him. There was no one in sight, apart from two old ladies on a distant bench feeding the pigeons. He knew the peace would be short lived, though. It wouldn't be long before Ian would be back, no doubt with additional members of his team, ready to scour the area. It was clear from the desperate way that the man had chased him that they were firmly focused on bringing him in.

Kester quickly made his way to the other side of the gardens, slipping past the crumbling remnants of the castle gate and back down to the high street. Somehow, he needed to find a payphone, even though most of them were out of use these days. Using his mobile felt too risky, though he supposed he'd have to if there was no other choice. Then, he needed to phone for help. Staying in Exeter wasn't an option, not now they knew he was here.

He vaguely remembered walking past a payphone by the bus station. It was only a five-minute walk away, less if he hurried his pace. Swiftly, he made his way down the road, checking the surrounding landscape as he went. Thankfully, there was no sign of Ian anywhere.

The phone booth looked worryingly decrepit the closer he got to it. The windows at the side had been smashed in, and graffiti covered the walls inside. He peered through the jagged glass, then cursed under his breath. The phone had been ripped out, probably years ago.

"Damn it, what do I do now?" he muttered, running a hand through his hair. He moved back instinctively as a car slowed to a halt by the pavement beside him, then realised with horror that the person in the driver's seat was staring straight at him.

His heart sped again. Studying the driver more closely, he braced himself for the sight of Ian's face staring back at him, ready to haul him into the back seat and drive off into the distance. But he quickly realised that it wasn't Ian or any other member of Infinite Enterprises.

Instead, he found himself staring at the unmistakably oily, delighted face of Crispian, Mike's brother.

"You've got to be kidding me," he muttered, as Crispian leaned over and threw the passenger door open.

"Kester! Fancy seeing you here. Well, not so funny, actually. I've just visited your home, but your housemate said they hadn't seen you for a while. What luck I spotted you on my way back!" He patted the vacant seat beside him. "Come on, in you get. I sent you a very important text message earlier, but I suppose you've been too nervy to reply."

"You expect me to trust you?" Kester took a step back, arms firmly folded. "You stole my father's company data, betrayed your own brother, and now you've used our agency to launch your own business. Besides, how do I know you're not working with *them*?"

"I'm working for myself, which is the most sensible thing by far. Now, do you want to get in or not?"

"Are you going to take me straight to Infinite Enterprises?"

"No. I want to talk to you about that job offer I sent you."

Kester sighed. He didn't want to get in Crispian's car, and he especially didn't want to hear him gloat about how clever he'd been, stealing the information from Dr. Ribero. He'd tricked them all, and he'd certainly had a hand in the agency's downfall. But what choice was there? It was only going to be a matter of time before Infinite Enterprises contacted all the hotels in Exeter and discovered where Kester was staying.

He climbed in, shut the door, then pointed a finger at Crispian's face. "Here's what's going to happen," he said firmly. "You take me where I need to go. You wait outside while I collect my belongings. Then, you drive to the destination of my choice. Once you've done all that, I'll listen to you."

Crispian beamed. "My word, this is exciting. I feel like James Bond."

"Well, you don't look like him," Kester retorted. He recited the address of the bed and breakfast, which Crispian dutifully typed into the satnav system. A moment later, the car engine revved into action, and they began driving along at a satisfyingly speedy pace.

"Can I tell you about my business plans while we travel?" Crispian asked plaintively after a few seconds. "It's better than sitting in silence, don't you think?"

Kester sighed. "If you must."

"My company has only been in operation for a few days, and already I'm in high demand. It seems a spirit-sighter is a much-wanted thing, Kester! All those years as a child, when Mike used to tease me about my talent, well, this shows what a moron he was, doesn't it? After all, what can he do? Make useless equipment for a failing supernatural agency, that's it. Hardly much to brag about, in my opinion."

"Leave Mike out of this," Kester snapped. "Remember that he let you stay at his place when you had nowhere else to go."

"Fair enough. The thing is, my old chum, if you were to join me, we'd make a formidable team. I know how rare spirit door openers are; I'd say your skills might even be regarded as *slightly* more valuable than my own. Only slightly, of course, but still."

Extremely, more like, Kester thought but kept his mouth shut. It was probably better to let Crispian get the bragging fully out of his system, then let him down gently.

"I'd make sure you were well-paid," he continued, turning a corner. "I'm an excellent businessman; I'd haggle for the best jobs and highest prices. You've had a while to get used to working in the industry, so that'll help. We could subcontract our services to Infinite Enterprises, and—"

"You mean the same Infinite Enterprises who are currently hunting me down as a wanted criminal?"

"Ah, that's just a misunderstanding. I heard about what happened with that daemon fellow; I'm sure it will all blow over."

Kester shook his head. This was the problem with Crispian. He had no understanding of the supernatural world nor of its complex politics. He merely viewed it as a money-making opportunity and nothing more.

"The bed and breakfast is just up there on the left," Kester said, pointing. "Can you wait while I run in? I'm hoping to speak to some people while I'm in there, so I may be a while."

"No worries," Crispian said. "I'll check out the stock market on my phone; that'll keep me amused."

"Thrilling," Kester muttered darkly, as he opened the car door.

As soon as he entered his room, Dr. Barqa-Abu materialised, bony hands anxiously wrestling the air in front of her.

"Where have you been?" she snapped, soaring close to him.

He recoiled. Despite having got used to her presence, he was still finding her sudden movements hard to adjust to.

"I've got to go," he explained, reaching for his bag. "Ian Kingdom-Green chased me down the high street, but I managed to get away."

"Why were you even outside? You were told to conceal yourself."

"It was a mistake, I know. Don't worry, someone's giving me a lift to somewhere else. I'm going to Dawlish; I'm sure at least one hotel will have a spare room to stay in. Will you and Hrschni be able to find me?"

The djinn's face came into focus, emphasising her incredulous expression. "Kester, you're referring to two ancient spirits here. Yes, I think we can track down a twenty-two-year-old man in a deserted seaside town in winter, but thank you for checking."

He grinned. It was becoming increasingly more apparent that, for a sinister ancient djinn, Dr. Barqa-Abu had an excellent grasp on twenty-first century sarcasm.

"I'll see you later, then?" he said, as he grabbed his clothes and books.

"Of course," she confirmed. "Now go. Infinite Enterprises are closing in on you, and we cannot have you taken to their headquarters now. It would be extremely difficult for Hrschni and I to be present there without being detected."

He saluted, then made his way to the door. "So far we've stayed one step ahead of them," he reminded her.

"So far. Don't get complacent, though. They've already shown how resourceful they can be."

Kester hurried back to the car, where he found Crispian in exactly the same position he'd left him, still staring avidly at his phone.

"Stocks and shares performing well, are they?" Kester asked, clambering into the passenger seat.

"Oh, mine always do." Crispian said without looking up. He switched on the engine. "Where to?"

"Dawlish. I need to find a place to stay."

"Very well. As I'm acting as honorary taxi service, perhaps you'd do me the honour of accepting my kind business offer?"

"Kind? I think what you're doing is immoral."

Crispian revved the accelerator a touch too hard. "Oh, morality. Where does that get anyone? If you want to succeed in life, do what you want. That's my motto, anyway."

Kester sighed. So far, Crispian's motto had got him booted out of his house due to cheating on his wife and had cost him his previous job too. Still, it wasn't worth saying any of this aloud; he knew the man would never understand. And he was helping Kester to escape, which counted for something.

They sat in silence as the car raced past the outskirts of the city and out onto the hedgerow-lined country roads.

"The thing is," Crispian said after a while, "you let people take advantage of you, Kester. Take my brother, for example."

"Mike's never taken advantage of me."

"Oh, but he has, and the rest of them too. They're riding on the coattails of your success. I found out all about it from your father's notes in his diary. That dangerous spirit hiding in a painting? The case was only successful because of you. The same goes for that *what-d'ya-ma-call-it*, the one you got rid of in Scotland."

"That was a fetch, and don't use the expression *got rid of*. It's offensive to spirits."

Crispian snorted. "Anyway, my point is this: both cases would have failed if not for your talents. Ribero's precious agency would have gone under a long time ago, but they used your prodigious reputation as a spirit door opener to stay in business. Goodness me, Kester, how can you be so naive!"

Kester shook his head. He knew Crispian was only trying to twist things, though he suspected there might be a nugget of truth buried within his manipulative spin.

"Aren't you trying to take advantage of me too?" he said, raising an eyebrow. "You already said you wanted to work with me because I'm in hot demand as a spirit door opener."

"Ah yes. But the difference is that I'll admit it to you. Yes, I want to make huge amounts of money off the back of your spirit door opening skills. But unlike your father and the rest of them, I'll be honest about the fact. And most importantly, I'll make *you* lots of cash too."

They sped along the open road. Kester leant back and closed his eyes. There were already far too many other things for him to worry about at the moment, without Crispian adding to the list.

"Well?" Crispian asked eventually.

Kester shook his head. "You've made one major error of judgement."

"Really? Enlighten me."

"You presumed that we value the same thing, but we don't. I couldn't care less about being rich. I have no interest in cashing in on my ability. I'd rather use it to do the right thing."

"Oh, how tedious."

"Why?"

"Well, you know. *Doing the right thing*. That's just the rubbish schoolteachers fill our heads with when we're younger. Doing the right thing never gets you results."

Kester groaned. "It depends on what results you want. Don't you want to make a difference to the world?"

"I'd like to make a difference to *my* world."

"Your talent as a spirit-sighter could be used for good. Instead, you've chosen to profit from it, and where has it got you? Your own brother hates you, your new colleagues are disgusted by your actions, and the one person you'd like to work with wouldn't *dream* of accepting your job offer in a million years. It hasn't really panned out well for you, has it? Yes, you'll have money but not a lot else."

Crispian frowned. "So that's a no, then, is it? You might have said, before making me drive all the way out here."

"You're doing a good deed, Crispian. Embrace the moment; you might even learn to like it."

After depositing Kester by the nearest hotel in Dawlish, Crispian raced off without so much as a departing wave. Kester watched him go with conflicting emotions. He felt guilty about giving him such a hard time, but only slightly. It was about time someone told him some hard truths, though he hadn't relished being the one to do it.

Once the car was out of sight, he examined the hotel behind him. The façade had a faded Victorian glamour to it, but a vague sense of dereliction too—of a building left to fend for itself against the relentless sea breeze for far too long. He stepped through the door and gladly shut out the cold behind him.

A young woman looked up from the reception desk as he entered, then frowned in confusion at his presence.

"Have you got a room for the night?" he asked.

"You want a room? For tonight?"

"Er, yes please, if you've got one."

She laughed. "Of course we have; no one stays here over winter. I'm only downstairs because we've got family coming to visit; they'll be here any moment." She pulled a key off the board behind her, then handed it over. "Fifty pounds a night, breakfast included. I mean, we haven't got anything in for breakfast, but I can pop out to the shops later. Sign into this book, please."

Kester rummaged in his pocket and handed over the cash. "Thank you. If anyone asks, I'm not staying here, okay?"

She eyed him suspiciously. "Are you in trouble with the police?"

"Absolutely not. I'm just desperate for some peace and quiet."

"If you say so. I won't tell any lies to protect you, though. What with my uncle and his brood coming over, I've got enough to deal with as it is."

"There's no need to lie."

"Alright, then. Your room is on the top floor, three flights up— hope you're feeling energetic. Nice view though. I've put you in the one overlooking the sea."

He thanked her, picked up his bag, then made his way in the direction of her pointing finger. She'd been right; he would need energy to get up the stairs, which like those in all Victorian properties, were narrow and steep.

Oh well, he thought, as he started to climb. *Perhaps here I can get some proper rest for once, before I have to hare off to the next hiding place.*

He found his room, then entered, taking a moment to absorb the sight in front of him. *Another day, another hotel room,* he thought glumly. Already, the novelty was wearing thin, and it didn't help that this room looked almost identical to the one he'd previously departed. Still, this place, as promised, did have an impressive view of the sea, which at present, was thrashing angrily against the promenade below.

He fished out his copy of *A Historie of Spirits* again and dumped it on the dressing table. There was nothing else to do for now; he might as well get back to reading. Sitting down and ignoring his exhausted reflection in the mirror in front of him, he opened at the chapter *Early Spirit Relations*.

The sound of the waves provided a soothing backdrop, along with the distant shrieking of the gulls, whirling in the wind outside. Soon, he'd lost himself in the text, oblivious to everything aside from the words in front of him.

The book stated that shamans often summoned higher orders of spirits, who were then tasked with preserving the peace. Kester read with fascination about how they monitored the conduct of their fellow spirits and even taught lesser spirits the ways in which they could assist humans.

He moved onto the next subsection, which focused on witches. He smiled to himself. Only a few months ago, he'd thought witches only existed as Halloween inspiration: hook-nosed, warty hags that flew around on broomsticks and cackled a lot. Now, of course, he knew better.

However, he hadn't realised they'd also been spirit door openers, back in those early days. He read on, becoming more engrossed with every paragraph. Apparently, the witches had used familiars to assist them. He chuckled to himself, remembering the exuberant familiar he'd encountered in the pub in Topsham. Having a giant spirit dog leap in his face had been an intimidating experience, but as far as spirits went, it had been fairly endearing.

"The witches also worked alongside more ancient spirits," he muttered aloud, following the words with his finger. "They summoned them in a ritual referred to as the Sabbat. Some of the witches also had children with the spirits: halfling creatures that were gifted with powerful supernatural abilities. The offspring of the witches and spirits were able to pass directly into the spirit realm and helped to foster positive relationships between the two worlds."

He paused, tapping the page. *Sounds heavy,* he thought. *Who'd want to venture into the spirit world?* Continuing with the chapter, he wasn't surprised to discover that the witches' practices had been used against them as evidence during the trials of the fifteenth century. After all, the persecution of the witches was famous, even in non-supernatural circles.

"Shame," he mumbled, with a frown. "They were only trying to do good, and once again, people cast judgement without really understanding the matter."

He heard a low chuckle behind him and wheeled around immediately to face the source of the noise. It came as no surprise to see Hrschni and Dr. Barqa-Abu hovering behind him, both wearing matching expressions of amusement.

"I think you're beginning to see things as I do," Hrschni said, drifting over to the dressing table. "All it takes is some understanding, isn't that right?"

"Hrschni, don't try to influence the boy's thoughts," Dr. Barqa-Abu scolded. "You and I see things differently, and we are polarised in our opinions. He, on the other hand, might be able to see a middle path." She turned her attention to Kester. "We will continue your training first. Then, Hrschni will show you more of your mother's memories. Now, stand up and demonstrate how much more control you have over opening spirit doors. Your improvement has been impressive."

"You want me to show off my skills?" Kester said, shutting the book. "Now, at this instant?"

"I do."

He stood, then breathed slowly in and out. It helped when his mind was calm and his thoughts were permitted to drift. Almost immediately, he felt the familiar *tension* to the air, the sense that the particles around him were tightening, then readying themselves to part.

A few moments later, the air shivered and started to split. Hrschni muttered approvingly, and Kester glanced over, distracted. At once, the door sealed itself shut again.

"You put me off," he grumbled.

"It doesn't matter," the daemon replied, weaving excitedly in the air. "I have never seen anyone open a spirit door so swiftly before. However, it doesn't surprise me, given who you are."

"Was my mother as quick?" he asked.

Hrschni shook his head. "She wasn't, but there's a reason for that."

"What was the reason?"

"It's easier if I show you, rather than tell."

Kester shrugged. "There's no time like the present."

"Very well," the daemon agreed. "This time, we must progress a few years further, after your mother had completed her education at the SSFE. She qualified with flying colours and developed a formidable reputation as a spirit door opener. Unsurprisingly, she went to work for Artemis Wellbeloved, Jennifer's father. In the very same office where you work now, actually."

"What about you?" Kester asked. "Were you and her still . . . ?" He didn't know how to phrase it; the very notion that they'd had any sort of intimacy was still difficult for him to accept.

"We were. Even after seeing me in my true form, Kester, she still wanted to be with me. It's important that you understand that. I know that she never stopped—"

"Hrschni, let Kester see for himself," Dr. Barqa-Abu said gently.

The daemon nodded. "You're right." Without saying another word, he pressed his finger to Kester's forehead, and at once, the room dimmed to black.

Chapter 7 – The Wellbeloved Agency

The door to the office slammed open, nearly knocking a nearby potted plant off its stand. Gretchen raised her head, just in time to see Julio parade through the doorway, hands held aloft in triumph. Then, after a surreptitious nudge, he moved aside to let Artemis Wellbeloved enter.

"I take it that appointment was a success, then?" The pair of them reminded her of Olympic athletes celebrating a victory.

Julio grinned wolfishly. "Ah, another day, another contract won. It is too easy. We tell them that we can get rid of their spirit within twenty-four hours, and they want to hire us, just like that." He bowed in her direction. "It is down to you, of course. You and your formidable gift."

Artemis hung his coat on the hatstand, then joined them both. "I've said it before, and I'll say it again," he said, squeezing her shoulder, "you're a powerful asset, Gretchen. Now, where's Jennifer?"

Jennifer poked her head from the stockroom as soon as she heard her name called. "When's this job booked in for, then?" she asked, emerging with several files tucked under one arm.

"Tomorrow," Julio replied. "It's very nice, very easy. Just a little nixie, hidden in the bottom of a pond. Very sharp teeth, though." He held up his hand, revealing several minute indentations around the fingers.

"I did tell you not to stick your hand in the water," Artemis said, retreating to his private office. "You must learn to listen. It's every bit as important as talking, you know."

After their boss had shut the door behind him, the three of them laughed.

"We should celebrate with a drink tonight, yes?" Julio said, wrapping his arms around the pair of them. "We are putting this agency on the map. Young blood, that's what we are. Powerful and strong, like the raging bull!"

"Or persistent and loud, like the overeager terrier?" Gretchen muttered, making Jennifer chuckle even more.

Julio kissed them both on the cheek. "It is nearly the end of the day; shall we go to the pub? I always enjoy an English pub. It is the one thing that this country does *right*."

"That's a good idea," Jennifer agreed. "Daddy might want to come too; he's got something to show you. An exciting surprise."

"What is it?"

"The architect's plans for our house. I had a sneaky look while you were out; they're amazing. It's a ranch, Julio, just like you wanted."

Julio wrung his hands with delight. "With the wood and the porch, yes? The porch is very important. I remember my dear Mama sitting on her porch and watching me play in the grass."

"It has the porch, yes. Daddy said it'll be ideal for children." She blushed, then looked away.

Gretchen stifled a sigh. She'd heard all about the proposals for the house several times already. It wasn't that she wasn't happy for them; after all, they'd waited long enough to be married and live together. It was just that once again, she felt like the odd one out. There was no ranch waiting for her in the future, or wedding, or even children. In fact, as far as she could tell, her future was just one tangled, complex mess.

Still, at least I'm not alone, she reminded herself. Since she'd moved out of the Wellbeloved house and into her own tiny apartment in town, it had been far easier to see Hrschni. Sometimes he came to her in Billy Dagger's body, always under cover of darkness, for fear of being recognised. At other times, he travelled to her as *himself*: a form that had frightened her at first but that she'd now adjusted to. He was still the same, after all. The creature that she loved, regardless of what he looked like.

It was undeniably hard loving a daemon. Sometimes, his intensity overwhelmed her, made her feel as though she were drowning, without any way of saving herself. At other times, the force of his will made her feel brittle, liable to snap under the pressure. His sheer age was daunting to her too; he'd experienced things she could only dream of, and she felt like a mayfly by comparison, impermanent and flimsy.

Sometimes, she believed they'd be together forever. But then, she imagined herself growing older. Never being able to confide with anyone about their relationship. Gradually filling with bitterness and resentment as she became wrinkled and grey, and Hrschni failed to change at all.

It couldn't last, and she knew it, but that didn't stop her from wanting him. Life without Hrschni seemed like an impossibility, and that was all there was to it.

Julio nudged her in the ribs, making her jump. "Are you coming to the pub?"

She shook her head. "I'll go home, I think. You two go and have fun."

"Always the same, sneaking off to do your own thing." He raised a hand before she could protest. "It's okay, you've told us before. You like your own space. We understand this."

"I'm sorry. I'll see you tomorrow." She knew they were worried about her, and in some ways, they were right to be. She felt *overstretched*, anxious that her relationship with Hrschni, the double life she was living, and all the pressure of continually keeping secrets would somehow corrupt her spirit door opening ability and that she'd fail them all.

It was a silly thing to be concerned about, of course. Hrschni had helped her to hone her skills over the years, until she could make a door materialise in the air within a minute, if not less. There was no chance of failure. As far as she was aware, she was the most competent spirit door opener in the country.

Even so, she couldn't shake off the feeling that the happiness that surrounded her was nothing more than a cheap veneer, casting a sheen over the truth. And that it could be snatched away from her at any time.

She sensed Hrschni's presence, even before she'd stepped through the narrow front door of her flat. It was a barely discernible vibration in the air that gave him away, plus a level of heat, radiating from somewhere ahead. She rubbed her arms reflexively, then made her way through to the living room.

"You decided to come, then," she said, conversationally to the empty room.

Hrschni materialised a few seconds later, curling around her like a silk scarf, submerging her in bright flame. His glow illuminated the surrounding walls and created a perfect circle of light on the rug below.

"I had things to attend to in Exeter," he said, touching her skin with his fingers.

She nuzzled her cheek against his. "Oh, those mysterious *things* again," she said, throwing her coat over the back of the sofa. "When are you going to tell me what these things are, Hrschni?"

"Meeting with old friends and discussing important matters. Challenging new conceptions too."

"And who are these old friends?"

He smiled, coiling lazily around her. "I have many old friends. Too many to mention."

Yet another tricky answer, she thought, as she headed to her tiny kitchen to make herself a drink. She adored him, but sometimes, trying to untangle his words felt like a full-time job.

"You're upset about something," the daemon said, following her. "I should have come in Billy Dagger's body; I could have offered better physical comfort."

She raised an eyebrow. "Physical comfort only goes so far. Anyway, Billy Dagger has a sold-out concert tonight in Manchester, so I presume you won't be staying long."

"Regrettably, that is the case, and I mustn't let Billy down. It's Julio and Jennifer, isn't it? I can sense that your emotions are tainted with the jealousy of—"

"It's not jealousy," she said curtly. "I'm happy for them. It's just difficult, hearing about their perfect life all the time. The plans for the ranch house have arrived. It's so ostentatious, and it's costing a ridiculous amount too. And what do I get? A basic salary and the occasional pat on the back, when I'm the sole reason the agency is performing so well."

"I always said your talents could be put to better use elsewhere." He hovered beside her as she poured milk into her tea. "You have a natural affinity with spirits, and they need you badly."

"Spirits don't need me, Hrschni."

"*I* need you."

She sighed as she felt his essence flow over her skin, *through* her body. It was intimate, thrilling, and she was embarrassed at how quickly she felt herself responding to it.

"A spirit door opener sends spirits back into their own world," she mumbled, closing her eyes with enjoyment. "It's a skill that's useful to humans, not spirits. We covered this time and time again, back at college."

"That's not always the case. In the ancient times, people like you helped to create larger, more powerful doorways to the spirit world."

"Hrschni, not now, please. I'm tired. I just want to spend the evening relaxing with a good book."

Reluctantly, he pulled away from her. "I understand. But we need to talk about this properly, and soon. I feel it's what you are destined to do, Gretchen. You were born for better things than working for a regional supernatural agency."

Maybe I am, she thought, as she collapsed on the sofa. Her head felt overstuffed with thoughts, and all of them were too large and complicated to concentrate on. She knew that Hrschni wanted her to work with him, that he had *plans* to change the world for the better. So far, however, he'd been reluctant to share the details.

That was the thing, she realised, when in a relationship with a powerful spirit like Hrschni. The relationship tended to operate on his terms, not hers.

The next morning, Artemis pulled up outside Gretchen's apartment, alerting her to his presence with several cheery toots of the car horn.

After waving out the window, she raced down the communal staircase, then slipped outside. Jennifer shifted along the back seat to make room for her, giving her a warm smile as she did so. As usual, Julio had assumed his place in the front passenger seat, even though he was scarcely much taller than his wife-to-be. The patriarchal hierarchy was well-established in the Wellbeloved Agency, a fact that irked Gretchen, regardless of how wonderful both of the men were.

"It's not a long journey," Artemis chorused, as they headed off. "Just beyond Broadclyst. As for the briefing, there's not much you need to know, ladies. The nixie is disgruntled, but not to the extent that she's causing any major problems. However, she's eaten all the fish in the pond, which has ruffled some feathers. They were koi carp, apparently. Rather expensive too."

"The nixie's probably frustrated, being trapped in such a small space," Jennifer said.

"It is a big pond!" Julio protested. "The spirit has nothing to complain about. Only a few ducks to share the water with, it is a luxury palace, I think. But you know what these spirits are like: they are never content with anything; they always want more."

"Julio," Artemis said warningly. "We don't talk about spirits in that way; you know that."

"I know, I know. The nixie is a living thing, and we must respect her, yes, yes."

"Correct. Anyway, it's a simple job, Gretchen," Artemis continued. "Just do your thing, and we should be in and out in about fifteen minutes."

Once again, it's down to me, she thought, fixing her attention out of the window. *What a surprise.*

She peered into the murky waters below. Julio's earlier description had been a fair one; for a garden pond, it was positively palatial. Jennifer knelt beside her, whispering soft words in an attempt to calm the nixie.

"Sweetheart," Artemis said quietly, "you're not going to have much luck. This little spirit is quite overwrought, and no amount of conversing will change that."

Jennifer stood, then rubbed the mud off her knees. "I thought it might make Gretchen's job a little easier."

"I don't need help, don't worry," Gretchen said, as she began to focus her energy on the air directly above the pond. "This hardly requires any effort at all."

After a minute or so, she felt the familiar *tensing* of the world itself preparing to split open. The air began to tear apart, and she relaxed into the sensation, knowing that the fastest way to achieve results was to be passive—to *accept* the power that flowed through her and let it do its job.

Soon, the rip was large enough to serve its purpose. The nixie drifted upwards from the depths, dark and wet as eel skin, its tiny eyes sparkling like soap suds, before erupting from the pond's surface in a splash of water. A few moments later, it slipped silently through the spirit door, which Gretchen promptly sealed up behind it.

It's all ridiculously easy, she thought, straightening her legs.

Artemis nodded with delight. "Perfectly executed, Gretchen, as always. Let's go and tell the client, then we can get back to the office.

Julio, we'll start working on that bid for the ghoul in Crediton this afternoon." He patted his future son-in-law on the shoulder. "Here's to another success, eh?"

Jennifer caught sight of Gretchen's expression and smiled sympathetically.

Why does she just accept it? Gretchen thought, as they wandered back towards the house, leaving the now vacant pond behind them. *Our talents are ignored, while Julio gets all the credit. It's ridiculous.*

When they returned, the men retreated to Artemis's private office, presumably to go through the latest jobs that had arrived through the post that morning. Gretchen watched as Jennifer filled out the paperwork, nibbling the tip of her fountain pen as she worked.

"Boring job?" she said, after a while.

"It always is," Jennifer replied. "Someone has to do it, though."

"That someone's always you though, isn't it? Or me."

"Julio's useless at anything like this. You know how frustrated he gets if he has to sit at a desk for any length of time."

"Unless he's having a mid-afternoon nap, you mean." Gretchen got up from her desk and strolled over to her friend. "You should be firmer with him."

Jennifer looked up. "What do you mean?"

"You always let him get his own way. Stand up to him. Make him do some of the rubbish jobs for a change."

"But I don't mind doing them for him."

"You're a doormat, Jennifer. Stop letting him walk all over you."

Jennifer stiffened, then put her pen down on the desk. "I'm not a doormat," she said quietly. "It's called *loving someone*."

"Love isn't being someone's willing servant," Gretchen snapped. She knew she was being cruel, but Jennifer's submissive nature was starting to irritate her. How could her friend be so accepting of the way she was treated? It was the nineties, not the nineteenth century.

"I'm not his servant," Jennifer said. "I just want him to be happy. And he is, which means I've done my job well."

"What about your happiness? Is this all you want in life? To do your father's bidding until you're an adult, then your husband's bidding after that?"

Jennifer said nothing, only bit her lip and focused on the papers in front of her. With a sigh, Gretchen returned to her desk. She knew she'd gone too far; she'd upset her friend, and the guilt was already setting in. But she loathed the way Jennifer put Julio on a pedestal. Julio was wonderful, that was true. He was energetic and exhilarating, and life was never boring in his presence. But by pandering to his whims, Jennifer was turning her fiancé into a pampered dictator.

Gretchen sighed and returned to her notes on the ghoul case. It was inevitable they'd be awarded it, regardless of what they bid. They won every job they offered their service for, and it was all down to her.

A while later, Julio and Artemis emerged. Julio had the remnants of a cigarette between his fingers, a growing habit, thanks to Artemis's insistence on offering him all the time. *Offering him, not us,* Gretchen thought, watching Julio disappear into the stock cupboard. It was yet another way in which they were treated differently.

She slipped out from behind her desk and went to join Julio, closing the door quietly behind her. He'd put the kettle on, which was no surprise. She knew how he liked a strong Argentinian coffee at this time of the day.

"Gretchen? You made me jump," he said, spooning the coffee into the nearest mug. "Why have you closed the door?"

"Because I'd like to talk to you."

He placed the teaspoon carefully on the little kitchenette unit beside him. "Is something wrong? I *knew* there was something wrong, Gretchen, because I have been worried about you. You are not yourself; you are holding something troublesome deep within you, and this is causing you pain, I can tell."

Gretchen's eyes widened. "That wasn't what I was going to say."

"But it is true, is it not? You are not happy."

She frowned, before shrugging. "I don't know. But Julio, that isn't why I came to talk to you. What I wanted to say was—"

"Ah, I hate to hear that you are sad. Please, you can tell me anything. I am your friend; I would do all I can to make you feel better again."

"What about helping with the menial tasks in the office, then?"

He tilted his head to one side. "That's not what I expected you to ask. But yes, I can do these menials. I do not know what the word means, but—"

"It means the boring stuff that you always leave to Jennifer, because you don't want to do it."

"But she likes those jobs."

"No, she doesn't, not really. She does them because she's sweet, and you're taking advantage of that." Gretchen folded her arms and glared at him.

His eyes twinkled. "Look at you. All fire and passion. We are so alike, Gretchen. When we feel something, it is deep and powerful, right inside us."

She took a deep breath. Somehow, it was impossible to remain irritated with him, despite her best efforts. "I don't mean to sound cross," she replied, softening. "But it's important. Jennifer is destined for better things than being your obedient housewife."

"I know that." He pulled her into a hug, and she leant her head against his shoulder. The scent of his aftershave reminded her of being a student again, all three of them lying on the lawn, laughing over a silly joke. She inhaled deeply, closing her eyes, and felt his hand resting on the small of her back.

It was nice to be held by a human, for a change.

Hrschni, she thought, eyes snapping open. *And Jennifer. I mustn't forget myself.* "Anyway," she said brusquely, pulling away, "I'm glad we had this chat."

He nodded. "Was it a chat? I am confused. You came in like the whirlwind, and now I have forgotten what I came in here to do."

She pointed at the kettle. "Make coffee."

"Ah yes. Coffee." He grinned at her. "Of course."

After work, Gretchen deliberately walked in the opposite direction of her apartment. She couldn't bear the thought of spending yet another evening sitting on the sofa, staring out at the busy street below. Nor could she tolerate the idea of watching passersby as they went about their everyday lives, without any idea of how much effort was involved in keeping the spirit world separate from their own.

She knew Hrschni would find her in the end, no matter where she wandered to. He always did; there seemed to be an invisible chain between them both, binding them together. She knew that he couldn't come in his human body tonight; Billy Dagger was performing several gigs across the country, and Hrschni was only able to slip away in his daemon form. She admired his dedication to the human he'd chosen to inhabit. Elevating Billy to greatness was something he took very seriously indeed.

Without thinking too much about where she was headed, she wandered through the public gardens, just behind the city museum. An ancient castle had stood there once, and the tumbledown remains of the wall and tower were still standing, though the stones were coated in moss and ivy. It was quiet, apart from the lilting notes of a blackbird somewhere in the trees above and the rustling of the wind in the surrounding bushes. The solitude and peace were soothing; they were what she needed right now.

Finally, she sat on the nearest bench. Her head was overstuffed with whirling thoughts—and doubts too. It was difficult to put them into any sort of rational order or arrive at any resolutions. When she'd started work at the agency, she'd been swept up in the excitement of it all and the prospect of making Artemis's business great again. Praise had been heaped on her, and she'd been thrilled by the attention, by the sudden *respect* she was earning.

But already, the cracks were beginning to show. Removing spirits from the human world no longer excited her. After all, they were the same as Hrschni in many ways; did that mean they also had something to contribute to the world? She hated the way they were referred to as *lesser beings,* as though their existence were an inconvenience and nothing more.

Her relationship with Jennifer felt increasingly strained too. She missed their cosy conversations back in their room at the SSFE. Though she loved her friend, she wasn't sure she understood her as well as she once had. Jennifer had no real ambitions beyond keeping her father's business going and marrying Julio. It was baffling, not to mention frustrating. Jennifer was intelligent and fiercely passionate about many things, like spirit rights. However, when it came to standing up for her own rights, she was utterly hopeless.

After a while, Gretchen rose from her seat. The cold was seeping through her clothes and numbing her body. She strolled through the doorway in the old castle wall and out to the open gardens on the other side. A little path ran alongside the steep, muddy banks, and she paced along it. Up here, it was easy to remain unseen while watching those below, like a circling bird of prey.

He's here, she realised suddenly, stopping in her tracks. It always felt the same to her: first, an anticipatory tension in her body, then, the tingle of heat against her skin, announcing the daemon's arrival.

A second later, the air shuddered before her, and Hrschni appeared soon after—a more muted form of his usual self, to avoid detection. Despite his attempts at concealment, she could still make out the writhing fire that formed his body and the black pits of his eyes.

"Your mind is in turmoil," he said, without preamble.

"Good afternoon to you too," she replied.

He wound around her, warming her skin, resting his fiery lips upon hers for the briefest of moments before retreating.

"You're confused," he said finally, hovering beside her. "Melancholy too. You feel more alone than ever." He stilled for a moment, his energy dimming further. "This worries me, Gretchen. You have *me,* so you don't ever have to be lonely. Don't forget that."

"You're hardly ever here. This isn't a normal relationship."

"But we are not normal creatures."

She sighed. It was impossible to explain her feelings, especially as she didn't really understand them herself. "I had to expel a nixie today," she said, eventually.

"Expel? That's a nasty way to put it."

"But that's what I do, isn't it? I throw spirits out of our world, without knowing anything about them."

He brightened again and touched her gently on the arm. "That is why you're different, Gretchen. You *want* to know them. You want to make a difference."

"The nixie wasn't doing any harm. She was living peacefully in the pond, though I suppose she did eat all the fish. But that aside, she wasn't haunting anyone. She wasn't making anyone's life a misery. Yet I forced her away, anyway. It all feels so pointless."

"Help me to make a better world, then."

"Hrschni, you keep talking about this, but I don't know what you mean."

"Spirits can help humans, but only if we're allowed to move freely in this world. If we created some permanent sun doors, this could happen."

She stopped walking and faced him. "You're suggesting that I quit my job and help you? This is the real world, Hrschni. I have to earn money, otherwise I'd be living on the streets."

"You would be fine. I would make sure of it. I wouldn't let you suffer."

"You mean you'd be yet another male protecting the poor helpless female who couldn't fend for herself?"

He reeled away from her. "That is not what I meant. Males, females, I see no difference."

"Isn't it?" She forced herself to take a deep breath. "I'm sorry. My head is all over the place at the moment."

"Then let me help you. Leave the agency. Be with me—properly, I mean."

"What, travel the world as the long-suffering girlfriend of a rock star?"

"There are worse things to be. It's the perfect opportunity to reintroduce spirits to the world. Every destination we arrive in, we can erect a sun door, as the shamans used to in the ancient times. There might be chaos at first, but this can be controlled. Spirits listen to me; I will ensure that they don't run amok and—"

"Hrschni, that isn't about me. That's about *you* and your dreams."

He flickered uncertainly. "It's about both of us. Our future. What we are destined to do."

"No." She took a deep breath, then reached for him, steeling herself for the resistant burning before he relaxed and let her *in.* "I'm getting so tired of helping other people achieve their goals. What about mine?"

He met her gaze evenly, and as always, she found herself trapped in the unfathomable darkness of his eyes. It would be so tempting to give into it, as she always did, to relax and pass herself over to him, and to feel the warmth of his love radiate through her.

Not this time, she thought, steeling herself. The daemon flinched.

"I need some time alone," she told him and looked away.

Time passed. He was waiting for her to continue, she sensed, but she didn't know what else to say. Her mind had turned to stone: immobile and cold.

Eventually, he nodded. "If that's what you want. How long do you want? A few days? A week?"

"You don't understand. I need *a lot of time,* Hrschni. We've lived like this for too long, and I can't bear it anymore. I hate leading this secret life, and I hate knowing that I can never really *have* you. This relationship—it can never go anywhere, can it?"

He dimmed, almost to nothingness. "But we love one another," he said softly. "Isn't that enough?"

"I'm sorry," she replied, wiping her eyes. "I need more."

The idea of facing her colleagues at work was intolerable, especially after a sleepless night spent mostly thinking about Hrschni. As the sun rose, she texted Artemis to let him know she wouldn't be coming in, then spent the day in bed, curled up on her side, staring at the wall beside her.

She already missed the daemon, with a raw, hollow ache that refused to diminish, no matter how hard she tried to think about something else. Perhaps it would get easier with time; everyone always said that breakups were painful. Maybe it was normal to feel this desolate, though somehow, she didn't think so. She wanted nothing more than to stay here and *shut down,* to stop everything from hurting so much.

I've made a mistake, she told herself. But she knew it had to happen, at some point. Relationships between humans and spirits were too complicated; their natures were just too different.

The next day was no better, nor the following one. She had no motivation to move—or to even exist, for that matter. Her world had faded to a washed-out grey, and it seemed there was no colour in anything anymore, nor life either.

I've made a mess of everything, she thought, over and over again. She wondered what Hrschni was doing at that moment, while she was lying here in her apartment. He'd no doubt be nestled deep within Billy Dagger's body, signing autographs, giving interviews, and performing on stage. The arrangement with Billy Dagger was mutually beneficial. Thanks to the daemon, Billy was now one of the most celebrated musicians in the country, if not the world. She'd heard tales about his home in London, with its indoor swimming pool and expansive landscaped gardens, his private jet, the wild nights on tour. That life could have been hers: the excitement, the luxury, the fame, even. But she'd turned it all down, for this lifeless existence in Exeter.

Her mobile phone beeped loudly, bringing her back to the present. It was another text message from Jennifer, asking how she was, then begging her to return her calls. After considering it for a few seconds, she stuffed her phone under the pillow. She couldn't face any sort of interaction with her friend now, especially if it involved hearing about the wedding plans or the construction of their new ranch-style house.

Face it, she told herself sternly, *you can't cope with the fact that she's happy and you're not, and that's a shameful thing. She's your best friend, for goodness' sake.*

The next day, she forced herself to have a shower and make something substantial to eat. She felt wispish and frail, a creature made of antique plaster and dust, ready to blow away in a stiff breeze. Her hair was a wreck, and her usually rosy cheeks were pale and hollow.

What the hell am I going to do with myself? she wondered, staring at herself in the mirror. *And more to the point, do I even care?*

Later that evening, the doorbell rang. She ignored it. If it was the postman making a late delivery, he could leave the parcel on the doorstep. However, much to her irritation, the trilling didn't stop. Someone's finger appeared to be glued to the button, pressing it repeatedly to get her attention.

It's Jennifer, she guessed, pulling on her cardigan with a sigh. It didn't surprise her; she'd suspected that her friend would turn up sooner or later. Stepping reluctantly out of her front door, she traipsed down the communal staircase to let her in. After all, there was only so long she could continue hiding away from them all.

Pulling open the heavy entrance door, she peered out, then gasped. The person standing on the doorstep most definitely wasn't Jennifer. Instead, she found herself locking eyes with Julio, whose finger was still hovering over the doorbell. He removed his hand slowly, then grasped her by the shoulder before she'd had chance to say a word.

"What has happened to you? Why are you not talking to any of us?" He stepped inside without being asked, then studied her intently. "You look so tired, Gretchen, and so sad! Tell me thing—I am your friend."

She rubbed her eyes. "Why are you here?"

"You mean why not Jennifer?" He started marching up the communal staircase towards her apartment, then beckoned for her to follow. "She thinks that you are upset with her; she said you had the row, yes? So now she is too scared to come round, because she thinks you will shout."

Gretchen sighed. "I'm not going to shout at her."

"That is what I said, but you know how she is." He reached her door, then barged straight through, making his way through to the living room. "So, I am here instead. That is a good thing, of course, because you are my friend too, and I have brought some good Argentinian wine. Now, you will tell me everything. Sit down, please."

She chuckled, in spite of it all. It was just like Julio to invite her to sit down in her own apartment. "I'd better get some glasses if you've brought alcohol," she said, nodding at the bottle-shaped bulge in his jacket.

"There is a hint of the old Gretchen I love so well. I will wait here, and then we will talk."

She fetched two glasses from the cupboard, then returned, sitting beside him on her tiny sofa. He popped the cork as reverently as a vicar performing religious rites, then poured them both a generous measure.

"Here's to you, Gretchen," he said, clinking her glass with his own. "And for everything you are about to tell me, because we are all sick of the secrets."

"How do you know I've got secrets?"

"Come now. All this scuttling off after work, never wanting to spend time with Jennifer and me? You were like it at college too. What is this big dark thing you keep from us? Whatever it is, I can tell it is tearing you open."

"Tearing me apart," she corrected.

"See, even you say it." He leaned closer, until his face was barely inches from hers. "I want to know, so I can help."

She sighed and leaned back against the cushions. A part of her longed to tell him everything, right from the start. But she suspected he'd be horrified once he learnt the truth. Repulsed, even. She knew how he felt about spirits and humans having relationships with one another.

"You've got it all wrong," she lied. "I'm just lonely and frustrated, that's all. I feel like my life isn't going anywhere."

He wrapped an arm around her shoulder and squeezed her tightly. "That is not true. You are so talented; you could go further than us all."

"That's just it, though," she said. "I don't know where I want to go."

They drained the bottle of wine far quicker than Gretchen had anticipated. Afterwards, she retrieved another bottle from her kitchen, then poured them both another glass. It wasn't Argentinian, which generated the usual round of grumbling from Julio, but as she pointed out, at least it wasn't German—wine that he professed to loathe more than any other. Personally, she always liked the Rieslings that her mother used to drink, but she recognised that now wasn't the time to defend them.

"I've drunk far too much," she said after a while. A glance at her watch revealed that it was only nine o' clock, yet here they both were, already slurring their words and giggling too much. She appreciated Julio's presence, though. There was something about her friend that always managed to lift her mood, whether she wanted it lifted or not.

"It is okay. It's a Saturday, and that is the day people get drunk, right?" He raised his glass. "So, let us do the British thing."

"Even though neither of us are British?"

"We live here, and we both love this place. So, we are British, in a way. The country, she has adopted us both, yes?"

"That's one way of looking at it." She put down her glass and studied him closely. "Do you ever feel like an outsider?" she asked.

He considered the question carefully. "Sometimes I do. When people call me the rude name in the street; that is not nice, is it? When I get told to *go home*, that hurts me too, because I cannot go home, can I? I brought shame to my family, because I was the strange one who sensed the spirits. They said I had the devil in me. So I am not wanted there either."

She nodded. "I'm the same. Mutti used to talk about her parents back in Germany, but that's not a place I can ever go. I don't know them. I can't even speak German very well."

"Well, it is the slippery language, yes?"

"No more so than Spanish."

He laughed. "English is the most slippery of them all. All these words that look one way but are said another. It is a mystery to me."

"Maybe we're more like spirits than we know," she said, stroking the armrest thoughtfully. "They're outsiders too, and they know how it feels to be unwanted."

He paused. "I have not thought of it like that before. Gretchen, you are a wise woman. You make me see the world a different way, sometimes. It is good."

"I don't know, sometimes I wish I had your singular vision. You know what you want, and you go for it."

"I don't always know what I want. Sometimes, I am very torn."

"Torn?" She met his eyes, only to find that they were fixed upon her.

"Always."

The word came out like a caress. She stiffened, then quickly looked away.

"You look so sad," he whispered, placing his glass on the coffee table, then resting a hand on her shoulder. "I wish you would tell me what you are feeling. Don't shut me out, Gretchen."

"I can't help it," she replied. To her embarrassment, she felt hot tears prickling at the corners of her eyes, threatening to spill over at any moment. *It's just the alcohol,* she reminded herself, fighting to get hold of her scattered thoughts. *It's making me feel things that I shouldn't.*

He pulled her into a hug, and she pressed her head against his collar, savouring the solidity of him, the reassurance of a human presence, someone who wouldn't disappear without warning. That was what she loved best about this man: the sheer *earthiness* of him and his intense passion for the world and everything in it. Her hand rose to his chest, quite without her meaning it to.

Jennifer enjoys this every day, she thought darkly, then pulled away.

She met his gaze. His eyes were startlingly dark, even in the warm light of the lamp. He placed a hand on her knee, and she shuddered involuntarily.

"Julio," she whispered, a protest locked somewhere in her throat, unable to emerge. *This is wrong,* a small voice echoed in her head. It was drowned out by the sound of breathing, which was suddenly fast and shallow.

"I'm here," he said simply and moved closer.

His lips pressed against hers, seemingly without either of them moving. The pressure was so reassuringly solid, so unlike that of a daemon, that she sighed with pleasure. This was what she'd wanted, all this time. Someone with his own body, who was entirely himself at all times. His hand found its way through her hair, and her own hand moved to answer it, lacing a trail around his neck. All she could focus on was the heat of his breath, the scent of his aftershave, his entire body, so gloriously human and flawed.

Suddenly, her lips touched nothing but air. Julio stared at her, eyes wide, hand pressed against his mouth.

"This is terrible of us," he whispered.

"I know," she said, choking back a sob. "But God forgive me, I want it anyway."

Afterwards, she gathered her T-shirt from the floor, then her cardigan. She couldn't look Julio in the eye, couldn't even turn her head in his direction. Disgust filled her entirely, an intense revulsion aimed at him—and herself too.

I'm a horrible person, she thought, as she pulled on her clothes. *There's no other explanation. Otherwise, why would I do something so terrible?*

"Gretchen?" Julio's voice sounded broken, frightened even. "Please, talk to me."

"What is there to say?" she replied, keeping her gaze focused on the floor.

"I don't know. *I don't know.* But you will make it worse if you block me out."

She turned to see that he'd lowered his head into his hands. To her horror, she realised that he was sobbing. Her eyes stung in response.

"Julio," she said slowly, handing him his shirt. "We can't undo what we just did. But we were drunk, it wasn't planned, it just—"

"Do not say it *just happened*," he hissed. "We made it happen! We could have chosen differently; we could have stopped ourselves."

"But we didn't. We can't change things."

"It would kill Jennifer to know this happened. I cannot do that to her. As for her father? Think of everything he has given me, Gretchen! And I repay him like this?"

"We won't tell them," she said. The words sounded cold and hard, even to her own ears. "They don't need to know."

"But I know! How will I live with myself?"

"We'll both have to learn how to, won't we?"

He swiftly buttoned his shirt, then looked at her. "I want you to know that it was not just a physical thing, right? I would not risk everything for a roll in the hay-barn or whatever it is that you say." He clasped her hand swiftly, then dropped it. "I do care for you. When I am with you, it is energy, it is fire, it is like I am full of electricity."

"Stop saying things like that, please." Wincing, she gestured firmly to the door. "You have to go. We both need to think about this."

"I cannot bear to think about it, and I cannot bear *not* to think about it."

"You're a good person, Julio. In spite of this. I promise you."

He flinched, then turned away. "You are a good person too," he said, walking across the room. "But sometimes good people do very bad things."

She nodded in agreement as she watched him close the door quietly behind himself.

CHAPTER 8 – THE GAME IS UP

Kester's eyes flew open. He cried out—a garbled protest that brought him firmly back to the present. At first, the only thing he could see was Hrschni's face, barely inches from his own.

"Leave me alone. I don't want to see anymore!" he shouted, flinging his arms outwards.

The daemon flew into the air, landing against the opposite wall with a whiplash crack of energy. Kester gasped. He hadn't meant to do it; in his desperation to *stop seeing*, he'd reacted instinctively, still entangled in that strange darkness between the present and the past.

Hrschni's form shivered for a few moments before returning to its usual steady glow. However, his expression showed concern. Unsettlement too, and Kester couldn't help but notice that he remained a safe distance away.

"I've never seen anything like that before," Dr. Barqa-Abu said, from her position by the window. She drifted towards Kester, holding her hands over his body as though trying to detect some sort of static charge. "How on earth did you manage it?"

"I don't know," Kester said shakily. "I was so *angry*, I couldn't control myself. I'm sorry."

"It wasn't your fault," Hrschni said. "I should have known that seeing those things would upset you."

Kester sat weakly on the bed. He felt sick, feverish almost. Of course he'd known that his mother and Ribero had been together, but he'd had no idea that it had been *like that*.

"I always presumed Dad had seduced Mum," he said bleakly. "I thought she'd just been swept along by his charm. But it was her fault as much as it was his. She *chose* to do it, even though Miss Wellbeloved was her best friend."

"That's true," Hrschni said, resting beside him. "But you know as well as anyone that life is never a simple case of right or wrong. It exists in the cracks in between, the messy areas of truth that are hard to define."

Kester lifted his head. "How did you feel? You must have known about it; you're a daemon."

"I did, as soon as it happened. But don't feel pity for me, Kester. Spirits don't feel things the way humans do, so I didn't feel betrayed. In fact, I understood. She craved humanity, and that's what she got."

"They don't come more human than Julio Ribero," Dr. Barqa-Abu said wryly.

"You were different to what I'd imagined, too," Kester said to Hrschni. "I always presumed you'd tried to force her into opening permanent spirit doors. But it wasn't like that at all."

"She was correct, though, when she said I only thought of myself," the daemon said sadly. "I was so immersed in what I wanted, I forgot to think of what Gretchen needed. Again, you can blame that on my spirit nature. Sometimes, I fail to understand human emotion."

"Why were you so different towards me, then? You were gentle and kind to Mum. But you kidnapped me, trapped me in a cave, then tried to force me into doing what you wanted."

"Call it desperation if you like. All those years, I could see the human world slide into desolation, and I felt powerless to stop it. It was for all those reasons and more."

"I call it overstepping the mark," Dr. Barqa-Abu said, though her tone was gentle, not harsh. "I've said to you so many times over the years, Hrschni: you can't force people to bend to your will. Nor is your opinion the only one that matters."

"My ancient friend, on this matter, we always disagree." His fiery form shuddered for a moment before settling again. "Aside from that, we are united on every issue."

Kester smiled slightly. "I always believed that Mum was an angel, when I was younger. She made me feel safe. Whenever I was being teased at school or upset about having no friends, she made it better. I presumed she must have been perfect as a little girl and that she'd spent her whole life being wonderful."

"That's how she wanted you to see her," the daemon said softly. "For years, she'd felt like an outsider. Then you came along, a beloved child who loved her unconditionally and accepted her as she was. One thing I can tell you, Kester: you made her unbelievably happy. She thought you were the most marvellous creature alive. And she knew that one day, you would become a great man."

"I don't feel like a great man right now. I feel like a pathetic mess that's ruined everything for everyone."

Dr. Barqa-Abu raised an eyebrow. "That's defeatist. I expected better from a Lanner."

"A Lanner or a Ribero? What am I, anyway?"

Hrschni glanced back at the wall, which only minutes previously, he'd been thrown against. "You're more than you know," he said quietly. "I hope you'll understand that soon."

After a time, Kester left the hotel and wandered towards the main high street. He needed the bite of the sea air to rouse him and some time away from the stuffy confines of the room, which was now full of disturbing memories of what he'd witnessed. He also needed to buy something to eat or else run the risk of becoming too weak to function properly.

His mother hadn't been perfect. That part wasn't so hard to understand. The thing he struggled to comprehend was how much anger she'd hidden within herself. She'd raged against those who'd deserved it, but also against those who certainly hadn't, like Miss Wellbeloved. He wondered if that fury had ever been directed at him in the past.

I wouldn't have known, he realised, as he arrived outside the supermarket, then stepped through the automatic doors. *She might have hated me, and I would have been oblivious. Not because I was stupid, but because she was so good at hiding her true feelings.*

He picked up a container of pasta salad and an apple. It wasn't much, but it would keep him going. However, by the time he'd carried it back to the seafront and perched on one of the benches overlooking the beach, he realised his mistake. The scent of fish and chips, emanating from the take-away just behind him, was much more appetising. Still, pasta was sustenance, which was all he needed at present. With that thought firmly in mind, he started to shovel it in his mouth.

His mother had talked about being an outsider, his father too. He'd never really thought of either of them in those terms, but after hearing them discuss it, he could see things differently. Although he himself was half Argentinian and half German, he'd never felt anything other than British, and naively, he'd imagined they'd both felt the same.

It must be difficult feeling like you don't belong, he thought. His mother had been right; that must be what it was like for spirits, ancient creatures who had once been welcome here. The hurt and rejection he'd experienced recently, knowing that Ribero's team didn't want anything more to do with him—perhaps that was how the spirits felt. Many of them apparently wanted to be helpful but were abused by humans, then forcibly removed from the place they loved.

This was a skewed way of viewing it, he knew that. No one in one's right mind would argue that the fetch had been trying to help.

Instead, the murderous spirit had been hellbent on eradicating as many humans as possible, to whet its appetite for fetching people to their deaths. The fetch would be described as an outsider, and perhaps rightly so.

He stuck his fork into the container, then realised it was already empty. He must have been hungrier than he realised. On impulse, he stood up, headed towards the take-away, and ordered a large portion of chips and a pot of mushy peas.

I have a few missed meals to compensate for, he reminded himself, as the woman behind the counter handed him a pile of greasy, vinegary chips, neatly wrapped in paper.

Returning to the bench, he started eating once more and fixed his stare on the horizon. The sea rolled and tumbled against the cliffs in the distance—a violent, unpredictable motion that echoed his own turbulent thoughts. Maybe this was what real failure felt like: a messy situation and no clear path out of it. It all felt utterly hopeless.

A gull landed beside him, yellow eye fixed on Kester's food, and he threw a chip towards it, smiling as the bird gulped it down whole. A second gull landed soon after, closely followed by a third, and they began to circle him, beaks jabbing insistently at the pavement under his feet.

What's a congregation of gulls called? he wondered vaguely. Various other terms for groups of birds came to mind: *a murder of crows, an asylum of cuckoos, a parliament of owls.*

Parliament. The word triggered a memory of something he'd read about in *A Historie of Spirits:* meetings between spirits and humans, much like a parliament session, to discuss affairs and resolve issues.

The word *parliament* echoed once again in his mind. There was already a minister of the supernatural in the Houses of Parliament: Lord Bernard Nutcombe. So already, the spirit world was something that was acknowledged and accepted by the government, albeit secretly.

What if there were more elected officials? A person to act as spirit representative in every local council? Someone to monitor spirits on a regional level and to assess their behaviour individually, rather than getting rid of them all without discovering first if they were benign or malevolent?

He shoved a few more chips into his mouth, then frowned. There was something to the idea, a nugget of something promising. The only thing was, how could he ever convince anyone to give it a go? The budget required for hiring that many more people, let alone training them, would be mind-boggling.

But still. It was a start, and now that he'd discovered a starting point, he wasn't going to let it go.

He spent the rest of the evening ambling along the seafront, losing himself in the surroundings. The waves crashed beside him, threatening him with a soaking each time they slapped the side of the promenade, but he managed to nimbly duck out of the way each time.

The occasional train whizzed past on the tracks to the other side of him, but other than that, the path was deserted. After another few minutes, he arrived at Dawlish Warren. The irony of the location didn't escape him—ending up in this place, after everything that had happened. It was here, after all, at the end of the dunes, that Hrschni and Fylgia had battled against each other, where Serena had used her extinguishing skills to try to trap the daemon, and where Kester had stopped her, enabling him to escape.

Here's where it all went so badly wrong, he thought, staring past the parade of shops and amusement arcades. But even if he could somehow turn back the clock and make the choices over again, he wouldn't do anything differently. It had to be this way, for better or for worse.

His phone vibrated inside his pocket. He whipped it out, then scanned the message quickly.

Don't know if you'll read this. Your dad and Miss W have been taken in for questioning by Infinite Enterprises. Because they helped you, I reckon? Call if you get a chance. Mike.

Kester froze, then read the words again.

"You've got to be kidding me," he muttered, shaking his head.

He knew that Infinite Enterprises were determined to get to him, but he'd never imagined they'd drag his father and Miss Wellbeloved into it. Were they trying to use the pair as bait, to get him to surrender himself? Or were they going to grill them both until they cracked?

It was important to remain calm, though instinctively, he wanted to call Mike straight away and start coming up with a plan to free them both. He had to remember that the staff at Infinite Enterprises weren't evil. Intimidatingly professional and efficient, most certainly, but also friendly, approachable, and always happy to help. He couldn't envisage any of them causing harm to either his dad or Miss Wellbeloved.

But then, there was clearly a lot that he didn't know about them. The secret room where they annihilated spirits might just be the tip of the iceberg, for all he knew. How many other secrets were they keeping from the rest of the world? It didn't even bear thinking about.

I'll be back in Exeter very soon, he texted back. *Don't worry. It's me they want, not them.*

A reply pinged on his screen soon after.

Good. Miss W called me from Infinite HQ and she was in tears. It was horrible. I've never heard her cry like that before.

Kester gulped. The Miss Wellbeloved he'd come to know through the visions of the past had been trusting, kind to a fault, and she'd remained that way as an older woman too. She'd gone through enough in her life; she didn't deserve this.

It was time to take action. However, he didn't relish the prospect of doing so, nor the trouble that might follow afterwards.

"I have to go back," he told Hrschni as soon as he entered his hotel room. "We've got a big problem, and it needs to be dealt with right now."

Quickly, he outlined what Mike had told him. The daemon listened carefully, stalking from one end of the room to the other, then back again.

Finally, he paused and examined Kester intently. "You realise that's what Infinite Enterprises want you to do, don't you?"

Kester nodded glumly. "I know. But what choice do I have?"

"You could stay away. They won't harm your father or Jennifer. They reserve that type of treatment for spirits."

"There are other forms of harm. Ruining their reputation even further, for example, or causing them emotional distress."

"They're resilient; they'll survive it."

Kester took a deep breath. He knew it would be dangerous to act rashly. "If I talk to Infinite Enterprises and explain the situation," he said, "there's a chance they'll understand."

"They never have in the past. Why would they now?"

"I had an idea earlier, about how we could resolve things. If spirits were monitored more closely, as they entered and exited the human realm, then perhaps it would work. But I'd have to—"

"Kester, that gives humans too much control, as always! What right has a human to say which spirit is worthy and which is not? Who would decide the criteria?"

"Please, just give it some thought. A compromise is the only way out of this."

The daemon growled. "*Compromise*. We've discussed this before. For humans, compromise means that spirits give, and they take."

"What if we help them to see things in a different light?"

"I admire your tenacity, but it won't work. It's been tried before."

"Well, I'm going back to Exeter anyway," Kester said heavily. "I'm going to let Infinite Enterprises find me, make sure they release my father and Miss Wellbeloved, and see if I can figure out a deal with them."

Hrschni wheeled closer. "If you go now, you lose the opportunity to hear the final part of your mother's story."

"Haven't I heard enough? She was talented, but she lied about everything. She kept secrets from everyone. She stole her best friend's fiancé and even had a child by him. Don't worry, you've shattered any remaining delusions I might have about her."

The daemon stopped weaving and stared at him. "That was never my intention," he said quietly. "Your mother was a great woman. Don't ever doubt that."

"Everyone keeps saying that, but there's a lot of evidence to suggest the contrary."

"Very few humans have ever affected me as your mother did. She *glowed*, Kester. Her exuberance, her passion for life—she kept me captivated for far longer than most humans do. She was special. Unique, even."

"Yes, but she wasn't very nice," Kester said, leaning against the wall. As soon as the words left his lips, he regretted them. That was *Mum* he was talking about, not a stranger. Yet the young woman he'd seen through Hrschni's visions felt like an imposter, someone he couldn't equate with the kindly parent he'd loved so much.

The pair stood side by side for a while, each lost in his own private thoughts. There was no point in trying to discuss the matter further; he knew that Hrschni saw things differently to him and probably always would. *Once again, I'm on my own,* he thought, with a grimace. It seemed to be his default status, these days.

"Where's Dr. Barqa-Abu?" he asked, after a time.

"She had to return briefly to the SSFE," Hrschni explained. "Someone is covering her lessons, but she still needs to check in from time to time."

"It must be useful, being able to travel around in the blink of an eye." Kester sighed. "I'm so sick of being driven around here, there, and everywhere. I feel like I've only existed in cars or hotels in the last few days."

"Cars are dreadful things. I much preferred travelling by horse and cart. The clatter of hooves on the cobblestones was very soothing."

"Were you around when humans invented the wheel?"

"Not personally, but I heard about it, naturally. It was less thrilling than the history books suggest. Apparently, they'd been trying to design a circular pillow with a hole to rest the head in, then someone tried to roll it down a hill and realised it moved rather quickly."

"Did you like humans, even back then?"

"They weren't fully developed at that point. Rather difficult to communicate with at times, too. But sweet, like playful children. Full of curiosity, though occasionally slow on the uptake. The number of times I had to stop them eating poisonous berries—it got quite tiresome."

Kester smiled. "You really did care for humans, didn't you?"

"I still do, despite their brutal treatment of my kind. They've lost their way, and I want to help them to find it again."

"Then you understand."

"Understand what?"

"Why I have to go back to Exeter. Why I've got to let Infinite Enterprises find me again and talk to them properly. They're lost too; we all are. But if we don't dare put a foot back on the path, how will we ever be able to walk on it again?"

The daemon frowned. "It's a weak analogy, if you don't mind me saying."

"It sounded better in my head."

"Very well. I sense you have a plan, Kester. Maybe you can bring some sort of balance to this mess."

"So, you won't stop me?"

"I won't stop you. I wish you'd reconsider, but I can tell there's no persuading you."

"No," Kester said, as he started to gather his belongings for what felt like the hundredth time. "You're right."

"Just like your parents," Hrschni said with a wry chuckle before fading out of sight.

After packing his bag again, Kester headed to the local station. Ten minutes later, he was on the train back to Exeter and wondering what on earth to do next. He fixed his attention out of the window, watching as the waves continued to thrash against the coastline. It seemed a good metaphor for his life, he felt: restless, thrown this way and that with no control over any of it.

He should have known that Infinite Enterprises would find a way to get him in the end. It had been foolish to imagine that they'd ever stop their pursuit, especially when so much relied on his capture. He wondered if they'd arrest him straight away or question him first. Perhaps they'd put him on trial, then sentence him to time in prison. It was impossible to guess; after all, supernatural cases were never featured on the news, and he didn't know the government's stance on such matters.

Knowing his luck, assisting dangerous spirits was probably regarded as a major offence. He wondered if they had special jails for those who committed supernatural-related crimes, or whether he'd be placed in a normal prison, with every other criminal in the country. If that were the case, he was doomed. A pasty, bookish man like himself would be demolished within days, if not hours.

Probably best not to think about it, he reminded himself. His anxiety was threatening to overwhelm him, which wouldn't help the situation at all.

The train pulled into Exeter Central station twenty minutes later. As he hurried along the platform, he pulled his phone out of his pocket. The battery was down to a few percent, but it was probably just enough to call Mike.

He held the phone to his ear, then waited. Thankfully, Mike answered shortly afterwards.

"Kester? You're not meant to be calling people," he said gruffly.

"It doesn't matter now," Kester said. "The plan is to let Infinite Enterprises find me. What did my dad and Miss Wellbeloved say, when you spoke to them?"

"Not much, mate. Only that they were being held for questioning, that Infinite Enterprises were extremely concerned about the situation, that sort of thing." He paused, then added, "Where are you?"

"I'm just leaving the train station."

"Wait there. I'll come and join you. I'll phone the others too."

"Mike, you don't have to do that. This is my problem, not yours."

"Stop with all that. I was angry to begin with, but things have changed. Well, partly changed. I'm still a bit miffed about Serena quitting her job, I guess. Not that I care personally, of course, but—"

"Yeah, I get it," Kester said. At a recent New Year's Eve party, he'd caught Serena and Mike in a romantic embrace. He suspected that Mike was a lot more upset about her departure than he was letting on.

"Anyway," Mike continued stiffly. "I want to help. I've felt like a right useless git these last few days. All I've done is sit on my arse while the agency has gone down the pan, and I can't do anything about it. Even worse, I can't track down my brother either, which is a real shame, because I'd ram my steel-capped boots firmly where the sun doesn't shine. Getting a good kicking would be the least of his worries."

"I spoke to Crispian the other day," Kester interrupted, stepping out of the station and into the cold. "He offered me a job."

The noise that emerged from the phone receiver was something between a strangled gargle and an engine exploding. "That *git*. What job? What's he up to?"

"He's set up a new agency," Kester replied. "Don't worry, I declined his offer. I also told him a few home truths."

"What, like he's a nauseating twit who deserves a hiding?"

"Not those exact words, but I certainly didn't hold back."

"Good," Mike said, with obvious satisfaction. "Right, I'm heading out to the van now. I'll call Pamela and Serena, then make my way to you. Stay there, alright?"

"You'd better hurry," Kester said, studying the car park in front of him and wondering if any of the vehicles were lying in wait for him. "It wouldn't surprise me if Infinite Enterprises already knew I was here."

"Wait somewhere subtle, then. Don't stand in the entrance, gawping like a fish."

Kester reddened, because that was exactly where he *was* standing, and his facial expression had been distinctly open mouthed too.

"I don't know what you take me for," he said stiffly. "See you in a bit."

After hanging up, he scurried to the side of the building. The narrow path between the station and the neighbouring parade of shops formed a wind tunnel, buffeting him with ice-cold air. Still, at least from this vantage point, he'd be able to spot anyone from Infinite Enterprises before they saw him. Then, he could decide what to do once the others had arrived.

He waited. A taxi rolled up, and the driver eyed him first with hope, then with irritation. Kester buttoned his coat up to the chin and pretended not to notice. Finally, he caught sight of the agency van, rumbling into the station car park. The wheels shrieked in protest as it ground to a halt, and the bumper at the front juddered, hanging only an inch or so from the ground.

It's amazing that vehicle is considered road worthy, he thought, rushing towards it. Mike always claimed it was his remarkable mechanical skills that kept the van going, but Kester suspected it was more to do with sheer luck than anything else.

Mike clambered out, closely followed by Pamela. At once, Kester was enveloped in a tangle of arms, as both of them hugged him at once. He returned their hug fiercely, then finally prised himself away.

"This is all bit emotional, isn't it?" Mike said, adjusting his baseball cap.

"Oh, love, isn't it terrible, what they've done to Julio and Jennifer?" Pamela added. "I've been so worried. I keep calling Infinite Enterprises, but the snooty receptionist won't let me talk to anyone."

"Well, let's go there now," Mike said. "If we storm the building, they'll have to let us see them."

Kester remembered when he'd last been inside Infinite Enterprises headquarters. It was a shining tower of glass and metal, with sophisticated security measures such as advanced fingerprint-recognition systems and lasers on the upper floors. To be honest, he didn't much fancy their chances.

"Where's Serena?" he asked, peering inside the van.

"She's not answering her phone," Mike said. "I tried her earlier too, just to see how she was—left a really heartfelt, tender message. The old witch ignored it. You know what she's like."

"I guess she's still furious," Kester said. "I mean, she's always been suspicious of me, ever since I started working with you. Letting Hrschni escape gave her the perfect chance to express her loathing of me."

"It was never like that," Pamela said. "She was jealous, that's all. She saw it as just another man being handed a job he didn't deserve."

Kester bit his lip. Pamela's words uncomfortably echoed his own mother's opinions, back when she'd worked for the Wellbeloved Agency. *Am I part of the problem?* he wondered. But it wasn't as if he'd wanted his father to leave the agency to him. He hadn't asked for any of it.

"Are we going to drive to Infinite Enterprises HQ, then?" he asked, throwing his bag into the van. "You can hand me over to them, and they'll let Dad and Miss Wellbeloved go."

Mike shrugged. "I haven't got any wild parties to attend this evening, so why not?"

Pamela gave him the thumbs-up. "Count me in. Though I'm not sure about handing you over; there must be another way to resolve this."

"I don't think there is," Kester said. "And let's face it, they were going to catch up with me sooner or later. Are you sure you want to come? It's a long drive"

"I've nothing better to do; I was only listening to the radio and knitting a scarf. I suppose Hemingway might nibble the scarf while I'm out, but at least it'll give him something to do."

Kester grinned. At the very least, Hemingway was likely to slobber on it or else deposit a pile of hairs over the wool. Pamela's dog was easily the messiest creature he'd ever encountered.

"Great," he said. "Let's go to Infinite Enterprises, then."

A polite cough stopped him midmotion. He froze, one foot inside the van, one still planted on the ground, then turned his head, already knowing who he'd see behind him. Sure enough, Ian Kingdom-Green stood only a few metres away, accompanied by Lili Asadi. To his surprise, both of them looked slightly embarrassed—abashed even. They certainly didn't seem angry.

"Hello, Kester," Ian said, bowing slightly. "Mike, Pamela."

Kester stepped down from the van. He glanced at the others, who looked every bit as concerned as he felt.

"Alright, Ian?" Mike said guardedly, shifting from one foot to the other. "Funny, you being here. We were just talking about you."

They stared at one another. Everyone seemed momentarily lost for words.

"We overheard what you said," Ian said, after a long pause. "We're glad you've decided to come to our offices, Kester. It's far easier this way."

Kester frowned. "The decision was made for me, when you seized my dad and Miss Wellbeloved."

"Let me reassure you that they weren't *seized*," Ian clarified. "We've treated them with the utmost respect."

"You're holding them captive, and you won't let me speak to them on the phone," Pamela said, wagging a finger in his direction.

"That's only a temporary arrangement, madam."

"It's not a very nice arrangement."

Ian glanced at Lili, who shrugged.

"Anyway," Lili said, directing her attention at Kester, "I'm glad you've finally seen sense. You've run us ragged the last few days. I haven't had a proper night's sleep in over forty-eight hours."

"I'm sorry," Kester said. "There were things I needed to do."

"Daemons you needed to assist?" Lili held up a hand before he could answer. "Don't waste time telling me; it's our bosses you need to be speaking to. They want to know how far it's gone."

"How far?" Kester looked at the others in confusion.

"You know," Ian said quietly. "The sun door. Have you and Hrschni started creating one? We need to know urgently, because if you have . . ."

Kester shook his head. "I haven't. Look, I'll come quietly, but you need to promise you'll release Dad and Miss Wellbeloved. They didn't do anything wrong."

"Apart from helping you to evade us over the last few days," Lily grumbled. "They deliberately created obstacles and made our jobs so much harder. All of this could have been avoided if you'd just done the sensible thing at the start and talked to us."

Pamela squeezed Kester's arm. "Perhaps it's best if you go with them, sweetheart. We'll follow behind in the van."

Lili raised a perfectly arched eyebrow. "That thing? Surely it doesn't go much faster than forty miles per hour, does it?"

"She can move when she wants to," Mike said defensively, patting the bonnet, which groaned under the impact.

"She just doesn't want to very often," Pamela added.

Ian grimaced. "I know the feeling. Now, Kester, would you be so kind as to come with us? Please don't run away again. You left me quite exhausted earlier. I'm not a man built for physical exertion."

"Fine, I'll come with you." Kester turned to his colleagues. "Honestly, if you'd rather go home, I'd understand. It's getting late, and I imagine they won't let you in the building."

"Your friends will be made comfortable when they arrive," Ian stated firmly. "To be frank, I don't know why you've got such a negative opinion of us. Haven't we always treated you nicely in the past?"

"You have. But tracking me like a criminal, then pursuing me around Devon, has made me a bit wary."

Ian and Lili both sighed in unison.

"Fair enough," Lili said. "Come on, let's get on with it. Some of us have got homes to go to."

Kester had to admit that the Infinite Enterprises van was at least ten times more comfortable than Mike's. The seat was soft and smooth, and the heating actually worked, which was a bonus. Ian and Lili sat at the front, and Kester studied the backs of their heads as they cruised smoothly out of the station car park and onto the main road.

"I'm sick of travelling around," he commented after a while. "When I was a child, I hardly went anywhere. These last few days, I seem to have spent most of my time on roads."

"Some travel is pleasant, though," Ian said, craning around to look at him. "When we went to Italy, for example. That was a jolly trip, wasn't it?"

Kester smiled. It seemed so long ago, when in reality, it had only been recently. So much had happened since then, though; it was bewildering to think about.

"It was fun," he agreed, "in a nerve-wracking sort of way. But I wasn't wild about the haunted house. Having poltergeists lob saucepans at my head wasn't the best experience I've ever had."

"And that's where we found those letters, of course," Ian continued. "What a shock, to discover your grandfather knew Hrschni!"

Kester looked down at his lap. He knew what Ian was attempting to do: gently steer the conversation onto the daemon and pump him for information. He didn't blame him; Ian was naturally curious about everything and probably desperate to understand Kester's actions.

"It *was* a shock," he agreed quietly. "To be honest, the last six months have been one continuous shock to me, from start to finish."

Lili glanced at him in the rearview mirror. "Don't think we don't recognise that, Kester. No one wants to punish you. We all know this is new to you and that you don't understand the severity of your actions. But you *must* help us. Too much is at stake here."

"I want to help everyone," Kester said. "But to do that, we need to start listening to each other. There are always two sides to every story, you know."

"Wise words, my friend," Ian said. "Did you know that the phrase *two sides to every story* is believed to have dated back to ancient times? Protagoras said that—"

"Not now, Ian," Lili said, not unkindly. "The history lesson can wait."

Once they'd reached the motorway, Kester found it hard to stop yawning. The comfort of the car, combined with his exhaustion, eventually got the better of him, and he let himself drift into a deep, dreamless sleep.

He awoke just as the van slowed to a halt. For a moment, he was disorientated, taking in only snippets of details: The gentle amber light above his head, the rows of shining windows outside, illuminated from within by a series of large metal lamps. Pillars. A bronze plaque by the rear entrance, shining in the light of the van's headlights.

We've arrived, he realised, wiping his face. The building looked somehow larger at night, soaring high into the sky. Even though they were around the back of the building and not the front, it was still intimidating to behold.

"The sleepyhead finally awakens!" Ian said, reaching over and patting Kester's knee. "My goodness, you were unconscious the entire journey! You didn't even wake up when we stopped at the services. Lili required a toilet break, you see, so I took the liberty of purchasing a coffee to—"

"I'm sure he doesn't want all the details," Lili snapped. "Though I must say, Kester, your snore could break world records. I even had the music at top volume, and it still failed to drown out the noise."

"I was very tired," Kester said defensively.

Ian opened the door. "Come on, then, let's get you inside."

A blast of chill night air hit Kester immediately, and he flinched, reluctant to leave the womb-like cosiness of the back seat.

"Are Mike and Pamela here yet?" he asked, wincing again as Lili opened the door next to him.

She laughed. "In that van? We'll be lucky to see them before morning, I should think."

Kester climbed out, shivering with the shock of the cold, then followed them both to the door. A security guard was positioned just inside and, seeing them, hastily pressed a few buttons on a pad beside him. Immediately, the doors slid open with a low *whoosh*.

"Evening, Mr. Kingdom-Green, Ms Asadi," he chorused, tapping his cap.

"Can you let Mr. Philpot know we're coming up?" Lili said. "He's already expecting us."

"Right you are." The security guard quickly tapped at another few buttons, then muttered something through a microphone. "He's ready for you," he announced, pointing at the lifts at the far end of the reception area.

Without another word, Lili and Ian swept forward. Kester scuttled after them, feeling smaller and more inadequate with every step. He couldn't imagine working in a place like this; it was all far too opulent and too professional. Mistakes clearly weren't tolerated here; that much was evident in every polished surface and every austere metal pillar and post. The lift doors opened, and they stepped inside. A moment later, the lift began to rise.

"Don't worry," Ian murmured to Kester. "This will all be sorted out soon, I assure you."

Lili snorted but made no comment.

Finally, the lift came to a halt. *The top floor,* Kester realised, surveying the glowing display above the door. *Presumably where they do all the top secret, awful stuff that no one knows about.* The corridor beyond was white walled and featureless. Their footsteps chimed off the marble-tiled floor as they made their way to a doorway at the end.

"Here we are!" Ian announced, knocking loudly. His cheery tones rang false in the sombre surroundings, echoing loudly before fading into silence.

They waited without looking at one another. A few moments later, the door swung open, and the familiar, narrow face of Curtis Philpot peered out. He spied Kester, then shook his head like a disapproving headmaster surveying a repeatedly naughty child.

"What a merry little dance you've led us on," he said wearily, as he moved aside to let them enter. "I feel like I've taken up permanent residence in this building, thanks to you. Still, you're here now; that's the main thing."

"Tell me about it; I haven't been home in ages," Lili agreed, sitting down on a leather sofa by the wall. Ian rested beside her, and Kester eyed the chair in front of Curtis Philpot's desk. He didn't quite dare to presume he'd be allowed to sit down, or at least, not yet.

"Go on," Curtis said irritably, gesturing at the chair. "Lord Nutcombe needs to be updated on the situation immediately, so we need to get started."

"Will you release my dad and Miss Wellbeloved?" Kester said. "That was the deal. I mean, that's why you brought them in for questioning, wasn't it? So you could use them as bait?"

"Dear God, Kester, this isn't a Hollywood movie. Also, can you stop portraying us as the villains here? You're the one who thwarted the capture of a dangerous daemon, remember."

"Only because I knew what you'd been doing!" Kester blurted. "You can't deny it; I've seen the CCTV footage!"

Ian and Lili looked at each other in confusion, while Curtis shifted uneasily in his seat.

"I wondered if that might have something to do with it," he said eventually, leaning over his desk. "Lili, Ian, you can leave us now. Go home, get some rest. Goodness knows you've both earned it."

"What was he talking about?" Ian asked, pointing at Kester. "What footage?"

Curtis shot a warning glance at Kester. "We'll discuss it later. For now, I need to chat to this young man alone."

Ian frowned but didn't protest. With a final concerned glance at Kester, he and Lili both departed. The atmosphere felt even more uncomfortable in their absence.

"I'm not going to insult your intelligence by denying it," Curtis said quietly, after the sound of their footsteps had faded into silence. "We suspected Hrschni had stolen that footage, and it comes as no surprise that he chose to show you."

"It was horrible," Kester said. "I can't believe you could be so cruel."

"Firstly, it's not me personally. I don't operate the machinery, nor do I decide which spirit is dismantled and which isn't."

"Dismantled?" Kester's eyes widened. "The process involves scattering spirits into thousands of tiny pieces of energy, and then leaving them to spend the rest of their days in agony, trying to assemble themselves again. And you just call it *dismantled?*"

"We have no proof that spirits have feelings, Kester. They're not corporeal beings; they don't have a nervous system. So, it follows that they can't experience physical pain. It's science, my boy, basic science."

"You don't believe that; I can tell by your face. You're just toeing the company line, doing what they tell you, to ensure you keep your job. You *know* that spirits can feel things; you've spent your life working in the supernatural field."

"Enlighten me, then, as you know so much. What exactly can spirits feel?"

"Anger, for one." He thought of Hrschni's visions, the tenderness that had radiated from the daemon whenever he'd been close to Gretchen. "And love."

Curtis sighed. "Let me assure you, the dismantling process is as swift and humane as possible." He took a deep breath, then added in a softer voice, "I understand what it's like to be young and idealistic, you know. I was like that once. I had lofty ideas about how spirits should be treated with respect. But the truth is, when you get to know them, you realise they're not like us. They don't have our sophisticated thought processes or emotions. They're just like animals, really. You don't feel guilty when you're tucking into a juicy steak or a nice cup of milky tea, do you? You don't worry about the cow in the slaughterhouse or the calf being torn from its mother shortly after birth?"

"It's not the same," Kester muttered.

"A vegan may disagree."

Kester rubbed at his temples. Curtis was using rhetoric to twist his thoughts, and he was too tired to come up with a logical response.

"This is going nowhere," he said, after a time. "Let's cut to the chase. What do you want from me?"

Curtis studied him for a moment, then nodded. "Very well. It's straightforward, really. We'll release your father and Miss Wellbeloved. You too, of course. We'll make sure that your agency is still awarded jobs, so everything will return to normal. In return, you'll bring us the daemon."

"I'll bring you the daemon?" Kester echoed weakly.

"That's correct. Hrschni is a threat to the continued safety of the human race. You failed to do your job last time; you can make up for it now. I don't care how you do it, but it needs to happen. Until then, you'll be taken down to a room in the basement level of this building and held there until you comply."

"You mean, you're planning to lock me up."

"It's not imprisonment."

"If I can't leave, that's exactly what it is."

Curtis shrugged. "You can choose to view it that way, if you prefer. I didn't want it to be like this, Kester. I've enjoyed working with you in the past. But if you continue to protect a terrorist, then you must be regarded as a threat to national safety too."

"I'm the least threatening person I know! Look at me, I look like a mole that's lost its way in a meadow!"

"I'm sorry." Curtis picked up the phone receiver from his desk, then dialled a number. "Hello there," he said curtly, keeping his eyes fixed on Kester. "Send security up please. Kester Lanner needs to be escorted to the secure suites. Many thanks."

"This is a mistake," Kester said, rising out of his chair. "If you'd just let me explain, then—"

"Bring Hrschni here. Then we can talk." Curtis sighed. "More importantly, we can all relax again. Honestly, I've never been so tired in all my life. Please, Kester. This could all be resolved swiftly; then we can get back to normal."

"If I asked Hrschni to come here, you'd *dismantle* him."

"I never said that."

"What would you do to him, then?"

Curtis looked away. "It wouldn't be my decision to make."

I think we both know what you'd do, Kester thought, just as the door opened, and two security guards advanced towards him.

CHAPTER 9 – LOCKED UP

To be fair to Infinite Enterprises, the "secure suite" was more a hotel room than a prison cell. It was spartan—grey walls, grey concrete floor, no windows—but the bed in the corner was comfortable, there was a small shower room to one side, and an armchair rested against the opposite wall, with a bookshelf beside it. Kester inspected the selection and nodded approvingly, pleased to see that there were a few books in there that he hadn't yet read. Then he remembered himself and sat heavily on the chair. He was trapped. He'd suspected something like this would happen, but he hadn't predicted that his father and Miss Wellbeloved would remain locked up too. They may well be in the rooms next to his; there was no way of knowing for sure.

What a mess, he thought, staring at the wall ahead. He couldn't comply with their demands; there was absolutely no way he could condemn Hrschni to a *dismantling.* Even the word itself made him shudder. But what did that mean for him? Would they keep him here for years? That would mean he wouldn't see Anya for ages, and how long would it take for her to tire of waiting and start seeing someone else?

Glassy-eyed, he continued to stare without really seeing. The situation was hopeless; he had no choice but to sit here and hope that the situation would take a turn for the better.

Fat chance, he told himself grimly, sinking his head into his hands. He'd been in several difficult situations before, most of them while working for his father's agency, but he'd never encountered anything like this. The truth was, he was completely out of ideas, and hope too.

Idly, he focused his attention on the air in front of him. Immediately, it started to shudder gently, a fact that took him by surprise. Instinctively, he focused his energy more intently on the area before his eyes, watching with fascination as the air trembled in earnest before tearing apart, like a zipper slowly being unfastened.

I'm getting good at this, he thought, with a thrill of excitement. *I can even open spirit doors without intending to.*

A high-pitched wail startled him into alertness. It was coming from the corridor outside—a shrill siren that pierced through the silence with relentless urgency. He gasped, and the spirit door sealed itself once more.

The siren continued to blare outside, and Kester covered his ears, straining to block the sound out. After a few minutes, the room fell quiet again, and he exhaled heavily. Someone must have activated the system, and it didn't take much brainpower to realise what had set it off in the first place. As though answering his thoughts, the door swung open, and a heavyset security guard entered, scowling at him in irritation.

"What did you do?" he snapped. "You made the alarm go off."

"I didn't do anything," Kester protested.

"You must have done something. We'll have to go through the CCTV now."

"It'll give you something to do, I suppose. Things must get tedious down here."

"You have no idea," the security guard agreed, before remembering himself and glaring again. "Anyway. Behave yourself, please."

That was interesting, Kester thought, as the door slammed shut again. Infinite Enterprises' sophisticated monitoring systems must have been able to sense the energy produced by opening a spirit door. It made sense; he knew that they'd picked up Hrschni's presence in the past, and he was a daemon, highly adept at moving around undetected.

Kester took the opportunity to rest for a while, something he'd had precious little time to do during the last few days. The bed was soft and inviting, and he allowed his mind to drift. It was pleasant to empty his head entirely of all thought, even though it was an unusual sensation for him. He closed his eyes, then fell into unconsciousness almost immediately.

It seemed like no time had passed at all when he awoke again. However, there was now a tray of food resting on the narrow table beside him: a generous fried breakfast, with a pot of tea beside it, which suggested he'd been napping for at least a few hours.

It's better than a hotel, he thought wryly, as he tucked in. A glance at his watch revealed that it was past nine in the morning, though given the room had no windows, it was impossible to get any sense of what sort of day it was. It could be snowing outside, the wind could be blowing a hurricane, or the sun might be shining. He had no idea at all, which was disorientating.

After eating, he had a quick shower, then wrapped himself in a generously sized towel. It wasn't great to be locked up, but he had to admit, things could be a lot worse. Indeed, it was arguably slightly nicer than some of the places he'd had to stay in recently.

As soon as he finished dressing, he heard a polite knock at the door. Before he could call out, it swung open, and a woman he'd never seen before stood in the doorway, surveying him with casual interest.

Someone important, he realised at once, taking in her neat suit, tucked-in blouse, and perfect chignon bun, without a hair out of place. *Obviously they've decided to send in the bigwigs to deal with me.*

"Kester," she began, in a tone every bit as polished as the rest of her. "My name is Miriam Webster, and I'd like you to accompany me."

"Is this about the siren going off last night?" he asked.

She tilted her head to one side and eyed him shrewdly. "And the rest of it. Come on."

He followed her obediently out of the room, then down a narrow hallway, which was lined with identical metal doors on both sides. *More cells, perhaps,* he thought, as their footsteps echoed off the walls around them. *More people locked away, for goodness knows how long. Just what sort of operation are Infinite Enterprises running here, anyway?*

Towards the end of the corridor, Miriam stopped abruptly, then pushed against the door beside her. "Here we are," she announced, then entered the small, dark space, ushering him inside after her.

The stark desk, combined with the chairs flanking it on either side, marked it at once as an interrogation room. Kester had seen rooms exactly like this before in countless thrillers and crime dramas, and he knew what was coming next. Reluctantly, he sat at one side of the table as Miriam took a seat at the other.

"Don't you need to record the conversation?" he asked. There was nothing on the desk apart from his own hand, which was drumming nervously against the surface.

"It is being recorded," she replied, pointing at the corner of the room. "Cameras."

"Of course."

"So, do you want to tell me what happened last night, then?"

"I presume you already know."

"You tried to open a spirit door. Why?"

He shook his head. "There was nothing premeditated about it; it just happened."

"Spirit doors don't just happen, Kester. Were you attempting to escape?"

"What?" He straightened in his seat. "Into the spirit realm? Can humans do that?"

She frowned. "Don't be silly, that's not what I meant. I rather thought you might be trying to contact Hrschni through it. Anyway, let's not get off topic; we've got more important things to discuss. Where is the daemon now?"

"I honestly don't know. He's a spirit, so he could technically be anywhere."

"We're aware you've been in contact with him over the last few days. What has he got planned?"

"I suspect you already know."

She propped her chin with her hand, then surveyed him closely. "He wants to open numerous permanent sun doors around the world, and he needs you to help him. Correct?"

"See?" Kester leaned back, folding his arms. "You already knew."

"Were you going to assist him, then?"

"No. My motives for preventing his capture weren't to join his cause. I just didn't want him to be torn apart by that horrible machine you've got."

"That horrible machine," she said sternly, "has been keeping humans safe from dangerous spirits for years. We don't throw any old spirit into it, Kester. We reserve it only for the spirits that constantly break the rules, the ones who harm humans. As you know, spirits can sometimes be deadly."

"Hrschni has never harmed humans."

"Don't be naive. He's planning to flood the world with dangerous spirits, which is the worst harm he could possibly inflict."

Kester shook his head. "He's not like that. Remember, I know him well."

"Oh, countless people felt they knew him well over the years. He's charismatic, persuasive, charming even. He's quite capable of tricking people into helping him." She pointed a finger at him. "That's why you must tell us where he is. If you won't open those sun doors, he'll find another spirit door opener who will. You're nothing special to him, Kester. He might have made you feel like you are, but you aren't. You're very disposable."

"That's not true," he said with confidence. "And I'm not going to bring him here; you won't convince me."

"This is ridiculous. You're so young; you've got your whole life ahead of you. A glittering career in this industry too, if you want it. Infinite Enterprises would hire you in a heartbeat, with talents like yours. Please, don't throw it all away on some idealistic crusade. Besides," she added, smiling slightly, "you wouldn't be the only member of your team to have a career with us. As I understand it, your colleague Serena Flyte had her final interview yesterday and was subsequently offered the job."

Kester blinked. "Excuse me?"

"We approached her directly, after the unfortunate incident happened. She was more than willing to hear our offer. After all, she's an adept extinguisher; her abilities will be useful to us."

"Serena might change her mind and come back to us."

"I doubt it. It seems she felt undervalued in Ribero's agency for quite some time."

He took a deep, shuddering breath. He'd always imagined that he'd be able to convince her to return to her job, that her resignation was nothing more than an act of momentary frustration, something that could easily be overcome. Obviously, he'd been naive about it all. Her anger clearly went deeper than he'd realised.

"So," Miriam said conversationally, oblivious to his distress. "With that in mind, perhaps you'll consider your future too, Kester. The decisions you make today will affect the path you take in the years to come. They'll also affect your friends."

After Miriam, Curtis Philpot returned with yet more questions. This interrogation was followed by a session with another stern-looking man, failed to introduce himself and who remained surly for the entire interview. Afterwards, Kester felt wrung out, a husk of his usual self. Their interrogations left him floundering, unsure of how much to reveal and how much to keep hidden. One thing was certain though: his lack of concrete responses had infuriated them all.

Afterwards, a guard accompanied him back to the room. A fresh plate of food was resting on the table—pasta and a can of lemonade—but he couldn't face it. There seemed to be no way out of the situation, and he had no idea what to do for the best.

He needed to talk to Hrschni. If the daemon would only offer the government his promise that he wouldn't attempt to open any sun doors, they might be more willing to discuss options. But Kester had no idea how to reach the daemon from a locked room, miles away in London. He supposed he could try opening a spirit door again, but what then? The alarm would be activated, and the guards would be back, before he'd even had a chance to shout into the spirit realm beyond.

Hrschni, he thought, closing his eyes, *if you can sense me, in some small way, please help. You were right; I never should have let Infinite Enterprises take me, and now I'm stuck here, unable to do anything at all.*

He waited for a moment, breath held, then sighed. There was no sign of the daemon in the room, not that he'd expected there to be. After all, if Hrschni were to appear, even briefly, Infinite Enterprises would detect his presence in a matter of seconds. They might not be quick enough to catch him, but if they knew he'd visited Kester, they'd be even more suspicious than they were already.

"It was worth a try," he muttered, picking up the fork and spearing a piece of pasta. It was well cooked, but he hardly tasted it. *It's a sad day indeed when I lose my appreciation of food,* he thought glumly, putting the fork down again. But then, these were sad days, and he couldn't see any sign that they were due to improve any time soon.

Kester spent the afternoon reading one of the books on the shelf: a dark mystery that matched his own bleak mood. It wasn't particularly engaging, but it was something to do, to pass the long, meandering hours of imprisonment.

He wondered if Serena had already started work at Infinite Enterprises, if somewhere in this same building, she was settling at her new desk, placing her belongings in drawers, chatting to new colleagues. It was just the right sort of company for her, he supposed. She'd always been ambitious and had frequently complained about feeling held back in Ribero's agency.

At least here, she'll be given proper extinguishing equipment, not an old water bottle, he thought, with a wry grin. Despite his amusement at the thought, he couldn't help but take it all as a betrayal. They'd had their differences in the last few months, but he'd always believed she was devoted to the agency in her own way. Obviously, he'd assumed wrongly.

After dinner, he made his way into the shower-room to prepare for bed, even though it was barely past seven o'clock. There was nothing else to do, and all he wanted to do was let himself drift into unconsciousness, the only place where he could enjoy *not thinking* for a while. Even reading was starting to lose its charm for him, given he'd had his nose in a book for most of the afternoon. Besides, books reminded him of Anya, and again, he felt the sting of knowing he probably wouldn't see her for a long time. Even thinking about her crooked smile made him ache with longing for her.

He commenced brushing his teeth while studying his bleary-eyed reflection in the mirror. Suddenly, a low humming sound caught his attention. The sound swelled to a telltale crackle of energy, which seemed to be coming from somewhere in the shower cubicle, just behind him. *It's not possible,* he told himself, but he spun around anyway.

To his amazement, Hrschni flashed into visibility before his eyes. A moment later, the sirens sounded, filling the still air with a jarring, ear-piercing wail.

Kester instinctively clamped his hands over his ears, then glanced at the door to his cell, which was thankfully still closed. It would only be a matter of time before the guards burst in, though, and he didn't like to imagine what would happen if they discovered the daemon in here with him.

"What are you doing here?" he hissed over the din.

The daemon glided closer, the air shivering around him like a mirage in a desert. "Listen to me; we don't have much time."

"They know you're here; that's why the alarm has gone off. They're probably already on their way, and—"

"I know," Hrschni said. "Spirit door. Step through. I will guide you."

Just as swiftly as he'd appeared, the daemon vanished again. A few seconds later, the door to the room flew open, hitting the wall with a crash. Kester watched dumbly as two security guards raced inside, then seized him by the arms and pinned him against the wall, crushing his face against the cold, smooth surface.

"That hurts," Kester complained over the shrill whine of the siren as they pressed more firmly against his body. "Can you release me? I'm honestly not going to do anything silly."

The guards said nothing, only held him in place with grim-faced determination. Finally, the siren fell silent, and another few minutes later, Miriam Webster arrived. She groaned as she entered, shaking her head at the scene before her.

"You're determined to cause trouble, aren't you," she said, in a flat voice that suggested a statement, not a question.

Kester attempted to protest, but the guards had him too firmly pinned in place.

"It's not like that at all," he muttered—a difficult process, given most of his mouth was pressed against the wall.

Miriam stepped closer. "What did the daemon have to say?"

"What do you mean?"

She nodded at the guards, who released him, albeit reluctantly.

"Let's try again," she said tersely. "We saw a powerful burst of energy on the monitors, which we're presuming was Hrschni. Tell us what he said, please."

"Nothing much, he didn't get a chance."

"You're telling me he went to the effort of materialising here, putting himself at great risk, only to say nothing at all? Come on, we both know that's ridiculous."

Kester put his toothbrush down. It was now rather bent at the top, thanks to its sudden impact with the wall.

"Hrschni wanted to see if I was alright," he said. "He wanted to check you hadn't harmed me."

She slammed her fist against the door, making him jump. "Rubbish! Tell me the truth and stop these foolish games!"

"It's not a game! Anyway, what does it matter? You know I can't escape from here. Hrschni might be able to slip out of locked rooms, but I can't."

"I'm going to fetch the others," she said, clicking a finger at the guards. "Then we're going to talk to you properly, until we get some real answers. You've wasted enough of our time as it is."

He opened his mouth to protest, but the woman had already spun on her heels, taking the guards with her. Presumably, it would only be a matter of time before she returned and before he was subjected to even more interrogation.

Quickly, he recounted what Hrschni had told him. *Spirit door. Step through. I will guide you.* It was clear what the daemon wanted him to do, but the mere thought of it terrified him. He'd glimpsed what lay beyond the rip in the air and seen the dark, unnaturally slick landscape that lay within. It wasn't a place for humans; he knew that for certain.

He also knew that he didn't have much choice in the matter. *I have to trust him,* he realised. *I can't waste time thinking about it, because then I'll talk myself out of it, and the chance will be lost. I just have to act, and fast.*

He thought of his mother. For everything that she was, he knew that she'd been gutsy. She would have stepped through, into that strange spirit world, and she wouldn't have let anyone stop her.

If Mum could do it then so could he, and there wasn't a moment to lose. He directed his attention on the air in front of him, aware that the door to his room was likely to burst open at any moment. *Come on,* he urged himself, fighting the rising panic within himself. *Now isn't the time to lose your nerve.*

He allowed his mind to drift, to let the invisible particles around him slide and tighten, to watch passively while they began to separate themselves before him. Dr. Barqa-Abu had told him how important it was to remove himself mentally from the process, to let his conscious thoughts disengage while the subconscious part of himself took over.

A few seconds later, the air began to rip: a small hole to begin with, which soon started to race like lightning down to the floor. In a matter of seconds, it was done.

He stepped back and admired his handiwork: a raw, shimmering doorway leading to a place that frightened him more than anything else in the world. Even now, he could sense the spirits that hid themselves through that door and their curiosity at his actions.

I can't do this, he thought. The edges of the door rippled, sensitive to his doubts. In another few seconds, it would seal itself up again; he knew this from experience.

The siren began blasting again, distracting him from his thoughts. He *had* to step through. But what if it killed him? What if the spirits dragged him through, what if they—

The door to his room slammed against the wall. The spirit door quivered then narrowed, readying itself to close. He heard someone shout, then another person yell something in response.

A hand settled on his shoulder. He had to act *now*. With a yelp, he leapt through the rip and out of the human world.

Darkness enveloped him in an instant, and straight away he realised his error in judgement. This was much, *much* worse than he could have possibly imagined. This was a nightmare brought to life—a terrain that defied all logical explanation, where nothing could be defined or relied upon.

The first thing he noticed was the resistance in the air around him: a spongy, damp pushback that pressed against his entire body. He gasped with relief; the spirit world was *expelling him*. In a few moments, he'd be back in his cell at Infinite Enterprises, and he would never, *ever* set foot in this place again.

Then the air shifted. It *relaxed* itself, like a mattress giving under pressure. With an eager sucking motion, it yanked Kester forward.

"Help!" he cried out, reaching backwards, praying that one of the guards would haul him to safety. But instead of touching familiar human bodies, his fingers made contact with thick, syrupy mist, which whirled and danced around him.

He'd been pulled through and was now fully inside the spirit realm. Standing in the semi-darkness, he stared at the shifting skies above him, then at the purple-bruise softness of the land beneath his feet, which was oozing around his feet. He turned, ready to scream again, just in time to see the spirit door seal itself behind him.

Kester felt himself seized by rising panic. He closed his eyes, and told himself to just breathe. Slowly, he opened his eyes again, and attempted to process his surroundings.

It was a landscape, of sorts, but unlike anything he'd ever seen before or could even begin to understand. There was land around him, some clouds above his head, and he supposed the things sprouting from the ground might be plants. But other than that, he could find nothing to anchor him to the world he'd come from.

A violet sun burnt a rapid path through the sky, rising, setting, then circling around again only a few seconds later. Asteroids of some description raged past the distant mountains, glowing a fierce pink before hitting the rocks below.

His feet sunk deep into the mud— if that's what it was. It felt alarmingly cloying and *alive,* like a creature testing his person with a multitude of wet tongues. Within the muck, root-like things snaked and coiled, patting at his socks before diving beneath the ground again. The trees around him were skeletal yet flexible, and their branches dripped with moisture. He could have sworn that they were reaching towards him, sniffing at his body then retreating, unsure as to what conclusions to draw.

Something cold brushed past his cheek, and he choked back a shout. He knew what it was; he'd felt it before, back in the other world. It was a spirit, drifting too close. Sure enough, a lithe, oily body appeared in front of his face a moment later, two sharp pin-prick eyes staring hard into his own before vanishing again.

He knew that would only be the start of it. Sure enough, the temperature started to drop, as seething mass of spirit creatures began to circle around him, now alert to his presence.

I'm in their realm, now, not my own, he realised, struggling not to scream. *Anything could happen here. The usual rules don't apply.*

"Please don't hurt me," he whispered. "I didn't come here to cause harm."

He sensed understanding, albeit on a basic, intuitive level. The spirits continued to reel around his body but moved more slowly now, less aggressively too, he felt, though there was no way to be sure. It seemed they'd somehow realised that he posed no threat.

Suddenly, a vivid red flash tore through the landscape. Its bright glow dimmed the rest of the surroundings to darkness, and the spirits reared away, retreating into the whirling mists around them. Kester immediately stopped shivering with cold. *Hrschni,* he realised, overwhelmed with relief. The daemon had been true to his word and had managed to find him here.

In the human world, Hrschni had always been intimidating, a bright, burning, serpentine spirit, exuding energy with every movement. However, that paled in comparison to his appearance here. Lava heat oozed from every inch of his form, which was too bright to look at directly.

"I didn't realise it would be like this," Kester squeaked, shielding his eyes.

"You're the first human to have come here for a long time," Hrschni replied. "It's an important moment; you'll understand just how significant with time. But I sense you're overwhelmed, so let's return to your world. Open a door, and we'll leave this place for now."

"How will I know where to make the door appear? I don't want to end up back in Infinite Enterprises' headquarters."

"You know how to do it. Focus your thoughts in a passive manner. Let the *feeling* of your home run through you."

Kester looked around himself. The spirits were watching, some visible as mist or liquid, others out of sight but *there*, nonetheless. However, now that Hrschni was with him, he felt less frightened. They hadn't intended to hurt him; that was obvious now. They were remarkably accepting of his presence—something he hadn't anticipated.

He turned back, then let his thoughts turn towards creating a door. It took longer than usual, as it was hard not to be distracted by the erratic movements of the sun circling overhead and the twisting forms of countless spirits as they passed by. Also, the environment was different here; everything was denser and wetter, and the particles responded more sluggishly to his will. Squeezing his eyes closed, he focused on the *feel* of being in his bedroom back in Exeter: The happiness of snuggling under his duvet with a book. The safety of being inside those four walls, despite the draughty window, the dubious stains on the carpet, and the continual noise from his housemates.

Finally, he felt the air begin to part, zigzagging a jagged line to the ground. He peered anxiously through the widening gap and was astonished to see his bedroom back in Exeter, just as he'd left it. From this vantage point, it looked like a movie set, the bed too narrow and artificial, the little desk flat and two-dimensional. *Is this how it looks to spirits when they slip through?* he thought wonderingly, extending a hand through the gap. *It seems so small. Trivial almost.*

He stepped forward. The swirling mists of the spirit world tugged at his limbs, reluctant to let him go before releasing him abruptly. He stumbled, barely keeping his balance, and at once felt familiar carpet and floorboards beneath his feet, rather than the eerily sucking mud. He was back in the normal world, as easily as that.

How is any of this possible? he thought, looking around himself in wonder. In a matter of minutes, he'd travelled from a cell in London to his room in Exeter—a journey that would usually take several hours. Even more dauntingly, for a brief period of time, he'd also been an inconceivable distance from everything he'd ever known.

I might be one of the only people alive to have visited the spirit realm, he realised, with both horror and awe. Now that he was back in the safe confines of his bedroom, he wanted to know *more*. Why had the spirit sun moved so quickly? Where did the spirits live? What were those writhing roots under his toes?

Hrschni emerged beside him just as the door sealed itself, leaving the bedroom as it had always been: small and unremarkable.

"How did you find the experience?" he asked, mouth twisting in what might have been amusement.

Kester pressed a hand against the wall, partly to check it was real and partly to steady himself. "I'm not sure it'll ever be a top holiday destination," he replied. "It's so *strange*."

"That's how your world seems to us. It's just a matter of perspective."

They paused, both noticing the music drifting from across the hallway. Judging by the erratic techno beat and discordant bleeping, it was one of Pineapple's dance tracks, which he liked to play at full volume to help him unwind.

The normality of it all took some getting used to. Kester wasn't sure which place felt more like a dream: the eerie world of the spirits or his own room, which the laws of physics stated he couldn't possibly be standing in.

"It will take Infinite Enterprises a while to find out where you are," Hrschni informed him. "Stay here for now, and I will keep a secret watch outside."

"Don't you think they'll be on their way here now?"

"No. They'll be confused, wondering what on earth happened."

Kester frowned. Infinite Enterprises didn't usually stay confused for long, in his experience, but he knew better than to question Hrschni further. The daemon *knew* things, and more often than not, his assertions were correct.

"Before you leave, can I ask something?" he said, as the daemon started to fade. "Infinite Enterprises said I was nothing special to you. They said you'd use another spirit door opener to achieve your goals if I didn't work with you and that I was a fool to be so trusting."

"What do you think?" Hrschni asked, sharpening to visibility again.

"I don't believe them. But then, I've been a naive idiot in the past; I'm worried that—"

"Are you aware of the daemon code of conduct? Humans occasionally accuse us of manipulating the truth, but we never lie."

"So, am I special to you?" Kester asked, biting his lip.

"You are. Now, go and spend some time with your housemate, even though he is a peculiar creature. I sense that he's missed you."

"He's probably missed someone buying food for the fridge. He usually relies on my supplies to keep him alive."

"Go and feed him, then. I will come back soon enough, then we will decide what action to take. It may be best to take you somewhere far away for a while. Now that you've travelled in the spirit realm, this should be easier."

"I can't just leave Miss Wellbeloved and Dad, you know. They're still stuck in Infinite Enterprises' cells." He brightened. "Can I take them with me? We could open a spirit door in their room, get them to step through, and then we'd all be free."

Hrschni shook his head. "It doesn't work like that. But we will speak more about it soon. Don't be afraid; I will warn you if you're in danger."

Kester waited until the daemon had vanished, then headed to Pineapple's bedroom. It wasn't a room he tended to frequent much. There was usually a riot of clothes and knickknacks scattered over every available surface, plus it had an alarmingly *overripe* smell, as though something problematic might be growing underneath all the clutter. Still, he'd just survived a brief visit to an entirely different world, so he supposed Pineapple's room would be relatively tame by comparison.

I've travelled into another dimension, he thought. The enormity of it was still sinking in, and even now, so soon after, he was starting to doubt the experience. Because it just wasn't possible, was it? Those sorts of things didn't happen to extremely normal people like him.

"Perhaps I'm not as normal as I thought," he muttered to himself, just as Pineapple's bedroom door swung open. To Kester's surprise, his housemate wasn't alone. Lying on the sagging futon in the corner was his other housemate, Daisy, and even more shockingly, she was only wearing a T-shirt and a pair of floral boxer shorts.

Oh boy, Kester thought, surveying the scene and drawing the only logical conclusion. *This is something I hadn't predicted.*

"Kester, my man!" Pineapple chorused, dragging him inside before he could protest. "Where have you been? These last three days we've missed your vibe, that killer Kester vibe, right?"

"Er, my killer Kester vibe has been a bit busy," he explained weakly.

Daisy scrambled to her feet, then enveloped him in a hug. "Oh, Kezzy-wezzy," she said, planting a wet kiss on his cheek. "Life is *good* at the moment, and you've been missing it all."

"I thought you were still upset after that bloke abandoned you in Thailand?"

"That's history. Remember, we don't hang onto history, because it's terrible for our chakras."

Kester thought of *A Historie of Spirits* and how useful it'd been but didn't contradict her. Instead, he watched with a blend of fascination and horror as Daisy snaked her arm around Pineapple's waist, then kissed him squarely on the lips.

"I see," Kester said awkwardly. "Pineapple's your new bloke, then. That's nice."

"He's my soulmate, Kester."

"Yeah," Pineapple agreed, fixing his new girlfriend with a dopey, somewhat sickly gaze. "When we come together, it's like proper *soul,* you feel me?"

"I don't want to be involved in any of the *feeling,* thanks all the same," Kester replied. He stepped firmly from the room. "I'm delighted for you both; I really am," he added sincerely. "Now, I'm off to make some food. Do you want me to cut to the chase and make you something? Rather than you sneaking downstairs ten minutes after and stealing whatever's left over in the fridge?"

"Man, that'd be proper sweet. I haven't eaten in days."

"You ate that tub of chocolates left over from Christmas," Daisy pointed out. "And all those crisps that had gone out of date."

"Ah, but that's *empty* food," Pineapple said emphatically. "*Empty* food isn't really there; you know what I mean?"

As usual, Kester didn't. With a weary shrug, he made his way downstairs to the kitchen. His housemates should consider visiting the spirit world; they'd probably fit right in. Knowing Pineapple and his blissful lack of awareness, he might not even notice he was anywhere different until he started to wonder where his next meal was coming from.

The next morning, he awoke with a start. Sitting upright in bed, he took a few minutes to shake off the remnants of his dream, then looked around the room. All appeared as it should; he was safe. Nobody was waiting to drag him back to Infinite Enterprises headquarters. There were no spirits ready to pull him into their own peculiar realm. It was just him, his narrow little bed, and the clank of the central heating, as the ancient pipes strained to distribute a trickle of lukewarm water around the house.

He cast his mind back to just a few weeks ago, and it seemed like another lifetime, events that had happened to another person, even. At the weekends, he used to enjoy crawling out of bed as late as humanly possible. It had been his habit to cook breakfast, settle onto the sofa, then watch daytime television until he couldn't bear the pong of his own pyjamas anymore. He couldn't imagine doing anything as indolent as that now.

"Hrschni?" he whispered. He could sense the daemon close by, though as usual, he didn't understand how. Other humans were oblivious to his presence, apart from those with psychic abilities, of course. He wondered if it was because he'd got to know the daemon well; perhaps they'd formed a connection.

Hrschni appeared shortly after, towering over his bed like a flaming torch. Despite their familiarity, Kester still flinched. He knew Hrschni's body wouldn't set anything alight, but he was rather alarmingly close to the bedsheets.

"Infinite Enterprises are on their way to Exeter," Hrschni announced, in a conversational tone. "But they're concerned, not angry. They believe you must be lost forever in the spirit realm. In fact, they're only checking Exeter as a formality."

"What, so they think I'm dead?"

Hrschni shifted closer, until his sharp features were barely inches from Kester's own. "Humans can't enter the spirit realm, Kester. Infinite Enterprises have carried out experiments in the past. On every single occasion, the humans were forcibly repelled by spirits. It was for their own good, you see; otherwise, they would swiftly die."

"But that's nonsense. I went in, and I'm not dead. Is it different for spirit door openers?"

"It's different for *you*, Kester."

"What do you mean?"

The daemon paused. He shifted from side to side—a sure sign that he was uneasy about something. "It's easier if I show you," he said eventually. "That way, you'll understand better."

"I don't want to see my mother again, if that's what you mean. The last time was horrible. I don't want to think of her and my father *like that*."

"It's important to face the truth, even if it causes us pain. Remember what I said all along, Kester. I am the key, and you chose to unlock this path. We must see it through to the end."

Kester met Hrschni's eyes and saw his own, reflected deep in their black, fathomless pits.

"Is this the last time?" he whispered.

"It is. Your mother and Julio had an affair that lasted two years. In all that time, Jennifer never voiced any concerns, though I believe she had her suspicions. When Artemis Wellbeloved became ill, it threw the agency into turmoil, not least because he sickened so quickly."

"Were you back on the scene at this point?" Kester asked dryly.

"I never left Gretchen. I often visited her, to see how she was. But I never made myself known, if that's what you mean. She never knew I was there. It wasn't the right time, Kester. Events must be allowed to happen when they *need* to happen. They cannot be forced or hurried. Do you see?"

Kester didn't, but he knew there was no point saying so. "Shall we start?" he asked instead, sitting up. "I don't mean to be rude, but I want to get this all over and done with. Especially as I suspect this vision will make me more ashamed of my mother than ever."

"Give her a chance," Hrschni whispered. "For all our sakes." With that, he reached out and placed his finger firmly on Kester's forehead. The now-familiar darkness descended almost immediately, and with a sigh, he allowed himself to sink into it.

Here we go again, he thought wearily, as he passed into one state of consciousness to another.

CHAPTER 10 – LOSSES AND NEW LIFE

Gretchen stood at the foot of Artemis's bed, watching silently as her boss struggled for breath. She wasn't sure if he was aware of her presence or not; some days he was better than others, and this was definitely not one of those days. Jennifer sat on a stool beside him, her hand resting over his, face twisted in torment.

"Can we get him something?" Julio asked eventually, from the corner of the room. "It is terrible, seeing him like this."

Gretchen jumped. She'd forgotten he was there, but she refused to turn around to face him. It was easier this way—to ignore his presence as much as possible. Then, she could pretend things were as they had been before and that she had nothing to be ashamed of.

Free from shame until I'm lonely again and ask him to come over, she reminded herself, then blushed. Now wasn't the time to think about it—not here, in a room with a man who was so obviously dying.

"Julio, you know there's nothing else we can do," Jennifer said softly. "There's nothing more he can take. They've already given him more painkillers than they should."

She let out a quiet sob, then covered her mouth. Awkwardly, Gretchen moved to her side, wrapping an arm around her shoulder. She desperately sought to find the right words, something that would show how much she cared, but she felt empty, sucked dry of any emotion, aside from numb horror at seeing her boss reduced to *this*. His pain was awful to watch, but more terrible was the pity she felt for him—to see such a vital, buoyant man transform into this frail, helpless creature.

"This is crazy, yes?" Julio muttered, pacing up and down the room. "This is the modern day, not the medieval times! They have medicine; they can treat this illness, can't they?"

"Don't make it worse," Jennifer muttered. "I can't take it."

"Why do you accept this? You must fight these things, not just let them win!"

She looked helplessly at him, then frowned. "Just leave us, please," she said, turning back to her father.

"I was only saying that we should—"

"Julio, go away. I want to be with him, alone."

Gretchen tensed, sensing her friend's rejection of them both, not just her fiancé. She took Julio by the arm, then led him firmly out of the room.

"What did I say?" he asked eventually.

"Give her some time," Gretchen said quietly. "Don't take this the wrong way, but your bombastic approach isn't helping right now."

He allowed himself to be guided down the narrow corridor, to the guest bedroom at the end. Gretchen took a seat at the little dressing table and waited for Julio to settle down too. She could still remember the first time she'd stayed in this room, all those years ago, back when she'd been a student at the SSFE. Jennifer's parents had welcomed her with comfortable ease. In fact, every time she'd stayed here, every day she'd worked alongside them, she'd always felt cared for and part of the family.

She glanced at Julio, then shuddered. This was how she'd repaid them: by betraying their daughter and potentially ruining everything they'd ever worked for. It didn't bear thinking about.

At least she and Julio didn't see one another so often now. The last time he'd come to her apartment had been over a month ago, just after Artemis had received his diagnosis. He'd sobbed, then so had she. He'd talked about his *shame,* how he couldn't meet Jennifer's gaze anymore, and then before she'd realised, his hands were around her waist, and his lips on her own.

We've become one another's sordid secret, she realised, swallowing hard. It had to stop, before it completely destroyed everything that mattered the most.

"You are thinking deep thoughts," he said, breaking her concentration. "Gretchen, we need to talk about this; it's—"

"We don't need to talk," she said curtly. "Not about that, and certainly not here. Let's discuss something else, to take our mind off things. How are the wedding plans going?"

"You know it's all going wrong; why do you go on about it?"

"Because I can't believe you're still going to marry her."

"It matters to Artemis; he wants to see his daughter wed before he—" he faltered, then rubbed his face with his hands. "You know how it is. I cannot let him down; he deserves a last piece of happiness, right?"

"Then after he's passed away and you've married her, you'll get your agency," she hissed, turning away.

"That is not why I'm doing it; you know me better than that."

"Give the agency to her, then. She's his daughter; it should be hers."

Julio rose. "She *won't take it,* Gretchen! I have asked, and she says that her father insists it must go to a male. This is how the supernatural industry works; agencies are passed down to sons, not daughters."

"So, change things then. Be the first to do things differently."

"People will snub the Wellbeloved Agency if it is run by a woman. We will not win so many cases. We will start to lose money."

Gretchen sighed. She knew it was true, but she was so *sick* of it.

"You need to stop coming to my apartment, then," she said in a low voice. "You owe Jennifer that, at least."

"I have already. I said last time; it will never happen again."

She sighed heavily. He'd said that the previous time too, and the time before that. Often, she found herself mourning for the time she'd spent with Hrschni. He was a daemon, but in many ways, their relationship had been far simpler. At least he had been hers, and only hers. Whereas this man standing in front of her, she'd always had to share.

"I've booked the church," Jennifer announced, later on in the evening. She dimmed the lamp beside her, until the rest of the kitchen was dark, save for the pool of light on the table in front of them.

Gretchen said nothing, only nodded, then poured herself another glass of red wine. Julio had already retreated to his room to read, which was a relief. The atmosphere was tense when the three of them were together—a painful contrast to the comfortable companionship they'd all enjoyed before.

"Don't you want to know which one?" Jennifer pressed.

"Go on, tell me."

"St. Michael's, the one just outside town. It's not the nicest building, but it's all I could get at short notice."

"What date?"

"Eight weeks' time. I just hope Daddy can hold on that long."

Gretchen patted Jennifer's hand. The gesture felt like a betrayal. "Do you think he will?" she asked softly.

"He's a fighter. On good days, he's out of bed, moving around, and he seems nearly like his old self. We just have to hope that the wedding is one of those days."

Not like today, Gretchen thought miserably. *On days like this, he looks like he won't even last the night.*

"Are you sure you don't want to postpone it?" she said aloud. "I know it means a lot to have your father there, but—"

"No," Jennifer said firmly. "I know Daddy would be devastated if he didn't get to see it. Besides, I want to. I've waited so long; it's about time it happened. Then Julio and I can start living together properly. After all, the house is finished now; it's just waiting for us to move in."

"What about the agency?"

"Daddy has already prepared the paperwork. All it needs is Julio's name on the dotted line, and it's done."

Gretchen sighed. Julio would come out of this with everything—the devoted wife, the house, a business of his own—and she'd be left with nothing.

That's just the way this world works, she thought bitterly, as she rose to her feet. *I suppose I should try to get used to it.*

The day was already warm when Julio and Jennifer picked Gretchen up outside her apartment block, even though it wasn't yet eight o'clock. She climbed into the back seat of the car, then reached forward and squeezed Jennifer's arm.

"How is Artemis?" she asked.

Jennifer shrugged. "He had a bad night. The new medication is making him hallucinate; he kept crying out. But when we left this morning, he was better, wasn't he, Julio?"

"Much better. I had breakfast with him. He ate some egg; it was good. Maybe this new medicine will be the thing that makes him better?"

Jennifer said nothing, only kept her eyes fixed on the road ahead.

They drove to the outskirts of the city, then along a winding country lane, which led past countless hamlets and farmsteads. It was clear that Jennifer wasn't in the mood for conversation, not that Gretchen blamed her. This was the seventh case they'd taken on without Artemis at the helm, and it wasn't getting any easier. Their conversation was stilted at best, nonexistent at worst, and every so often, she caught a look in Jennifer's eye that made her heart quicken with dread. *Suspicion*—that seemed to be the only way to interpret it. But then her friend would smile, and the moment would pass, leaving Gretchen doubting whether it had been real.

She stared out of the window. The sun was already merciless, the sky a brazen, piercing blue. It was a strange sort of day to be hunting down a spirit—but then, every day was rather strange in this line of work, she supposed. She'd never considered any other career and couldn't imagine what it would be like to do something more normal, to open a shop, for example, or work as a doctor or teacher. She felt sudden pity for Jennifer and Julio's future offspring. They'd have no choice but to work in the agency; the supernatural would be woven into their DNA, their future determined the moment they left the womb.

Julio turned the car into a narrow driveway, and she glanced out the window, surveying their surroundings. Thick pines flanked them to either side, obscuring much of the landscape, and the red-brick house ahead was sizeable.

"The client is called Verity Bilby," Jennifer said, tugging a bundle of notes from her satchel. "Since our initial meeting with her, she's seen the will-o'-the-wisp several more times. It seems to be bolder now, circulating within the house, rather than just out in the woods. We may have to split up so we can search more quickly."

"This bright sun does not help," Julio grumbled. "We will not be able see the little light of the spirit, will we?"

"We'll just have to do our best," Jennifer said, as they pulled to a halt outside the house. "Come on, let's get this over with."

Gretchen had never heard Jennifer sound so unenthusiastic before. Her moroseness was understandable but worrying, nonetheless. In fact, she couldn't remember a time when she'd seen her friend this unhappy before.

"Would you like me to do the talking?" she offered, as she pressed the rusty doorbell.

Jennifer paused, then nodded gratefully. "It's probably for the best."

They waited, each of them deliberately keeping their gaze turned from the other. Finally, the door swung open, and a square-faced, matronly woman stood before them, skirt pulled up to her bosom, flowery blouse pluming over the waistline like a sagging balloon.

"I'm relieved you're here, I must say," she announced, without giving them a chance to speak. "That damned *thing* leapt out of my oven, just as I was about to put my apple pie in. It made me drop the dish on the floor. Pie everywhere, absolute carnage."

"Wasted pie is a terrible thing," Julio said gravely. "We will catch this *pie-crushing* spirit, then you can make a fresh one without fearing its ruin, yes?"

The woman raised an eyebrow. "Er, yes, I suppose that would be good."

"Are you happy with us moving freely around your house and the surrounding land?" Gretchen asked. "That way, we can get on with things, then let you know when we're done."

"Be my guest. I'll be in the lounge watching *Jerry Springer.*"

She wandered off down the hallway, leaving the three of them alone.

"I'll take the house," Jennifer offered, composing herself swiftly. "It's too hot out here. I don't like working in the full sun."

"I suppose that leaves the woods to you and me," Gretchen said to Julio. There was an uncomfortable silence, before he finally nodded.

Gretchen wasn't sure if it was the trees brushing continually against her skin or the sunlight beating through the foliage, but something was making her feel claustrophobic. The woods had a watchfulness to them, as though numerous unseen eyes were appraising her every move. Despite having wandered for over twenty minutes, there was still no sign of the will-o'-the-wisp anywhere.

This is stupid, she thought, yanking a branch out of her path. It was such a small spirit; they weren't usually a problem to anyone, and she was willing to bet this one was the same. Generally speaking, they kept out of the way of humans, only appearing to light a path on dark nights. This one had probably wandered off from its usual spot and ended up here by accident.

She heard a low rustle to her left and turned, just in time to see

Julio emerge from the undergrowth, looking distinctly sweaty and dishevelled.

"Have you sensed anything yet?" she asked.

"Not a thing. This little spirit, he does not want to be found, does he?"

Gretchen paused, forcing herself to be calm. She found that it sometimes helped to be still; spirits seemed to trust her more when she was peaceful and when her thoughts weren't tearing around like racing cars in her head.

"Are you giving me the silent treatment? I do not have the time for this; we need to—"

She silenced him with a finger, then squinted into the distance. "I think our little spirit might be over there," she said softly, nodding in the right direction. "I can sense something; can you?"

Together, they peered through the bristly branches. A few seconds later, they both spotted it: a weak blue light, bobbing and dancing before them.

"Finally," Julio said, with satisfaction. "Now, do your spirit door thing, Gretchen. I need to go home and soak this shirt in cool water. The sweat and the silk, it does not mix well."

"Next time, wear a cotton shirt instead." She focused her attention in the vicinity of the will-o'-the-wisp, making sure to keep her thoughts present, but also remote. The spirit door appeared a few minutes after, slicing lazily through the air until it almost reached the ground.

The will-o'-the-wisp quivered, bounced to and fro, then serenely floated through the door, back into its own realm. Gretchen quickly sealed the rip in the air, then nodded at Julio.

"Job done," she said. "I wish they were all that easy."

"Magnificent, as always. You have a great talent, my friend."

"Friend?" she repeated, raising an eyebrow. "That's a funny word to use, given the circumstances."

Julio glanced around. "Don't talk like that, not here. What if Jennifer hears?"

"Heaven forbid you ruin your wedding plans, eh?"

"I don't want to start this again. How many times do I need to say it? If I tell Jennifer, I break her heart. I break up the agency. I ruin her life. Is that what you want?"

"I want you to stop pretending it's all about her," Gretchen snapped, jabbing a finger in his face. "*You* want this, Julio. You enjoyed the thrill of being with me, but you didn't want the responsibility of it."

"That's not fair, and you know it. I care for you deeply. I hate to see you hurting like this, but I cannot—"

"Oh please, spare me. The deed is done, and now we've all got to live with it."

"Live with what?" Jennifer's voice rang through the trees behind them.

Gretchen and Julio froze, then turned together, far too quickly.

"Jennifer, you startled me," Julio said with a forced laugh. "The spirit is gone; that is what we were talking about."

She clambered through the dense foliage, then studied them both intently. Gretchen fought hard to keep her expression neutral, fighting the urge to simply *run*. Anything would be better than having to endure her friend's scrutiny, especially as she felt she'd crumble beneath it at any moment.

"I don't know what to make of you two, sometimes," Jennifer said eventually, folding her arms.

"Ah, we are like two silly children, with all the bickering," Julio said, brushing his hair out of his eyes.

"Or an old married couple." Jennifer's eyes narrowed, then she waved behind her. "Come on. If the job's done, we should get back. I want to see how Daddy is."

"Yes, I would like to have lunch with your father; he is talking me through the accounts at the moment, and—"

"I'd like to spend some time with him," Jennifer interrupted, jaw tensing. "Alone. You can talk to him later." Without waiting for an answer, she turned away and started marching back in the direction she'd appeared from.

Julio gave Gretchen a stricken glance, which she ignored.

"Jennifer, wait for me," he chorused, then ran ahead, leaving Gretchen behind—not that she minded. She couldn't bear to be around him anymore or even to have to *look* at him. She also felt the same way about herself, which was ironic. After all, she could never escape herself, no matter how much she might want to.

Artemis was out of bed when they arrived back at the Wellbeloved house, though his exhausted posture suggested that it required immense effort. He raised his head as they entered the living room and forced a shaky smile.

"There you all are," he croaked, reaching for his handkerchief and carefully patting his mouth. "Another successful case, I take it?"

"Daddy, why are you up?" Jennifer said, perching on the footstool beside his armchair. "You're worn out; you should be in bed."

"Sweetheart, I need a change of scenery." He inhaled again, with obvious effort. "I must say, I never imagined dying would be such hard work."

Jennifer's lower lip trembled, and her father reached down to stroke her hair.

"I'm sorry," he continued in a gentler voice. "I forget myself sometimes." He looked up at Gretchen and Julio, who were still standing awkwardly by the door. "Julio, I'm glad to see you. We need to get your signature on the agency documents, don't we?"

Julio glanced at Gretchen, then quickly back to Artemis. "Is now a good time?" he said reluctantly. "I think we should talk things through, make sure this arrangement works for everyone."

"Who could it possibly not work for? You and Jennifer will do admirably with the business. Gretchen will continue as spirit door opener. You'll hire a reputable psychic, just as we always planned to do. The agency will grow, and it will all be splendid. Then one day, your sons will take it over."

Jennifer dabbed at her eyes and said nothing.

"Please?" Artemis said, voice cracking. "We must get this done sooner rather than later. You understand, surely."

Unable to mask her anger anymore, Gretchen strode from the room. It was all too much—the lies, the sight of her friend's misery, and Artemis's desperation too. Storming through the kitchen, she shoved the back door open, then stepped out into the small walled garden at the back. She knew they'd question why she'd left so suddenly, but she was past caring. The truth was, she couldn't remain a passive observer. Their torment was horrible to watch, especially Jennifer's. She was always so accepting, even though she obviously suspected something. Calm too, though her emotions must be raging as wildly as everyone else's.

Slumping onto the bench at the back, she rested her head against the wooden slats of the shed beside her. As she looked around, she noticed the garden was looking overgrown and unloved, and she wondered who would tend it in the future, once Artemis was gone. For the last few years, Jennifer's father had loomed large in her life: a lively, emphatic figure who provided a firm anchor for all those who worked with him. It was difficult to imagine him not being there anymore.

Without his steady presence, she, Jennifer, and Julio would drift alone. A few years ago, that wouldn't have been a problem. Their friendship could have tied them together, and they would have muddled a path through it all. Now, she wasn't so sure. In fact, she was struggling to see a future for herself here, alongside her soon-to-be-married friends. When they had children, as they inevitably would, she'd have to play the role of the indulgent maiden aunt, all the while knowing that she'd once been their father's lover.

No, it would never work, she realised miserably. Everything was ruined, and it was partially her own fault.

"I miss you, Hrschni," she muttered. "I know you're still enjoying the celebrity lifestyle, and you've probably forgotten all about me—but nonetheless, I wish you were here."

That evening, she stripped off her T-shirt and skirt and lay on the sofa, staring at the ceiling. The day was still hot and her skin felt clammy and warm to the touch. Perhaps she was sickening for something. She certainly felt feverish and disorientated too.

There was nothing on the television, and she knew it would be impossible to concentrate on a book. Instead, she let her mind go blank. It was a blessed relief to stop thinking for a short while. A storm of emotions was building up inside her, and she knew she'd break, sooner or later. Everyone had their limits, and she was no different, regardless of how outwardly calm and self-contained she might seem.

Stroking the cushions under her fingers, she remembered Hrschni being *here*, on this sofa, right beside her. She'd always enjoyed it most when he visited in Billy Dagger's body, when they'd been able to touch one another freely. In the early days of their relationship, the combination of human physicality and spirit energy had been a revelation to her, and she'd grown to crave it.

In his daemon form, their connection was spiritual only. A meeting of minds, of thought processes and philosophies. Over time, she'd grown to value it as much as the physical, realising that both entities were equally him, only in two different forms.

Of course, he wasn't the only one to have touched her on this sofa. Julio had too, that first time, when he'd come to her apartment to comfort her and ended up doing far more. But she didn't want to think about that now; she couldn't bear the guilt of having those memories in her mind. *I'm a terrible person,* she thought, sitting up. *And the worst thing is, I'm not sure I'd do things differently, even if I could. I still would have slept with Julio, over and over again, because something binds me to him. Even if it's something I don't truly like.*

"Everything's gone wrong," she whispered aloud.

Her doorbell rang, almost as soon as the words left her mouth. Her eyes widened, and she looked instinctively towards the front door. It was late in the day; she was sure it wouldn't be Julio or Jennifer. They'd been busy planning the catering for the wedding when she'd left—a task that sounded like it would take some time.

Hurriedly, she pulled her clothes back on, then raced out of her apartment and down to the main entrance, pulling the front door open.

A man stood on the steps, shoulders hunched, face obscured by an oversized hood. However, seeing his face wasn't necessary. Her instinctive response to the person in front of her, visceral and powerful, revealed immediately who it was.

How is it possible? she thought, staring, half expecting him to disappear at any moment, like a mirage in a desert.

He stepped into the light and gently lowered his hood.

"Hrschni," she gasped. "It can't be you."

"It is."

What are you doing here?"

He glanced around himself, then drew nearer. "You've been reaching out to me, these last few days. So here I am."

"What, you mean you heard me, somehow? Are you always listening to me? Why would you—"

"Can I enter quickly?" he interrupted. "If any fans see Billy Dagger here, they'll cause a fuss."

Gretchen stepped aside quickly, ushering him in. She closed the door firmly, then without thinking about it, kissed him squarely on the lips. His breath was warm, and his arms quickly snaked around her waist.

It was easy to give into it and to subside against him, feeling the heat of his spirit self radiating from Billy Dagger's body. Then an image came to mind. *Julio.*

She'd betrayed Hrschni. It wouldn't be fair to do this.

"Sorry," she said, pulling away from him. "I had no right to do that."

"But that's what you want, isn't it?"

She didn't know how to reply. A part of her wanted to collapse in his arms and to beg for things to go back to the way they had been, even though she knew they had no future together. But she'd pushed him away for so long; she didn't deserve to be happy with him. Not after what she'd done.

"The last few months have been horrible," she whispered, turning away. "You shouldn't be here; I'll only hurt you again."

"You're lonely," he said, reaching for her again, then pulling her close. "And in pain."

"I've done terrible things."

"It doesn't matter."

His lips found hers again, and she started to cry.

"I need you," she said, burying her head against his shoulder. "Is that wrong?"

He shook his head, then allowed himself to be led up the stairs, into her apartment.

"Do you want me to leave?" Hrschni asked, afterwards. He stood, then moved to the window. The gleam of the streetlamp made Billy Dagger's bare skin shine and brought each tattoo to life, like a series of creatures in motion.

She pulled the duvet over herself and said nothing. There were so many words inside her, countless things she wanted to say, but none of them seemed right to say aloud. She just wanted him here, more fiercely than she'd ever wanted anything before. She yearned for it to be just the two of them, in this room, forever. No intrusions from the outside world, no complication caused by other people— just him, and only him.

But she wanted nothing to do with his plans. The implications were too huge, potentially damning to the safety of the world. Hrschni loved being with humans, that much was obvious. But sometimes, she wondered if he *understood* humanity. How could he, after all? He was a spirit; he came from a strange world that she could never enter, because she was human. There was so much about him that was unknowable; he only ever gave her a miniscule part of himself.

He turned, sensing her silent turmoil. "I'll go."

"I'm sorry," she said, hugging her knees tightly. "It's all so complicated."

"Don't worry."

"Stop being so *kind* to me! I don't deserve it."

He drew nearer, then placed a hand on her cheek, catching the tear that rolled down it. "I will never stop loving you, Gretchen," he said softly. "But don't see it as a burden or a debt to be repaid. You must follow your own path, wherever it takes you."

"I love being with you. I've never felt this way about anyone else. But it's too *big* for me, do you understand? You want me to be like you, capable of great things, ready to change the world. I don't think that's me, Hrschni. I've got a rare talent, but I don't want to be a saviour or a scourge."

"I know," he said simply. "I put too much pressure on you. You're right; perhaps this isn't the path for you."

He sat beside her, then incomprehensibly pressed a hand against her stomach. The heat spread over her skin, down through tissue and muscle, right to the very core of her. His eyes met hers, and his expression froze, just for a moment.

"What are you doing?" she whispered.

"It doesn't matter. I'll leave you now." He stood, then kissed her gently on the forehead. "Don't feel bad, Gretchen. Good things will happen to you in the future. You'll feel a love that's far greater than any you've experienced before."

She thought of him, and of Julio too, though comparing the two was impossible.

"You're wrong," she said.

He touched her reflectively, for a final time. "Wait and see," he said.

After Hrschni had departed, Gretchen lay in the dark staring up at the ceiling, though her thoughts were far away from her bedroom. The daemon's words had sounded so final; did that mean that she'd never see him again? Maybe it was for the best; she knew there was no way they could ever enjoy a long-term relationship. She'd age, he'd move on to another human body, and then they'd part. However, the thought of living the rest of her life without him was a dreary, colourless prospect. How would anyone else ever compare?

Maybe I shouldn't try to compare anyone, she thought bitterly. *I should just find a normal human to be with. Settle down and have children. Give up my career, stay at home, cook, clean, buy the weekly shopping. Then spend the rest of my life wondering what could have been if I'd made different choices.*

Her phone rang. Quickly, she groped around on her bedside table, then scooped it up, hoping it wasn't Jennifer checking up on her. Her friend was always so dedicated and *concerned,* but it only served to make Gretchen feel worse about herself. She was the one who should be worried about Jennifer, not the other way around.

She glanced at the screen. It was Julio, not Jennifer. She couldn't decide if that was better or worse. He hadn't called her in a long time. In fact, they'd both gone out of their way to keep their interactions to a minimum.

Finally, she answered. "Why are you calling?" she said, by way of greeting.

Silence rang down the line. "Are you at home?" he replied, eventually.

"It's past ten o'clock; of course I'm at home. Why are you calling me?"

"I need . . . I just need . . ." His voice broke, and a hoarse sob filled the line.

She sat up immediately. "Julio, what's the matter?"

"I'm sorry. I should not have come, it was a bad idea."

"Where are you?"

"I'm outside, on your doorstep. I didn't know where I should go. I don't have any other friends, and Artemis, he was talking to me about loyalty and trust, and I felt so terrible."

She took a deep breath. He was right; he *shouldn't* have come, and she was in no state to be his emotional support. But this was Julio. Despite her reservations, she couldn't just leave him out there on his own.

"I'll come down and let you in," she said wearily, reaching for her dressing gown. *This isn't wise,* she thought, as she slid her feet into her sandals and headed to the door. But she didn't have a choice. Once again, the situation felt completely out of her control.

The communal hallway was dark, but it didn't matter. She knew each step by heart and ran nimbly down to the front door. As she pulled the door open, she took a moment to compose herself. It wouldn't do to be too kind, or too soft. She needed to maintain an emotional distance, for everyone's sake.

He stood on the doorstep, wet and shivering, suede jacket dark with moisture. Gretchen looked up at the sky. She hadn't even realised it'd been raining. The electric tension of a summer storm, somewhere in the distance, made her skin tingle.

The contrast between Julio and Billy Dagger, who'd stood on the same spot only hours before, was stark. She took a deep breath. It wasn't a good idea to dwell on Hrschni now, not with Julio here. The two resided in very different worlds and elicited entirely different emotions from her.

"Come in, quickly," she said, waving him inside. "You look like a kitten that's been thrown down a well."

"That is what I feel like too." He hung back uncertainly, until she forcibly ushered him up the stairs. "I should throw myself off a cliff, Gretchen. What sort of a man am I?"

"Don't talk about that now," she said, peering up the stairwell. She couldn't see any of her neighbours up there, but that didn't mean no one was listening. "Let's get you dried off, otherwise you'll get sick."

"It doesn't matter. Nothing matters."

His fatalistic attitude disturbed her. It was unlike him; his usual approach was to rage and complain, then return to his usual optimistic self. This nihilism threw her off course, knocking her off balance. She led him through to her apartment, then settled him on the living room sofa.

"Thank you," he said simply, slipping his damp jacket off, then draping it over the armchair.

"I'll make you a cup of coffee."

"I don't want one. Gretchen, please. We need to talk; this cannot continue."

This wasn't the conversation she wanted to have right now, not so soon after Hrschni's departure, when her mind was already in disorder. But seeing Julio's stricken expression, she knew she couldn't refuse him. She'd never seen him so desolate, and she couldn't see any evidence of his usual spark, no matter how hard she searched for it in his face. He reminded her of a spent candle: limp, lifeless, and no longer able to serve its purpose.

She sat beside him, hands clamped between her legs, and waited.

"I cannot marry her," he said, finally.

"Don't say that."

"It's true. I am going to tell her tomorrow."

"Julio, why would you do such a thing?"

"Because I'm not good enough for her. This evening—it was torture, listening to her and Artemis. All they talk about is the wedding and how bright the future of the agency is. And there I was, the traitor sitting beside them, grinning like a nasty villain. I don't deserve her love, and I cannot take her family business."

Gretchen shook her head. "If you break the wedding off, you'll also break her heart."

"But she would be free. She could find another man, someone who would be faithful and true, like she is. If I marry her, I will ruin her life."

"Her father is already close to death. If you leave her too, that'll be a blow she won't recover from."

He raised his head. "What about *us*? Sometimes I think I mean nothing to you."

"Julio, stop it."

"Why? You never talk of these things, but they are important. Always, you have been like this; you keep your secrets, you don't share your feelings. I share mine with you, but it is one sided."

"You share yours with everyone," she snapped. "Too much, sometimes."

He flinched, then hung his head. "You're right," he agreed, after a time. "I am a selfish man."

"You are, but I'm selfish too," she replied, thinking of Hrschni, how she'd called him to her, only to reject him soon after. He was a spirit, but that didn't mean he couldn't be hurt by her actions. She slumped against the cushions. "We're as bad as each other. We believe ourselves to be remarkable, when actually, we're nothing much, in the grand scheme of things."

He leant his head close to hers. "What a situation, eh? There is no way to make it right."

"There's always a way," she said firmly. "You just have to have the vision to make things better."

"Better, eh? I don't even know what *better* is. You are a strange person, Gretchen, do you know that?"

"Of course I do."

"But you are wonderful as well. That is the problem; always I think you're wonderful, whenever I am with you."

She kissed his forehead: a chaste, motherly gesture. "You're wonderful too, Julio. I didn't mean what I said just now. You're a good person, really."

He returned her kiss, pecking her on the cheek. "So, what should we do?"

"What do you want to do?"

The comment hung in the air. She blushed, knowing that the words carried a certain ambiguity with them, an allure that was inappropriate, given the circumstances.

"I want to make you all happy," he said quietly.

"You make everyone happy. Don't call your wedding off. I'll disappear, then you and Jennifer can focus on each other."

"If you leave, the agency will be broken. *I* will be broken, Gretchen." He studied her carefully, then touched her cheek with his thumb, stroking it softly.

"I am sometimes lost in your eyes," he said, wonderingly. "They go deep; there is so much going on behind them."

"Don't say that."

"I already did. I have missed you, these last few weeks. And you have missed me, I can tell."

But what about Jennifer? she thought, wishing she had the integrity to say it aloud. She opened her mouth to speak, just as his lips found her cheek, then the tip of her nose. She pressed her hand against his chest, preparing to push him away.

"Julio, we can't."

The heat of his breath warmed her face. She looked up, and his stricken expression broke her, somewhere deep inside.

"I am so sorry," he whispered.

"I'm sorry too."

Somehow, her hand found his face. She stroked it by way of comfort, then froze as he took her hand in his own and pressed it against his heart.

He met her gaze. "I don't want to leave you. I *can't* leave, because I am all tangled up in you, do you understand?"

This is horribly wrong, she thought, passively accepting his lips against her own, then responding, despite the knowledge that she would feel terrible about it afterwards.

Maybe a final time is what we need, to say goodbye, she told herself. Then, they could both agree that it was done.

The day was sombre, the clouds above heavy with rain. Gretchen raised her head as the church bell chimed above: once, twice, three times. It sounded like an omen, ringing her doom, and the others.

The rest of the crowd had already moved on, congregating in a cheerless huddle around the open grave in the distance. She noted the crooked elm tree, looming over it like a watchful sentinel. Artemis would have approved of the spot, she suspected. It was suitably scenic, with just a touch of Victorian gothic—something he always enjoyed while he'd been alive.

She braced herself against the wind and wished she was anywhere else but here. The funeral reminded her too much of her own father's, back when she'd been a student. It was the stillness of the event that unsettled her, that and the way everyone seemed reluctant to meet one another's eyes. It seemed so incongruous too. Artemis had been energetic, full of laughter before the disease raged through his body. This silence and sobriety didn't seem right, somehow.

After a while, she made her way towards the grave, remaining concealed at the back of the crowd. She could see Julio at the front, arm wrapped around Jennifer's shoulders. Gretchen had never seen her friend look so thin or so broken.

She sensed *others* too. Spirits, lurking at the back, just like her—invisible, but there, nonetheless. Perhaps they'd wandered over out of curiosity; churchyards were popular with certain types of spirits, thanks to their tranquillity. Or maybe they were paying their respects. Although Artemis's agency had focused on removing them from the human world, he'd always gone to great lengths to treat them kindly. Perhaps some of the spirits remembered and thanked him for it.

The vicar's low voice rumbled on. Finally, Jennifer and her mother were asked to throw a flower into the grave, followed by a trowel-full of soil. Jennifer's cry was high and sharp, Carole's a ceaseless, defeated sob.

Gretchen felt a sob rise in her own throat and swallowed it back down. She couldn't let herself weep, not here, because she suspected if she allowed herself to start, she'd find it difficult to stop.

After the service, the rest of the well-wishers scattered. Jennifer and her mother were soon swamped by multitudes of people: neighbours, friends of the family, and representatives from other agencies around the country. Julio stood awkwardly to one side and stared down at the coffin in disbelief.

Gretchen joined him, maintaining a respectful distance from his side.

"Are you alright?" she asked quietly.

He bit his lip. "What will we do without him? He was like a father to me."

"He was a good man."

"He was. Better than me, anyway."

Not more self-pity, she thought, looking away. It was exhausting, continually trying to make Julio feel better about himself. To her relief, he raised his head, jaw firm, and nodded in the direction of his fiancée.

"Jennifer is so sad," he said. "It is a torment that she cannot bear, and I don't know how to help her."

"It's awful seeing her like this. Look, I'm sorry to do this now, but we need to talk."

His head swivelled round. "This is not the place; can't you see that?"

"I have to tell you something."

"It can wait, Gretchen. We are burying a dear friend today; that is the only thing that matters."

She sighed. He was right, of course, though the sombre atmosphere would have been appropriate for what she had to say. "Of course," she said stiffly, as she retreated. "We'll talk some other time. But it needs to be soon."

He waved a dismissive hand in her direction, then turned back to the grave.

Gretchen sat on the edge of Julio's desk and stared down at him, waiting for some acknowledgement.

She understood that he wanted to be left alone, that he was already overwhelmed with thoughts of running the agency, preparing for a wedding, and moving into a new home. She knew the guilt was consuming him from the inside out too; it was evident in every awkward pause and unnatural conversation that they shared. But she needed to talk to him, and already, it had been too long.

"Julio, please," she said eventually. "Just a few minutes, that's all I ask for."

"I have things to do," he replied, squinting at the paperwork in front of him. "These accounts, they make no sense to me. I see the numbers, but they don't add up to *this* number, down here." He jabbed the bottom of the sheet, as though it had personally offended him.

"That can wait."

"It cannot. None of it can. That is why Jennifer is on the phone now, because we cannot find your father's private login, so we must beg the government to tell us." He waved at Artemis's private office. Of course, it wasn't his anymore, though it was impossible to imagine it as anyone else's. The air carried the lingering scent of cigarettes and aftershave, and the desk was still covered with his files and folders.

"You've been ignoring me for weeks now," she said. "You won't take my calls, and you walk away when I try to speak to you. I've been patient, because I know you're grieving. But I have to tell you something."

"It is over," he said, in a low voice. "You told me to marry her, so I will. But I cannot be around you anymore. I don't trust myself to be the good man."

"You have to hear what I've got to say."

"I don't, Gretchen. That's what we agreed, remember?"

"You don't understand. It's not about that, it's—"

"Please, stop doing this to me. Don't you see, I am already pulled so tight. I am like the elastic band, and I may snap at any moment. It is not fair, not when you—"

"Julio, I'm pregnant."

His head whipped upwards, lightning fast. She'd expected to see disbelief, shock, even anger perhaps. But the intense horror, etched deep into his expression, shocked her to her core.

"You can't be," he whispered.

"I am."

"No, this is not right. It is a mistake. Please, tell me this is a sick joke. This is the British sense of humour, yes? In a moment, you will click your fingers and laugh, and say 'I got you good' or something."

She stood. "Of *course* it's not a joke. I took a test several weeks ago."

The blood drained from his face. In a heartbeat, he looked ten years older. "You can't have a baby," he said, shaking his head. "You must get rid of it."

"I don't want to."

"You *must*. This will ruin me, don't you understand?"

"Then you shouldn't have slept with me! I don't know if you're aware of how basic human biology works, but getting pregnant is always a risk!"

"Keep your voice down; Jennifer will hear."

"Don't you think she needs to know? You're going to be a father; you can't pretend it's not happening."

The low, unmistakable sound of a door creaking brought them both to silence. They turned as one, to see Jennifer standing in the doorway of her father's office.

"Jennifer," Gretchen and Julio said in unison.

"I heard what you just said," she said quietly.

Gretchen closed her eyes. The truth had to come out, but she hadn't wanted it to be like this, especially not while her friend was still grieving. *She deserves so much better,* she thought, wishing the floor would split apart and swallow her down, or that she could simply create a spirit door, then slip through and never return. *She deserves a better friend than me, and a better fiancé than him.*

"I'm sorry," she muttered. The words were scarcely audible, although the room was silent.

Julio leapt out of his chair, which toppled backwards, hitting the carpet with a reverberating thud. Gretchen jumped. Jennifer remained statue still and stared at them both.

"My love," Julio began, scrambling to set the chair upright again. "You've got it wrong. Whatever you are thinking right now, that's not how it was; it wasn't—"

"You slept together," Jennifer interrupted. Slowly, she brought her hands to her face, covering her mouth. "You cheated on me."

Julio advanced towards her, arms outstretched. She held her hands out in response—to ward him away, not welcome him closer.

"How long has it been going on?" she whispered.

"I never wanted you to find out like this. I didn't want to upset you so soon after your father had—"

"How *long*?"

"Tell her," Gretchen said. "Don't insult her by lying."

Julio's agonised expression would have been tragic in any other circumstance. He took another step towards Jennifer, then stopped.

"I don't know what to say," he said quietly. "Only that I love you."

"Love?" she repeated. "This isn't love. You've been having an affair with my best friend, and now you've got her pregnant?"

"It's my fault too," Gretchen said.

Jennifer wheeled around, face contorted with emotion, arm raised. For a moment, Gretchen thought her friend would hit her, and she braced herself for the blow. It would have been a relief. She knew she deserved no better.

"You're having a baby," she said instead, fist dropping to her side. "You. It was meant to be *me*, Gretchen. That's my future, not yours."

"It was never meant to happen."

Jennifer shook her head, too fast, as though trying to force the knowledge from her mind. She pointed at Julio. "We were meant to get married, have children, grow old together. That's what I clung onto, for all those years. And now, you've taken it from me."

Gretchen bit her lip. "You can still get married. I'm leaving anyway; I'm going back to Cambridge. You two can carry on running the agency and forget I ever existed."

"But you are our spirit door opener!" Julio exclaimed. "If you leave, what will we do?"

"Get a professional extinguisher, like every other agency."

Jennifer sat on the nearest desk, then started to sob. "You've ruined everything," she said, cupping her face in her hands.

"We will sort this out," Julio said desperately. "We will have the wedding as we planned. We will move to our new home and be happy, I promise. Please, Jennifer, don't give up on me."

"What about your baby?" She pointed at Gretchen's stomach. "Are you just going to pretend it doesn't exist?"

"Yes, he is," Gretchen said simply. "Julio, I don't want you to be involved in my child's life. I'll raise it alone. I always worked better on my own, anyway."

"You do not get to make those decisions," Julio flared. "If I am the father, I have a right to—"

"No, you don't." She turned to Jennifer. "I hate myself for what I've done to you. I only hope one day you can forgive me, though I wouldn't blame you if you didn't. You're one of the kindest people I've ever known."

"Is that it?" Jennifer said dully. "You're just going to leave?"

"What choice do I have? I can't stay here; it'll tear you and Julio apart."

"You've already torn us apart."

"That might change, one day. You won't forgive him any time soon, nor should you. But you may feel differently in the future."

"Don't tell me what I will and won't feel."

Gretchen felt the sting of tears at the corners of her eyes. She'd fought hard to stay strong, but there was only so long she could maintain it for. The guilt was unbearable.

"I think this is goodbye," she said slowly, turning away. "I'm so sorry."

She opened the entrance door and walked out, closing it softly behind her.

I've broken Jennifer's heart, she realised, as she made her way to the stairs at the rear of the building. *I've ruined her one chance at happiness. And I've misled them both.*

She held her belly protectively and immediately felt the telltale warmth radiating from within. It wasn't a normal baby; she could already tell. When she placed her palm against herself, she felt the *energy* of a child that wasn't quite human.

But she must be mistaken. The hormones raging through her were muddling her mind, making her suspect things that couldn't possibly be true.

It's probably Julio's baby, she told herself, stepping out into the car park and taking a deep breath. It was easier not to think about it too much, to simply love the child for who it was and forget about the world of the supernatural. In the few years she'd been immersed in it, it had changed her life irrevocably—and not always for the better.

Chapter 11 – Finding a Father

Kester felt himself drowning—or choking, rather—breath stolen by a tangle of emotions that he had no control over. For a moment, the darkness held him tight, and he wondered if this was what it was like to die: helpless, despairing, and desperately sad.

Then, his vision cleared. The remnants of the past faded away, his mother's face the last thing to disappear. He found himself back in his cold, cramped bedroom.

"The baby," he murmured, heart thumping against his ribcage. Pressing his hands to his forehead, he felt the warmth radiating from his skin. *Heat.* Just feverishness, perhaps—or something more unnatural.

"Kester," Hrschni said, seemingly from a great distance away. "Sit down. I believe you're in shock."

He felt the daemon's warm hand guide him down to the bed, then the reassuring resistance of the mattress beneath him. His ears began to ring, signifying the worst was over.

"It's not possible," he whispered after a while, pressing his hands against his belly, an echo of the movement he'd seen his own mother do, all those years ago. "It isn't true, is it? I mean, it can't be. I'm a human, a one hundred percent normal, uninteresting human. Right?"

"When I first saw you as a baby, I wasn't sure *what* you were," Hrschni said, drifting closer. "You were very human in appearance, certainly. Chubby-legged, rosy, and sticky—you looked like every other human infant I'd ever seen. But over the years, it started to become more evident, especially in your eyes. That's why your mother called you *Kester*, after a little kestrel, I believe. It was that sharp, all-seeing gaze, which you had even when you were young. The perceptive, knowing stare of a spirit."

"But I'm *not* a spirit," Kester protested. "Look at me! There's no mystery to me, no intrigue or spiritual grace. I'm as dull as it gets. You've got it wrong, Hrschni."

The daemon sighed. "I'm not wrong."

Kester thought it through, then realised how *ridiculous* it was. Somewhere along the line, a mistake had been made. He couldn't deny that his mother had been in love with Hrschni, nor that they'd slept together, but to claim the daemon was his parent was ludicrous.

"You're not my father," he said quietly.

"Spirits can produce offspring with humans."

"You were in Billy Dagger's body at the time. So that would make me Billy Dagger's child, not yours."

"That's true, in a way," Hrschni said patiently. "But making a spirit is an entirely different process. It requires a transfer of potent energy, which—"

"I don't want to think about of your potent energy, thank you." He stared at the daemon, then said quietly, "Is there any chance that you're wrong about this?"

"No. It's *there*, Kester: that burning spirit force, nestled within each of your pupils. And, if I ever had any doubts before, those were erased as soon as you stepped into the spirit realm. Only a spirit can pass through, you see. If you'd been fully human, you would have been repelled, straight back into the human world."

Kester's heart sunk, because he felt the truth of Hrschni's words. When he'd been in the world of the spirits, he'd felt some resistance, but also an acceptance too. The spirits had been wary at first, then curious about his presence, once they'd realised what he was.

He thought of all the cases he'd worked on with the rest of the team, how the spirits had always seemed to lock onto him, rather than the others. They'd sensed his kindred nature, even though he'd had no knowledge that it existed, back then.

"What about Dad?" he said suddenly. "Dr. Ribero, I mean. He's provided financially for me, all my life. He'd be devastated to know the truth."

Hrschni flickered like a broken torch, before glowing once more. "He will be upset," he said. "But we can't change the truth simply by wishing it was different. That's why we daemons never lie; there's no point in doing so."

"This is all too much." Kester stood abruptly, even though it made his head spin again. "I don't know what I feel about this. Mum lied to me, and you've hidden things from me too, regardless of how much you claim to value the truth. You're telling me that I'm a half spirit, but all my life I've been *nothing!* I went through school being told I was pathetic, cowardly, scared of my own shadow. Now I discover that I *am* the shadow?"

"You need time. This is a lot to take in."

"Damned right I need time."

"Go for a walk. I can sense the urge within you, to be alone and to be in motion. But be warned, Infinite Enterprises are on their way."

Kester shrugged. "What does it matter? I can just create a spirit door and escape again. They can't contain me."

They can't contain me. A rush of realisation flooded his body, and his eyes widened as the enormity of it hit him. There was nothing to be scared of anymore. All those years that he'd wasted being nervous about every little thing, his hesitancy to leave the safe confines of his childhood home—now it had come to an end. Nothing should be able to frighten him now.

Hrschni nodded, as though guessing Kester's thoughts.

"Embrace it," he whispered. "Your mother wasn't able to, and neither was your grandfather. But you're the son of a spirit door opener and a daemon. I don't know of a single other human like you. You're unique, and you can change the world."

He's right, Kester acknowledged, as he paced towards the door. *But I still have no idea how I feel about it.*

Kester strode down the street, hands stuffed in pockets, lost in thought. A fine mist left moisture over his skin, and he wondered which part of him felt it—the human or the spirit. Was this why he'd always been able to sense things around him as a child and why he'd feared doors so much? Sometimes, the doorways he'd seen in his dreams had seemed to be sucking him nearer, threatening to envelop him entirely. Maybe that was the spirit part of him, reaching out towards home.

In Hrschni's visions, he'd listened to Dr. Ribero and his mother talk about being outsiders. But at least they'd known there were others like them. According to the daemon, Kester was the only one of his kind: the ultimate alien, a creature that was unlike anyone else. Earlier, he'd felt the power of it. Now, all he was left with was a sense of intense loneliness. No one could ever understand how it felt, because no one was like him. He was completely, entirely alone.

Pacing past the station, he remembered boarding the train there, not so long ago. Heading to Dawlish, not knowing whether he'd assist with capturing Hrschni or help him to escape. If he'd permitted Serena to trap the daemon in her bottle that day, none of this would have happened. The agency would have been celebrated across the country for successfully eliminating a national threat. They would have won more jobs and improved their reputation beyond measure. Serena would have stayed. His father would have been happy, and the others too. More to the point, he never would have known the truth. Instead, he would have spent the rest of his life believing he was half a Lanner, half a Ribero.

However, he would have also had to live with the fact that he'd helped to slaughter a great daemon. A daemon who, he now knew, was actually his parent.

He was half one thing, half another. A mishmash of things, incapable of fitting into either world. Where did that leave him?

Maybe I should give in to it and help Hrschni after all, he thought. *Let the spirits flood into this world and see what happens. Who knows, maybe Hrschni and the Thelemites were right after all; maybe it would all turn out for the best.*

The reality of it was all too easy to imagine. The spirits would cause widespread terror and chaos. They would destroy technology, simply because their nature jarred against it, and bring down industry, forcing humans to find a new way of living. But would that be so bad? Spirits had lived peaceably among humans in the past.

And I'd live alongside my father, he thought, kicking at a stone on the pavement. *My real father, I mean. I wouldn't have to put up with being shouted at all the time or called a silly, lazy boy. There'd be no more dragging me out of bed at the weekend for frantic meetings. No more dealing with the squabbles and sarcasm. It would be an entirely new way of living.*

A new way of life—but the truth was that he'd miss his old life horrendously. The agency was his family, and to leave it would be to cut off a vital part of himself. He didn't believe that he could do it, not for one second.

There's a middle ground, he thought, staring up at the buildings around him. *It's just a matter of finding it.*

He sensed a looming shadow approaching close behind him. Turning, he took in the sight of a tall man, hands extended towards him, but his reaction was too slow, too stunned by the suddenness of the events.

Ian Kingdom-Green, he realised, staring upwards at the familiar face. Cardigan Cummings stood beside him, staring with open concern. With abrupt, fluid grace, Ian seized Kester by the arms, holding him firmly in place.

"Kester, it's a relief to see you," Ian said breathlessly. "What's going on?"

Kester shook his head. "You have no idea."

"You stepped through the spirit door," Cardigan added, frowning. "We've got witnesses who saw you. By rights, you should be dead."

"How did you find me so quickly?"

Both the men smiled, albeit tightly.

"We figured you'd return to Exeter, if you'd really managed to survive in the spirit world," Cardigan said. "You're a predictable chap."

"Can you let me go?" Kester asked, as the enormity of the situation started to hit him. "I won't run away, I promise. You have to trust me."

Ian shook his head, then started to push him gently down a side street. "I wish I didn't have to do this," he replied, with genuine regret. "But you're now listed as a Level One threat."

"Also, we know what you're capable of," Cardigan said, walking alongside him, but not too closely. "The news is all over Infinite Enterprises, and the government too. You weren't forcibly thrown out of the spirit world, like anyone else would be. Instead, you used it to escape. Nobody should be able to do that."

"Where are you taking me?" Kester asked. "Back to your headquarters?"

"That's right," Ian said, hurrying his pace. "Though it's a real nuisance, Kester. I've been driving all over the place these last few days. And I have a ticket to watch Macbeth at the Royal tonight, which I now won't be able to attend. The Guardian rated it as the definitive adaptation of the twenty-first century, and—"

"Let's just focus on getting Kester in the van," Cardigan said, pointing ahead. It was a different vehicle to the one he'd previously travelled in. This one was larger, less comfortable-looking, and had bars in the back window.

He watched as Cardigan opened the rear door, revealing two metal benches against both walls.

It's a prison van, Kester thought, with detached horror. *I'm under arrest.*

"I hate to do this." Cardigan stepped inside, then withdrew a pair of handcuffs from a box under the bench. "But we've all heard how easily you can create a spirit door now, not to mention slip through it."

Kester entered the van, then sat down with a sigh. "You have my word I won't open a spirit door."

"We can't take that risk." Cardigan grimaced as he clamped the cuffs on Kester's wrists. "I want you to know I'm really not comfortable with this, though."

"Nor me," Ian said sadly. "I do wish you'd just stayed put at Infinite Enterprises. They wouldn't have harmed you."

"They tricked me," Kester said bitterly. "They said they'd free Miss Wellbeloved and Dr. Ribero, and they didn't. They just wanted to use me to lure Hrschni to them."

"You're painting us as the bad guys," Cardigan said, settling beside him. "When in fact, we're trying to keep everyone safe. Including you."

"Do you know what your organisation has been doing to spirits? That's what Hrschni's protesting against, you know."

Cardigan shrugged at Ian. "Let's get going; this is unpleasant enough as it is."

"I'm not driving again, am I?"

"If you wouldn't mind."

"I've been back and forth between London and Exeter so many times now; could you take a turn?"

Cardigan sighed. "You know they asked me to talk to Kester. I can't do that while I drive, can I?"

"I manage to converse while handling a vehicle." Ian pressed his lips together, then sighed. "Fine. Yet another journey up the M5 for me, what fun."

Kester smiled slightly. It was good to see that even the country's most illustrious supernatural agency had its petty squabbles from time to time, just like Ribero's.

"I won't help you to capture Hrschni," he said, as Ian closed the door behind him. "And I presume you can't keep me locked up forever, either."

Cardigan raised an eyebrow. "We could, if we had probable cause. The government would approve the decision, I'm sure." He studied Kester, then exhaled heavily. "Please, just cooperate. We've always got on well in the past, and I respect you. Let's not make this more unpleasant than it needs to be."

Kester settled back against the hard surface, cuffed hands resting on his knees. He felt strangely removed from it all, his thoughts still whirring through everything he'd discovered and the implications for the future. After a while, Cardigan gave up trying to make conversation and sat in silence beside him, as the van drove onwards towards London.

Kester was escorted through the back entrance of Infinite Enterprises headquarters again—this time in a far less friendly manner. The security guard was the same man who'd been working the previous night, and he stared with open fascination as Kester was escorted through the reception area.

Kester lifted his head defiantly. His newfound criminal status mortified him, but he was determined not to show any shame. He refused to feel guilty for his actions, even though he wished they hadn't caused so much stress for those around him.

They entered the lift, then stood in silence as the doors hissed shut behind them. This time, rather than going up, they descended, far below the ground. Kester remembered the previous time he'd been down here, back when they'd been researching the Thelemites. Infinite Enterprises' cavernous archive department was the stuff of legend: a vast subterranean space filled with files dating back centuries. He'd have given anything to be heading there now, but he knew that his destination was somewhere far less pleasant.

The lift slid past the archives level and continued downwards. Finally, it stopped, and the doors slid open. As he stepped out into the low-ceilinged hallway, Kester could sense the weight of the building above bearing down upon them all. It was warmer down here too, and far less well ventilated.

This is where they keep their hardened criminals, he thought, surveying the featureless metal doors that flanked the walls to either side of him. It was nothing like the area he'd been imprisoned in before, which had been spartan, yet comfortable. This place was severe, with uniformed guards standing at intervals along the dark corridor.

One of the guards sprang into action at the sight of them and immediately unbolted the nearest door. Kester stepped inside reluctantly. His previous room at Infinite Enterprises had felt like hotel accommodation. This one was unmistakably a cell, with a metal toilet in the corner, a wooden bench against the wall, and a plastic water bottle beside it. The sight of the bottle reminded him painfully of his team.

"Why is the air crackling?" he asked. It felt as though an electric current was being run through the cell, making his skin tingle.

Cardigan and Ian glanced at one another.

"I'm surprised you can detect it," Ian replied, frowning. "It's a sensory blocker; it prevents anyone from conducting any psychic, telekinetic, or otherwise supernatural activity in here. That means no opening spirit doors either. Spirits are deterred by it too; it disrupts their natural energy, and if they're exposed to it for too long, it'll destroy them. It's enormously expensive to run, though fortunately, we don't have to use it much. Usually, people with supernatural abilities are working with us, not against."

"I'm not against you," Kester said, sitting on the bench. "Does that mean you can take the handcuffs off now?"

Cardigan nodded and swiftly slipped the key into the cuffs. "You'll have to put them back on once you leave this room, though," he said. "Just to warn you."

"So, what happens now?" Kester asked, massaging his wrists.

"You'll just have to wait in here, I'm afraid."

"For a few hours? A day? A week? How long are we talking?"

"I can't tell you that," Cardigan replied. "Hopefully it won't be too long. Good luck, Kester. I mean it."

Ian checked his watch. "I wonder if they'll let me head off? Macbeth starts in twenty minutes or so; I should be able to make it, as long as they don't give us yet another task to do."

Cardigan shook his head, then ushered his colleague out of the room. A moment later, the door slammed behind them with a dull, metallic thud, and Kester was left alone.

The bench was hard. The cell was cold too, and he wasn't looking forward to the inevitable moment when he needed to use the toilet, as it looked like it hadn't been cleaned for quite some time. However, these were mild discomforts when compared to the low buzzing of the air around him. It sounded like someone using a power-drill somewhere far away, and the vibrations were carrying through the floor and the walls, directly to where he sat. After a while, the noise seemed to travel, rising through his body and entering his skull, where it nested like a hive of angry bees.

Maybe this was Infinite Enterprises' way of getting their prisoners to break. It was becoming increasingly intolerable, and he rubbed his brow firmly, in a bid to massage the buzzing sensation into submission.

Tentatively, he focused on the empty space before him. Nothing happened, regardless of how hard he tried to connect with the particles or envisage the air splitting in front of his eyes. Ian had told the truth: all supernatural abilities were off limits here. He'd also mentioned that spirits hated it.

Maybe that's why I loathe it so much in here, he thought. *The spirit in me is disturbed by it, just like any other spirit.* Then, with dawning panic, he remembered the other piece of information that Ian had shared. Spirits could be destroyed by the sensory blocker if they lingered too long in the cell.

Could it destroy me? Kester wondered. He leaned back against the wall, forcing himself not to think about it. He had to tell himself he'd be fine; otherwise fear would overcome him. He was trapped in here, regardless of how he felt about the matter, and there was nothing he could do about it either way.

After a few hours, his head started to throb in earnest. Electric tingling raced through his body too, a sensation that made him twitch and wriggle on his seat. The vibration had ceased to be a mere irritation; now it was unravelling him and making him feel as though he was going mad. He started to pace up and down. Then, he started to moan.

"Please, let me out!" he called, aiming his attention at the tiny CCTV camera in the corner of the cell. "You don't understand what this is doing to me!"

Someone could hear him; he was certain of it. He knew how well Infinite Enterprises monitored their captives, thanks to his last stay in the building. However, they probably presumed he was trying to trick them into opening the door—a thought that did nothing to quell his panic.

I could tell them the truth, he thought, staring wildly around the cell. But being honest would have dramatic repercussions. He'd be treated like a freak of nature and never permitted to live a normal life again. They might even take him to be *dismantled,* and what would happen then? Would the machinery rip him apart like a smashed watermelon? Or would he be left as some sort of half person, devoid of his spirit energy?

This is unbearable, he thought, sinking back down to the bench. He started to rock backwards and forwards, aware that he couldn't take much more. It had only been a short while, and already, he was breaking apart at the seams.

All of this is Mum's fault. The thought came to him, swift and hot as a spark of fire. If she hadn't told so many lies, if she'd been honest from the start, then her friends would have advised her not to get involved with a daemon. He knew Hrschni wasn't evil, but he was *different,* and his lack of humanity now flowed through Kester's veins.

"I'm paying for your sins, Mum," he moaned, clutching his face. "You did this to me. You and Hrschni and Julio too." He pressed his head against the cold wall, raised it, then brought it down again as hard as he could. The pain was sudden and jarring, but it stopped the maddening electric buzz, at least for a short while. He drove his head into the wall again, harder this time, then again, and again— anything to distract him from the torment. After a time, his vision started to blur, and he slumped to his side with a stifled sob.

The cell door crashed open, and a pair of black shoes appeared in his line of vision. Hands hauled him upwards, then shoved him back against the wall. Something warm and wet trickled over his eyelid. He presumed it must be blood.

"Just let me out of here," he whispered, closing his eyes. "Please, I'm begging you. It's tearing me apart."

In terms of appearance, this cell was no better than the last. But it was mercifully free of the *buzzing*, and for that, he was grateful. Now that his mind was free from the vibrations, he could think again, without feeling as though his brain was about to short-circuit.

He waited patiently as two guards cuffed him to a chair by the wrists and ankles. They each gave him an experimental tug on the shoulders, then nodded, satisfied. There was no chance he was going anywhere, even if he did somehow manage to open a spirit door.

"Wait here," one guard said, then winced at his own foolishness.

"Don't worry," Kester mumbled. "I'm not going anywhere."

The guards stepped back, and Kester studied his new surroundings in greater depth. It was yet another airless, windowless room; only this time, there was a large desk at the back, and an equally formidable leather swivel chair behind it. It was designed to be uncomfortable and to elicit nervousness; that much was obvious.

His head ached. No one had bothered to clean him up, and the blood from his wound had dried, forming a sticky trail down his cheek. The door opened behind him, and he didn't bother to turn around.

"Good lord," a familiar voice muttered. "What on earth have you done to yourself?" A figure strode past, and Kester followed his path with interest. The man was recognisable from the hair alone, a bristly mass of black, which Mike often enjoyed comparing with a toilet brush. It was Lord Bernard Nutcombe: a mere MP back-bencher as far as the general public were concerned, but to the industry he worked in, the minister of the supernatural.

Lord Nutcombe settled on the swivel chair, hands folded on the desk in front of him. Then, he proceeded to study Kester hard, as a scientist might observe particularly virulent bacteria on a petri dish.

"I understand you've been causing trouble," he said eventually. "Big trouble, in fact; is that right?"

Kester sighed. "That depends on your perspective."

"Hmm. Aiding and abetting a spirit terrorist, that's pretty defin-itively wrong, wouldn't you agree? And running away from our team. Stepping through a spirit door too, though no one has any idea how you did it. What have you got to say for yourself?"

Kester started to laugh. The ludicrousness of it all was impossi-ble to ignore, especially with Lord Nutcombe glowering at him in disapproval.

"I hardly think this is a suitable time for chuckles, Kester. Things could get diabolical for you very quickly."

"Nothing could be more diabolical than that cell you put me in."

"Yes, I heard about that." He leaned across the desk. "What on earth was going on? They said you were banging your head on the wall and pacing around like you'd completely lost your mind."

"I didn't like it in there."

"Seems like an extreme reaction, if you ask me. But now, let's get down to business. I'm here now; I don't wish to be, but I am. Curtis will be joining us shortly, and then we will sit down as grown men and resolve this situation as quickly as possible. Then I shall return to my home, as I have guests coming over for dinner."

"Yes, I get it; everyone's got plans for this evening," Kester muttered.

After another minute or so, the door opened again, and Curtis Philpot slid inside, looking every bit as flustered and overworked as he usually did. He was carrying an additional plastic chair, which he placed by the side of the desk.

"I do wish they'd get better seating down here," he grumbled, nodding curtly at Nutcombe.

"It could be worse; try being cuffed to your chair," Kester said, rattling his handcuffs for good measure.

Curtis looked abashed. "Yes, that does look unpleasant. But really, you gave us no choice."

"That's enough chat about chairs," Nutcombe said, pressing an emphatic finger on the desk. "Kester's here. He can't escape this time, so what the hell are we going to do with him?"

"Offer him a job," Curtis said dryly. "Seriously. The lad has talents far beyond anything we've ever seen before; he'd be a valuable asset to the company."

"Yes, if he wasn't so intent on helping daemons unleash chaos upon the world."

"Which is why we'd offer him something he can't refuse."

Nutcombe raised an eyebrow. "Such as?"

"A huge pay packet. Bonuses every year. A large house, fancy car, time off whenever he wants it. A senior job title, people working for him. His own subdepartment." He glanced at Kester. "How does that sound?"

"You sound just like Mike's brother, Crispian," Kester said. "Both of you mistakenly think I crave money. I really don't."

"Alright, then," Curtis said, undeterred. "A chance to make the world a better place. That's what you want, isn't it? Help us to keep the spirits in order, and the world will run far more harmoniously."

"I'm not sure I agree with your definition of *harmonious.*"

"See!" Nutcombe waved his hand in Kester's direction. "He admits it himself: his vision for the future is aligned to Hrschni's, not ours. He's a danger to us all."

"No, I'm not," Kester said patiently. "I'm not about to open loads of permanent sun doors around the world, don't worry."

"This is hopeless," Nutcombe said heavily. "We can't trust this boy, because he's far too powerful for his own good, and he's friends with an unpredictable spirit. The only option is to keep him locked up in the disabling cell, to ensure he can never open a spirit door again." He shook his head sadly. "It's a horrendous waste of a talent, but what choice have we got?"

"Don't put me back in there," Kester said swiftly. "Please. You have my word that I won't open a spirit door again."

"What's so bad about that cell?" Nutcombe said, then turned to Curtis. "Have you tweaked the sensory blocker levels? I thought you said it had no ill effects on humans?"

Curtis shrugged. "I can only assume he was hamming it up, in order to get out. He's proved himself to be very resourceful in the past, after all." He gave Kester an admiring glance, then quickly straightened his features.

"Well, you'll have to go back in there for now," Nutcombe concluded. "We've got nowhere else to put you, and I can assure you that it's perfectly safe."

"It isn't. Not for me." Kester leaned forward as much as his cuffs would permit. "Please, hear me out. I think I know how we can resolve all of this. All I ask is that you arrange a meeting, sometime soon. Get everyone to attend: every agency that's involved, every government official working on the case. The Thelemites too, if possible. I also ask that you allow Hrschni to be present, without trying to capture him."

The minister scoffed. "As if he'd attend. He wouldn't trust us any more than we'd trust him."

"He'd be right not to trust us," Curtis added. "How could we not seize him, Kester? We'd be foolish not to."

"No, you'd be foolish not to take this chance to put things right."

"A meeting won't magically make the situation go away!" Nutcombe snapped, slapping the desk. "Do you seriously expect us all to sit down with Hrschni and make polite conversation, after all the trouble he's caused?"

"Just this once," Kester said. "That's all I ask. What have you got to lose?"

Curtis sniffed. "Hrschni won't come, nor the Thelemites. It's pointless."

"They might, if I ask them. The meeting will have to be somewhere neutral, though. It's too easy for you to double-cross them if they come here."

They all stared at one another in silence, trying to read the other's thoughts.

"Why do you think a meeting will help?" Nutcombe leaned back in his chair and folded his hands across his stomach. "Go on. You've got two minutes to convince me."

Kester nodded. "I think an agreement can be reached, but we all need to discuss it in person."

"An agreement? What sort of agreement? If it involves letting Hrschni get his own way, it's not going to happen, let me tell you."

"I feel the same. But I think we're all missing a trick here. We could find an arrangement that's mutually beneficial to everyone."

Nutcombe snorted. "Tell me what this arrangement is."

"We all need to discuss it first. There's no point in me making you a promise on Hrschni's behalf that won't be kept."

"How do we know he won't try to harm us?"

"Come on," Kester said, shaking his head. "You know him better than that. Anyway, he could have harmed you at any point over the last few weeks, and he hasn't. The idea of hurting humans is abhorrent to him."

Curtis nodded. "That's certainly true. He's dangerous, but he's not psychopathic. But what about the Thelemites? They might attack us."

"What, Barty Melville and his crew?" Kester said. "They'd consider it beneath their dignity, and you know it. They're no real threat. They just represent an ideology that you don't agree with."

Lord Nutcombe rolled his tongue over his lips, mulling it over. "Normally, I'd say no," he said finally, fixing Kester with a hard stare. "But to be honest, I'm out of ideas, and I want all of this to be over. So, I'll arrange this meeting, just like you've requested. Be warned, though: if it's a waste of time or if anyone's hurt, you'll be held fully responsible. I'll make sure you're put back in that cell and that you never see daylight again."

Kester swallowed hard. Even now, his suggestion was starting to seem flimsy, with far too much potential to fail. "I understand," he agreed, trying to inject some reassuring confidence into his voice.

"You better. Curtis, sort it all out, will you?" Nutcombe clicked his fingers in his colleague's direction. "It'll need to happen very soon, as we all want this over and done with, don't we?"

"We do," Curtis and Kester agreed in unison.

Nutcombe pointed at Kester. "We'll keep you cuffed for now," he said, "and put you in a normal cell. Quite simply, I don't have the energy to argue about whether or not the other room was causing you genuine problems. Is that alright with you?"

"Thank you," Kester nodded. "Honestly, I mean it."

"You're an odd one, you are. Right, Curtis, you'd better get to work. Kester, will you be contacting Hrschni and his Thelemite chums? You seem to be able to communicate freely with him, though goodness knows how you're doing it."

"Leave it with me."

"Lock this lad up again," Nutcombe ordered, standing up. "I'm off home, though I shan't enjoy my dinner party at all now, not with all this hanging over me. It's absolutely typical; I even purchased a beautiful Châteauneuf-du-Pape, and now I won't be able to drink much of it, because the last thing I need on top of everything else is a hangover." He sighed, then stood. "Sometimes I wonder why I took this job on. Actually, that's not quite true. I wonder that *all the time*. Every single bloody day."

Just wait until your party's voted out of government; then it will all go away, Kester thought, with a wry smile. He strongly suspected Lord Nutcombe wouldn't much like *that*, either.

Still, despite the minister's complaining, Kester had managed to secure a meeting. Quite what he was going to say at the meeting was still a mystery, but it was a start. Right now, he had the inklings of a plan, but he needed to think it through properly. He supposed that was the one advantage of being locked up in a room. For once, he had plenty of time to think. Indeed, there wasn't much else he could do, really.

The new cell looked uncannily like the previous one, with its hard bench and rusted toilet, but at least this time, there were no sensory blockers to torment him. The guards even supplied him with a blanket and a pillow, which he guessed was a particularly rare perk for criminals imprisoned down here. He made himself as comfortable as possible—no mean feat, given that one of his cuffed wrists had been attached to the leg of the bench.

He lay on his back and stared at the ceiling without really seeing it. Thoughts raced through his mind, some too quickly to grab hold of. However, certain phrases stuck fast, repeating over and over with freight-train urgency.

Outsider.

Two halves.

Secrets.

He tried to relax, to let the thoughts form some sort of logical pattern. *Spirits are seen as outsiders,* he began, closing his eyes. *These days, an outsider is often regarded as a bad thing. But it wasn't always like that.*

He thought back to what he'd read in *The Historie of Spirits*. It had discussed the symbiotic nature of the human-spirit relationship. Why had it stopped? What had changed to make humans see spirits as nuisances instead of friends?

I'm an outsider too. But he didn't regard himself as a negative force, despite how others might view the matter. In fact, his *otherness* meant that he could achieve great things.

"It also means I could be a threat," he muttered. "Even though I would never do anything bad, I understand why they'd be suspicious.

It's because they know they couldn't stop me unless they kept me permanently locked up."

But how could suspicions be changed into trust? Not just trust in him, but in spirits too? The situation was complex, especially as some spirits behaved badly, and others were downright dangerous. Their existence was a secret, and that created tension too.

Secrets haven't served any of us very well, he thought, shifting to ease the cramp in his arm. His mother, Hrschni, Infinite Enterprises, they'd all kept secrets, and it hadn't benefitted any of them. Perhaps it was time for transparency instead and for the current systems to be reviewed.

Hrschni, he thought, this time focusing his attention outwards and hoping the daemon would hear him. *There will be a meeting tomorrow, and you need to come. The Thelemites too, this involves them as well. Please be there. If you're really my father, then you owe me this much. Please.*

Kester felt a little better afterwards. He believed, though couldn't say why, that Hrschni had heard him and would continue to hear him, whenever Kester needed to get in touch. He'd long since suspected there was a hidden part of himself that was in tune with spirits and able to reach out to them. Again, his mind took him back to that duality inside himself: the *two halves* that existed within him. Human and spirit. Overwhelmingly average and uniquely exceptional.

Maybe that was the key to all of this. Bringing the two halves together somehow and reuniting everything that had become so fractured over time.

"Who am I kidding?" he muttered to himself, placing his free hand behind his head. "It's far too challenging." But he had to try because there was no other option. He needed to either reconcile the two conflicting factions or accept his fate in the *buzzing* cell. One thing was for certain: he wouldn't last the night in there, and it would be a miserable way to end his life.

Change the world or die alone, in torment. *It's not the greatest of choices,* he thought, laughing humourlessly, then closed his eyes.

Chapter 12 — The Meeting

In dark and muddled dreams, Kester stood in the spirit world once again. This time, he saw a myriad of spirits weaving around him like tossing waves: a sea of dark eyes, all fixed upon him. Hrschni was there, somewhere behind him, and Fylgia too; he could sense them. Dr. Barqa-Abu was hovering above, waiting for him to speak.

I don't know what to say! he shouted, in a voice that was almost lost in the dense, liquid air. *Can't you tell me?*

The daemons shook their heads. Dr. Barqa-Abu tapped at her forehead, then pointed at his. He took a deep breath, then realised he had no lungs to breathe with, nor a chest to rise and fall. He stared down at himself and saw that he was smoke and flame, shifting to and fro and fading in and out of sight.

I'm like you, he whispered, raising an arm to the sky.

A bony finger prodded him, hard. Then again, even harder.

Don't hurt me.

Please, stop it, you're—

Kester's eyes flew open, and he sat upright with a gasp—quite forgetting the handcuff on his wrist. With a yelp of pain, he snapped back down again, head hitting the pillow with a dull thump. Then he realised that a finger was still poking him, even though he was now fully awake. He turned to find himself face to face with the owner of the prodding finger, who was perched at the foot of the bench and eying him with mild distaste.

"Serena?" he said, squinting in disbelief. "What the hell are you doing here?"

She raised an eyebrow. "Nice to see you too, Kester. I've got a job here now; what's your excuse?"

"But this is a cell," he muttered. "You don't work in a cell."

"That's correct, I don't. But I heard you were down here and asked if I could say hello."

He eased himself awkwardly into a sitting position, with one hand still trapped against the leg of the bench. She certainly looked the part, in a smart tailored dress and her trademark towering heels. Professional. Composed. *Also a traitor,* he thought, uncharitably.

"I suppose you're feeling rather pleased with yourself," he said gruffly. "Now you've got your ideal job."

She glared at him. "Don't take that tone with me. If you hadn't royally mucked things up, I wouldn't have needed to find a new job, would I?"

"Yeah, but Infinite Enterprises? It's not even like it's convenient for you to work in London; you live in Exeter."

"I'm staying with a friend. It's fine."

"It's not fine." He took a deep breath, the dregs of his dream still clinging to him. "We miss you. The agency won't be the same without you there."

"Kester, there *is* no agency. It's ruined, after what you did."

"I know. I believe I did the right thing, but it was horrendous for everyone else. I'm sorry."

She took a deep breath, obviously keen to say more, then thought better of it. "Look," she said finally, "I didn't come down here to have an argument. Everyone's buzzing with the news that you've requested a nationwide meeting and that you've got something important to announce."

"Have I?" he said weakly.

"Apparently so, though I'm not sure who nominated you to be our personal saviour."

"I didn't ask for any of this."

"That's probably true, but you really have an uncanny knack for disrupting things. Have you and your daemon chum managed to destroy the world yet?"

"I've no intention of doing that." He pointed to the bottle by her feet. "Can you pass me that water? I'm parched."

With an exorbitant sigh, she swept the bottle up, unscrewed the lid, then handed it to him. "So, what's your big plan, then?" she said. "Tell me, oh mighty leader."

"I haven't got one yet."

"Why doesn't that surprise me? You really love to wing it, don't you?" She snatched the bottle from his hand and took a hearty swig. "They're saying you went through a spirit door, you know. I keep reminding everyone that it's impossible, and besides, it's *you* we're talking about, not anyone special."

"I *did* go through the spirit door," he said quietly.

"Don't be silly. It's a commonly known fact that humans are forcibly repelled from the entrance, before they even—"

"Yes, I know. But I went through, nonetheless."

She met his gaze, then frowned. "You're a liar."

"You know me better than that."

"Only spirits can enter. You're not a spirit, so it's not possible."

"I'm half spirit," he said, dropping his voice to a barely audible whisper. He couldn't keep it from her any longer, but the last thing he wanted was for his revelation to be picked up on the CCTV footage.

She snorted, ready with a sharp retort, then froze. "Excuse me?"

"Whisper, please." He nodded up to the corner, where the tiny red light of the camera was flashing in their direction.

"Half a spirit?" she hissed, edging away from him. "You mean—?"

"Yes, that's exactly what I mean," he muttered. "I only found out recently."

"But Gretchen wasn't a spirit, and Dr. Ribero is about as human as they come." Suddenly, she clamped a hand over her mouth. "It's *Hrschni*, isn't it? Bloody hell. That's why you're protecting him."

"Please, keep your voice down. Everyone will know soon enough anyway, but I'd rather the news wasn't leaked via a security camera."

"It makes sense," she said wonderingly. "Your eyes, the pupils always bothered me. Like there's something monstrous inside you, just waiting to get out. And the way you always accuse me of being spiritist, it's because you're protecting your own kind, isn't it?"

"Serena, can you please be quiet?"

"You *infiltrated* our agency," she said. "How long have you been working against us, then?"

"Let me see, for approximately zero months, zero weeks, and zero hours?" He sighed with exasperation. "You're forgetting something. Up until yesterday, I thought Julio Ribero was my father. Do you have any idea what it feels like to have yet another parent taken away from you?"

"I do, actually," she whispered. "My mother was tortured by a spirit, then my father drank himself to death soon after. So, you'll forgive me for not being too fond of *your kind*."

He shook his head in disbelief. "I've just given you yet another reason to hate me, haven't I? That's all you've ever wanted, right from the start."

She flinched. "I don't *hate* you, Kester. I never have. It's just that you blundered into our lives a few months ago, and since then, everything has been so much harder."

"I didn't mean for it to be that way."

"No, I suppose you didn't. It's in your nature, isn't it, to be troublesome. Or half your nature, anyway." She rose, then stepped towards the door. "Oh, I don't know what to think, Kester. Every time I feel that I'm right about something, you make me doubt myself. And you can stop giving me those pathetic puppy eyes too; that doesn't help."

"I thought you said they were monstrous a few seconds ago?"

"I can't figure out what you are, really. Look, I've got to get back to my desk. I'll be at the meeting later on, though. Don't worry, I won't tell anyone what you've just told me, though don't be surprised if Infinite Enterprises run the footage through an audio-magnifier or something like that. They've got a wealth of sophisticated technology, in case you haven't noticed."

"I had," he said dryly, thinking of the cell in which he'd been locked, shortly before this one. "Serena, before you go?"

"What?"

"Whatever you feel about me, I want you to know that I respect you. You're a mean sod sometimes, and every word that falls from your lips is usually an insult, but in spite of that, I really do care about you."

Her mouth twisted, then relaxed into a small smile. "Me too," she said tightly. "Though I wish I didn't. You're an absolute pain in the backside, to be honest."

"Ditto," he said, with a grin.

She rolled her eyes, then opened the door and stepped out.

He twisted his head to the camera. "Don't bother sharpening up the audio," he said loudly, emphasising each word. "You'll find out what I said soon enough."

And much more besides, he added silently, as he settled back down on the bench.

The door opened again a few hours later, and Miriam Webster stepped through, flanked by a couple of security guards. She was carrying a packet of sandwiches, which she deposited beside Kester.

"Tuna?" he said, wrinkling his nose.

"It's sustenance, isn't it?" she retorted. "I see you've already finished the water. The meeting is arranged; it is taking place at Larry

Higgins' agency headquarters, down in Southampton. For some reason, everyone decided that would be a low-risk location, even though it's a devil to get to."

Kester grimaced. He remembered the last time he'd been there, back when they'd been working on the case of the murderous fetch. That particular meeting hadn't gone well at all. He could only hope that this meeting would be a little less stressful. He also knew he needed to convey the time and place to Hrschni as swiftly as possible. The daemon needed to be there—his absence wasn't an option.

"Who's coming?" he asked, sitting up.

"As many people as we could contact in such a short time frame. You really could have made life a *little* easier on us, Kester. This has all been exceptionally challenging."

"When are we leaving?"

"Soon. Firstly, we're taking you to speak to your father."

Which father? he wondered. Was it possible that they'd already found out about Hrschni? Maybe Serena had already told everyone; he knew it had been a risk to tell her. Then he noticed Miriam's irate expression and realised she meant his *other* father. Julio Ribero.

"Is he okay?" he asked, as one of the guards started to unlock his handcuff.

"Perfectly fine, just complaining about every single thing," she said. "Miss Wellbeloved will be present too. Serena Flyte informed us that it was absolutely vital that you spoke to them before the big meeting today."

It made sense. Serena hadn't wanted Dr. Ribero or Miss Wellbeloved to find out about Hrschni later on, not with several other people in attendance, watching their reaction. *It's unusually thoughtful of her,* he thought, massaging his wrist as the blood flowed back into it. *Still, I'm sure the pleasantness won't last. It never does, with her.*

"What do you need to talk to them about?" she asked, unable to conceal her curiosity.

"Something important."

"Is this the same important thing you were whispering about to Serena, earlier today?"

"I thought you might have been listening."

"Of course we were," she snapped. "We have to, in case you hatch any other nasty little plans. We haven't had a chance to run the conversation through an audio-magnifier yet, but we shall."

"There's no point; it'll all come out at the meeting anyway," Kester retorted, rising as she clicked her fingers and gestured to the door.

Together, they marched out of the cell. He left the tuna sandwich where it was and hoped someone would think to retrieve it. He remembered Mike leaving a tuna sandwich in his desk for several days a while back, that the resulting stench had been stomach-churningly repulsive.

She led him down the corridor, then towards the lift. "We'll have to handcuff you again when we get there," she warned him, as they squeezed into the cramped space.

"Excellent," Kester said. "My wrist was starting to get cold without it."

She grunted with displeasure but didn't reply. Kester smiled inwardly. He knew he was being far more sarcastic than he'd usually dare to be, but the difference was that now he had absolutely nothing to lose.

Dr. Ribero's cell was several times more comfortable than his own, and for that, Kester was grateful. Although he and Miss Wellbeloved had been imprisoned, at least they hadn't been made to suffer—or at least, not that he could tell. He obediently extended his arm, letting Miriam cuff him to the metal bedframe, then sat on the mattress.

As soon as Kester was settled, Ribero lurched forward and wrapped him in an exuberant hug. Miss Wellbeloved, who'd been waiting anxiously by the armchair in the corner of the room, leapt over too, her thin arms lacing around his shoulders.

"Kester, we've been so worried," she said, dabbing at her eyes. "It's such a relief to see you. We've heard all these rumours, and some of them sounded too crazy to be true."

"Yes, what is this silliness about you entering the spirit realm?" Ribero barked. He sneered at Miriam, who was hovering awkwardly by the door. "What a load of nonsense, eh? Infinite Enterprises are making it all up to paint you as the criminal."

"Dad, it actually happened," Kester mumbled, wincing at his choice of words. Now that he was here, enveloped in the safety of the two people he trusted most in the world, he felt horrified at the magnitude of the task ahead. There was no easy way to tell them the news, and he knew that it would break Ribero's heart. Miss Wellbeloved's too, probably.

Miriam coughed loudly. "I'll leave you to it," she said. "Kester already knows that the conversation is being monitored, though I suspect he's going to do his whispering act again." She turned to Kester and gave him a pleading look. "Could you just say it aloud? It'd save my team a lot of time and effort."

"No," he replied firmly. "I've got my reasons, which will become clear in the meeting later."

"Fine. I can see there's no convincing you. You've got ten minutes max, then we need to be on our way. It takes a while to get to Southampton, you know."

They waited patiently until she'd closed the door, then faced one another. Kester took a deep, shuddering breath. Ribero and Miss Wellbeloved were wearing matching expressions of anxiety, and he knew that he was about to make them feel a lot worse.

"You didn't slip through to the spirit world," Ribero said, nudging him hard in the belly. "Humans cannot do that. So, explain yourself, because we want some answers."

"I'll do my best," Kester said miserably, then dropped his voice to a whisper. "Look, there's no point beating around the bush. I've got to tell you something, and it's not going to be pleasant. Think about it carefully. Who *can* enter a spirit door?"

"Only spirits, silly boy!"

"Julio, keep your voice down," Miss Wellbeloved murmured. "Kester needs to say something important, and you need to calm down and listen."

Kester met her steady gaze. Beneath the hollow cheeks and fine lines, he could see the young woman she'd once been: the delicate, pretty student that had trusted her fiancé implicitly, and the stricken twenty-something-year-old, devastated at the loss of her father, her husband-to-be, and her future.

"You already know, don't you?" he said softly.

"I have my suspicions. To be honest, there were a few times I wondered in the past, but I convinced myself it couldn't be true. Tell us, Kester. Just say it."

He nodded, steeling himself. "I'm a half spirit. My mother was in love with Hrschni."

Dr. Ribero roared with laughter, then stopped abruptly. He stared at his hands, which had started to shake. "That is a mad thing to say," he whispered. "She didn't even *know* the daemon. Why would you say such a thing?"

"Think about it," Kester said patiently. "Her father, my grand-father, he knew Hrschni. Doesn't it make sense that he'd eventually find Gretchen too?"

"No, this is not right. She loved *me* and no one else. I have carried the guilt of it for years, but it is the truth."

"Julio, listen to me," Miss Wellbeloved interrupted, taking his hands into her own. "We both knew Gretchen had her secrets. Remember how she used to disappear in the evening, back at college? And when we all worked together? She never told us what she was doing; she always gave a vague answer and said she was going for a walk or doing some work."

Ribero kept shaking his head. Then suddenly, he stared at Kester, as though seeing him for the first time. "Are you saying that you are Hrschni's son?"

Kester braced himself. The conversation was more awful than he'd imagined, but it couldn't be avoided.

"That's exactly what I'm saying," he said. "Please, keep your voice down. The others mustn't know, not yet."

Ribero shifted away. "It's not possible. Crossbreeding does not happen anymore; that is a fact. Right, Jennifer? You must back me up here because these things he says, they are ridiculous."

"If the daemon told Kester that he's his father, then it must be true," she whispered, glancing anxiously at the flashing camera in the corner of the room.

"Why must it be true? Hrschni cannot be trusted!"

"Daemons don't lie. You know that."

Kester hung his head. "I'm sorry," he mumbled. "I know this must be a terrible shock."

Dr. Ribero's mouth opened, then closed again. His shoulders slumped.

"If you are *his* son," he said heavily, "that means you are not mine."

"That's right." Kester felt his eyes burn with tears. "I wish things could be different."

"But I *loved* you, I really did. Gretchen wouldn't let me see you when you were growing up, but I thought of you all the time. She sent me letters, sometimes, telling me how you were. I kept them all; they are in a box under my bed."

"I believe you, and I *hate* that I had to tell you this. I'm so sorry!" With that, Kester started to sob. He couldn't help it; Ribero's anguish was unbearable, especially on top of everything else. The stress of the last few weeks broke through like a burst dam, and he willingly let Miss Wellbeloved pull his head to her shoulder.

"You poor thing," she said tenderly. "You don't owe anyone an apology."

"Look how much pain I've caused!"

"Not you. This isn't your fault."

"Hrschni showed me the past," he whispered. "I asked to see it, because I wanted to know the truth. Now I think I made a huge mistake."

"It's always better to see the world with open eyes," she said. "My father always used to tell me that. Make sure your vision is clear, because that's the only way to see the path forwards."

"Your father was a good man."

"Hrschni showed him to you, did he?"

"Sorry," he said again, wiping his nose on his sleeve. "It was nosey of me to look."

"You saw me as a young man too?" Ribero said.

Kester nodded.

"I was a handsome thing, yes? Very manly and full of character."

"Only *you* could be worried about your manliness at a time like this, Julio," Miss Wellbeloved said, giving him a squeeze. Kester smiled ruefully. He knew Ribero was trying to put on a brave front.

Ribero sighed. "So, I am not your father after all." He was pressing his hands against his knees to stop them from shaking.

"I still think of you as my dad," Kester said. "I know it's odd, but I can't imagine you any other way."

"Of course you can't," Miss Wellbeloved said briskly. "A person can be a father without having biologically produced you."

He hugged her as best as he could with one arm. "I think of you as a mother too, you know. You're the kindest person I know."

She lifted her glasses and patted her eyes. "Thank you, Kester. That means more to me than you'll ever know."

"What do we do now?" Ribero said. "You cannot take over the agency if you are half—"

Kester nodded at the camera. "That's the least of our worries. The meeting will take place in a few hours. I've got to figure out how to solve this mess, and I don't feel at all qualified to do so."

"Not qualified?" Miss Wellbeloved examined him carefully. "Given what you've just told us, Kester, you might be more qualified than anyone."

"What do you mean? I'm not even twenty-three yet; I'm a bumbling nobody who's in big trouble with just about everyone."

"Do you remember what I said earlier, about clearing your vision and seeing the path ahead?"

He nodded.

"Think about what Hrschni has shown you, and *why*. Think about what you've learnt from Dr. Barqa-Abu—not just in the last few days, but in the entire time you've known her. And what you've learnt from us and the spirits you've encountered." She patted his chest. "You know the truth in *here*, Kester. The hard work is already done; you've gathered all the parts of the puzzle. Now, you just need to work out how to put them together."

"This puzzle metaphor is very confusing," Ribero said gloomily.

She smiled at him. "If he understands it, then that's all that matters."

"Perhaps I do," Kester said. He tilted his head to one side, thinking, then nodded. "Put the pieces together and see the path ahead. Thanks, Miss Wellbeloved."

"As you've browsed extensively into my past," she said primly, "you should probably start calling me Jennifer, you know."

"And call me Julio," Ribero added.

Kester nudged him. "Can I just keep calling you Dad?"

The old man smiled wanly, then, after a while, gave a nod.

Kester wasn't surprised that he was escorted to Southampton in a different vehicle than the others. Nor did it come as a shock when they cuffed his wrists and ankles again, nor when a particularly broad-shouldered guard sat beside him, then glared menacingly at him at regular intervals.

However, the presence of so many other members of Infinite Enterprises was something of a surprise. Soon, the back of the van was full to the brim with various members of staff, including Lili Asadi and Tinker, who both looked rather put out to be travelling in such cramped conditions.

"Why are we all wedged in like sardines?" he whispered to Tinker, as the van pulled out of the car park.

Tinker blinked at him earnestly. "There are rather a lot of us attending the meeting, so we're trying to fit as many of us into as few vehicles as possible. I believe there are over twenty from Infinite Enterprises alone, and of course, your father and Miss Wellbeloved make another two, and—"

"I see," Kester replied quickly. Tinker was a nice enough man, who had the general demeanour of a mole that had accidentally emerged into broad daylight, but he did have a tendency to waffle on at times.

It was an uncomfortable journey, made worse by the fact that several of the Infinite Enterprises team seemed intent on glowering at Kester, as though it was all his fault. He supposed their opinion was fair. He *had* caused this upheaval, even though he hadn't intended to. He kept his head down and focused his thoughts instead on what he would say and how on earth he'd manage to put things right.

The van pulled into the car park about two hours later. As the back doors opened, Kester took a few grateful breaths of fresh air. Being trapped in an enclosed space with so many others had certainly been a stuffy experience. The guard beside him unlocked his cuffs, then ushered him outside.

Nothing had changed at Larry's premises, as far as Kester could tell. The office block was as bland and businesslike as he remembered it, and the surrounding landscape was as flat and featureless. He was shoved unceremoniously in the direction of the doors, where he joined the rest of the crowd of Infinite Enterprises employees fighting to get inside.

I bet Larry Higgins loves the fact that they selected his office to hold an urgent national meeting, he thought, walking down the wide corridor, listening to the sound of numerous shoes clipping against the tiled floor. Not that there would be tiles in Larry's office. When Kester had last been there, Larry had gone to great lengths to emphasise the quality of the lambswool carpet, which Mike had promptly mocked.

Eventually, he reached the door of the office, complete with a polished metal plaque announcing that *Larry Higgins' Supernatural Services* lay within. He forced himself to breathe calmly, even though it was proving difficult. Then, he stepped through with the rest of the crowd.

The room was already alive with the hum of conversation. People jostled for space around the desks, bumping into one another and looking generally rather uncomfortable, not to mention bewildered. Kester studied the sea of faces before him, recognising several of them straight away. Dr. Barqa-Abu hovered in and out of focus at the back of the office, while Fylgia lounged casually beside her, casting a green glow against the wall behind her. He spotted Mike and Pamela too, right at the front, and both waved cheerily when they noticed him. He was amused to see that Mike had already located the buffet at the back and helped himself to a paper plate of biscuits.

Larry Higgins was present too and was pacing fretfully from person to person, muttering something that sounded suspiciously like an order to *not touch anything*. Luke and Dimitri were both perched side by side on one of the desks and were busy chatting to an elderly man dressed in a smart grey suit. Kester wondered if it was Mr. Whilshin, the owner of one of the most prominent northern agencies. If so, it was a miracle he'd managed to get down here on time.

His gaze landed on Barty Melville lurking in the corner, plus Parvati Chowdhury and two other Thelemite Lodge-Masters, Felix Taggerty and Reggie Shadrach. It was difficult to raise a smile for them—after all, it had been the Thelemites who had trapped him in a cave, pursued him through the darkness, then threatened him with violence. He was surprised they'd dared to turn up, given that their conduct had been so closely investigated by Infinite Enterprises. Presumably, they were just as curious about what was going on as the rest of them.

Gradually, the room fell into silence, as everyone was alerted to Kester's presence. He shrank against the wall, aware of the pressure of all those eyes boring into him, waiting to see what he would do. Hrschni was nowhere to be seen.

He has to come, Kester thought, chewing his lip. Without the daemon, it'd be a whole lot trickier to put his plan into action.

Curtis Philpot, who'd been deep in conversation with a member of his team, cleared his throat loudly.

"Thank you everyone for attending today," he said loudly, hands clasped in front of him. "I know it was a challenge for many of you, and I want you to know we appreciate your dedication."

"I'll say it's a bloody challenge," Larry chimed, barging his way to the front. "Whose idea was it to supply biscuits? There are crumbs all over the carpet now; it's an absolute mess."

Kester stifled a smile. Obviously, Larry's obsession with his carpet hadn't yet abated.

Ignoring the outburst, Curtis continued. "You know why we're all here," he said, "so I won't waste time going through it again. Our industry is in crisis, humanity is under threat, and we urgently need to resolve the matter." He gestured to Kester. "This young chap here, despite being the source of much of the problems, believes he has the answer. He's requested this meeting, and given the nature of his talents, not to mention his connections to a very powerful spirit, we decided to give him this chance."

The elderly man in the suit stepped forward. "How do we know this isn't a trick? You assured our safety, Curtis, but I see no evidence that we're being protected. What's to stop the daemon from launching an attack right now?"

"Mr. Whilshin, we know this is a delicate situation, and we've taken measures to—"

"What rot and balderdash!" Barty Melville chorused from the corner. "Hrschni is a noble daemon; he has no intention of harming you. It's just this sort of outdated view that's causing the problems in the first place."

"I disagree, sir!" Mr. Whilshin retorted. "I've devoted my life to maintaining order while always showing spirits the utmost respect. Without this order, society lies in tatters! Is that what you want?"

"Respect? Do you know what Infinite Enterprises have been doing to spirits?" Parvati interrupted. "Why don't you ask them? Let's hear it, straight from their own mouths."

"Please, will you all remain calm?" Curtis said desperately. "This is exactly the sort of thing I wanted to avoid. If we start fighting amongst ourselves, we won't make any progress at all."

"Parvati has a point, to be fair," Pamela piped up, waving a hand in his direction. "If it's true that you're exterminating spirits, you ought to tell everyone."

Silence fell over the crowded room. Mouths fell open, bereft of words. Gradually, everyone turned to Curtis and waited for an explanation.

He gulped, then pointed at Kester. "Look, *he's* the one who wants to talk to you all. So, without further ado, I'm going to hand this over to him."

Kester's eyes widened. He spluttered to say something, which came out as a garbled mumble. Now was his time to start speaking; only now the moment had arrived, he was at a loss as to where to start. He scanned the room, searching for encouragement, but found none—only expressions of horror, anger, and from his colleagues, complete confusion.

Where's Hrschni? he wondered. Even though he had no way of knowing if the daemon could reliably hear when he mentally reached for him, he'd always *felt* the connection between them. He'd trusted that Hrschni would be here, but so far, there was no sign of him. Without Hrschni, there could be no resolution. Without Hrschni, he was in big trouble.

Still, he had to start somewhere or risk looking like a complete idiot.

"Infinite Enterprises *are* exterminating spirits," he announced eventually, over a fresh round of gasps. "I've seen the CCTV footage and heard it from Curtis Philpot's own lips. They refer to the process as *dismantling*, and they use it against spirits that they regard as a threat."

"But that's murder, plain and simple!" Luke called out. "That isn't what I got into this line of work for. I want no part in it." Beside him, Dimitri nodded in agreement.

"You're right," Kester said, warming to the task. "And Infinite Enterprises need to stop, because it's barbaric."

"What do you propose we do instead?" Curtis said, placing his hands on his hips. "None of you have any idea how difficult it is, having to make the final decision on how to deal with unruly spirits! They cause unspeakable pain to humans; we send them back to their own realm, then lo and behold, a few months later, they're back again. It may take them a while, but they always manage it in the end. That's why opening a permanent door would be a disaster; they'd be back in our world in a heartbeat."

"So, if we could ensure that only decent spirits came through, would that eradicate the problem?" Kester said.

Curtis frowned. "It'd make life easier. But the problem is, people don't want spirits here anymore, even if they are nice spirits with friendly intentions. It's our job to keep them out, or at least make sure they operate without detection. That's what our entire industry is based on."

"Quite right," Serena shouted out. "You've already ruined my career at the agency, Kester; don't try to butcher the entire supernatural sector."

Several others laughed at her joke. Kester winced. He sensed the room wasn't entirely on his side, which wasn't a comfortable sensation.

"Look," he said desperately, "We need to change our perspective. I was reading *A Historie of Spirits* recently, and it talked about the relationships between spirits and humans. It was very different back then, and—"

"Goodness me, this is preposterous," Larry bellowed. All eyes turned to him, and he grinned, basking in the attention. "This young whippersnapper is barely out of nappies, and here he is, spouting nonsense about a musty old book that isn't even on the SSFE curriculum anymore! Why are we standing here listening to him? He's way out of his depth."

"Larry, could you just be quiet, for once in your life?" Miss Wellbeloved said, jabbing a finger in his direction. "All your life, you've loved to stir up ill feeling. It doesn't serve any purpose, apart from making people angry!"

"I'm merely stating the truth, madam. Kester has an impressive door-opening talent, I'll give him that, but he's been led astray by Hrschni. He doesn't have a clue what he's talking about."

"That's not true," Kester flared. "I'm merely saying that our current system doesn't work."

Curtis sighed. "It's the system we've always used. It's served us well so far."

"Has it? Look at you all." Kester waved around the room. "You're exhausted. You spend too much time bickering amongst yourselves. You keep secrets from each other, because you all have different opinions and ideas. It's not working, not anymore."

"Well said," Miss Wellbeloved muttered.

"That's what we've been saying all along!" Barty Melville chorused. "But would you listen? No, you would not. Your outdated views on the spirit world are calamitous."

"Says the man wearing a medieval wizard's dress," Larry scoffed.

"You are a fine one to talk," Ribero interrupted. "Your shirt barely fits around that big round belly of yours."

"I'd rather an ill-fitting shirt than a ridiculous fedora and pinstripe suit. Dear god, man, those clothes ceased to be fashionable about a century ago!"

Kester rubbed his temples, watching as the room erupted into arguments and sarcastic comments once again. It was useless to even try to make a difference; he'd badly underestimated their resistance to change. As far as the supernatural industry was concerned, preserving the status quo was the ultimate goal. Anything else was regarded as unnecessary at best, dangerous at worst.

He caught sight of Mike and Pamela, who nodded at him earnestly. A moment later, Miss Wellbeloved joined him at the front of the room.

"Don't give up," she said quietly, surveying the chaos before them.

"I thought Hrschni would be here," he replied miserably.

"Perhaps he felt it was too much of a risk. After all, can any of us guarantee that Infinite Enterprises wouldn't try to capture him?"

"Look at what I've risked, though. If I fail to get anywhere in this meeting, they're going to throw me in a locked cell again." He lowered his voice. "They've got a special cell for blocking spirit abilities, which they kept me in before. The only problem is, it's toxic for spirits; it tears them apart after a while. That's the place they're planning to imprison me in. Do you understand why that might be a particularly big problem?"

She paused, then her eyes widened. "What happened when you were last in there?"

"At first? It was just uncomfortable. But after a while, I started to feel like I was going mad." He pointed at his forehead. "That's how I got this cut; I started headbutting the wall, in an attempt to make it stop. That was after just a few *hours*, Miss Wellbeloved. Imagine what it'd do to me after a few days?"

"You need to tell them," she whispered. "Kester, it's not an option; you can't risk your life to—"

"If I tell them, and Hrschni isn't here to protect me, what do you think they'll do?"

"I don't know."

"Neither do I, and that's the problem. Suppose they decide to put *me* in that machine of theirs, as an experiment? What would happen if they tried to dismantle *me*?"

She shook her head. "They wouldn't. We wouldn't let them."

"You wouldn't necessarily know about it. They're good at operating with complete secrecy."

Curtis Philpot stumbled over to join them, cheeks flushed, posture suggesting extreme agitation.

"This isn't going well," he said, prodding Kester in the chest. "You promised this would resolve things, and it's done the reverse. Worse still, you've made my organisation look foolish. This sort of ineptitude is usually reserved for agencies like yours."

"Well, welcome to our world," Miss Wellbeloved said breezily. "Cock-ups and schoolboy errors are just a daily routine for us. However, if we had better support from well-funded organisations such as Infinite Enterprises—"

"Come now, Jennifer, don't start with that. We've done plenty to support the small-time players like yourself. It isn't our fault that you're not very good at what you do."

"Just stop it!" Kester shouted. His voice carried far further than he'd intended it to, and immediately, a shocked hush fell upon the crowd. "This arguing is futile," he said, as his face reddened.

"We wouldn't need to argue if you presented us with this wonderful solution you were promising," Mr. Whilshin said, folding his arms across his narrow chest. "Come on, let's hear it. I've travelled a large distance today, and goodness me, you have no *idea* how I loathe public transport. So, make it worth my while, boy. Remember, I've met your mother; it's thanks to her formidable reputation that I'm even bothering to *listen* to you right now."

"Please, don't talk to me about my mother," Kester said. "Not now."

"Your mother would have shown better sense, lad."

"I assure you, she wouldn't." He stepped forward. "You want to talk about sense? For me, good sense is always tied up in the truth; wouldn't you agree?"

"Of course," Mr. Whilshin said. A few others nodded in agreement.

"A few days ago, a daemon offered to show me the truth, so I could see sense. I could have refused him. I could have let Infinite Enterprises seize him, then tear him apart in their *dismantling* machine. But I chose to listen to him instead. I wanted the truth, because without it, it's not possible to make the right decision."

He paused and surveyed the room. For the first time, everyone listened in silence, giving him their undivided attention. But he knew it wouldn't last forever, that all it would take was one voice of dissent, then the crowd would erupt into chaos again.

His eyes fell on Dr. Ribero. He noticed how his hands were shaking again, despite the man's best efforts to keep them pinned against his stomach. But it wasn't just the Parkinson's disease that was causing him pain; Kester knew it was the knowledge, too, that a daemon had fathered his son and that his agency was now without an heir.

Everything that mattered to him has come crashing down, he realised. *But he's still here, supporting me. He still believes in me, in spite of everything. I can't let him down.*

"Hrschni showed me the past," he continued, forcing himself to speak calmly. "Through him, I saw my mother. Julio and Jennifer too. I also saw Hrschni, when he was living within Billy Dagger. He asked my mother to open a permanent spirit door, but he never forced her. He never applied any pressure, and when she asked him to leave, he did."

"That's right," Barty chimed in. "He's a noble spirit. Although he believes passionately in our cause, he would never make humans act against their own free will."

"What about kidnapping poor old Kester and trying to trap him in those caves?" Serena snapped.

Poor old Kester? Kester thought with a smile. He was almost certain that only a few hours ago, she'd declared him to be a *pain in the backside.*

"I don't think Hrschni intended for things to happen like that," he said. "Also, he was getting desperate. But let me continue, because I *have* to say these things, whether I want to or not."

"Go on, my boy," Ribero said encouragingly.

Kester smiled at him, an overwhelming fondness rushing through him as he locked eyes with the man. *Not my father, but a parent in all the ways that matter,* he realised. He nodded, then looked up.

"My mother was in love with Hrschni," he said loudly. "They had a secret love affair for many years, and he's the one that fathered me. Not this wonderful man standing here today, I'm sad to say."

A hum of astonishment burst out, as everyone started talking at once. Kester shrank backwards, unable to meet so many gazes, all fixed upon him. He was frightened of what he might read there, knowing how some people regarded intimate relationships between spirits and humans.

"Before you ask," he announced over the noise, "that makes me a half spirit."

The room fell silent again. *There*, Kester thought, with something like relief. The secret was out at last, and finally, people knew what he really was. *He* knew what he was too, which perhaps mattered even more.

"So, let me get this straight. You actually did enter the spirit realm?" Curtis said after a while, stepping away instinctively. "We presumed you and Hrschni had pulled off some sort of complex telekinetic transportation or something; we never imagined that you'd *stepped through the spirit door.* Kester, do you know how unnatural that is?"

"Unnatural and freakish," Larry added. "Good god, are you telling me I've been working alongside a creature like this without knowing it?"

"Larry!" Luke exclaimed, standing up. "Don't be so rude."

"Hang on a minute," Mike added, dropping a biscuit on the floor in his surprise. "When we went to watch Billy Dagger perform, Kester, you were actually watching your *dad?* You lucky git! Billy Dagger was a total legend!" He eyed Kester with respect, then screwed up his eyes. "Not that you inherited his looks, though. No offence intended."

"None taken," Kester said.

"You're missing the point!" Larry exploded. "Billy Dagger was only the receptacle that impregnated Gretchen; it was Hrschni that *made* Kester. Ugh, what a thought. I'd always been so fond of Gretchen as well; we got on ever so well when we were studying."

"No, you didn't. Mum thought you were a prat, like everyone else," Kester replied. "I should know; I saw it through Hrschni's visions.

Also, you *did* steal my dad's idea for his thesis. So technically, the prize you won for it should be his, not yours."

Larry scowled. "I fail to see what you're so cheerful about," he snapped, turning on Ribero, who was currently slapping his knee with open delight. "You're not even his father anymore. You've been raising a half-spirit cuckoo!"

"Will you stop being so horrible!" Luke shouted. "Larry, I've put up with so much from you in the past. You get my pronouns wrong on purpose, you *never* pay us for overtime, you're always complaining about stuff that doesn't matter—but I won't keep listening to you being spiritist!"

"Bloody hell, you can't say anything these days," Larry groaned. "Look, I didn't mean it rudely. I'm merely pointing out the truth: he's half spirit, half human. Which isn't what nature intended."

"How do you know what nature intends?" Miss Wellbeloved asked, glaring at him over her glasses. "Just because it's unusual doesn't mean it's wrong."

Larry laughed. "You're defending all of this? Come on, Jennifer, stop being a doormat. Your so-called friend Gretchen not only stole your bloke, she also let him believe he had a son when he didn't. Not exactly what I'd call friendly behaviour."

"Can we move on from my parentage?" Kester urged, waving his hands to get attention again. "I don't feel like this is getting us anywhere."

"To be honest," Curtis said, hissing in his ear, "I think you might have lost them. They didn't trust you when they thought you were fully human, and they trust you even less now."

Kester paced to the wall and slumped against it. He surveyed the people in front of him, observed the delight in the expressions of the Thelemites and the revulsion in Larry's. Even his friends looked somewhat bemused, as though they'd purchased a pet dog, only to discover it was actually a slightly unpredictable wolf cub.

"I'm sorry," he said loudly. He waited until everyone was focused on him again. "You're right, I'm an oddity, and I don't fit in anywhere.

It's strange; I've never felt like I did, even before I found out I was half a spirit. Why should you listen to anything I've got to say? I've wasted your time, and we may as well all go home. Mr. Philpot, if you want to lock me up again, there's not much I can do about that. I'm not a threat, but I understand why you think I am."

"If you lock him up, you'll have me to answer to," Pamela said.

"And me," Mike added. "He's an oddball, but he's *our* oddball. If you lock him up, I'll smash your head so far into the nearest—"

"Mike, you don't need to prove your manliness," Serena said snidely, as she slunk beside him. "But just for the record, I won't let you imprison Kester either. He's hugely annoying, not to mention the biggest, wettest wimp I've ever encountered, but he doesn't deserve to spend the rest of his days rotting in a cell."

"You're our employee now, so you'll do as you're asked," Curtis snapped. "Besides, we're not monsters. We wouldn't leave him to rot, thank you very much."

"Only trap him in a cell that maddens him so much he's forced to hurt himself in order to make it stop?" Miss Wellbeloved said. "I'd call that monstrous."

"Please, everyone," Kester interrupted. He could sense another fight brewing, and although it was heartening to see his colleagues defending him, he knew it would only make matters worse. "Shall we end the meeting here? Mr. Philpot and his team can decide what to do with me later."

"Don't give in like this!" Pamela said. "You've got a grand plan, Kester, I can tell."

"I thought I did," he said sadly. "But now, I can see that it'd never work. Especially as Hrschni hasn't turned up. I needed him here, to prove that he has no intention of causing harm."

"That's daemons for you," Larry sneered. "They witter on about their trustworthiness and integrity, but when it boils down to it, they either trick you or let you down."

"Is that so?" The hot, gravelly voice resounded through the room, causing everyone to freeze.

Kester's head snapped up. *Hrschni,* he realised, with relief.

"You finally came," he whispered, and waited for the spirit to appear.

The air in the centre of the room started to quiver and shake. People stepped aside quickly, each of them wearing matching expressions of panic and wonder. Finally, Hrschni's familiar form came into view: a raging torrent of red flame surging and twisting around itself. His serpentine head turned slowly as he met every person's stare in turn.

"Apologies for being late," he said smoothly, as he drifted to the front of the room. "Perhaps, as I'm so prone to *tricking* people, I should claim that I was held up by traffic. What do you think, Mr. Higgins?"

Larry blushed, a deep shade of maroon that almost matched the daemon's own fiery colour. "I was merely referring to the fact that daemons enjoy puzzles," he muttered, "which is a well-documented fact."

"That's true," Hrschni acknowledged. "Though I found the Times crossword devilishly difficult this morning, I must confess."

Kester chuckled. This was a side of the daemon he hadn't seen before, and he rather liked it.

"I'm sorry," the daemon said to him, once he'd reached his side. "I had to ensure it was safe for me to enter first. I didn't mean to make you feel abandoned."

"It's okay," Kester replied, then smiled at his colleagues. "I didn't feel abandoned at all, really, thanks to some friends of mine."

The daemon clapped his skeletal hands together. "Shall we begin?" he said. "I believe Kester is going to present us with a solution, and we'd all benefit from listening to it."

"Is that my cue to start?" Kester hissed.

"It certainly is. Good luck."

Here goes. He took a deep breath and began.

Chapter 13 – Changing Paths

"Some of you believe that spirits should be brought back to this world," Kester started, gesturing at Barty and the other Thelemites. "While others think that it belongs to humans, and no one else."

"Too right," Larry muttered.

"Many of you aren't sure *what* to think," he carried on. "I often felt like that too. On the one hand, I could see that some spirits were pretty decent. But then, it was obvious how dangerous they could be. Like humans, in fact."

Curtis frowned. "I'm not sure they're like us, Kester. We're very different in nature."

"You've talked in the past about how threatening spirits can be and how they're capable of murder. But aren't some humans too? The point I'm making is that there are some good spirits and the occasional bad one. We're missing out on the benefits of welcoming good spirits to our world, because a few problematic spirits have made us wary."

"Yeah, but we can't tell which is which," Mike said. Somehow, he'd managed to pile several more biscuits on his plate, though quite when he'd sneaked off to replenish his supplies, Kester wasn't sure.

"That's true," he acknowledged. "At the moment, anyway. I was reading *A Historie of Spirits*—"

"Not this again," Larry groaned. "Yes, we all know you can read, well done, you. Gold star for Kester. Now, can we hear about something else instead?"

"No, because this is important," Kester said patiently. "In the past, spirits and humans produced children together, and those half-spirits were able to enter the spirit realm, just like I can. They worked to promote relations between spirits and humans. Presumably, they were also able to identify difficult spirits and keep them at bay."

"Are you proposing to live in the spirit realm and monitor spirits on behalf of the human race?" Barty called out, eyes shining. "What a prospect! So bold, so innovative! It could really work, don't you think?"

"That's not *quite* what I was proposing," Kester said. In fact, the prospect of living permanently in the world of the spirits wasn't appealing in the slightest, but he didn't want to voice his opinions aloud. "Though I am suggesting that Hrschni and I act as a *bridge* between their world and ours. We'll create a permanent sun door, but it'll be monitored carefully, and only spirits with good intentions will be allowed to come through."

"But humans won't be able to cope with *any* sort of spirit," Curtis protested. "This isn't the old days, you know."

"You're right. So, we'll need to develop an integration process. We hire a spirit as a representative in the Houses of Parliament. Slowly, we introduce well-respected spirits to work for local councils, in a limited way to begin with, of course."

"What you're proposing is insanity," Larry said.

Mr. Whilshin waved a fist in the air. "What you're proposing will put us all out of work. Without problematic spirits, there's no *us*. We'll all be unemployed the moment this plan is put into action."

"You're wrong," Kester said. It's just the nature of your job that changes. You've already got the expertise and the knowledge of how spirits behave. Instead of ridding the world of them, supernatural agencies work hard to promote positive relations between spirits and humans in the local community. They visit schools, local businesses, festivals, and events, and make sure people are educated about the benefits of having spirits in our world. And, if any spirits do misbehave, you'll be right there, ready to put the situation right."

"What about technology?" Dimitri asked. "Spirits hate it, but our whole world is run by computers."

Kester scratched his head. "You know, I've *never* liked computers. Maybe that's why." He thought of all the times his laptop had crashed while he'd been writing an important essay for the SSFE and the occasions where the internet had run at the pace of an arthritic snail for seemingly no reason at all. It made good sense, now that he knew what he was.

"We can't have spirits blowing up our systems," Larry scoffed.

"They'll have to stay away from technology," Kester said. "Maybe, in time, it might encourage humans to step away from their computers too, even if it's just for a while. Don't you think we might all be a bit happier if we weren't constantly staring at screens?"

No one replied. One Infinite Enterprises employee, who'd been checking his phone, blushed, then hastily stuffed it back into his pocket again.

"You're proposing a complete overhaul of our entire society," Curtis said slowly.

"He is," Hrschni said. "But you'll have powerful assistance. From myself, from Fylgia, from Dr. Barqa-Abu, plus many other higher orders of spirit who haven't visited this world for a long time. They may have given up on humans for many centuries, but I'm confident I can change their minds again and bring them to our cause."

"Then humans will enjoy the benefits of working alongside powerful spirits," Parvati said, pressing her hands together in excitement.

"I've experienced it myself, working with Hrschni and Fylgia, even though we've had our disagreements recently."

"What benefits?" Ribero said. "If this is such a good idea for everyone, we must know what the advantages are."

"You remember the spirit that lived in the tree in our garden," Miss Wellbeloved said, nudging him. "She looked after me as a child; she had a marvellously kind, benevolent way with her. It gave my mother a welcome break from having to keep me entertained, I can tell you."

"Spirits can assist with many things," Hrschni added. "We can help you to see situations more clearly. Guide you with making tough decisions. Help you to express, to build, to change things for the better. This is what I have been trying to say for many years. We *love* you all, and we have missed you so badly. Being apart from you is like losing a valuable part of ourselves. Without the vitality of humans, we are more shadow, less light. We are more likely to behave badly when we are sad."

Miss Wellbeloved nodded. "And without spirits, we lose our spirituality. We lose ourselves in industry and technology, and we forget our real selves. We get depressed, without understanding why, and we feel lonely because we don't understand what we've lost."

Hrschni smiled at her. "That is exactly it, Jennifer. Of all people, I knew you would understand."

"This is all very well," Curtis said, "but how on earth do you think I'll convince Lord Nutcombe? I can only imagine what he'd say, if I suggested we make a spirit a Member of Parliament."

"Unless we all present the idea to him?" Miss Wellbeloved said. "If he sees we're all on board, he might be more inclined to give it a try."

"Are we all on board?" Larry asked incredulously.

"I'd happily lob you *over*board if we were on a boat," Mike offered.

Barty Melville raised a hand. "We're most certainly in agreement. Personally, I'm delighted that the younger generation seem to be viewing spirits more positively."

"It helps if they're related to them," Larry glowered. Everyone ignored him.

"We'd need to review things carefully," Mr. Whilshin said, stroking his chin. "We can't launch hastily into anything. There are a number of issues that must be examined first."

"I agree," Kester said. "We all need to talk it through. That's what I've been saying all along; we achieve far more when we're discussing ideas, not shouting in each other's faces."

Curtis paced along the carpet, then stopped. "Very well," he said. "I'll present your proposal to Lord Nutcombe, who will discuss it with the Prime Minister. I can't say I'm convinced, and I have no idea what they'll say, but I can convey the message, at least."

"I will assist," Dr. Barqa-Abu offered. "I can offer the historic perspective, having existed through most of it."

Kester beamed. "It's a start, anyway. Let's all try working together for a change. We might have differences of opinion, but that could be a strength, not a weakness. It'll ensure we view things from all angles."

Hrschni glided closer, then whispered in his ear. "That's exactly the sort of thing your mother would have said. That's why she was wonderful, Kester, in spite of what you might feel about her at present."

Kester shrugged, feigning disinterest, but stored the comment in his mind, nonetheless. He'd already realised that the world existed in complex *maybes* and *possiblys*, rather than absolute rights or wrongs. He supposed that his mother had been the same—selfish and secretive in some ways but wonderful in others.

I wish you were here, Mum, he thought, for the first time in a while. *I think you would have quite enjoyed witnessing all of this.*

"So, does this mean you're not a free man, after all?" Mike asked Kester, after everyone had headed out to the car park. The wind was brisk, carrying with it the cold, sharp scent of the nearby sea, but they lingered by the entrance, nonetheless, along with the rest of the team.

Kester grimaced. "I offered to go back with them to Infinite Enterprises headquarters. Regaining their trust won't happen overnight, and

I have to show them I'm willing to cooperate. Hrschni's doing the same."

"You mean your father," Ribero said sadly, kicking at the side of a nearby concrete bollard. "You and your father will be doing the parent thing, yes? The bonding and the chatting about the good times and all of that?"

Kester rested his hand on Ribero's back. "Life is always complicated. I don't see it as swapping one father for another. I've just got two of you, now. An ancient spirit and a very cool human; it could be a lot worse, you know."

"It is true; I am very cool. I should have known you were not biologically mine, because there is no coolness to you at all, is there?" He poked Kester's stomach. "You are all warm, soft and sweet, like a jelly baby."

"What I want to know," Serena said, zipping her jacket up to her chin, "is where this leaves us. Crispian stole all our sensitive information, which won't go down well with—"

"Hang on, what's all this *us?*" Mike said. "You scampered off to Infinite Enterprises the minute our backs were turned. You've got your dream job, so what are you worried about?"

She kept her eyes on the ground, feigning great interest in the tip of her shoe. "I panicked," she replied quietly. "I thought it would be good for me to get a better job, one that earned me a lot more money, but—"

"Hey, I always paid you very well!" Ribero interrupted. "And I let you pillock around a lot without telling you off, which is worth more than money."

"Mike and Kester did all the pillocking, thank you very much!"

"Serena," Miss Wellbeloved said gently, "are you saying you want to come back?"

Serena glanced at Mike. "Possibly."

"The agency needs to be signed over to someone else," Kester reminded them. "I've just offered my services as a mediator between this world and the spirit realm, remember?"

"It should be Miss W's," Mike said.

"It shouldn't," Miss Wellbeloved replied quickly. "I'm too old. The agency needs new blood, someone with the energy to move it forward."

Ribero flapped a hand at Kester. "But we don't have the spirit door opener anymore! We lost one, many years ago, and now we lose another. It is embarrassing, right?"

"You don't need one, not now," Kester reminded him. "If the new system is introduced, you won't be focused on chucking spirits out of this world, but on helping them to settle in." He could tell by examining the old man's face that he wasn't entirely convinced.

"Who's going to take over the agency, then?" Pamela pressed.

Kester looked at each of them in turn, then grinned. "All of you," he said. "Larry and his lot as well, if they want to."

"There must be a boss!" Ribero exploded.

"Make it a cooperative organisation instead. You're all capable of running it together. Equal partnerships, equal shares—no more squabbles. Then, when Serena and Mike have kids, they can pass the agency on to the new generation."

"We are absolutely not going to produce children!" Serena said. "Just because I'm a woman, you automatically presume that I want to make babies, which I don't. Especially not with this hairy ape."

Mike winked. "That wasn't the impression I got at the New Year's Eve party at the museum."

"You promised you'd never mention that again, you rotten lout. I was tipsy, I wasn't thinking straight, and—"

"Let's not forget what the Bloody Mary spirit showed you in the mirror," Kester reminded her. On their first case, Serena had helped to expel the dangerous spirit by chanting her name in a mirror. She'd seen her future husband in the reflection, which Kester had witnessed too. Unfortunately for her, it had unmistakably been Mike's face, beaming out leerily from the glass.

Without warning, Mike enveloped her in a bear hug, nearly lifting her off her feet. "I'm glad you want to come back," he said, planting a wet kiss on her cheek. "Things wouldn't be the same without your mean, venomous presence in the office."

Kester caught Miss Wellbeloved's eye and smiled. He believed his work here was done, for now.

After saying his farewells to the others, Kester headed back to the Infinite Enterprises van, where Curtis Philpot stood waiting. To his surprise, Hrschni hovered beside him, and it looked as though they'd just finished their conversation.

"As far as solutions go," Curtis began, folding his collar up to keep out the cold, "this isn't what I expected, Kester."

Kester winced. "I admit, it's rather unorthodox."

"However," he continued, "I'm prepared to admit that life evolves. Things change. And perhaps, our current way of doing things isn't terribly effective. If there's one thing Infinite Enterprises cannot abide, it's being ineffective, you see."

"I got that impression, yes."

"You know that this is a momentous task to take on? The spirit realm is the great unknown. Are you really willing to put yourself at risk by entering it time and time again?"

"He won't be alone," Hrschni reminded him. "He will have my protection. Besides, Mr. Philpot, I believe it's time that you adjusted your view on spirits. I know we seem strange to you, but very few of us wish to harm humans. Those who do tend to be broken, unhappy creatures, who may yet be saved simply by being around people once again."

"Well, those *broken, unhappy creatures* need to show they can behave, or otherwise, this whole concept comes crashing down around our heads."

The daemon nodded. "I understand."

Curtis gestured inside the van, which was already full to bursting with Infinite Enterprises employees. "Come on," he said. "I'm freezing out here, and to be honest, I'm looking forward to getting home and forgetting about work for a while."

"Kester can travel by spirit door," Hrschni said. "We'll meet you there."

Curtis scoffed. "You expect me to trust you?"

"Yes, I do. That's the purpose of all of this, isn't it? Rest assured, Kester and I shall be waiting in the main reception area when you arrive."

"If you're not, you'll cost me my job."

"Why would I bother running away?" Kester reminded him. "There'd be no advantage to doing so. Also," he added, "if I'd have wanted to, I could have done it already. I don't mean to show off, but I can literally escape whenever I want to."

The daemon's mouth twisted into what might have been mirth.

"Very well," Curtis said wearily. "But please, don't let me down. This week has been rough enough without having to deal with more problems."

Kester gave him a thumbs-up. "We'll see you there."

With a grunt of disapproval, Curtis opened the front door and climbed into the passenger seat. Kester looked across at Hrschni, then nodded.

"Shall we?" he asked, gesturing at the air in front of them.

"Absolutely," Hrschni agreed. "But there's one place you might want to visit before you return to Infinite Enterprises, you know."

Kester frowned—then smiled. "I think I know where you mean."

The spirit landscape was slightly less alarming on the second visit, as now he knew what to expect.

Kester crept tentatively along the spongy, boggy ground, feeling the strange tentacle-like roots sucking and pawing at his shoes. All around him, spirits surged and circled, their curiosity piqued by his presence. Although he wasn't one of them, he felt some sort of kinship on a deep, primal level. There was an *understanding* there, between them all. They weren't malicious or determined to cause pain. They were simply creatures living their lives, just like humans.

"Are you sure Curtis Philpot won't be cross that I'm doing this?" he said to Hrschni, who was glowing brightly beside him.

"You promised you'd be waiting for him in the reception area when he returned," the daemon reminded him. "You never said anything about travelling straight there."

Kester grinned. His spirit father was an honourable creature, but like all daemons, notoriously adept at trickery and wordplay. "Can you remind me how I get back to the human world?" he asked, as the dense air oozed and slipped around his body.

"You know already. Have confidence in yourself. Focus on where you want to be."

It wasn't hard. There was one place he'd yearned to be for a long time now, somewhere that he associated with pure happiness. Closing his eyes, he envisaged a particular front door, the red-brick façade that surrounded it, and the neat narrowness of the Victorian architecture. The building he imagined was much like his own home, only tidier.

It's working, he realised, as the air crackled in front of them both. Although it took more effort to open the spirit door here, he felt he was getting the hang of it. The landscape tore slowly before his eyes, the gap widening to a long gash that revealed a slither of the world beyond it.

He peered through, then sighed with satisfaction as he glimpsed the house he'd been thinking of.

"She might not be home," he muttered to Hrschni. "Perhaps she's still at work."

"There's only one way to find out," the daemon said.

Stepping through the hole, Kester staggered slightly, disorientated by the sudden hardness of a front-garden path beneath his feet. He peered behind himself, studying the still-open spirit door at his back.

"Are you coming through?" he said. "I can't leave it open, you know. Imagine what her neighbours would think?"

"I'll wait here until you've done what you need to do," Hrschni replied. "Go on."

With a deep breath, Kester sealed up the rip in the air and the daemon with it, then reached for the doorbell. He listened as it chimed dully down the hallway inside, then waited.

I probably look a mess, he realised, straightening his glasses. He hadn't slept properly for a long while, and the stress of the last few days would surely be etched across his face. Still, there was nothing to be done about it now. All he could do was hope for the best.

A few seconds later, the door opened, and Anya's familiar face peeked out. She was wearing an apron and covered almost entirely in white powder.

"Kester!" she said, mouth open in surprise. "I'm so glad you are here. The bag of flour exploded all over me, and Thor is eating it right now. It's probably not good for ferrets, is it?"

"Probably not," Kester said, then pointed to the wriggling creature at her feet. "But he seems fine, look."

She scooped up her pet, who looked remarkably like a furry white sausage, thanks to the liberal coating of flour. "How are you?" she said. "When you came to see me in the library, we couldn't talk properly. Are those people still chasing after you? Are you okay?"

"I'm fine," he said. "Everything is being sorted out, I think. I've got some things to tell you, which is why I'm here. It's probably better if I just blurt them out without thinking too much about it, because they're pretty big things, you see."

"What is it?"

He took a deep breath. *Here goes nothing,* he thought.

"I found out that I'm only half human," he said, in a rush of words. "Hrschni's apparently my father; he had a love affair with my mother, you see. Everyone was angry at me, because they thought I was trying to unleash spirits all over the world, but now they know the truth. And now, things are going to change. We might even get a spirit MP in the government, can you imagine? And I won't be working here anymore, because I've promised to travel regularly into the spirit realm, and work on building spirit-human relations. And . . ." He faltered then took a deep breath. "Does any of what I just said make any sense?"

She shook her head. "Not really."

"Hmm. That's a shame. But to be honest, Anya, that's not the big thing I wanted to tell you."

"It's not?"

"No." He stepped forward and reached for her. "I came here to tell you that I love you. I suppose, compared to telling you that I'm only half human, that's quite a small thing, actually. But—"

Her face lit up with a smile. "No, that's a very big thing, Kester."

"You don't have to say you feel the same way, of course; I mean—"

His next words were muffled by the pressure of her lips against his. Eyes widening with surprise, then intense relief, he kissed her back. *This is what really matters,* he realised, pulling her closer. *When we're together, everything is better.*

Finally, she pulled away, then laughed. "Now you're covered in flour too," she told him, patting him down.

"I've been covered in worse things."

"Kester?" she said, taking his hand.

"Yes?"

"I love you too. Even if you are the weirdest person I have ever met."

"Half person," he corrected.

She wrinkled her nose. "That might take some getting used to. But I've had a daemon living inside me, so I get it."

They started to laugh, then kissed again. This time, Kester didn't *think*; he just *did*.

"I think this will all work out," he whispered in her ear. "I really do."

"I believe you," she whispered back. "And I believe *in* you."

Belief. Sometimes, that was all it took to make things better.

About the Author

Lucy has enjoyed inhabiting worlds of her own creation from a young age. While her initial creations were somewhat dubious, thankfully, her writing grew as she did. She takes particular delight in creating worlds that closely overlap reality . . . with strange, supernatural differences.

Lucy lives in Devon with her husband and two children. She immerses herself in the wild, rural landscapes and loves seeking out hidden locations. More of a book-python than a bookworm, she devours at least one novel a week, and loves the written word so much that even her day job involves writing and editing.